HASHTAG
GOOD GUY
WITH A
GUN

JEFF CHON

Sagging
Meniscus

Printed in Great Britain and the United States of America.
Set in Williams Caslon Text with LaTeX.

ISBN: 978-1-952386-02-2 (paperback)
ISBN: 978-1-952386-03-9 (ebook)
Library of Congress Control Number: 2020934219

Sagging Meniscus Press
Montclair, New Jersey
saggingmeniscus.com

For Dina, Mia, and Avery

Contents

I.

All That David Copperfield Kind of Crap

The Sad Tale of Old Hwang

There once was an old general named Hwang Hyun-soo, who was known throughout the village as a coward, a man who hid as his battalion was slaughtered by soldiers of the Tang emperor. Of course, no one could prove he'd lost his nerve on the battlefield, but how else could a general return home unscathed while his men were captured or murdered by Chinese dogs? Because of his cowardice, none of his seven sons—all handsome, refined young men—could find families willing to give their daughters away as brides. Until the winter of his sixty-sixth year, many thought this was his curse.

On that fateful winter, while his virgin sons slept in their rooms, old Hwang stepped onto his porch to find Jeoseung Saja, envoy of the afterlife, waiting for him at the gates of his home, and Hwang, coward that he was, fell to his knees and wailed.

"Oh frightful emissary," Hwang cried, "Is it truly my time?"

The emissary stood silently in his black robe and wide-brimmed black hat. A great wind tossed old Hwang to the dirt. Dead leaves rose from the cold earth, danced and twirled about his head, vengeful spirits mocking the end of an old coward. Hwang begged and clawed at the earth, praying someone would hear his cries and rescue him from his fate.

"My entire life, I have avoided death," Hwang lamented. "But I only did so for my sons, to watch them grow into men, and husbands, and then fathers! Yet I have been cursed with the burden of seven virgin sons! I have failed in life! Surely the afterlife deserves better than the likes of me! I beg you—I am not worthy to walk alongside you!"

Jeoseung Saja stroked his beard. He regarded the sad sight of old Hwang, who wept as the barren branches above him clicked and rattled in the wind. Many say the emissary took pity on the craven old man—how could anyone not pity the father of seven virgins? The breeze weakened, and the air was still, and the emissary laughed.

"You speak the truth," the emissary said. "You are not worthy to walk among us. When you are worthy—if you ever shall be worthy—our paths shall cross again."

And with that, the wind roared, louder and louder until it rumbled the old coward's heart. Hwang shut his eyes and hid his face.

When Hwang opened his eyes, he saw he was in his bed. Believing this dream to be a good omen, he put on his robe and sent a servant to gather his sons, so he could tell them of this dream. Jeoseung Saja had spared him because he had not achieved his one true purpose: to see his sons married off to good women. Once his sons were married to suitable girls, he knew the emissary would come for him, and old Hwang told himself he would go gladly into the underworld with courage and gratitude.

What other meaning could there be for such a dream?

He heard his servant scream, and then the cook, and then the maids. He bolted from his room to see them all gathered in the courtyard, weeping in one another's arms: his sons, all seven of them, had died in their sleep.

Old Hwang was so heartbroken, he ran to the mountains, where he spent the rest of his days as a hermit. Some say, when the night is especially silent, you can still hear the moans of the seven virgin ghosts, tormenting their father for his cowardice.

The Pizza Galley Shooting

One moment is not just one moment—it is a cluster of past moments affixed to a cluster of future moments. Scott Bonneville understands this long before pulling the trigger forty-five seconds, into the fifty-fourth minute, of the twenty-second hour, of the fourth day, in the first week, of the eleventh month. Everything that's ever happened leads to everything else that ever happens. There is no one thing connecting them all because they're already tangled together—and that tangle of past and future is what we call the present.

After the Pizza Galley Shooting, people will say losing his job was the exact moment that inspired Scott's actions. Others will say it was his broken heart. Another group will say it was something to do with his father. Some will even blame J.D. Salinger. The rest of us will ask why anyone cares—isn't the fact he took a human life all that matters here? How are we supposed to focus on *this* when *that man* is the president? And then the conversation will shift toward *that man* because the present is a cluster of past moments affixed to a cluster of future moments.

Forty-three minutes after closing time, an embittered man named David Brightman stormed into the Pizza Galley restaurant in Torrance, California with the intent of killing his wife Darcy, who worked as a head cashier. His 9mm had three bullets in the clip—one for Darcy; one for Christian Gibbard, the assistant manager she was sleeping with; and the final one for himself. Unfortunately, Gibbard had the night off, having traded shifts with the store manager, Yu-jin Walker, so she could begin her maternity leave a week earlier than scheduled. David demanded everyone sit calmly at the tables closest to the prize booth, while he called Gibbard on the phone, telling him to come alone, that if the police showed up, he'd kill everyone in the restaurant, even though he'd only loaded three bullets into the handgun—but Gibbard had no way of knowing that.

The entire night had been a disaster for those working at Pizza Galley, as they'd been short-handed for most of the night. Mark had been scheduled to work the kitchen, but called in sick because it was his birthday and no one would swap shifts with him. Abhay, who was set to work the kitchen with him and wear the Captain Pete Pizza costume for two birthday parties, called out with strep throat. As the night wore on, two drunken mothers got into a fistfight, one hurling a beer mug at the other. She missed, and the mug hit a server named Amber in the face, and after the police reports were filed,

4

Amber was sent to the Emergency Room with a broken nose. After closing, Yu-jin sent Ryan home early because he'd agreed to clean the shit streak in the tunnel slide for Rachel, who couldn't bring herself to do it. The agreement was Rachel would assume all of Ryan's clean-up duties as long as she didn't have to climb into the slide. After Ryan left, only Yu-jin, Darcy, Rachel, and an owl-faced woman named Morgan remained. During her maternity leave, Yu-jin would have to answer for closing the store with an all-female staff, which was against company guidelines.

David paced the carpet, which had a wood paneling pattern in order to resemble the deck of a pirate ship, muttering to himself about lying bitches and cheating motherfuckers, while Yu-jin held a sobbing Darcy. She was seated in between Darcy and Morgan, who kept asking everyone to pray with her. Rachel sat alone at a table to their left, staring at the napkin holder in the center of the table, her arms crossed. David's hands trembled as he cried and shouted and told Darcy sorry didn't cut it.

"I loved you," he said. "I loved you fucking bitch. And you cheat on me with that cocksucker?"

"It's not what you think," Darcy told him.

"Please, Dave," Yu-jin said. "You have to calm down. Think about—"

"You don't tell me to calm down Jinny. I'm calm as shit. I know exactly what I need to do."

As this was all happening inside, Scott Bonneville stood at the dumpsters behind the restaurant with a homeless man named Jae, demanding to know why Jae had called him Jeoseung Saja, Korean folklore's emissary of death. Jae didn't seem frightened of Scott in any way, even though Scott had placed a gun to Jae's forehead. He simply stared into Scott's eyes, eating a slice of leftover pizza, sipping Pepsi through a straw.

Scott pulled the gun from Jae's head and looked up at the Waxing Crescent moon. Earlier, Jae had pointed out that a rabbit lived on the moon, pounding rice cakes with a mortar and pestle, and now Scott couldn't unsee it, even though the rabbit was only visible when the moon was full. Jae pointed over Scott's shoulder, and Scott lowered the gun and turned to the back door, which was cracked open.

"They're waiting for you in there," Jae said.

How did Jae know Scott was Jeoseung Saja? How did he know about his plans for Pizza Galley, that he'd come ready to kill, to die, for the truth? Was this a sign? No, only his father believed in signs. Signs were random accidents, and Scott was a man who understood patterns—he knew Jae was another link in the chain that led him here. Scott stared at the door. He couldn't believe his luck, that it was open, just like that.

"Can you do me a favor? There's a girl in there, Korean like me and you. Her name's Yu-jin. Don't hurt her, okay?"

Scott walked in through the back door, into the warehouse. His eye caught a pallet in the right corner of the store, stacked with shrink-wrapped boxes which read *DOUGH-BLOONS*, boxes and boxes filled with the horrible little gold tokens Pizza Galley had used to entice children into their lurid trap. He tightened his grip on the gun as he stared at the door leading into the restaurant. On the door was a poster with Olive-head the Buccaneer, telling kids to stay away from drugs. He walked up to the poster, stared at it, and his guts raged and tightened with hatred. He turned the door handle slowly.

On the other side of the door was the stage, where the animatronics danced and sang for the kids. He peered in and stifled a gasp. David Brightman raged in his biker jacket, waving his gun, shouting at a group of women cowering at the tables. Earlier in the night, Scott had seen the agitated Brightman smoking a cigarette in the parking lot. Scott then realized he and this man had been circling one another, waiting for the other to leave, so one of them could enter the restaurant and fulfill their mission. For the rest of his life, Scott would wonder why the two of them had been in the right place at the wrong time. He'd never come to anything that made sense in any way.

Seated in between an attractive middle-aged woman and a stout, owl-faced girl, he saw Yu-jin, the Korean girl Jae had told him not to hurt. Yu-jin was pregnant, and this made Scott think of his own mother—not Wilma Bonneville, the woman who'd adopted him, but the young Korean girl who'd abandoned him all those years ago. Yu-jin's hands clasped the hands of the two women on either side of her. Their eyes were closed, and they seemed to be praying, and they'd never know how disgusting Scott had found their prayers. The young blonde girl seated at the table next to them looked up, noticed him. Her hands shot up to cover her mouth. Scott brought his finger to his lips, told her to be quiet.

The last thing David Brightman would see is Scott coming toward him, out from behind the animatronic Calico Jacqueline—who was holding an up-right bass—gun raised, the muzzle flashing twice in succession. As Darcy wailed, as the young blonde girl screamed, David Brightman dropped to his knees, his arms lowered, blood seeping from his chest and stomach. Police sirens blared—Christian Gibbard had chosen to call the police, rather than come down himself—and David Brightman dropped face-first onto the carpet, blood seeping into the faded wood panel print.

And that was how Scott became *#goodguywithagun*, a hashtag used by people who pushed horrible, stupid ideas. If all of those people had known the truth, logic would have dictated the multitudes would never have extolled Scott's virtues the way they had, but that's the problem with logic in an age of foolishness, in these interesting times that make us lose all sense of perspective.

An Alleged Chinese Curse

In 1966, Robert F. Kennedy gave a speech in which he invoked the existence of a Chinese curse: *May he live in interesting times*. And while no one has ever been able to authenticate this curse's Chinese origin, these were indeed the interesting times those fictional men of China spoke of. Three days after the Pizza Galley shooting, a man many felt was grossly unqualified was elected President of the United States. There isn't much else to say about that, really—at least not right now—other than this:

A year before this man's inauguration, the site where a women's crisis center was being constructed was vandalized by a group of sad, hopelessly stupid young boys. The vandals spray-painted *Slut* and *Whore* on the sidewalk in front of the newly installed glass door, which they'd shattered so they could make their way inside. Once inside, they shat on the carpet, smeared their shit on the walls and windows. The next afternoon, the papers reported the culprits were three sixteen-year-old boys who belonged to an internet messageboard known as the Half-Minute Brigade, calling themselves by this unfortunate name because, as one of their ranks had so elegantly put it, MINUTEMEN TAKE TO FUCKIGN LONG! (sic) Because these were all angry boys who'd been mocked their entire lives, they'd never once considered the comedic implication of young men bragging about doing anything in thirty seconds. And that's the issue with boys like this: they always ask for it, always make it so goddamned easy. To not rake them over the coals would almost be a disservice.

These particular young men had planned their desecration of the crisis center in plain sight on the Half-Minute Brigade messageboard, declaring their disgust over the construction of the crisis center, claiming it was an indoctrination camp for radical feminists before their conversations devolved, as they always did, to musings of sexual violence. But these posts weren't how they were discovered—half the reason boys like this are so bold is because they're convinced no one is ever paying attention. These three boys were caught because they had used the fiberglass insulation they'd found on the site as toilet paper. All it took was for the Redondo Beach Police to see which Emergency Room had admitted three boys with inflamed and bleeding anuses. An hour after the news broke, the Half-Minute Brigade messageboard crashed, and the Half-Minute Brigade as we knew it ceased to exist. Of the three vandals, one of the boys hanged himself, while the other two were sent off to live with relatives in Oregon and Alaska.

No one would think of these boys again until the day after the Inauguration, when one of them, a boy named Walton Pabst, will open fire at a rally against the President-Elect, killing three and wounding nine before taking his own life.

What a Fool Believes

Scott Bonneville lay on his stomach with his hands up. The police rushed into Pizza Galley, their guns trained on Scott, who dropped to his knees and raised his hands. A police officer, a tall man with a shaved head named McGill, placed him in cuffs and pulled him to his feet, read him his rights. None of the hostages protested. None of them told the police how Scott had saved their lives. Scott watched Darcy Brightman kneel on the wood-panel carpet, sobbing by her husband's body. Paramedics gathered around Yu-jin, the pregnant Korean woman, who was doubled over and clutching her belly. Scott turned around to see if she was okay. McGill snapped him forward and out the door, into the parking lot, awash in red and blue lights from the squad cars. The commotion outside was broken by the sound of a helicopter flying overhead. The choppy pulse of its propeller merged with the red and blue lights until Scott could no longer separate the two—they were all he could see and all he could hear.

"Move it," Officer McGill said.

"What?"

"Move. Don't make me repeat it."

Officer McGill shut the door and radioed dispatch to let them know he was coming in. He told them he was transporting the shooter, as if he were some kind of criminal, as if he were David Brightman. Scott noticed McGill's tattoo, a spiderweb on his right elbow. He'd once read white supremacists had that tattoo to signify they'd done time. The police department had even tried to ban those tattoos until the union got involved. Was this man a Nazi? Is that why he was being so belligerent? Scott didn't believe in racism, not like a lot of his old colleagues had, that it was still prevalent the way everyone said it was—especially when it came to Asians—but this was different. This man had a Nazi prison tattoo. What if he took Scott to some alley and murdered him? What if the holding tank was full of Nazis, and this cop would let them rough him up?

"By the way," McGill said. "Mrs. Walker, that pregnant woman—she just went into labor."

"I know," Scott said. "I was there."

"How much stress do you think your stunt put that poor woman under? She's a nice lady. I take my kids to this place."

"If I hadn't been there, she might be dead."

"Of course, of course. Tough guys like you are the real heroes."

They stopped at a red light in front of the 7-Eleven. A young woman stood in the parking lot with her pug. She smoked her cigarette and the pug wore a service vest, which was complete bullshit as the pug was clearly not a service dog. Earlier that evening, he'd had a run-in with this woman inside of Albertsons over her fake service dog. Scott tried to turn away so she wouldn't see him. But their eyes locked as the light turned green, the cigarette dangling from her mouth. She smiled as her pug crapped on the asphalt. McGill sped away.

"That dog just took a crap in the parking lot," Scott said. "Service dogs don't go willy-nilly like that. She's committing fraud."

"Yeah, that's exactly the sort of thing I should be worried about tonight."

McGill ran a red light. Why run through this one and not the one in front of that bitch at 7-Eleven? It was clearly a red light—the light had gone yellow fifteen yards ago—and while the way he blew through the intersection was amazing in and of itself, Scott was more struck by how the other drivers, drivers who had the right of way, slowed their cars. He wondered if every driver was this deferential when cop cars were present. When he first learned to drive, Scott had to fight the urge to pull over every time there was a cop car behind him, as if the mere sight of a policeman would trigger a traffic violation. McGill began to whistle the first verse of "What a Fool Believes" in a very unconscious way, as if he'd forgotten Scott was in the back seat, as if it didn't matter even if he hadn't forgotten there was a man in his backseat who'd shot another man in the chest and stomach. McGill turned on the siren. Scott leaned forward.

"Why turn on the siren now as opposed to when we pulled out?"

"We're done talking. That means you stay quiet."

And why wasn't Scott thinking about the fact that he'd killed another man? A man was dead because of him, and all he'd done so far was try and convince Officer McGill he didn't belong in the back seat of a squad car, that he'd saved lives. All he'd done so far was wonder if the police presence had rendered commuters spineless. All he'd done so far was try to keep Michael McDonald's falsetto from replacing Office McGill's whistling. And why was he whistling "What a Fool Believes" anyway? Was he taunting Scott? Was Scott the fool?

He thought of Dave Brightman lying on his back, how the two of them had been staking out the same Pizza Galley. He looked at his hands, which weren't shaking. Why weren't they shaking? Why wasn't he more upset? Why wasn't he upset at all? Scott had never fired a gun until that night, had never even held a gun until days before. The young blonde girl had clearly pissed her pants—Scott wondered if anyone else had noticed. Yu-jin had gone into labor. A new life was being brought into this ugly, stupid world, yet all Scott could do was stare out the window, try to mask the rage induced by McGill's whistling.

The next day, Scott would learn the reason Dave Brightman walked into Pizza Galley with a gun, how Darcy Brightman had been fooling around with a coworker, and he'd remember sitting in the back of McGill's car, the red light obeyed and the one that wasn't, the dog shit that probably wasn't cleaned up, how he couldn't get "What a Fool Believes" out of his head until the next afternoon.

"Could you please stop whistling?"

"What the hell is wrong with you? I thought I told you not to talk."

When Scott first moved to Oregon, people had asked him what he'd missed most about California. He'd always had trouble answering that question, as he'd spend more time thinking about what he hadn't missed. He'd never cared for beaches and had no opinion on sunlight. The pretty girls in Portland had ignored him the way they'd ignored him in California. What was left? Wildfires? Earthquakes? Everyone's strange obsession with In-N-Out Burger? He stared out the window of the squad car as one palm tree swept past his eyes, only to be replaced by another, and then another, in succession. Scott had been in Oregon two days before he'd noticed its lack of palm trees. He'd driven past a tropical-themed trailer park outside of Portland when he finally saw one again. Next to a weather-beaten sign, *Key Largo* written in pink neon cursive lights, a palm tree stood dying, its fibrous trunk practically staggering from the weight of the brown, withered fronds. Standing next to the tree, a pregnant woman in flip-flops and a green sundress smoked a cigarillo. He remembered how they'd locked eyes as he slowly drove past, the way she placed her hand on the swollen mound under her breasts as if to say, *Mind your own business.*

Scott hoped Yu-jin was okay. He prayed for her, something he hadn't done in years because he didn't believe in God—but he didn't just pray for her, but for her baby as well, who would come into a world where men tried to murder their wives to prove their love and other men, good men who acted in the name of justice, were placed in cuffs as if they were the real criminals. Scott prayed that someday, his mission would be completed—maybe not by him, but some other truth-seeker—imagined a world where Yu-jin's baby would know the truth about the world he or she was raised in, that men like Scott had exposed all of the liars, and murderers, and rapists, that men like Scott had made all of them pay. Quite simply, he prayed her baby would grow up in a world that was better than the one it had been born into.

The Worst is Always Behind Us

Four years into his time in Korea, where he'd gone as a missionary, Cary Bonneville had been visited by two angels who told him the world was to end on September 11, 2000. He then left the Wesleyans and travelled up and down the Korean countryside with his wife Wilma, helping converts prepare for the end times. Travelling through Seoul, he met Reverend Park Min-kyu, who'd been expelled by the Unification Church for having a vision in which angels told him Kim Il-sung, who'd sold his soul for immortality, would march an army of demons into Seoul in the ninth month of the two-thousandth year.

Discovering their shared sign from God, the two men formed the Church of the New Millennium, preaching on soapboxes and storefronts all over Gyeonggi Province, eventually building a megachurch in downtown Seoul. Scott was found the night after they'd officially opened their doors in late October of 1981. Wilma had supposedly found him in a basket, with a note written in Hangul asking God for forgiveness, and that was enough for her to keep and raise Scott as her own.

When Scott was three, Cary Bonneville built another church in Lanai, Hawaii. There in Lanai, he impregnated Noelani Fielder, his secretary, leading to the birth of Scott's brother Brian. Scott didn't know all of the particulars—he was only six at the time—but one day his mother came home with a little baby and moved into what would become Brian's nursery. She would live in that room until Brian was three years old, at which point she took Scott and moved in with her sister in Redondo Beach, leaving Brian and Cary behind. On the plane, she told Scott it was their chance for a normal life, their chance to be normal people.

Scott stared out the window, the plane's wing wobbling as it passed through a cloud, and he remembered going door to door to pass out leaflets with Wilma, remembered the way doors would slam in their faces, the way the mothers standing on their porches shielded their children from them, the way the children placed hands on their mothers hips and peeked out at him, how their little eyes narrowed when they caught him looking.

"Are we different?" Scott asked.

"No," Wilma said. "Not anymore. The worst is behind us, Scotty. The worst is always behind us. My mother used to say that all the time. It's sad, but I don't think I ever believed her."

Scott heard the captain's voice through the speakers. The plane was making its approach into Los Angeles, so he asked everyone stay buckled in their seats. The wing sliced through another cloud, and Scott was fascinated by how fluffy they were. The year before, Wilma's mother had passed away in San Bernardino, and Scott and Wilma had taken a plane to pay their respects. On the flight back to Hawaii, he remembered looking out at the clouds stumbling over the wing of the plane, just as he was doing now, how much they'd reminded him of the dandelions he'd blown apart with Aunt Margaret before the funeral, how a tiny puff of air had made them separate and disperse. When they went back into the church, Wilma knelt in the vestibule and picked the tiny florets off his tie and collar.

"Do you know what that means, Scotty?" Wilma asked. "Do you know what the worst is always behind us means?"

"Does it mean we're gonna be happy?"

"Yes. That's exactly what it means."

The plane shook and Wilma pulled Scott's hands to her lips. She placed it on the arm rest and squeezed. After the plane landed and Aunt Margaret took them home, Scott ran through the front lawn with a bouquet of dandelions, watching the tiny florets trail behind him, fragments of a broken cloud.

Wake Up Sheeple

Detective Ramirez, Holly was her first name, sat across from him in the interrogation room. It was just like in the movies, except the room was cold, which the movies had failed to mention. Detective Ramirez also looked like a movie cop, a severe woman with a bob haircut and a tiny scar on her chin. Scott imagined she was probably a lesbian. He had no way of knowing if she was, but it made sense at the time. Ramirez looked at the notes and sighed, over and over again. Scott found their silences agitating, but he knew they were supposed to be. He was quite familiar with this kind of silence, as he'd used it every day in his classroom. Perhaps Ramirez didn't realize he, too, used silence as a weapon. He, too, understood someone was eventually going to speak up as long as he said nothing.

"So you went to the back of Pizza Galley at approximately ten-forty five or so," Ramirez finally said, "and noticed the back door was open. Then you went in, saw Mr. Brightman threatening those women with a gun, and shot him in the chest and stomach about a minute or so after."

They'd already been through this five times in the past hour. Yes, Scott went to the Pizza Galley dumpsters to have a cigarette. He'd noticed the back door hadn't been shut properly. He knocked on the door to see if anyone was around. Then he went inside to inform them they'd left the back door open. Why not just go around front? Because, what if they didn't answer? It felt like the right thing to do at the time. As he made his way in, he heard a woman begging for her life—Yes, Mrs. Brightman—and then noticed Mr. Brightman brandishing his gun. After that, everything was a blur as he was acting on pure instinct. How much clearer could he be?

Scott hadn't mentioned Jae. The last thing he wanted was more questions. All he wanted was to go home and think about what he and David Brightman had done. Not in any remorseful way, of course—what did Scott really have to feel sorry about? What Scott had wanted was to contemplate what had happened that night, why things had fallen in place the way they had. What he'd needed was to regroup and not only think about what he'd done, but why he'd done it. Mostly, Scott wanted to sit alone and curse his rotten luck, wanted some time to actually feel sorry for himself—was that too much to ask?

Had Yu-jin shut the door tightly behind her, Scott wouldn't have had such an easy path inside. Had Scott not begun hyperventilating, had he not taken up smoking because he'd wanted to always be by Lisa's side, he wouldn't have gone to the dumpsters for a smoke, which would have set off a different chain of events. Maybe he would have had to force his way inside—David Brightman would have seen him and panicked. Maybe they would have had a shootout, or Brightman would have just shot his wife and them himself, but only after shooting Scott first. Perhaps he should've been more forceful with Brightman in the parking lot. What if they'd had an encounter that brought Brightman to his senses and made him go home? Had Darcy Brightman actually been a faithful wife, perhaps David wouldn't have been there at all.

How did Jae know about Jeoseung Saja? How did this homeless man know who he was? It was as if he were expecting Scott to be there. None of this would have made any sense to Ramirez.

"Your gun," Ramirez said, "why was it on you at the time?"

"It's registered."

"That's not what I asked, Mr. Bonneville. Okay, let me start again, just to make sure we're on the same page. You went to the back of Pizza Galley at approximately ten-forty five or so to have a cigarette. You noticed the back door was open. Then you went in, saw Mr. Brightman threatening those women with a gun, so you pulled out your gun—"

Scott panicked and told Ramirez he'd been thinking about killing himself. It wasn't the best answer, but what else could he say? That he'd come to expose the child sex-trafficking ring run in the basement of the Pizza Galley? That Pizza Galley was the front for a nationwide, possibly even global, order of pedophiles? That he'd come to hold the Pizza Galley employees hostage until someone finally revealed the secret kill room? Of course all of this was the truth—Scott had done the research—but now that David Brightman had thwarted his plans, who'd believe him? Certainly not the complicit police department Ramirez worked for.

The truth was, Scott had gone to Pizza Galley after months of investigating the disappearance of children across the country. They always seemed to come in threes, and every time he pinpointed the places they'd disappeared and then drew a line connecting the sites—every single time—they always formed a triangle which surrounded a Pizza Galley location: a triangle, the shape of a pizza, these people were taunting him. Beyond being the shape of a pizza slice, the triangle has a much greater significance. The mascot for Pizza Galley is a cartoon pirate named Captain Pete Pizza. He wore a tricorne hat, the kind worn by 18th century military men. Affixed to the tricorne's brim was a gold Dough-Bloon token, the currency used in all Pizza Galleys. Heads was a pirate ship; tails was the company logo, another triangle, which surrounded a slice of pizza—a triangle containing a smaller triangle also happens to be secret pedophile code for "Boy Lover," the larger triangle representing the man, while the smaller one signified the little boy. Others have even said the triangular logo represented the Eye of Providence, the eye topping the Freemason pyramid on the back of every one dollar bill. Of course, he couldn't tell Ramirez any of this. She'd either think he was crazy, because she was blind to the truth—or if she wasn't blind, she'd have to make his execution look like an accident. God damn you, David Brightman.

"So there it is," Scott said. "Happy? I wanted to kill myself. For what it's worth, I don't want to anymore. I don't want to kill myself. I want to live, okay? I want to live my life."

They—and we all know who *they* are—liked to call people like Scott conspiracy theorists, paint people like Scott as lunatics, losers, unproductive members of society who desperately grasp at nonexistent causal chains to prove the world is rotten, simpletons looking for scapegoats for their own failure to function normally in the world. But Scott knew in his heart he wasn't a conspiracy theorist—the Earth is round, we did in fact land on the moon, and there is no such thing as Bigfoot. In Scott's mind, he was a free-thinker, a seeker of truth, an explorer of possibilities. He's highly educated, eats healthy and exercises regularly—he'd even had a very good job and a loving girlfriend until his life had gone off the rails. Critical thinkers such as Scott were only demonized because of their devotion to the truth and their determination in exposing lies.

Wake up, Sheeple LOL! they'd say in mocking terms, as if this were something people like Scott would actually say. Yet the half-wits who mocked him always described themselves as "woke" at every turn so they could harvest Likes and Shares on social media, while defending the systems put in place by the Global Elite, like the good little serfs they were. He'd always sneered at the term "woke," a preterite verb, a colloquial one no less, representing a past action or state, and with most of these sheep it was always the recent past they were describing. True individuals such as Scott described themselves in the more active "awake." He wanted to ask all these "woke" people if they've seen photos of the Pizza Galley kill room—the drainage hole in the middle of the floor for all the blood, white walls smudged with dirt, a black poster on the wall which read *D.A.R.E. to resist drugs and violence.* He wanted to ask if they knew about Aiden Iwakuma, the autistic twelve-year-old John Cena fanatic who'd disappeared while camping with his family, found on a riverbank by a group of city councilmen on a fishing excursion. What about Tasha Bennett, who had dreamed of becoming a pop singer, her body discovered behind St. Lawrence Church by an elderly nun? Then there's the mysterious case of Hunter Moxley, a buck-toothed kid whose dream was to quarterback the Patriots to a Super Bowl. His foot—his severed foot—had been found on the steps of the County Sheriff's Department during a massive power surge. Isn't it convenient there's no surveillance footage?

Why is it these three children were discovered by local government, clergy, and law enforcement? The government, the people who make the laws; clergy, the people who keep us good and stupid; law enforcement, the people who punish those who aren't good and stupid—what shape has three lines and three vertices? How was it that Councilman Becerra-Hernandez, who'd found Aiden's body, had gone to college with the current C.E.O. of Pizza Kingdom? Was it any coincidence that this C.E.O., Daniel Patrick McDougal, was a devout Catholic who'd allegedly started a legal fund defending priests accused of sexual abuse? How convenient is it the local Sheriff's department, where they found Hunter's foot, and Pizza Galley worked hand-in-hand, sending a deputy and some child-rapist in a Captain Pete Pizza costume to school assemblies in order to teach children how to—and this is a direct quote from the brochure—*RESIST DRUGS AND VIOLENCE?*

Why was it that when he'd pinpointed the spots where Aiden, Tasha, and Hunter's bodies were found, Scott could draw a line from one to another until they'd connected to form a triangle—three lines, three vertices—around the Pizza Galley location he'd decided to investigate that night? Had these "woke" little boys and girls even read the numerous accounts of men flipping Dough-Bloons to see which sex act they were going to inflict upon the children—heads meaning one thing, tails meaning something just as obviously crude and horrifying? Did they know that when police raided the homes of pedophiles, they'd often found the gold Dough-Bloons used at Pizza Galley, sleeved in rolls, disguised as quarters, as to not arouse suspicion? What despicable creatures these "woke" people were, laughing and mocking men like Scott, while predators sat in the basement of Pizza Galleys across the nation, flipping coins and laughing as drugged children lay curled in cages.

"I'm very sorry to hear that," Ramirez said. "I'll refer you to a counselor after we're finished. Thank you for your honesty. It was a brave thing to admit."

Of course, none of the things Scott knew to be true, none of the truths Scott wanted to expose, came to light that night because of David Brightman, a sad man who'd only gone into Pizza Galley because of a broken heart. Brightman had gone in after the restaurant had closed, just as Scott had planned, because neither wanted to harm anyone they felt didn't deserve it. The next day, everyone would call Scott the Good Guy and Brightman the Bad Guy, but Scott would feel Brightman deserved maybe the tiniest bit of consideration here. He knew how that felt, having your heart broken, knowing the person you loved maybe didn't love you as intensely as they should. A man in a gray suit and an American flag necktie walked into the interrogation room and Ramirez sighed, threw her hands in the air.

"Mr. Bonneville," he said, "not another word."

"I guess your attorney's here," Ramirez said. "We'll be in touch."

She touched Scott's hand, told him to be strong, to have a good night. After she left, the man introduced himself. Mills Burghardt told Scott not to worry—not only would Scott never see the inside of a cell, but together, they were going to change the world.

"I'm going to be very honest with you, Scott," Burghardt said. "I saw you on the news—you're all over the news, by the way—and rushed over from Pasadena. I just knew that you needed me on your side. I need you to know you're in very good hands here. I'm not some low-level P.D.A. I have over fifteen years' experience dealing with self-defense cases like yours. And you know what? I also happen to be a firm believer in the Second Amendment—did that woman ask you about your gun?"

"She did."

"Of course she did. Did any of these cops thank you for saving all those lives?"

"Look, Mr. Burghardt, I'm honestly not much of a gun nut—"

"Mills. And of course you're not. No one is. There's no such thing as a gun nut, Scott. It's just some fake, made-up term used to demonize gun owners. You may not see yourself as a gun nut, most reasonable people won't see you as a gun nut, but what do you think the media is going to do? They're already talking about how you lost your job in Oregon. CNN had your former principal on the phone and honestly, he's not as complimentary as he probably should be. They're already planting the seeds to make this about you and your gun—disgraced former teacher who became a gun nut—I know their game, Scott, and that's what they're doing right now."

They talked to Jed Birkenstein? What did he say about Scott? Did Jed push Blake Mesman's lies? Blake Mesman, that lying little shit. Oh, if only their paths could cross one more time, Scott would really make it count.

"Okay," said Scott.

"Good. Let's get you out of here."

They left the interrogation room. Scott's mother was waiting for him on a bench, next to an elderly man with a black eye and a young woman with a sleeping child.

Inertia Got Us Here

The truth was, Scott had in fact contemplated suicide before killing David Brightman, but it also happened to be the moment he'd been saved, the moment he was finally given another sense of purpose, so he didn't think much about how low the world had crushed him. Three months before the Pizza Galley Shooting, he was trapped in one of those moods that swung back and forth, from sentimentality to resentment, with the violence of a drunk with a baseball bat. He sat at the computer in his bedroom—his fucking childhood bedroom—searching for the one thing that might bring him peace, or at least coax him back to bed, promise to stop the memories scraping the insides of his skull, memories that quickened his breath and made him toss and turn. He hadn't slept for three days, and often wondered if death might be his only escape.

He spent a little time looking at Lisa's Facebook page. He knew it wouldn't help him in any way—he knew, in fact, it would hurt him—but inertia is a tricky thing that takes you exactly where you're supposed to go. Everything lands where it's supposed to land, even when we believe our aim to be true. In the end, gravity takes everyone down, and Scott followed his arc of descent clicking on thumbnails of selfies of Lisa in her new yoga pants, to photos of kale tossed with quinoa and garlic, to close-ups of manicured toenails lacquered red like a brand new car. Lisa posted an update about a young girl in Beaverton who'd gone missing two weeks earlier. Accompanying the post was a photo of the young girl, smiling in an Oregon Ducks cheerleader outfit, wisps of blonde hair glistening as if conducting sunlight—she couldn't have been more than twelve, fifteen at the most.

Thoughts and prayers for Caitlyn Oliynik and her family, the post read. *Please bring this beautiful angel home to her mom and dad.*

It was a harmless post, and that was the problem. It may have done no harm, but what possible good could this post have done for anyone? What good were Lisa's thoughts and prayers? Was this post even for Caitlyn, or was it for Lisa? The comments underneath were from Lisa's yoga friends, all of them telling Lisa she was a beautiful person for bringing Caitlyn's disappearance to everyone's attention, and Lisa responding with how heartbroken she was for this little girl she didn't even know, how she cried just thinking about her.

What good are your tears, Lisa?

You think Caitlyn's parents care about your broken heart?

Scott was ready to finally break his radio silence, tell Lisa where she could go with her thoughts and prayers—he'd be dead by sunrise anyway, so what was the difference?—when he ran across a comment from "Rahni Sage," one of the execrable New Age shitbags Lisa liked to call her friends, a deplorable phony of a man whose real name was fucking Ronald. Scott had seen the way Ronald had looked at Lisa with his stupid smile and rat's nest of a manbun— he'd even do it right in front of his girlfriend Sasha—the way he'd leered at Lisa and flirted with her, the way she limped her wrist, as if Scott had no right to say anything. Sasha had once even come onto Scott, drunkenly put her hand on his crotch, assuring him "Rahni was cool with it." What kind of couple is cool with that? Absolute trash people.

Here's what's happening, Rahni wrote, *and every word of this is Gospel truth. This poor girl was kidnapped for Adrenochrome. People in Hollywood are addicted to it. They harvest it from our adrenaline glands and take it to get high. The purest form comes from children.*

Scott should have used this opportunity to humiliate Rahni, to make him look like the crank he was—no one else was pushing back—Lisa had even liked the comment. But something told him he should research Adrenochrome, at the very least he could use factual inaccuracies against Rahni, so he opened a new tab and looked it up. One of the first results was a video link about Adrenochrome, which traced it back to the drug "drencom" (the Nadsat trans- lation for Adrenochrome) in *A Clockwork Orange.* From there, the video went on to make ridiculous claims, showing grainy clips from a supposed snuff film recorded at an unnamed Hollywood producer's mansion. They never showed the child being tortured or killed, thankfully—instead pivoting to Before and After shots of Hollywood actresses, showing the severe weight loss they'd suffered as a result of their Adrenochrome addiction. Scott hated himself for watching the entire video. Scott hadn't even realized the video had ended, and gone straight into another video, "The Truth About Millie DuFresne," a fif- teen minute clip tying J.D. Salinger and MKUltra to the Millie DuFresne In- cident, which Scott had personally lived through during graduate school. The man who made this video, a talk radio host named Gordy French, confirmed everything Scott had already known about Millie—her father's connections to global banking interests, the fact the pipe bombs she'd used were the same ones used by CIA-influenced counterculture terrorists in the early 70's, her obsession with *Catcher in the Rye.* And for the first time all night, Scott felt something close to comfort. He watched the next Gordy French video, one about Masonic rituals in *Catcher in the Rye* (which he'd already known about), and then another about Salinger's time as a counter-intelligence officer during WWII (which he'd also known about), and then another about the history of *Catcher in the Rye* and high-profile assassinations (which he'd also known about). For the next three hours, he watched video after video—new knowledge was gained, and old knowledge was validated—until he finally came to the end of his rabbit hole, the video clip that would change his life: "The Concentric Triangle: Pizza Galley and Pedophilia." Of course, not all of it was useful—the notion pedophiles worshipped Satan seemed a bit farfetched—but everything else made perfect sense. It made so much sense, that after it ended, Scott was able to crawl into bed and finally sleep for the first time in days, the rising sun and chirping birds be damned.

That night, he dreamt he and Sasha were once again in her kitchen, while Rahni and Lisa lay passed out on the couch. This time, when Sasha said "Rahni is totally cool with this," Scott realized he too was totally cool with it as well. He slid his tongue into her mouth and they lowered onto the dirty checkerboard laminate tiling, which then opened up and sucked them down into the darkness. He and Sasha descended into the abyss—their tongues, and limbs, and sex-parts tangled together—floating downward like a dying balloon.

"You're the second woman I've done this with," Scott said.

"Inertia got us here," Sasha said.

And he never questioned her response, the way he might have were he awake—he won't even remember she said this when he finally awakens and sneaks his underwear into the trashbin.

Scott finally came to a little after noon. He took a long hot shower and then went back to the computer, watched "The Concentric Triangle" four more times before spending the rest of the day watching music videos of Lisa's favorite songs. His mother came home from work and asked him about his day. She was happy to hear he slept like a baby.

It Doesn't Mean What You Think It Does

A year after Song Jae-dong—his friends called him Jae—retired from IBM, his soul (they prefer the term "Earthly Occupant") wriggled out of his palm, and floated into the backyard. Before it disappeared into the sky, it told Jae Jeoseung Saja, the Emissary of Death, was on his way, told him to run away and lay low until it was safe to come out, told him the emissary couldn't take him as long as they were separated. So he's spent the past four years running up and down the west coast while his Earthly Occupant hid out in an old IBM 2314 stored in the basement of the Almaden Research Facility in San Jose, scouring data in an attempt to understand the nature of death and how to avoid it. Jae had a wife, Miri, and an adult daughter, Nina, and it hurt him to know they were probably worried sick about him. But his soul had asked for his trust, and if can't trust your own soul then can you really trust anyone?

Here's one thing Jae had learned in those four years: ghosts do exist. The dead do, in fact, wander among us. But it's not their souls that wander aimlessly—it's the bodies that wander, emptied of their Occupants. He'd see them all the time, men and women—even some children—shambling through the day like everyone else, empty shells, blood pumped through empty hearts, into empty minds.

On November 8, 2016, the America we'd fooled into existence vanished right before our eyes. No one thought he stood a chance. She was supposed to win by a landslide—our first female president. All the Thumbs-Up, Heart, and Angry Face reactions we'd accumulated were for naught. For all our righteous anger, our irreproachable scorn for that cretin, all of us so busy applauding ourselves and each other, we'd failed to see we were all like Charles Foster Kane in his futile attempt at starting a round of applause for Susan's opera performance, clapping loudly after everyone else had decided they'd had enough (dot gif)—convinced everyone around us was every bit as sensible and every bit as good as we knew ourselves to be. Looking back, his narrowest of victories makes perfect sense. Look at who we are, where we live—this is who, and where, we've always been. We were living on borrowed time, but feeling clever certainly was nice while it lasted.

The day after the election, four days after Jae sent Scott Bonneville through the back door of the Pizza Galley, people wandered the streets in a daze. Of course, there were still people with smiles on their faces, people who'd run into neighbors or relatives, still hoping for the kind of consideration they'd refused others for the past eight years, but for the most part, people tried to keep to themselves—what could they really say to one another? What could anyone possibly say to make that feeling go away?

Jae watched them from the bus stop on the corner of Hawthorne and Lomita Blvd, the sad way they pumped their gas, the way they stared vacantly into their phones, the way their jaws clenched when another person said "good morning," the way they wondered if that person had voted for him—what the fuck was so good about this morning?

For the first time in months, people had acknowledged Jae's presence. They stopped to offer him money, to ask if he'd had anything to eat, to tell him they were sorry the country was the way it was, sorry they had created a world where a man lived the way he was living. Jae would stare at them, confused, until he realized stopping and talking to him wasn't an act of kindness. It was penance, and once he realized that, he'd wished they'd go back to the way things were—back to when they'd forced themselves to ignore him the way they'd tried to ignore the seagulls picking through the dumpsters.

In another life, Jae would have judged these people harshly—called them soft, called them childish self-centered liberals—but only because he'd lacked an understanding of their sickness. He now knew they'd lost the will to live, and they'd only spoken to him because their Occupants had compelled them to do so, drawn to him as a cry for help. He'd always hated when the Occupants called to him, how swelling domes of stretched skin ballooned from necks, or wrists, or cheeks as they tried to escape their bodies. These encounters had intensified during the weeks leading up to the election. On good days, Jae invoked memories of little Nina pushing against her mother's womb, the outline of her little hand brushing against Miri's swollen belly—and doing this usually helped him cope with the curse of knowing these people were as good as dead. On bad days—and they were mostly bad days—he'd remember the last time he'd gone to that little diner in San Jose, the one Nina had loved since she was a child. It was on Lanai Street, and they used to go every other Sunday morning for brunch. On that fateful day, Jae noticed the scoop of butter on his pancake bubbling in and out as if it were breathing. Finally the bubble popped and a fat housefly emerged, desperately rubbing its front legs together in an attempt to clean itself. At those times, Jae curled into a ball, moaned into the concrete, until the people backed away, their hosts begging Jae to stay with them. He'd sometimes look up, and watch the people turn back in pity—this crazy homeless man who no longer had the capacity to appreciate charity—their Occupants cursing him for turning his back on them.

That morning, the morning after the election, a young man dressed for his business casual job stopped next to him and took a seat. They stared at the empty building the Democratic party had rented as a call center during the election. A group of young volunteers stood with police officers, shaking their heads at the red graffiti sprayed across the glass storefront: *#GOODGUY-WITHAGUN*.

"That place used to be a toy store when I was a kid," the young man said.

"You don't say," Jae said.

"The guy who owned the building jacked up the rent, and they went out of business. I went to high school with his son."

"The guy who owned the toy store or the guy who owned the building?"

"I used to ride my bike to that store with my paper route money. Star Wars, pro wrestling action figures, that place had everything. It's like, I had so much money to burn back then. And now, every time I go to work, it's like I'm chasing that feeling, you know? You could buy a lot of useless pieces of plastic with paper route money."

He looked like he was going to cry, this young man. He seemed like a nice kid, the kind of boy Jae would've been happy to see Nina bring home, rather than the ponytailed ingrates she'd usually introduced him to. Jae asked the young man what he did for a living. The man closed his eyes, and the side of his neck began to twitch in and out as if something were poking at it from the inside.

What do I do? a voice called out from beneath the skin.

Jae looked away, even closed his eyes for good measure. The first time Jae had seen an Occupant push through the skin like this was four years ago—in Truckee, fifteen miles outside of Lake Tahoe. He'd been on the run for a mere eight hours when he ran into a young Korean couple vacationing from Daegu. As the husband spoke about the fresh mountain air, Jae noticed a small lump along the wife's jawline—he wondered if she'd contracted the mumps. Before he could ask if she was feeling well, the lump began to move, and a shrill Korean voice called out to him in the same harsh, sharp-pitched southeastern accent his father had also spoken with, telling him all she'd ever wanted was a child, that this husband was too selfish to notice, how sorry the husband would be when Jeoseung Saja came to end her sorrows and left him to a life of loneliness. Jae fell backwards, held up his hands, shielding his face until the couple slowly backed away. He ran into the forest, abandoning his car and all his belongings.

Please, the voice whined. *Tell me what to do.*

It chilled his blood, their horrible voices. Sometimes, he'd even tried to tell himself he was losing his mind, but he knew he wasn't. The young man asked Jae if he was okay. Jae concentrated on the empty building across the street, focused his eyes on the graffiti, asked the young man to tell him about the toy store, begged him to keep talking.

"Uh, sure," the young man said. "Okay. Anyway, when the store finally closed down, I was way too old for toys. But knowing that it was closing down forever, I couldn't help but go in there. It was so fucking empty, and so big, and sad. The owner's son was in there. We talked for a little bit, and I left with three packs of hockey cards. I don't even like hockey. I just couldn't leave empty-handed, you know?"

The poking swelled into a lump, and moved slowly from the side of the neck to the back of the young man's hairline—whenever it moved like that, Jae was reminded of a cartoon mouse running under a carpet, like those old *Tom and Jerry* cartoons he used to watch with Nina. Although Jae had been seeing these occupants push and stretch for years now, it was still every bit as unnerving as it had been with the poor housewife from Daegu. In those moments, thinking about *Tom and Jerry*, the way Nina laughed every time Jerry tunneled through the carpet into the mouse hole cut in the baseboard, soothed the horror of watching the human soul pushing against its restraints. The young man watched as more campaign volunteers showed up to help break everything down, every single one of them making their way to the graffiti—their Occupants wailing in confusion.

"Look at those fucking people," the young man said. "They might as well have opened a toy store because they sure as shit couldn't win an election."

And Jae looked at those fucking people—the way they held one another, the way they pinched the bridges of their noses, the way they cried as hand trucks moved boxes and boxes of crap that no longer mattered—blood pumping through broken hearts, into bitter minds.

The bus came, and the young man pulled out his wallet and handed Jae all the cash he had—a ten dollar bill, a five, and three singles. And as he stepped onto the bus, his Occupant pushed out the back of his neck, begged Jae to tell it what to do. Jae turned away, placed his chin on the back of the bench, pulled his legs under him and stared at the seagulls gathering in the empty lot behind the bench, cringing every time the Occupant demanded he listen. He shut his eyes tightly, until he could only see black spots floating in the darkness behind his eyelids, and groaned until a police officer roused him and told him to move along.

Gwishin Samchun

She'd met him eight months before the Pizza Galley Shooting, and at the end of every shift, Yu-jin Walker brought Jae leftover pizza and a drink. He'd always told her not to trouble herself—that he'd only come to hear her voice—but he always came and she always had pizza. The first night they'd met, she'd stayed a bit late as the manager till had an overage of $18.73. After walking Darcy to her car, she walked to hers, parked in the employee spots on the side of the restaurant, when she saw Jae sitting on the stoop in front of Receiving. She placed a bag of leftovers she was taking home to the twins on her car, reached into her coat pocket to make sure she had her pepper spray ready, just in case.

"Hello?" she'd said. "Are you okay?"

"Korean girl," the man had replied.

"How did you know?"

The man stood up and walked over to her. She slowly reached into her coat pocket, fingering the pepper spray attached to her keys. He smiled, held up his hands.

"Don't shoot," he said. "I'm just an old man. My name is Jae. What's your name, Korean girl?"

"Yu-jin."

She grabbed the bag of pizza from the hood. The twins were sick of pizza for lunch. Every day they complained—who'd heard of children complaining about pizza? What kind of child begged for tuna sandwiches?

"There's pizza in here," she said. "Would you like it?"

He took the bag. Looked inside of it, closed his eyes and breathed it in. He turned back to her. He was very clearly Korean, like her—even obscured by that white beard—it was very plain to see. Her mother had once told her to look at the jaw and cheeks to see who was Korean and who was Chinese, and this man had a Korean jaw, Korean cheekbones. Adam had once asked her how she could tell people apart, and she joked there was a secret code amongst Asians. She looked at this man's face and smiled, remembering Adam's frustration.

"What's that smile about?" Jae asked.

"I'm thinking about my husband," she said.

"White boy, right?"

"How did you know?"

"We just know, don't we?"

She texted her mother-in-law to let her know she was running a bit late, then sat with Jae. A policeman stopped to ask if everything was okay. She told him she was fine. He didn't seem to believe her, so she told the policeman Jae was her uncle. She stared at him, trying to will his skeptical face away from Jae's and toward hers. He appraised Jae, who began to squirm and wince. Jae stared at the policeman, and his eyes slowly widened. His hands began to shake.

"Sir," the officer said. "Sir? Sir? Sir, I need you to look at me."

Jae's shoulders hunched. He lowered his head, a feeble whine seeping from his lungs. Yu-jin put her hand on his arm. When he finally looked at her, it was as if he'd seen a ghost.

"I'm sorry, officer," she said. "My uncle's not well."

The officer apologized for any distress he might have caused. He got in his car and wished them a nice evening. After the officer left, Jae and Yu-jin sat and spoke, mostly questions and answers. It didn't matter how crazy he'd sounded. She just missed having an actual conversation in Korean:

"Why did that police officer upset you?"

"I saw something happening to him, something that only I can see."

"What was it?"

"It's better if you don't know."

"Are you homeless?"

"I have a home and I'll go back as soon as Jeoseung Saja stops chasing me."

"Why would Jeoseung Saja come for you? Are you dying?"

"Not quite. My soul is hiding in San Jose. I'm here because he can't take us if we're separated."

"Was Jeoseung Saja coming for that police officer? Is that what you saw?"

"I'd rather you didn't know the horrible things I see."

"Do you have a family?"

"I have a wife and a daughter who just turned twenty-four three days ago."

"White wife?"

"How did you know?"

"We just know, don't we?"

"That's very funny."

"Don't you think they're worried about you?"

"I'll see them when it's time. What brought the Korean girl to California?"

"It's a long story."

"Good. I like long stories."

"I met my husband while he was stationed in Seoul. He got stationed in Oklahoma and we didn't want our sons to live there, so he shipped us here to live with his mother."

"It's not good for boys to be away from their father."

"He's in Afghanistan right now. He's leaving the army once he gets home."

"So he knows you're pregnant?"

"How did you know I was pregnant?"

"I see things, now that I'm beyond life and death."

"Does that make you a ghost?"

"I told you I'm not dead."

"This is very confusing."

"If it's easier for you, then I'm a ghost. I'm your ghost uncle."

She laughed at the thought of a ghost uncle. It sounded like a terrible TV show about a young, single woman haunted by the ghost of her uncle— *AIGOO! Why aren't you married yet? Don't you know I can't leave this plane of existence until you find a husband?*

He told her he should get going, that she should go home to her boys. And she told him to wait, so she could run to the 7-Eleven and buy him a drink. He told her not to bother, so she insisted.

"I may not be here when you get back," he said.

"Then you should come with me."

"I don't go to that place. There's a horrible woman with a dog. It's always barking at me because it knows what I am."

"Then wait here until I come back."

"I'll see what I can do."

On the way to 7-Eleven, she thought about whether it was possible Jae was a ghost. Brenda, her mother-in-law, would have been horrified to know she was sitting with a homeless man. She stepped around a pile of dog crap at the 7-Eleven the parking lot and went into the store, came out with a Dasani and an orange juice. What had happened to this man? How could a retired software engineer become homeless? How could anyone lose their minds the way he had? And where was his wife? His daughter? They had to be worried sick. There was a homeless shelter next to her church. As soon as she got back, she'd make sure to mention it to him. She passed a group of teenage boys walking toward the store, and told them to be careful of the dog poop.

"Yeah we know," they said. "Some dumb lady and her pug. The guy that owns the place keeps telling her to knock it off."

"Every night he comes out here and hoses it down," they said. "It's all so stupid."

They voiced their hatred of the dog, telling one another of its horrible bark, that it barked all the goddamn time, that they'd love to kick it onto the roof of the 7-Eleven, each of them snapping high kicks that lifted them off the ground, laughing. Yu-jin smelled the pot on their clothes. They'd completely forgotten about her.

"Why doesn't someone complain?" Yu-jin asked. "Has he called the police?"

"A cop stepped in it once. He was so pissed off. It was hilarious."

The boys all laughed, mimicking the policeman scraping the heel of his boot against the concrete stop. Yu-jin made her way back to her parking lot.

Jae was gone by the time she'd returned. The next day, she finished her shift at 7:30. She knew he'd be there. She gave him the pizza, grabbed the Dasani and Orange juice from the cooler in her trunk.

"I can't stay today," she said.

"I know," he said." I'll see you Thursday."

"How did you know that was my next shift?"

"We just know, don't we?"

Son of the Geek

During his junior year of college, Scott had gotten drunk and set fire a dumpster outside the dorm. It was a little past midnight, September 11, 2000—the day Cary Bonneville had been preparing for during Scott's entire life had come and gone for Scott, but in Lanai, it was still three minutes after ten. What time zone had God observed? Was the apocalypse scheduled for the Hawaii-Aleutian time zone or the Pacific standard? What about in Seoul, where Reverend Park had gathered with his congregation? What time was it there? Was God waiting until the clock struck midnight in Seoul? Karachi? Moscow? What a joke it all was.

Because alcohol had been forbidden in his father's house, because he'd never felt any desire for a drink at his mother's, he thought he'd finally have a drink before the seven angels blew their seven trumpets, cracking open the skies, flooding the world with fire. This excuse was meant in jest, as Scott had become an Atheist by this time, knowing everything his father had to say about the end times was complete and utter bullshit. It just seemed like as good a time as any to get drunk for the first time. He sat in his dorm room, alone with a cheap plastic bottle of vodka, watching his father and a now teenage Brian on the news, singing hymns with their cult on Hulopoe Beach.

Earlier in the day, before a Victorian History class, one of his classmates, a frat boy named Jack, had asked Scott if he knew today was the last day on Earth, that there was some whack-job in Hawaii who'd predicted tomorrow to be the end times.

"That's my dad," Scott had said.

Jack laughed and wanted him to be serious—he'd even said, *Seriously*, a few times in order to redirect the conversation—and Scott told him it was seriously his father who was preparing for the End of Days in Hawaii. Jack laughed, and Scott almost told him it wasn't funny, before realizing the ways in which it was.

"Dude," Jack said. "I had no idea. Are you close?"

"If we were, I'd be hiding in shame right now."

"So, you're half-Asian then?"

"I'm—well, I guess I'm adopted."

"Cool, man. My mom's adopted. I'm sorry about your dad, man."

"Fuck him. He's an asshole."

Jack turned to the girls sitting behind them—both pretty girls, both wearing matching white sorority sweatshirts, the Greek letters Σ and K in blue and yellow plaid. He asked them what they were up to, and Scott was amazed at the ease with which Jack talked to these girls—*Hey, what's up?*—the way they responded with smiles—*Not much. What's up with you?*—unforced smiles, not like the ones Scott received when girls thought his gaze had lingered a few seconds too long. Their names were Victoria and Harley—what kind of name is Harley? And had Jack really not known their names? Had they really just met? Why were their interactions glossed with the patina of familiarity? Scott's mind reeled at the effortlessness of their commiseration.

"This is my boy Scott," Jack said.

"Hey, Scott," Victoria said. Harley said nothing, just nodded and forced a smile.

"You know that dude on TV," Jack said, "the one who says the world is gonna end today? That's Scott's dad. Seriously, isn't that crazy?"

They looked at Scott, shouted, *No way*, and that's when Scott realized what was going on. Jack was using him to break the ice with Victoria and Harley. Jack seemed friendly enough—far more personable than most frat boys Scott had encountered—but he still clearly suffered from the same dullness and lack of imagination his kind struggled to overcome. Of course he needed someone like Scott as a point of interest, as he had nothing interesting to offer on his own. So Scott didn't really mind too much, as the smiles that followed were the same unwittingly natural smiles they'd presented to Jack. It wasn't every day two pretty girls parted their mouths and offered wide-eyed, attentive smiles— at least not for Scott.

"So what's his deal, man?" Harley said.

"Angels came to him in a dream," Scott said, "at least that's what he says. They supposedly carried him to the sky, and he thought they were taking him to heaven. Then the entire sky burst into flames and the angels dropped him, so they could shield their faces. As he fell to the earth, he saw God's face—"

"What the hell," Harley said.

"And he heard God's voice. He said God's voice was like words typed out in his brain—I don't know, that's just what he told me—and those words were an instruction to prepare His children—God's children, that is—for, you know, today."

"So did you grow up in that cult?" Victoria asked. "I mean, no offense—"

"I did until I was nine. My mom left him and brought me here. We're just as confused by him as you are."

"It's so crazy that you're his son," Victoria said.

"Anyway," Jack said, "you should tell them what it was like. You know, having that dude as your dad."

So Scott told them what it was like having Cary Bonneville as a father—going door to door in an attempt to recruit new converts, being forced to memorize the Bible from Genesis 1:1 to Mark 3:35 (his mother having taken him away before the Parable of the Sower), watching church members converse (yes, converse) in tongues—and he had to admit it felt good to hold the fascination of these two pretty girls in their Sigma Kappa sweatshirts, even though they weren't necessarily fascinated by him, but by his father. Cary Bonneville was no more than a circus freak to them—he may as well have bitten the heads off live chickens. Scott understood being the object of morbid curiosity, as it was all he ever had going for him. In middle school, Scott had devoured book after book about urban legends, and realized that people paid attention to him when he told those stories he'd read as things that had happened to him or people he knew back on Lanai.

It's true, he'd once said. *Burger King uses wallaby meat in their Whoppers. That's why they taste different. There was a wallaby farm next to our old house on Lanai. Australian sailors brought them over on their ships and then let them loose, so my neighbor had to catch and kill them. Then he found out they tasted pretty good, so he kept them as livestock and sold the meat to Burger King.*

The only time his classmates had ever really enjoyed Scott's company was when he told these tall tales, as he was normally thought of as off-puttingly strange and a bit of a know-it-all. Every day, he thought of new lies to tell in order to keep them from avoiding him—that is, until high school, when he told the Tale of the Choking Doberman, trying to pass it off as his own, and a teacher pointed out how that story had been floating around since the early 70's. He'd gotten a lot of mileage from telling outlandish stories throughout his life. At least the things he was telling Jack and the sorority girls was the truth. After class, Jack told him good luck and left with the two girls to grab lunch.

Hey, Scott, you should come with us, no one said.

Yeah, no one replied. *Come hang out.*

Scott stared at his father's his face on the TV, uplit by torchlight. It was 10:04 PM in Lanai. The reporter said they'd been there for a little over thirty minutes. He hadn't seen his father in eleven years, and marveled at how old and fat he'd gotten. They were singing "We Shall See His Lovely Face," one of his father's favorite hymns. Scott marveled at how tall Brian had grown, towering over the other parishioners. He looked just like their father—had his eyes, his nose, even his small ears. Brian wept as he mouthed the words, *Trials cease, all is peace, when we see His face*, on the television screen, and for the first time in his life, Scott felt sadness for his brother. The way Brian's eyes turned toward the night sky, the way he clutched the tiki torch in both hands like a Little Leaguer choking up on the bat—if things had gone differently, Scott would've been on the beach with him, his arm around Brian, comforting his brother, letting him know that sorrow would be turned to joy very soon, that heartaches would be gone forever.

No more night, only light, when we see His face.

Scott winced as the vodka burned against his breastbone. He wiped his mouth and set the bottle on the floor. His father's eyes, closed in the gentlest of ways, his brows raised as he swayed back and forth to the hymn—he imagined his father on stage at a circus sideshow, speaking in tongues as the audience laughed and threw rotten fruit. Cary Bonneville's eyes would be closed in the same way they were now on the TV, mushy chunks of fruit sliding down his face like melting wax. Scott was dizzy. He could feel his face swelling, and every breath felt like a parched riverbed. He imagined tiny cracks forming in his lungs, the moisture being pulled from them, and remembered what drowning felt like, a man's hand holding his head underwater—*I don't want to hurt you, Scotty. Just trust me and you'll be A-okay*—the water filling his nose and lungs until he begged for his life, said he'd do anything. *Please make it stop. I'll do whatever you want. Please make it stop.* He took one more swig of vodka and stumbled outside, stealing a pack of cigarettes from his roommate's closet.

When the campus police found him in the bushes behind the bike racks, curled in a ball, crying in his own puke, they asked him if he'd lit the dumpster on fire. He told them he didn't remember. He didn't remember much after leaving his room, except that the cigarette was so awful he'd thrown it in the dumpster.

Adventures of Superman, Vol. 1, #428

Conflating Scott's drunken tears with his father's humiliation, the university took pity on him and decided not to expel him. Scott was placed on probation as long as he agreed to counseling. At that point, everyone in the dorm knew he was the son of that crazy doomsday preacher, the one they'd laugh about for days after September 11th had come and gone without incident. Some even took pity on him, confiding in Scott the shortcomings of their own fathers—things like drug addiction and spousal abuse. One girl even told him about her father's prison sentence for money laundering. Of course, she never spoke to him again—even went out of her way to ignore him when he asked if she'd like to hang out sometime—but Scott had to admit being noticed felt nice, until realizing what exactly he was being noticed for.

The fallout from Lanai lasted for weeks. Once midnight came and went without incident, two parishioners named Darren and Janine Korematsu smothered their children with pillows before slitting their wrists and bleeding to death in the center of the Kaumalapau Highway. Reverend Bonneville's bodyguard Neil "the Deal" McNeil, a man Scott had spent too much time hiking with, was arrested for trying to strangle the reverend with his belt. A woman named Carla Montes became a tragic profile on the news shows, as she was in financial ruin after the Rapture never came—*Where we're going, we won't need money,* the Reverend had told her—having spent all of her life savings visiting Mt. Rushmore, and Yellowstone, and the Grand Canyon, so that she could ascend without having spent her life only seeing them in books.

During a nationally televised basketball game, the Chicago Bulls burned all of their timeouts with nine minutes left in the fourth quarter, as they were up by twenty-nine. They ended up losing to the Celtics by two points. Conan O'Brien joked that Reverend Cary Bonneville had advised the Bulls to burn those timeouts because God had told him the game was in the bag. When the audience groaned, O'Brien retorted with a dry, *Yeah, you're right. How dare I make fun of that idiot?* and promptly won back the crowd.

Carla Montez walked into the ocean. Her body was never found. A postcard from Mt. Rushmore, George Washington in profile, washed in with the tide.

That his father was now a national punchline, that he was going bankrupt, was of little concern to Scott. What mattered was finding a way to turn his life around. Since leaving Lanai for Redondo Beach, Scott had wanted his father to fail. Although his mother had voiced sadness for what had happened to her ex-husband, Scott took a secret pleasure in watching his father fall on his face, and he knew his mother had as well. The universe had soundly defeated Cary Bonneville, and it felt as though that chapter in his life had closed. Even though his mother wasn't able to collect her alimony, even though his classmates and professors now knew all about his shameful parentage, even though he had to spend every other Thursday afternoon with Dr. Sheilagh Ong, all was right in the world. The man who'd cheated on his mother, the man who'd whipped him with a belt whenever he failed to recite Bible verses using the language of the King James Bible (he'd sometimes slip into the language used in the English Standard Version his mother had used to teach children), the man who'd continued sending him off on hikes with Neil McNeil (even after he'd complained of Neil pressuring him into skinny dipping "the way men like to do when they're alone")—that man had finally come to ruin. In spite of the issues his mother was having, in spite of his own issues, for the first time in his life, Scott felt something he'd come to call peace.

"We're about to turn a corner, Scotty," his mother had said. "I hope there's nothing bad waiting for us."

"It's like you always say," Scott said. "The worst is always behind us."

Years later, Scott would realize that his mother was wrong. The past isn't behind us at all. The past is all around us. When his pupils complained of hating history, usually during *A Tale of Two Cities*, he'd tell them to look out the window. A car would drive past, or a cyclist would pedal through, or an elderly woman in a tracksuit would walk her Labradoodle on the sidewalk.

"Well that just happened," he'd say after these objects left their frame of vision, "and that's history."

"I don't get it," they'd say.

"You hate history because you think it's the past," he'd tell them. "But the fact is, you're on one side of a chain and everyone in this book is on the other. You're connected by all those silver links. You need to realize how strong that connection is. For example, that old lady who always walks her dog past our window every morning, how does that make you feel?"

"I love it," a girl named Claire Cohen said. "I love that dog's face, I love how cute that lady is in her sunglasses and sweatpants—this is gonna sound weird, but sometimes when I don't see them, I worry about her."

"So the thing that happens affects your life in some way then. Well, that's history. If you can't connect with the things that happened, the things that are still happening, then you're not thinking hard enough."

Scott's mother had treated the past like a room she'd left, a door she'd closed behind her, and maybe she was right in her own way. But the things we experience in those rooms, the things we see, we carry with us into the present because we carry inside of us every room we've ever walked out of. There is no past. There's only the present, and those things we consider to be done and gone stay with us like barnacles clinging to the side of ship.

But that doesn't mean we always understand the past, or even remember it. And this was the issue during Scott's first few sessions with Dr. Sheilagh Ong. She kept asking him why he'd set fire to the dumpster, and when he'd say he didn't remember, she'd tell him to think about it a little more, and then he'd tell her it was because of the cigarette he'd stolen from his roommate's closet—a roommate who'd moved out a few weeks after the incident—she'd ask him if perhaps there was more to it than just the cigarette.

"I'm pretty sure it was the cigarette," he'd say.

An important lesson he learned in his sessions with Dr. Ong was that awkward silences were only awkward for him. She was very good at sitting and waiting things out, scribbling on her notepad, telling him to take his time, while the grandfather clock in the back corner ticked and tocked, ticked and tocked.

"I don't know," Scott said. "Maybe deep down, I was still angry with my father and embarrassed because of what he did."

"Do you feel abandoned by him in any way?"

"No. I mean, my mother left him and took me with her. If anything, he should feel abandoned."

"But your brother, Brian, right? He got to stay with your father. Do you have any contact with him?"

"My mother and I never mention him at all. As a matter of fact, that day on TV when they were all singing and waiting to die was the first time I'd seen him in about eleven years."

"So, eleven years. That would have made you. . . ."

"We moved to Redondo when I was nine years old," Scott said. "Because I'd been schooled in the church, my first few years in elementary school weren't very fun. The first day of class, I was asked to introduce myself."

Scott stared at the grandfather clock. As the pendulum on the grandfather clock clicked back and forth, he knew Dr. Ong wanted him to continue. He remembered his first day class, the confusion on their faces when he told them his name was Scott Bonneville. He looked more like a Logan Chang, or a Cecilia Tanizaki, or a Jason Hong—all classmates of his—than he'd ever look like a Scott Bonneville. At the time, he didn't realize why they'd looked so confused. On top of the cognitive dissonance that was his name and his face, when Mrs. Nelligan asked him to tell the class something that made him special, he told them his father had spoken with angels. To Mrs. Nelligan's horror, he told the room how the world was going to end on September 11, 2000, how seven angels would blow seven trumpets, and those not taken into the Kingdom of God would watch the skies shatter into a million shards of fire. Three of his classmates began to cry, and he was sent to the office, where a counselor, a young woman whose name Scott didn't remember, sat him down and asked him why he'd made up such a story.

Dr. Ong's phone rang. She told Scott not to worry, that she'd call them back, to just take his time, so Scott took his time, stared at his hands, at the scuff marks on the coffee table, the way his jeans bunched up at the crotch, without saying a word.

The counselor called Scott's mother, and Scott was asked to sit outside, on a bench in front of the reception desk, while the counselor and his mother spoke. The school secretary gave him a stack of word search puzzles to keep him occupied—even though they were insultingly easy and he was done with them in five minutes. When they finally called him into the office, it was clear his mother had been crying. He'd never seen her cry before—not when she begged his father to leave Seoul to come Stateside, not when his father brought Brian home, not when she carried him from his bed to the taxicab that took them to the airport away from his father.

As Scott's mother blew her nose, the counselor told him the things his father had told him weren't true, and that repeating those stories to his class-mates was going to upset them.

"He's a fraud," his mother had said.

The counselor smiled the best she could, most likely hoping he wouldn't know what fraud meant, and asked him if he was okay. He nodded, and his mother reached out for his hand. He pulled away.

That night, his aunt and mother took him to Pizza Galley, of all places, for dinner—the exact same Pizza Galley he and Dave Brightman had designated as the Ground Zero of the rest of their lives. He'd never been to any place like it in his life, having grown up on a small island where his entire life had revolved around the church. Earlier in the day, Aunt Margaret had even taken him to a comic book store right after school. He stood at the Whack-a-Mole, which at Pizza Galley was known as Whack-a-Troll, as trolls were the sworn enemies of Captain Pete Pizza and his brave crew: Alvin Albatross, First Mate

Calico Jaqueline, Sadie the Goat, and the buffoonish buccaneer Olive-head. As Scott smashed the trolls, who popped up from the holes dotting a deserted island, his mother rubbed his back and told him the truth about his life. His mother was a young girl named Soo-mi. She'd had an affair with the Reverend Cary Bonneville, the prophet of God, and had been banished from the church by Reverend Park and, of course, Wilma Bonneville herself. Ten months later, Soo-mi left him on the front steps of the church with a note explaining who Scott was, asking for God's forgiveness.

"So, Father is my real Dad?" he asked.

"Yes, he is."

"So I'm not adopted?"

"You are my son and I love you so much."

"How come I don't look like Father?"

"You have his mouth, and his chin. I think you look very much like him."

Scott thought about the comic book store he'd gone to earlier in the day, how Aunt Margaret had told him Superman had also been adopted by a family who loved him very much, how that had made Scott feel special—that this big, strong boy had been sent away by his real parents, how he'd overcome everything to become someone who could fly. Scott had read the comic in his bedroom while Wilma and Aunt Margaret talked in the living room, wondering if he could someday learn to fly. That was now all a lie.

A troll sprung from his hole and giggled. Then another. And another. Scott didn't even attempt to hit them.

"Is Brian my real brother?"

His mother nodded, but only after averting his gaze. It was as if she weren't nodding at him at all, but nodding as if finally accepting an inconvenient truth. She wasn't acknowledging Scott, but Brian. Years later, when he learned the meaning of the word Bastard, Scott would remember how he'd felt, standing in front of that Whack-a-Troll machine, wishing the mallet wasn't made of foam rubber, wishing he'd had the super-strength to really damage those giggling plastic trolls, the heat-vision to burn the entire restaurant to the ground.

Dr. Ong cleared her throat. When Scott looked up, she tried to reassure him, tell him that she wasn't clearing her throat to pressure him at all, that she simply had something caught in her throat.

"My first day of school," Scott said, "was pretty awful. So my Aunt Margaret took me to the comic book store. I'd never read a comic book in my life, so I had no idea where to even start. She picked a Superman comic off the rack and I stared at the cover. I remember he was in the desert fighting a giant made of sand."

"Do you think Superman being adopted had anything to do with her choosing that for you? Scott, I'd rather you not roll your eyes."

"I'm sorry. It's just, she probably chose it because it was Superman. What American kid hasn't read a Superman comic? Well, I hadn't at that point, so I'm sure she was just trying to help me be normal or something."

"What do you mean normal?"

"I grew up on a religious compound on a secluded island. My father thought he was a prophet of God. So I'm assuming normal to mean, you know, the opposite of that. Reading comic books, watching cartoons, eating at Pizza Galley—that sort of thing."

"So what made you think of this Superman comic?"

"I remember that comic. Every detail. Every March, my aunt has to call and remind me when my mom's birthday is, but that comic I remember."

"What do you remember?"

"Superman going to the Middle East with Jimmy Olsen. Rescuing a reporter, who turned out to have died in the desert a year ago, his body possessed by the leader of a secret society of aliens who've been living among us since ancient Egypt."

"So it sounds like this comic really spoke to you."

"You know what I remember the most? Actually, I didn't really think much of it at the time, but something just hit me. The comic starts with the front page of *The Daily Planet* and this photo on the front page of Superman destroying a tank. The caption talked about how Superman went into this country, they called the country Qurac ha-ha, and wiped out their entire military because of they were a terrorist state. The caption then said that leaders of other countries were worried Superman might one day turn his attention on them. Well, a few years later, we invaded Iraq. Qurac, Iraq—you ever wonder if little things like that maybe chip away at us until we're okay with doing bad things?"

"Can you tell me what you mean by bad things?"

"I remember when we invaded Iraq, I was caught up in all of the patriotism, like I cheered all those bombs being dropped on Baghdad. People died and I was cheering, you know? Maybe if Superman hadn't taught me that a country that rhymed with Iraq was bad, I might've felt different about it."

"Well, in all fairness, we did invade Iraq to liberate Kuwait."

"Sure, that's the official thing we like to say, but it's not like Kuwait was innocent in all of this. I read how there was an oil surplus in the 80's which lowered oil prices. This hurt Iraq which had war debts to pay off from the war with Iran. The country most responsible for increasing oil output, which lowered the value of oil, was Kuwait."

"Do you feel that justifies invading Kuwait?"

"Well, that's the thing. Saddam tried to settle things diplomatically, but then he also discovered Kuwait was using slant drilling along the Iraq Kuwait border to siphon oil from the Iraqi side. I'm not saying Saddam was a great guy, but we can't say this wasn't a war for oil. We wanted cheap oil, which Kuwait was willing to give us, and Iraq wanted to raise the price of oil. Sometimes, we have dig deeper than just what the media feeds us. The research is out there. We just have to look for it."

"Well that's interesting. So can you tell me how this ties back to Superman?"

"That's it. Just, propaganda's really subtle and I didn't even realize I was being fed a load of crap until just now."

"How so?"

"Maybe we're born with an immunity to bullshit, kind of. And they slowly break us down through books, and movies, and things like that until we're ready to accept the world they want us to live in. For example, my father used the Bible as a weapon. I had to read the Bible every day, and then once a week, he'd make me recite passages. It got to the point where the only thing I thought about was the Bible—I'd even dream about it. It's like conditioning, you know? Like Skinner's Box."

"I'm not sure if that's what the Skinner Box was doing, but I'd love to hear—"

"Well okay, maybe not literally, but I meant it was kind of like it."

"Let's see if we can tie your feelings on the Superman comic to your father and the Bible. Can we try that?"

At the end of the session, Dr Ong told Scott she felt they'd made a lot of progress. All they did was talk about Superman as a propaganda tool, how it made him feel good to buy into the illusion of good vs evil. Occasionally, she steered conversation back to his father, how the Reverend had used negative reinforcement to ensure Scott learned every verse down to the word. She'd even admitted that his Skinner Box allusion made sense in a lot of ways. So in the end, Scott agreed—they had made a bit of progress.

Prescribed Burn

On September 11, 2001, a year after Scott set the dumpster on fire, a year after angels told his father the world as we knew it was coming to an end, four planes bound for California were hijacked. What happened afterwards is all public knowledge—although Scott would point out everything else is still up for debate—but needless to say, Reverend Cary Bonneville and the Church of the New Millennium were able to turn their fortunes around. Scott's father was able to claim he misinterpreted the angels' words, as he's merely a mortal man, tossing out a jumble of numbers in order to prove his math was off. Reverend Bonneville then hit the lecture circuit, and Scott watched him on TV talking about how thrilling it was to go out and do actual missionary work again, meaning he was able to make enough money from his new writings and lectures, meaning his mother's checks once again arrived on time, meaning Scott no longer had to listen to her cry on the phone while she called his father a lying bastard.

That year, which was undoubtedly an awful one in American history, had actually turned out to one of Scott's best. With Dr. Ong's help, he was able to turn his life around and become a model citizen, making President's Honor Roll and graduating *cum laude* with a Bachelor's in Education. She'd even written a letter of recommendation for him, and along with his Statement of Purpose—which was about how literature saved him from his oppressive, religious background—Scott was accepted into a Master's Program in English Literature at a small school in Oregon.

The reverend had agreed to pay for graduate school on one condition: Scott would have to meet him for lunch. The summer after graduation, Scott met his father at the Marriott in Anaheim, where the reverend was to give a talk on radical Islam and the rapture. The reverend stood in the middle of the lobby, smiling broadly in a black Aloha shirt—a forest of palm trees in front of two blue mountains. For the first time, Scott could see the curl that rested at each end of the lips, the softly pointed chin—it was clear Cary was his father. He didn't want to hug him, but his father's grip was so tight he felt the only way he'd be free is if he's reciprocated. Gray stubble pricked against Scott's chin as the reverend kissed him on the cheek. His breath stunk of cigars.

"My son," Cary said. "After all these years. Let me get a look at you."

Cary held Scott by the biceps as he stepped back. His air-conditioned hands were cold against Scott's skin. Cary closed his eyes and tilted his head to the ceiling.

"Dear Father, thank you for reuniting me with my son. May I fulfill your mission so that I can be worthy of giving praise to you and all that you've created. Amen."

They walked through the lobby and out the sliding doors. The midday sun burned away chill of the Marriott's climate control. The steakhouse was a block away.

"So," Scott said, "Hula shirts on the mainland, huh?"

"This isn't any Aloha shirt. It's a replica of the one Montgomery Clift wore in *From Here to Eternity*. Your mother loved that movie. That was the reason we moved from Seoul to Hawaii."

"Why not move to Pearl Harbor then?"

"It was harder to get the permits in Oahu. Reverend Park, remember him? He had friends on Lanai. I think we built a pretty good life on Lanai."

"You and Brian?"

A red hand told them to wait. Scott pushed the crosswalk button over and over again, as if a lack of insistence was what was holding them back. Cary pulled a wad of saran wrap from his pocket, unwrapped a smoked cigar. He cut below the burnt ashes at the tip and lit it, sucked in, blew a puff of smoke into the hot, stagnant air.

"It doesn't matter how many times you push it, son," Cary said. "It's on a timer like the rest of the stoplights. That button's a placebo. I imagine there's some fella on the other side of that security camera up there laughing at us for pushing that damn button like lab rats."

Scott looked over at the benches across the street, the ones covered in shade. The sun beat down on his face. The next morning, the skin on his nose and forehead would begin to peel.

"Tell me about your life," Cary said. "I haven't seen you since, wow, two days before your tenth birthday. You know, I was going to get you a dog. Then your mother had to pull that stunt."

"You mean leaving the man who cheated on her?"

"I didn't cheat on her. Wilma wanted me to conceive with other women. She just didn't want to know them the way she did Noelani, Brian's mother. Your mother was a stranger. That was how Wilma wanted it."

Scott touched his forehead, feverish with sunlight, with the back of his wrist.

45

"And to be completely honest" Cary said, "I think she wanted Brian to be white. With you, she had no choice. We were in a foreign country. But I think she'd have preferred our second child to not be a native."

The traffic light went green, and the cars began moving, and then the red hand was replaced with the silhouette of the pedestrian—maybe it really was all just a timer. Scott would never push a crosswalk button again. They walked the rest of the way in silence, Cary puffing on his cigar, the skin on Scott's bare arms pulsing red.

The steakhouse was full of families in cargo shorts, and tank tops, and Mickey Mouse skullcaps. Cary made sure to tell every child how much he admired their Mickey and Minnie ears, made sure to tell every parent to have a blessed day. Scott wondered if it were true—that his mother's issue with Brian was his Polynesian mother. He remembered going to the store with her, people asking her if he was her child, how defensive she became when they merely mentioned adoption. How much easier would it have been for her had Brian been a white child, one that looked like her? The waiter took their order, a Porterhouse for Cary and a burger for Scott.

"You ever been to Disneyland?" Cary asked.

"No. Never."

"I came here with Brian about six years ago. We called your mother to see if maybe you'd like to come along. She told me—"

"It's fine. I never really had any desire to go."

"How could you not want to come? It's wonderful. You hear people complain about Small World, but I have to tell you it's wonderful. All the children of the world, coming together to put a song in your heart. And your head, of course. That darn thing never leaves."

"Did you wonder how many of those children were yours?"

Cary took a sip of water and looked around, caught the eye of a toddler in a high chair and engaged in an impromptu game of peek-a-boo. The little girl shrieked every time Cary revealed himself. The girl's mother smiled at Scott, probably thinking about of wonderful it was that such a kind-faced man had adopted him, probably grateful her child was born in the U.S.A. and not whatever third world backwater she'd imagined Scott had come from. Scott thought of all the other half-Asian kids he'd known, how they'd either had light hair or fair skin. He'd inherited all of his father's dark features—his dark hair, his dark eyes—no one ever would've believed he was part French, by way of Belgium. How much easier could life have been for him, for his mother,

46

had he looked more like the other half-Asian kids? At least then people would assume she'd married some Asian man.

"That was a joke, Father."

"Well, it's not funny. Good Lord, Scott. That's something your mother would say."

"Why are we here? Why did you want me to come here?"

"Tell me more about grad school. What do you want to do with it? I thought you already had a teaching degree. Why can't you just go and teach now?"

"If you don't want to give me the money, that's fine."

"I'm already giving you the money, son. You can leave any time you want. I just wanted to see you again. I missed you. Your mother refused to let me speak to you all these years. And I wanted to give you this."

Cary pulled a small photo from his wallet, an old black and white picture of a beautiful young woman—smooth skin and silky black hair, the most joyful smile he'd ever seen. Scott ran his thumb along the thick matted surface of the photo. He couldn't take his eyes off of her.

"Soo-mi," Scott said.

"Your mother said you knew. She's doing great, by the way. Back in the church, runs a really successful clothing boutique in downtown Seoul."

After all Cary and Wilma Bonneville had done to her, she'd gone back to the church. Scott was certain they'd made her beg to come back, that she'd had to humble herself. He looked at the photo—she couldn't have been over nineteen in the picture, twenty at the most. Scott handed the photo back to Cary, who told him it was his.

"I don't need it," Scott said. "I have a mother."

"Scott, I told her about you, how you're doing. Do you know how proud she is?"

"I really don't give a shit."

"Come on, Scott. Try to be a little forgiving here."

"She left me on your front steps like dirty laundry."

"Her father was going to ship you to an orphanage. She had no choice, other than give you back to me, your father."

"And then she went back to you people? After you deserted her?"

"Soo-mi left us, Scott. Let's not forget that. She left us, and kidnapped you. I could've sent her to jail."

"You're a fraud, you know that? The only reason you're doing well now is because some terrorists decided to hijack a plane—"

"God told me those terrorists were coming. You don't think I knew about the World Trade Center?"

The waiter brought their food, warned Cary his plate was hot. Cary thanked him by his name, William. William told him he was welcome, called him sir, asked if they needed anything else. Cary said they were fine. Scott turned to the little girl, who'd still wanted to play peek-a-boo, covering her eyes with her chubby little hands. Cary began cutting his steak, blood pooling on his plate, seeping the edges of his mashed potatoes.

"I really was raptured, Scott—just not in the way we'd imagined. Me and a few others were actually taken. We were lifted into the sky, and we just floated for what seemed like hours above the ocean. And then this voice told me it wasn't time, that I had to prepare for the Holy War. Then all of the sudden, I was back in my body and it was midnight."

Cary turned to the little girl. He wiggled his fingers and she laughed. The mother smiled at Scott. Maybe Soo-mi's father should have taken Scott to the orphanage. Maybe then, he'd have been adopted by some nice family in Cedar Rapids. Maybe then, Scott could've smiled back when mothers smiled at him. *You're right*, he would've thought, *I am lucky to have found such a kind family that totally isn't balls-out insane.*

"He showed me the towers falling. I saw them with my own eyes while I floated five miles off the coast. The others—Darren and Janine Korematsu, Carla Montez, they saw it but refused to believe. Neil McNeil, remember him? You used to go hiking together when you were little. He completely lost his mind. He tried to kill me, did you know that?"

"Neil molested me."

Cary stuck a forkful of mashed potatoes into his mouth. He chewed very slowly. The little girl began to fuss. Cary turned to her and opened his mouth, showing her the mashed potatoes. Even the mother laughed at that one. She placed her card in the leather check holder, handed it to her server. Cary sucked water through the straw.

"I'm sorry he did that, I really am, but it's all over now."

"For you, maybe."

"For all of us. It doesn't matter anymore, Scotty. None of this does. When the time finally comes, this will all be wiped clean. Whatever the world becomes after that, who knows? Maybe they'll rebuild, maybe they'll fall into chaos. We won't be there for any of that."

When Scott was thirteen, he went to Yosemite with his mother and her boyfriend Mitchell. During a guided tour, they'd come across a charred clearing, where the park ranger told them about prescribed burning. She said they'd occasionally set fires in the forest in order to reduce the risk of bigger fires happening later. She compared it to dams letting water spill out in order to manage flooding. A man in the group asked if this was like hunting seasons keeping the animal population down, and the ranger said it was very much like that.

Scott had often thought 9-11 was just that, a prescribed burn. War, famine, pandemics—letting water spill from the dams helped prevent flooding. But he didn't share this horrible thought with Cary, or anyone else for that matter. What would people say had they known he thought widespread death was necessary from time to time? What kind of awful person thinks such things?

The mother walked past with her stroller. Cary leaned into the stroller and said bye-bye to little girl, whose name was Clara. She told Scott what a great grandfather Cary was going to make someday. He smiled, finally made eye contact, said maybe. Cary turned to the mother, his finger still in Clara's tiny grip.

"Japanese, right?" Cary said.

"Yes," Clara's mother said. "My father is Japanese."

"Wow," Scott said, "I honestly couldn't tell."

"I get that a lot," Clara's mother said. "Most people think I'm Latina for some reason."

"Well I could tell," Cary said. "Clear as day to me."

The Horwitz Conundrum (Solved)

After graduate school, Scott took a job teaching sophomore and junior English at DuClod-Mann High School in a small town outside of Portland, Oregon. It was, all in all, not a terrible place to work, even though his colleagues were idiots, most of them having post-graduate degrees in Education, rather than their chosen subjects—none of them were experts in anything other than classroom management, and developing curriculum, and understanding education policy. Scott knew what had set him apart from his peers was his extensive knowledge of literature, and analytical theory, and close-reading—which led many of his coworkers to find him arrogant and pedantic. When they met for functions, without Scott, Dora Maragos, who taught sophomore English, loved to bring up the time Scott told her she was teaching *Fahrenheit 451* wrong, that it wasn't about censorship but the death of intellectual curiosity. She'd brought it up so much, even the other teachers rolled their eyes. And when the music teacher Andrea Sokolov mentioned she was teaching a unit on classical music, he'd criticized her choices, as Handel was Baroque, in fact, not classical music (as the classical era was from 1750 to 1820), while Edvard Grieg was a composer of the *Romantic* (emphasis hers) era—and why teach "In the Hall of the Mountain King"? Sure it was an elegant song, but wasn't it a bit simplistic for high school? It seemed he only had issues with female teachers, at least this was the consensus view, as most of the male colleagues were apt to shrug and mutter, *Well he's nice to me*.

And it was at DuClod-Mann where he'd met Lisa Mesman, his one true love, and her son Blake. Blake was in Scott's junior English class, his ninth year teaching at DuClod-Mann, and the only word to describe him was *unremarkable*. He wasn't stupid by any means—Scott had always entertained the notion Blake was probably bright enough, and had he been blessed with a more coddling teacher, he probably could've applied himself into mediocrity—but Blake was, as Scott had once overheard a colleague describe him, definitely the kind of boy born three credits short of an Associate's Degree in General Studies and cursed to die three credits short. This all sounds very unkind, but in light of the pain Blake had caused, Scott felt he was being charitable.

The fact was, Blake was dull. Perhaps not mentally dull, but spiritually dull with none of the psychological complexities and intellectual curiosity needed to truly go anywhere. Blake was so dull, he'd cultivated in others a delusion of adequacy. Children like Blake Mesman existed so other children could feel better about themselves, *Could be worse—at least I'm not Blake*, so other parents could feel they were doing their jobs, *Hey, at least I didn't raise that*. That Scott had agreed with this assessment only caused slight discomfort. Scott himself had been an outcast in high school, but Blake was different. He'd actually seen teachers cringe when Blake walked past, with his strange gait—*heel, tiptoe, heel, tiptoe, heel, tiptoe*—due to his general unpleasantness. And that was Blake's issue—there was nothing specifically horrible about him. Why he'd bothered those around him, why he was more bothersome than any other student, was very hard to pin down. He was a fog of unpleasantness. The end of every interaction felt like waking up in a bad mood from a dream you couldn't remember.

That all changed Christmas Break, December 2014, after Scott had assigned *Catcher in the Rye*. And it would turn out that Blake, a boy no teacher had ever mentioned as having any potential, took to the book in very interesting ways. In Blake, Scott felt he'd found the reader he'd been searching for. Scott thought he'd finally found one after all these years—the first since Millie Dufresne. And Scott became determined to find out whether Blake could be another Millie Dufresne.

In September of 2003, during Scott's first year of grad school, two years after he'd set that dumpster on fire, a young undergrad named Millie Dufresne set off a series of pipe bombs on campus, shutting down the school for eight days. Scott had seen Millie almost every morning, as she worked at the coffee shop right off campus. She was a friendly girl who'd always smiled when she asked how his day was going, which had always seemed like a stupid question, as it was 7:30am and the day hadn't even been given a chance to fully develop. But she'd always smiled and said *Awesome!* every time he told her his day was going okay.

After the school was evacuated, they found Millie's body floating face down in the duck pond behind the baseball field.

The day before, she'd left a final entry on her LiveJournal which read, *Tell Old Horwitz I know where the ducks go*, a reference to a scene in *Catcher in the Rye*, when young Holden Caulfield asks a cab driver named Horwitz where the ducks in Central Park go in the wintertime. Millie had cracked the code. Where do the ducks go in the wintertime? Of course, any lazy English teacher will tell you the ducks represent children, whom Caulfield believes no one really gives much thought to—even Scott held the line with this reading, to not raise suspicion. No one thinks to ask where the ducks go in the same manner no one thinks to truly understand the pain of children. But Millie understood what really happened to the ducks in Central Park. In her copy of *The Catcher in the Rye*, she'd scrawled in the margins on the first page of Chapter 12, *they stay put+huddle together 2 keep warm+try 2 keep from freezing 2 death you stupid motherfucker!*

After doing the research, he'd learned Millie was the daughter of Chuck Dufresne, a financier set to testify before Congress about a price-fixing scheme involving two U.S. banks, a German bank, and three from the Arab Peninsula. That was four days before she set off those bombs. Two days after she set off those bombs, her father was found dead in the garage with the car running, a garden hose affixed to his exhaust pipe wedged in the driver's side window. At the time, Scott found the timing of the father's death very curious, made more curious by the fact that the lifeless body of another man who was set to testify with Dufresne, Jacob Epstein, was found in a hotel room four hours after Dufresne's death, the high-end prostitute he'd spent the night with never found.

Two days after Epstein's death, Pencey Holdings, one of the banks embroiled in the price fixing scheme, very quietly liquidated all its holdings in the Carlyle Group—everybody knows the man who was President at the time of Millie's death had a father who held a seat with the Carlyle Group, and everybody knows the President's father, an ex-President himself, also happened to be the former head of the CIA. Pencey also happens to be the name of the fancy prep school in *The Catcher in the Rye*. The chief financial officer of Pencey Holdings at the time was named Horwitz—*Tell Old Horwitz I know where the ducks go*—and before Horwitz, the position was held by a man named Jerome Ackley, and before Jerome Ackley it was a man named David Stradlater. *The Catcher in the Rye* was written by Jerome David Salinger. Stradlater was Holden Caulfield's roommate at Pencey, Ackley was his neighbor. The man who holds the position now? A man named Holden Salinger. CFO Salinger always said his parents had a very literary sense of humor.

Yes, of course they did—Scott was sure they were laughing at all of us.

How many young Millie's were there? How many sleeper agents were awakened by *Catcher in the Rye*? Lee Harvey Oswald had a copy in his apartment. Mark David Chapman, who'd murdered John Lennon, would stare at a photo of Lennon and utter the Holden Caulfield-esque, *You phony, I'm going to get you*, and then pray for demons to give him the strength to pull the trigger. The police would find a copy on the coffee table of Ronald Reagan's would-be assassin John Hinckley. Robert John Bardo, who murdered a young actress in 1989, had a copy on him while he committed his crime. The young Korean boy who massacred his classmates at Virginia Tech had contemplated his crime at the school duck pond—even purchased thirty-seven rubber ducks on eBay.

Tell Old Horwitz I know where the ducks go.

they stay put+huddle together 2 keep warm+try 2 keep from freezing 2 death you stupid motherfucker!

The book's power was undeniable. Nine months after Millie's death, one of Scott's classmates had a birthday party at a quiet little bar outside of town. The discussion drifted to which books they'd considered aphrodisiacs. Sam Kittredge, Scott's thesis advisor, said he'd used *Catcher in the Rye* to seduce undergrads back in the early 70's. No one else seemed outraged by Sam's admission—a man, who'd been in his thirties during the 70's, abusing his power to bed eighteen and nineteen-year-olds. Instead, everyone seemed to agree on the book's power to smooth away inhibitions—the men all admitted they'd read the book to seem interesting to girls, and the women intimated they'd liked boys who read the book. Scott sat and nursed his beer—he'd never been much of a drinker—remembering Millie Dufresne, her father, the Carlisle Group, and Pencey Holdings.

"Did you know that book contains elements of Freemasonry?" Scott said.

The entire table fell into a hush. They'd never fallen silent when Scott spoke. Usually, the moment after Scott fishtailed a conversation with one of his strange turns of thought, someone would steer into the troublesome skid with a *Well, anyway*, and then everyone was back on track. But it was different this time, like one of those awkward silences in Dr. Ong's office. He may as well have asked them if they'd heard the good news, that Christ himself was on his way to save us all, the way his mother had when they'd gone door to door in Lanai. Sam gripped Scott's shoulder and shook it—Scott feared the pithy, rejoinder coming his way, as Sam had a penchant for cruel sarcasm.

"Scott," Sam said, "I've had a lot to drink. Keep talking."

"Oh. Okay. He says in the book, Holden Caulfield that is, that his favorite character in the Bible was the lunatic who kept cutting himself with stones, which is a story told in both Mark and Luke, both of which were composed in Greek. In Greek the word for one who cuts himself with stones is *Tekton*, which is another word for Freemason. It's actually kind of stunning how much Freemason lore Salinger worked into the book."

Directly across from Scott, Susan Vo the Milton scholar, sipped her beer. Joan Ehrenriech the Americanist quietly excused herself to smoke a cigarette, and Georgie O'Keefe—yes, Georgie O'Keefe—who specialized in 19th century queer lit, said she'd join her. Chuck Truman, the birthday boy, finally gripped the steering wheel with both hands and a brisk nod.

"Oh yeah," he said. "Stonecutters, like that *Simpsons* episode."

"Yeah," Scott said, "the Stonecutters—Tektons. They were making fun of Freemasons. Sure, absolutely."

And of course, the conversation drifted toward the goddamn Simpsons—the compositional nihilism of its art, the connotative symbology of Bart's haircut—and here Scott thought he was having an adult conversation. Scott turned to Sam, who sipped his beer as Scott tried to elaborate.

"Anyway, Holden even says that Jane Gallagher, the object of his affection, dated a guy named Al Pike, which also happens to be the name of one of the most famous Freemasons in American—"

"Scott," Sam said, "can I ask you about your father? I know it's personal, but I've always been curious."

"Sure, I guess. What do you want to know?"

"Well, to put it bluntly, how do you get rid of all that crazy? I mean, no offense, and I'm only asking because I know you reject what he says."

"Honestly, I don't think I ever really believed any of it. It was easy to overcome because it was never there."

"There he is, the Nature Boy."

Scott had hated that nickname. Sam had called him Nature Boy after Scott proposed using Sir Francis Galton, the Victorian scholar who'd popularized the phrase "Nature vs. Nurture," in his thesis: "Atavism in an Age of 'Upward Mobility.' " Sam had rejected the use of Galton in the thesis, as Galton was a racist. Of course, Scott had no idea as he'd never read Galton—only knowing about the popularization of Nature vs. Nurture—so he'd insisted everyone was a racist back then, feeling this was somehow a mitigating factor.

"Scott, the man's the father of eugenics."

"Oh," Scott had said. "Really?"

In all honesty, Sam had only laughed in that moment because he'd found Scott endearing—he always had. But he could see Scott's feelings here hurt. And something in the stammering way Scott had insisted he'd only wanted to talk about "Nature vs. Nurture," also amused Sam, who'd laughed at the mealy-mouthed way Scott had tried to implore him. Nature Boy had only become a nickname because he'd found Scott to be cute in many ways—he'd wanted to break the tension. Of course, Scott would refuse to see any of it this way. And as Sam patted him on the back, rubbed his palm up and down his spine, Scott wondered if this was how he'd touched those co-eds after feeding them crap about the purity of innocence, the heroic rejection of society's phony rules.

"Scott," he said. "I'm really glad you overcame what you did. Nature, nurture, whatever got you through it, I'm glad you're here, man."

"Thanks, Sam."

"Hey, Sam," Chuck said. "We're over here talking about the ducks in Central Park, and I realized something. No one ever talks about the fish. Now I've only read the book once, like in tenth grade, so I don't remember. But as an expert in the book, what about the fucking fish, man?"

Sam leaned over the table and talked about the fish in Central Park, how they stayed frozen in time while the ducks left for the winter. Scott sipped his beer and stared out the window. How could graduate students not understand simple metaphors like fish frozen in time? Joan Ehrenriech and Georgie O'Keefe puffed their cigarettes and laughed on the other side of the glass. Everyone at the table nodded, but Scott knew the ducks never left: they *stay put+huddle together 2 keep warm+try 2 keep from freezing 2 death.*

You stupid motherfuckers.

Absolutely Nothing to Do With Jodie Foster

The assignment was for everyone to have read the first six chapters over Christmas Break, and then write a one-page analysis on those chapters. Scott was in Redondo visiting his mother when he'd received notification someone had already uploaded their response on the portal. Never would he have imagined it was Blake Mesman, and that intrigued him, so he opened the document and read the response—tense shifts, fragments, typos, and all.

> *This book made me really angry but, I still liked it. I liked that he tried to fihgt Stradlater after STradlater told him to shut up. Sometimes I wish I could do that. I just shut up when people tell me to and it was cool to see Hodlen stick up for himself.*

That wasn't true by any stretch of the imagination. Blake never knew when to shut up, which always led to him getting into trouble. He was the kind of boy who'd always ask what he'd done wrong, and wouldn't stop talking even after being told exactly what he'd done wrong. But Scott was intrigued by that first sentence, that it had made him angry. Never mind that he'd liked it. It had made him angry. The unremarkable boy who'd hated and complained about every assignment had actually liked the book.

The subsequent analysis wasn't particularly insightful or smart—or particularly literate—but everything Blake had to say excited Scott. He talked of how Stradlater reminded him of the men his mother went out with, how his father had always talked about rules but had never followed them, how he would imagine bad things happening to the real-life humans attached to online avatars every time he'd lost while playing first-person shooters—when Blake managed to stick to the text itself, his analysis was superficial and, in many cases, wrong. It was the palpable rage in the digressions that kept Scott's attention:

> *Sometimes, I feel like he does. He being Holden All the phonies in the world who don't get that there are no rules for people like them. Only for people like me. Sometimes, I want to burn this school to the ground. Just to watch it burn. (Don't worry, I won't do it, I don't want to go to jail Lol) I think about that a lot. In conclusion, this book said a lot about today's society and how people don't understand that everyone is special in their own way. Also it was funny when he lied to that kid's*

mom on the train. *I know that was Chap. 8, but I still wanted to say
it was hilarious that he clowned her like that.*

Sometimes, I want to burn this school to the ground, Blake had said. *Just to watch it
burn,* he continued in a fragment. The economic brutality of that fragment—
if Scott hadn't known any better, he might have thought the fragment was
deliberate, rather than the act of a buffoon stumbling upon something important. Scott had seen that exact phrase before: Millie Dufresne had written
those words—fragment and all—on her LiveJournal. Even more remarkable,
she'd also referenced a world of phonies who'd figured out rules didn't apply
to them, that they only applied to honest people who were too stupid to realize rules were put in place to keep them dumb and docile. Of course, most
young people felt that way—Scott had taught this book enough to know this—
but how many of them admitted wanting to burn their school to the ground?
How many of them responded to Holden calling his red hunting cap a people
shooting hat? How many of them, in a class assignment, admitted to closing
one eye and pretending to aim a rifle at classmates, the way Blake had?

After the Millie Dufresne incident, Scott had become obsessed with
Catcher in the Rye, discovered J.D. Salinger was a counter-intelligence officer
during World War II. Salinger's contributions were instrumental to Operation Paperclip, the secret program that recruited Nazi scientists to work for
the U.S. government after the war. In addition to the strides made in the
fields of rocket science and chemical warfare, these scientists would go on to
create MKUltra, the CIA mind control program that experimented with LSD,
sleep deprivation, hypnosis, and sexual abuse. It's been said (mostly because
it's true) *Catcher in the Rye* wasn't so much a book as it is a series of neurolinguistic codes used to trigger CIA sleeper agents. Millie Dufresne had opened
Scott's eyes to everything.

He wondered if Millie Dufresne had been triggered by the government in
order to keep her father from testifying. It wasn't like they'd never done it before. During the Reagan Administration, Then-Vice President George Bush
and Secretary of State Alexander Haig were involved in a power struggle over
foreign policy. After Reagan recovered from his attempted assassination at the
hands of John Hinckley Jr., who'd had a copy of *Catcher in the Rye* on his coffee
table, he sided with Bush, signing an executive order handing foreign policy
power to a former head of the CIA and member of the Carlyle Group—the
same Carlyle Group that liquidated all its assets in Pencey Holdings two days
after the death of Millie's father. Let's not forget John Hinckley Sr. was a close
family friend of the then-Vice President. And Salinger was in league with all

of them. Bush had even once praised *Catcher in the Rye* as an inspirational book. He and Salinger must have had a good laugh over how "inspirational" the book truly was.

The press had claimed Hinckley was acting out scenes from *Taxi Driver*, that he'd wanted to impress the film's heroine Jodie Foster, but that itself was a cover story. The fact was, *Taxi Driver* been inspired by Arthur Bremer, the man who'd paralyzed Democratic presidential candidate George Wallace in 1972. None of this was hard to untangle:

1. President Nixon had risen to power through the Southern Strategy, grabbing as many white Southern votes as he could by cultivating their animosity toward African Americans.

2. His potential opponent in the next elections was George Wallace, a staunch segregationist, best known for his "Segregation Now, Segregation Forever" speech.

3. That Nixon would see this unrepentant racist as a threat was the kind of understatement that made Scott burst into laughter.

4. It was no leap of logic to deduce the Nixon administration had compelled Bremer to shoot George Wallace. Who would put this past Nixon? Richard Nixon, of all people!

5. *Taxi Driver,* the film inspired by Arthur Bremer, the film that supposedly inspired John Hinckley, was released in 1976

6. In 1976, the director of the CIA was none other than Hinckley family friend and Nixon loyalist, George Herbert Walker Bush.

And let's take a wild guess what book was found in Bremer's apartment. Catcher in the goddamn Rye, that's what book. As far as Scott was concerned, the dots connected themselves. How could no one else see this? How could so many people look the other way—did they not realize evil, true evil, was staring right at them?

Scott had also learned Salinger was a pedophile. He'd seduced Eugene O'Neill's fifteen-year-old daughter before shipping off to the war. He'd written stories of men on the beach, marveling at how she was nine years away from filling out her bikini; soldiers entranced by the beauty of ten-year-old girls, their conversation marred by his worry of not being attractive enough for them; Holden's overly affectionate relationship with his little sister, Phoebe—the way he said it drove him crazy when she touched him at the movie theater, how beautiful it felt when young girls touched him—was it any surprise Sam Kittredge was drawn to the book, that he'd act on his own ideations?

Neil McNeil, the man who'd taken Scott's own innocence from him, was a well-read man. Cary Bonneville had always joked Neil wasn't going to find a wife with his nose buried in books. Scott remembered Neil's room, how the books on his shelves were stacked in neat piles in order to maximize the space. He remembered Neil encouraging him to flip through those books, to borrow whatever he'd liked. Of course, Scott never did borrow any, but he did look through them, hold them, pretend to read in the hopes Neil would leave him alone. They were mostly adventure novels and mysteries, but surely he had a copy of *Catcher in the Rye* in there somewhere—at the very least, he's had to have read it at one time in his life. Of course he had. It would've made perfect sense for a man like that to have read a book like this. By the time Blake Mesman had uploaded his two page analysis, Scott had already convinced himself he'd seen a copy of *Catcher in the Rye* on Neil's shelf—in between *Conan the Warrior* and *Conan the Avenger*. He'd remembered the red cover, the gold lettering—it was unmistakably *Catcher in the Rye*. And he was right. There was a book with a red cover, gold lettering, just like *Catcher in the Rye*, but that book was, in fact, *The Black Stone*, by Robert E. Howard.

Every year, Scott suggested teaching another book, and every year he was told it was required by the district. Every time they sighed and shook their heads, and not once did their annoyance bother him because it was all an elaborate ruse anyway.

We go through this every year, they'd say every year.

I understand, Scott would say every year. *It doesn't hurt to ask.*

Really, Scott? they'd say every year. *Because it's getting to the point where it kind of hurts to ask.*

And every year, Scott would fight the urge to respond, *Well don't say I didn't warn you.*

The truth was, Scott didn't care one way or another about teaching *Catcher in the Rye.* Sure, it wasn't all that great, and he'd once joked to colleagues that it was literature for losers, that it was a dumb person's idea of intelligent storytelling—Scott was fully aware of how his peers viewed him, and why they reacted to him in such negative ways—but deep down, the prospects of teaching the book excited him. Scott knew he'd find another Millie Dufresne someday. He used to imagine that moment, sometimes it was a mass shooting, sometimes it was a bomb like Millie, and other times, the theoretical child would set themselves on fire in the middle of the cafeteria. Never once did he imagine he'd come to any harm, which would have made perfect sense, as these perpetrators would most definitely have blamed him for exposing them to the book. Not once did he ever conceive he'd be on the other end of that gun, or that he'd be caught in the blast radius—not once would he ever consider the blood on his own hands. These were flights of fancy—why ruin them with any thought of disaster befalling him?

Only when Blake Mesman finally ruins his life will Scott wonder why he'd never considered he could've come to harm. I guess life is just funny that way, he'll think to himself—even though it isn't funny at all.

Sometimes, I want to burn this school to the ground, Blake had said. *Just to watch it burn.* One of Millie Dufresne's pipe bombs had detonated in the Sociology department building, across from the English department. Before being ordered to disperse, Scott had watched all the bloodied, dirt-caked faces limp toward the firefighters and EMT's. Scott knew what he had to do. If there were to be any hope he'd have another Millie Dufresne on his hands, if there were to be any hope for validation, he had to observe Blake, keep him close.

Lisa

The first day after Christmas Break, Scott asked Blake to meet with him after school. Blake, being Blake, immediately told Scott he hadn't done anything wrong.

"I never said you did, Blake. I'm just really glad *Catcher in the Rye* affected you the way it did. For a guy who doesn't like books, you really had some strong emotional responses."

"I still don't like books, but this one didn't suck."

"Can we talk after school?"

"I'm not in trouble, am I? Because I didn't do anything wrong."

"I know that, Blake. Let's just chat."

Blake showed up ten minutes after the final bell, stinking from P.E. Scott asked him how it was, and Blake told him it sucked because he was supposed to run eight laps and only ran six, so Coach Belson called him pathetic.

"I hate that guy," Blake said, "and his dickhead son too. No offense."

"Why would I be offended?" Scott asked. "That's between you and them."

Scott had also hated Mark Belson, who'd graduated from DuClod-Mann and still held the school record for Doubles and RBI. This was a man Scott would never have anything in common with, and there was no teacher Scott hated interacting with more than Belson—even the idiot music teacher who'd spent her breaks humming "I Dreamed a Dream" without ever having read Victor Hugo. Belson's son, Colin, was the school's starting Tight End and Power Forward—Scott had witnessed Colin make palsy-hands as he followed Blake down the halls. At the same time, had Belson really called Blake pathetic, Scott would have been inclined to agree. Who can't run two miles in a half-hour? Even a middle school girl could run a ten-minute mile.

"I'm sure he didn't call you pathetic," Scott said.

"No, Mr. Bonneville, he really did."

"What did he say?"

"He said that it was pathetic I couldn't run two miles in 30 minutes, that even the girls could do it."

"So he didn't call you pathetic. Just your effort, which, you know, you're probably capable of doing more. That's all he meant."

"And his son's a dick."

"Yes, you said that. But the reason I called you in—"

"You've seen the way he picks on me. You probably see it all the time."

There was nothing accusatory in Blake's tone, or in his eyes. Blake didn't seem to blame Scott for not speaking up when Colin mocked him in the halls. Any normal person would have been furious—a teacher not sticking up for a bullied student—but, sadly, boys like Blake are resigned to their fates. Blake wasn't looking for justice. He was simply seeking validation, which Scott was more than willing to offer.

"Yeah," Scott said. "It's really shitty and I'm sorry he does that."

"It's okay. It's not your fault. He's the asshole."

"So, *Catcher in the Rye*. It seems to have really struck a nerve with you."

"I know why you want to talk about it. It's because I said I wanted to burn the school down. That was a joke."

Blake's sweat spattered on the desktop. His shirt was soaked through and his hair clung to his forehead. Blake swirled at the puddles of sweat with his finger, then rubbed it on his lips—how could the Colin Belsons of the world not pick on such a strange and disgusting person? Scott could practically feel the steam evaporate from Blake's head. He smelled horrible. The entire room smelled horrible, like a leather watch strap at the end of a hot day. Scott made his way to the window, opened it. He took a seat on the ledge.

"I'm glad to hear that," Scott said. "But—"

"I read the whole book," Blake said. "I read it all after sending you the paper."

"Oh, what did you think?"

"It was interesting. All those people he talked to, they were so stupid. He did a good job showing me how stupid they were."

"How so?"

Blake swiped his palm against his forehead, then cupped his hand over his mouth, breathing very deep breaths as if wearing an oxygen mask. He only stopped when they locked eyes. Scott would've judged him more harshly, but he'd practically seen Blake lick sweat off a desk. Besides, it wasn't as if Scott's hand hadn't formed its own oxygen mask,

"Remember that scene in the hotel where he's watching that tranny and then watching that chick spit water in that guy's mouth?" Blake asked.

"Well, let's not call them trannies, huh? Maybe we find better words to use."

"You know what's weird? He called that chick after that. I don't remember her name."

"Faith Cavendish."

"I guess. Anyway, my mom gets calls like that sometimes. I don't know what the guys are saying on the other line, but she says the same stuff. Like late at night and she's wondering why they're calling her to come out and whatever."

The intercom speaker in the corner of the room sounded. Lori Moss, the perpetually inconvenienced school secretary, asked Blake Mesman to come to the office. His mother was waiting for him. Scott imagined the sighs seeping from Lori's lungs as she walked to the intercom.

"Crap," Blake said. "I forgot. We have therapy today."

Scott walked over to his desk and called the office, asked Lori for a few more minutes, and waited for Lori's sigh, followed by her melodically sarcastic *Okay*. Before they could get much further, Lisa Mesman, Blake's mother, poked her head in the door. Scott stood from the desk. As she was his mother, Scott hoped she'd recognize the smell was coming from Blake and not him, that his classroom normally smelled like a regular classroom, that he wasn't the cause of the stench.

"I'm really sorry," she said, "but we're running late. I don't know what he did this time, but if you'd like to call me about it, I'll be happy to talk to you."

"I didn't do anything, mom. Jesus," Blake said.

"I'm sorry, Mrs. Mesman," Scott said. "It was my fault. Over the break, I read Blake's response paper and was so impressed I wanted to hear more of his thoughts. I'm Scott Bonneville. It's very nice to meet you."

Lisa stiffened up, looked directly into Scott's eyes. He extended his hand, and she smiled and offered hers. Scott could see she was a bit thrown off, and would later conflate her body language with love at first sight. But the fact was, she couldn't believe Blake actually impressed a teacher, even though she did her best to hide it.

"I'm not Mrs. Mesman," she said. "Just Lisa. Mr. Mesman is way out of the picture."

"It's nice to finally meet you, Lisa. Blake talks about you all the time."

The truth was, Blake never talked about her. It was always the other boys, who liked making crude comments about her under their breath. Of course, Scott did his best to ignore those comments, rather than shut them down, just as he tried to ignore them while trying not to stare at her chest.

"We really do have to go," she said. "I'm sorry, Scott. Could we talk about this later?"

"I'd love that."

Lisa handed Blake the car keys and told him to start walking. Blake stood up and shuffled out the door, dragging his backpack behind him.

"Jesus, Blake," she said. "You stink."

Scott's head dropped in relief, exhaled. Thank God she didn't think he was the source of the smell. He sucked in through his nostrils, noticed the stink was replaced by a woman's perfume. He breathed in a few more times, as if meditating—thank God that smell was gone. Lisa noticed him staring at her breasts. Scott looked away, then at the ceiling, then the whiteboard.

"I'm sorry I kept him," Scott said. "I've been trying to engage him a bit more."

Did she really notice him staring at her breasts? Of course she did. A woman like Lisa doesn't go through life without realizing men stared at her breasts. But maybe she didn't. Scott told himself he was going to try and zone out a bit more when she's around, just to show her he stares at lots of things, not just breasts, lots of things. Desks, pen holders, oh look—a laptop.

"I do have to go," she said. "But why don't I leave you my number. I'd really like to hear your thoughts on Blake."

She wrote down her number, handed it to him. Scott immediately entered the number into his phone, making sure to concentrate on the screen the way an overly observant person might stare at a screen.

"Are you okay?" she asked.

"I'm fine. Sorry, I tend to zone out from time to time."

Scott watched Lisa leave the room, and then rehearsed the phone call he'd make over and over again in his head. *I don't mean to pry, but Blake told me he was off to therapy. It's none of my business, so I don't need to know anything, but I hope everything's okay. Just wanted to check in, you know, make sure he was doing okay.*

He must have repeated those words more than forty times. At least eighteen of those times, he was sincerely wondering about Blake, rather than Lisa.

It Never Leaves

Blake Mesman wiped the haze from the bathroom mirror, flexed his biceps. It had been about a year since he'd stopped taking his meds (Nelson had kept calling it *Dextroamphetamine Saccharate* with italicized contempt). He'd also stopped taking the Melatonin (Nelson always had to correct himself with that one, as he'd always call it Mylicon—although he'd never pass up the opportunity to make a joke about babies and their baby pills). Blake hadn't slept all that well in months, but he had to admit his thoughts were, in fact, more focused, just like Nelson had said they'd be.

Even now, he was amazed at how much his body had changed in eighteen months—had it really been eighteen months since he'd been expelled from DuClod-Mann? His shoulders had broadened, his posture stiffened, the belly—that goddamn belly had melted away. He made a fist with his right hand, the knuckles still swollen from three nights ago, flexed his wrist. A vein crackled down his forearm like moss pushing its way through cracked asphalt.

What had never melted away was the anger. He'd thought that once he'd built his body into the barest minimum of what a man should look like, he'd become better adjusted, that people might like him more, that girls might even find him desirable. Sure, they talked about how great he looked, told him they were happy for him, but in the long run he was still Blake Mesman, still the Sneetch. It seemed the anger would never go away. Maybe it never does.

He hitched his thumb into the towel around his waist, pulled it down to get a better look at the tattoo—a black star over his belly button. It was the first tattoo he'd gotten, one of the guys from the Brotherhood had given it to him. Since middle school, the kids had called him Sneetch, after the Star-Bellied Sneetches from Dr. Seuss. He did look like a Dr. Seuss character back then—long neck, rail-thin with a round middle, skinny little arms and legs—of course they'd picked on him. Looking back, he would've picked on himself.

He'd gotten the tattoo as a middle finger to all those kids who'd picked on him, ridiculed him, spit on him his entire life. But all it did was give him a bullseye to focus his rage upon. There were times he could still feel the burn of the needle on his skin, still feel the ink seeping through the scar tissue, and all he'd want to do was punch something.

Three nights ago, he saw Colin Belson, an old classmate from DuClod-Mann, at a punk show he'd gone to with his friends—he'd finally made actual friends. Colin had been one of those kids who'd literally spit on him—it was back in seventh grade. In high school, he used to follow Blake around, slapping a limp wrist against his letterman jacket, mimicking a retarded person. The black star had seared against his belt buckle, and before he knew it, he was on top of Colin, pounding Colin's face and shoulders with his fists. Colin's friends, all boys from the baseball team, watched helplessly as Blake's friends glared at them, begging for an excuse. A bouncer separated them, told them to get the hell out.

The next day, he saw Colin at Burger Town with his old man, Coach Belson. Colin's left cheek was badly bruised and Blake stared at his knuckles, marveling at the injuries they'd exchanged. Grandpa Don had once told him no one comes away from a fight unscathed, to make sure the other guy got it worse. He'd wondered if Grandpa Don was smiling down on him, finally having done something right.

He sat down for his burger, when his phone buzzed. It was a text from Colin. How did he get his number?

Look, it said, *I get why you did what you did. I was a dick to you back in the day. I didn't tell my dad & I'm not pressing charges. We're gonna let it go. Just between us. Cool?*

Blake looked up, stared at the back of Coach Belson's fat neck. Colin nodded. Blake stood up and walked over to the Belson family table, stared down at Colin, who refused to look up.

"Wait," Coach Belson said. "Blake Mesman? Jesus Christ, kid. Good for you. You've really been working out, haven't ya?"

"Let it go?" Blake said. "Maybe that's possible. Maybe you will let it go. But you'll never get over it. Trust me. If I could get over it, you'd still have that pretty little face."

"Wait a minute," Coach Belson said. "You telling me Mesman did this to you? You said you didn't know who did this."

"Some day, man," Blake said, "you're gonna be alone with your thoughts. And then you're gonna remember what I did to you last night. It'll just pop into your head like magic and stay there. Eventually, you'll be able to laugh it off and it'll be like this inside joke between you and your memories. But you're never gonna get over this."

Colin sucked through his straw. Blake glanced at Coach Belson's raging, red face. He remembered all the times Lisa cleaned the blood from his split lip, the way she'd cried every time one of them had hurt him. Knowing Coach

Belson was feeling even a fraction of what Lisa had gone through curled a smile on Blake's lips.

"Hey Coach," Blake said.

And Colin never will get over it. And it will become like a joke. In college, Colin will even laugh about it with friends, tell them about the time Blake Mesman jumped him at an all-ages punk show back home in Portland, how he had no idea he was even there.

"No fucking way," his friends will say. "You knew that psycho?"

"Since middle school," Colin will tell them. "That thing he did in SoCal—we all knew something like that was gonna happen. He was always weird like that. It's kind of sad, man."

Blake ran his hand over the mirror again—the haze always seemed to get worse the more he wiped it away. He held his fists, knuckles out, in front of the mirror, admired the bruises. His mother knocked on the door, told him dinner was ready.

"You got it, Lisa," he said.

"Stop calling me Lisa. I'm your mother."

He'd been calling his mother by her name for over a year now, ever since all the shit went down with Mr. Bonneville, that piece of shit. What kind of teacher fucks his student's mother? Last he'd heard, Bonneville had moved to California. He wondered what Bonneville was up to? Not out of concern, but more to speculate on where he was that exact moment. Blake had often fantasized about running into his former teacher in a restaurant, or an empty field, or a dark alley, where he'd make him pay for what he'd done. Was there a word like Cuck, but one for mothers instead of wives?

It would be another three days before Scott Bonneville would enter the Pizza Galley and become a goddamn folk hero. If only that motherfucker could see him now.

"I'll fuck you up," Blake said into the mirror. "I'll pound your face into a goddamn pulp. Try me, Scott. Fucking try me, bro."

Lisa called for him to move his ass. Blake stared at his knuckles on last time, then walked into his bedroom to dress for dinner.

The Killer of Ducks

Jan Mesman was a technical consultant for ANOdyne, a manufacturing firm that built industrial and light rail locomotives, among many other things. When his father, Brigadier General Donald Mesman, joined the firm after Vietnam, they'd strictly built tanks and military transport vehicles. ANOdyne products were used all throughout the first Persian Gulf War and back when Blake still visited his grandparents, the first thing he'd see when he walked through the door was the photo of his grandfather as a younger man with President Bush and the Emir of Kuwait.

"Grandpa, how many people did your tanks kill?" Blake had once asked.

"A lot," Don Mesman replied.

"Was it a million?"

"That's way too many."

"Could it kill a million if it wanted to?"

"Blake, that's a lot of people to kill."

"But it could, right?"

"I think your grandmother's baking cookies. Maybe she could use some help, huh?"

Cora, Blake's paternal grandmother, had always found Blake's questions alarming. A six-year-old boy's fascination with a tank's specific body count was a point of concern for sure, but Blake's fascination with death and killing were especially alarming because Cora had never believed Blake had the capacity for compassion. When he was three, Millie, Don's Duck Tolling Retriever, had a litter of puppies. They had to keep Blake away from the pups, as he couldn't stop wrapping his little hands around their throats and squeezing, laughing as they yelped. She used to fight with Lisa, her daughter-in-law whenever her fears of Blake's mental state were discussed.

"He's your grandson," Lisa would say. "How can you say these things about your own grandson?"

"I'm only mentioning it because I'm worried. What kind of child strangles puppies?"

"He's playing, Cora. He doesn't know what he's doing."

What Lisa didn't know, and never would, was that every time Blake touched a puppy, Don would yank him into his den and swat him on the diaper. Every time he wailed, Don would say it was because he'd taken the boy away from the pups.

"He's going to kill these dogs," Don had said.

"He's not going to kill any dogs," Lisa said. "He's a goddamn baby."

"So are they, and he's choking them."

There were many things about Don and Cora Lisa could never forgive, but the one she'd always go back to was being told they couldn't have any of the puppies. That they'd refuse to give their own grandchild a puppy crystallized their resentment of her and of Blake. She'd actually taken to the runt of the litter, a tiny little thing they'd begun calling Ike. Of course he was the one Don decided to keep for himself, the bastard.

Blake Mesman was conceived on Jan and Lisa's second or third date. It had to be one of those days, as Jan stopped calling after the fourth date, after she'd told him she wasn't in the mood. She'd been on the pill, as Jan kept reminding her, and yes the baby was his, so fuck you for even asking that. Because Lisa didn't believe in abortion, and because boys like him just didn't have children out of wedlock, Jan Mesman and Lisa Baker eloped two months after being told of the accident. The divorce would be finalized six days after Blake's fourth birthday.

Years later, when Cora heard what her eldest grandson had done in Redondo Beach, she wasn't all that sad or disappointed. She'd been expecting it his entire life, after all. The boy was deranged, and time had immunized her to heartbreak. The last time her husband had seen Blake was on his fifteenth birthday. Because Blake didn't have any friends, there wasn't going to be any party, so Don thought it might be nice to take him goose hunting. Maybe the outdoors would do the boy some good. Maybe he could teach him how to be a man, instead of whatever the hell it was that he was. Blake slept over so they could leave at four in the morning. Cora listened as Blake argued and whined about not getting enough sleep. She fell back to sleep, as her husband told the boy to quit his bellyaching for once in his goddamn life. Don came through the door at nine-thirty. She hadn't expected them back until the evening.

"He shot the dog," Don told her. "I sent Ike off to retrieve and the boy just aimed and pulled the trigger. He kept saying there was a duck. There was no goddamn duck. The boy's deranged and there's nothing we can do about it."

"Don't say that," Cora told him. "He's still your grandson."

"He's going to die in a goddamn prison riot. That's where he's headed. Mark my words, Cora. Let's just pray he finds some way to become one of the guards instead of an inmate. Otherwise, it's hopeless."

She always remembered the way Don laughed when he said prison guard. It was as though the only good outcome he could think of was still just a sad joke. Don would die of heart failure two weeks later. On the day of the funeral, Lisa would tell Blake how his father and grandmother thought it was best that he stayed home. She would sit on the couch while Blake played video games. They ordered a pizza for dinner, sat and watched a Japanese cartoon about a kids at a ninja high school. She asked Blake if wanted to share good memories of Grandpa Don.

"Not really."

"Really? None? What if I start with a good memory? Do you want to hear about the first time I met him?"

"I thought he was a duck, Mom. I didn't mean to shoot him."

"You mean Ike?"

"I just aimed the gun, and Grandpa Don kept telling me not to, but he looked like a duck so I shot him."

Lisa rubbed his head, kissed his scalp. She told him she believed he saw a duck.

"Do you think he's still mad?" Blake asked.

"No. I'm sure he's forgiven you."

Three years later, handcuffed in the back of a squad car, Blake will remember the time he told Lisa he'd thought Ike was a duck. He'll remember her saying she believed him, how she said Grandpa Don had forgiven him, and then laugh at how those lies were like mushrooms growing out of a giant heap of shit. He'll imagine his lie growing in between those two, how much bigger it had grown than theirs had, how it would eventually expand until it pushed their lies off the heap. The officer will tell him to keep it down, and Blake will tell him he's thinking about shit—actual shit, like poop—and then laugh again. The officer will tell him to be quiet and Blake will watch the disgusted man shake his head.

"Nobody fucking gets it, man," Blake will say.

"I'm not messing around, guy. Shut your mouth."

Blake will lean his head back—the killer of ducks, sweet fucking Christ—close his eyes and smile.

Something, Everything, Anything

King Solomon was the wisest man on earth. The wisest men of other lands would beg for his audience, ask him questions, and he gave them wise answers—the wisest answers—and those who came to him always brought beautiful gifts—the best gifts, tremendous gifts, all of Israel told him no one had better gifts than he, believe me. Then one day two women came to Solomon with a baby.

"Your Majesty, one woman said, "this woman and I live in the same house. Not long ago my baby was born at home, and three days later her baby was born. Nobody else was there with us. One night while we were all asleep, she rolled over onto her baby, and he died. Then while I was still asleep, she got up and took my son out of my bed. She put him in her bed, and then she put her dead baby next to me. In the morning when I got up to feed my son, I saw that he was dead. But when I looked at him in the light, I knew he wasn't my son."

"No!" the other woman shouted. "Your son is dead. My baby is alive!"

"The dead baby is yours," the first woman yelled. "Mine is alive!"

They argued back and forth in front of Solomon until finally he said, "Both of you say this live baby is yours. Someone bring me a sword."

A sword was brought, and Solomon ordered, "Cut the baby in half! That way each of you can have part of him."

It was a wise plan, the wisest plan—no one had ever come up with such a wise plan. Solomon had never planned on letting the baby be cut in half. He wanted to see what the women would do. He knew the baby's mother would not let her son be hurt for Solomon was a compassionate man—no one knew more about compassion than he did.

"Please don't kill my son," the baby's mother screamed. "Your Majesty, I love him very much, but give him to her. Just don't kill him."

The other woman shouted, "Go ahead and cut him in half. Then neither of us will have the baby."

And with that, Solomon came to a realization. The woman who begged for the baby's life was the child's true mother—this was true—but by not allowing the baby to be cut in half, was she not disrespecting the wishes of the other woman? After all, the other woman shouted for the baby to be cut in half—was her opinion not equally valid? Would a just leader ignore the wishes of those who'd wanted babies cut in half? Do all opinions not matter equally? And so what if the woman begging to save the child really was the mother after all? Does true ownership grant rights others don't have? After all, if these women had come forward tugging on a piece of clothing, both claiming it was theirs, did the law not dictate the clothing be divided with each party getting half? That was the law, was it not? And, folks, no one knew more about the law than Solomon. Everything there is to know about law, he knew it, believe me.

So Solomon ordered his servant to cut the baby in half. The mother, the true mother, watched the sword cleave the child's plump, grape-like flesh. It pained her deeply but she knew Solomon's decision to be wise and just. She stared with the dead eyes of a gutted fish until the child stopped screaming, and then dropped to her knees. Solomon listened to the woman beg for forgiveness, and then commanded her to her feet.

"Let it be known throughout the land," he said. "This child was killed because neither woman was worthy. Both sides are just as bad."

The evening after the Pizza Galley Shooting, Scott came out of his bedroom, his childhood bedroom, at 5:30, made himself a sandwich. He sat and ate alone in the dining room, sitting in the seat he'd sat in every morning with a bowl of oatmeal before school. After the incident with Blake and Lisa, Scott was forced to resign from his teaching post. He'd been living in Redondo Beach with his mother for almost a year now, working odd jobs as a tutor and freelance editor while waiting for things to right themselves. Exposing Pizza Galley was supposed to set things right, justify his existence in a world that had erased all of his accomplishments. Sadly, David Brightman and the world had other plans. Why had David Brightman chosen that night of all nights? Why had Scott, for that matter? What cursed them to be there together? What had cursed them to fail? Surely, one of them deserved a bit of satisfaction in their crappy lives. Scott finished his sandwich and sat at the table in silence.

Wilma came home at 5:45, asked him about his day. He told her Mills Burghardt had called in the morning, told Scott he was going to be on TV. After she changed, she told him about her day, and then they walked to the living room and sat on the couch, turned on the TV. They sat through a campaign commercial, endorsed by the man who promised to make this country great again, promising to cut the head off of ISIS and to take their oil.

"Absolutely vile," Wilma said.

"Sure, but so is she."

"I don't know how you can even compare the two."

"I get he's an incompetent moron, but she's absolutely corrupt and a literal murderer."

"You can't be serious."

"Look, I don't support him either, but she's just as bad. If anything, at least he doesn't know where the bodies are buried. She might be worse because he has no chance. He's just a distraction. In the long run, she's the one who's going to damage this country."

"He's not a distraction. He's a heartbeat away from the presidency."

"Mom, do you know what controlled opposition is? He's been manufactured to look like the enemy by those in power. He's a straw man. They built him themselves in order to retain power."

"Scotty, isn't being against everything exhausting? Sometimes, you expend less energy simply being for something. You can get a lot more done."

"Something, everything, those are really vague terms, Mom. You can't get anything done with something or everything."

"I just don't want you to be angry all the time."

Scott had tried reasoning with Blake, that it wasn't a big deal. Actually, it was a big deal. Scott was in love with Blake's mother, that this wasn't some fling, that it was serious. Scott promised Blake he'd be nothing like his father, that he was going to be around—*no, I'm not insulting your dad, Blake. I'm sure he's a good man. You're right. I shouldn't assume things. I'm very sorry. Please, if you'll just calm down, we can discuss this like men. Please, I love your mother. I really do. I have nothing but the best intentions for—please Blake, please listen to reason. I love her, man. I love her. No, it's not bullshit. Please don't call her that. I love her. No, I really do. I really do.*

Just listen.

Please, just listen.

We can work this out.

The Choking Doberman

It's been twenty months since Scott and Lisa met for their first cup of coffee. In all honesty, Scott didn't remember the exact date, January Something, but what boyfriend remembers anniversaries? It was on a Saturday—that much he knew. Did Lisa remember the exact date? Of course not. What sort of freak remembers things like that? They'd had such a normal relationship, the same as any other man and woman. How could it all have gone so wrong?

Under her leather jacket, she'd worn a black T-shirt with the pink Rush logo from their first album. They chatted a bit about their lives—her husband had left when Blake was four and was now nothing but a series of alimony checks, she worked as an Optometric Assistant at the Lens Crafters in the mall, that raising Blake by herself had been hard given his emotional issues— these were all things that shouldn't have bored Scott. These were all things he should have cared about.

"Sorry, Scott," Lisa said. "But my eyes are up here."

"Oh, sorry. No, no, I wasn't doing that. I was just admiring your shirt."

"You like Rush?"

"They were my favorite band in high school."

"No way. I love Rush. How much do you love Rush? This is a test, by the way."

"Well, for a project in English class, I wrote an extra verse for 'The Trees.'"

"Love that song. Please tell me you remember that verse."

In "The Trees" by Rush, from their 1978 album *Hemispheres*, the maples are unable to feel the warmth of the sun because of the oaks that tower over them. The maples beg the oaks for a chance at sunlight, while the oaks wonder why the maples can't just appreciate the shade they provide. So the maples stage a violent coup, and equality, so to speak, is now enforced with hatchets and saws. The lyrics made it clear the oaks were the aggrieved party. They'd only gathered up the sunlight because they'd had the strength to do so—everything they'd done was compelled by nature and nothing more. After all, they weren't the ones who'd brought weapons of murder into the fray. But in Scott's mind, if the oaks had truly been resolute, they'd have found a way to neutralize the treachery of the maples. In Scott's mind, both were weak: the maples were morally weak, while the oaks were spiritually weak. Neither knew the meaning of strength.

"Not really," said Scott said. "I wrote it so long time ago. I know that it involved a mighty redwood growing in that forest, overpowering both the oaks and maples. You know, eventually replacing them both with a redwood forest. I remember it was all about how the forest was much more majestic because of the mighty redwood forest that came from that one single tree, how all the woodland creatures came back to this new paradise after order was restored."

"Wow. That's pretty amazing."

She laughed. Scott didn't like that she'd laughed but it was, in fact, quite funny. The rhyme schemes were forced, his lines didn't quite match the harmony, and Scott had decided to sing his verse after a stentorian reading of the original lyrics. The entire classroom had burst into laughter and after class, his teacher told Scott he hadn't followed instructions. He was supposed to use a poem as the springboard for his new verse and Rush, by this teacher's estimation, wasn't poetry. Why hadn't he chosen the Shakespearean sonnet he'd originally asked to use? Sure, the teacher admired his ingenuity here, but failure to follow rules had to have consequences, didn't they? Scott nodded and said he understood, even though the entire time the teacher talked about how much he'd appreciated Scott's insights in the class, how he was one of the brightest students in the room, Scott wondered what consequence this teacher would ever suffer for stifling his creativity.

"Anyway," Scott said, "I sang it in class and got laughed out of the room."

"That's terrible. You poor thing."

Scott heard the sounds of baristas calling out people's orders. *Joseph, large Blended Mocha; Natasha, Espresso Macchiato; Rupinder, Flat Mocha.* He heard a woman on her phone talking about drinking too much around her boyfriend's wife. It was fascinating, this woman's story of puking in her boyfriend's bathroom, how the ugly wallpaper was the kind some old woman would put up, how the hand soap was Cucumber Melon—as if there wasn't any other fucking kind that unimaginative bitch could've chosen. He realized that if he could hear it, then so could Lisa, that if he was fascinated, then Lisa might also be fascinated, that if Lisa was fascinated by this woman's story, then Scott probably wasn't fascinating in any way.

"So in Hawaii," Scott said, "they have this holiday called Boy's Day. It was brought over by Japanese immigrants, and it's just this day where we celebrate young boyhood. Anyway, when I was six, my parents and I spent Boy's Day downtown flying kites shaped like koi and watching the parade with fire dancers and men dressed like samurai—you know, typical macho bullshit."

Lisa laughed. The fact was, none of this was true. Scott rarely left the compound at all, and he'd only heard of Boy's Day from Greg Kinoshita, the Chemistry teacher at DuClod-Mann. But she laughed. She laughed and she licked her lips and leaned forward when he'd said "typical macho bullshit," the way he sneered when he said it, as if he were somehow above the everyday foibles of modern manhood, even though, in the long run, everything every man does is macho bullshit. It's actually funny, the phrase macho bullshit. People like Scott usually ascribe it to things like boxers and lumberjacks, fire-fighters and quarterbacks, those toned Polynesian fire dancers and armored samurai warriors he'd supposedly seen in the parade he never went to. But in the end, everything every man does is macho bullshit.

Once during a session, Scott told Dr. Ong about Sandy Cuomo, a girl from Chemistry class he used to study with in high school. She'd told him she liked him because he wasn't threatening like the other boys she knew, the dumb jocks she'd actually preferred. But the truth was, he was no less a threat than any other boy.

"How so?" Dr. Ong had asked.

"Well, if you think about it, I was only helping her with balance equations because I wanted to get into her pants. I can lie and say it was more inno-cent than that, but yeah. All I wanted was to find a way for her to have sex with me. So there's no real difference between me and those jocks. They used their muscles, or whatever, and I was trying to use my brain. I was just using whatever tools I had, just like they were."

Some used an elaborate fire dance, while others used martial prowess. Scott was no different from all those men he'd sneered at—sneered at from a distance, of course. All of those romantic yearnings he'd felt for Sandy were simply a calculation, just as they were right now with Lisa: If I show her A, then it will lead to B.

"Anyway," he said, "we got home really late at night. We'd planned on staying out later, but my mom was feeling a little faint, so we headed home. Besides, it was about 10:30 at night, so I was a little tired too. My poor dad had to carry me in his arms and help my mother into the house. We unlocked the door and looked down to see our Doberman, Allie, choking on the floor."

"Oh my God," Lisa said.

"Yeah, so my dad set my mom on the couch and told me to watch her. Then he scooped up Allie and ran her over next door to our neighbor, who was a veterinarian. About ten minutes later, our phone rings, so I answer it. It's my dad, screaming, *Both of you! Get out of the house! Now!*"

Scott had no idea why he was telling the "Tale of the Choking Doberman." The last time it had worked was in Middle School. For all he knew, Lisa had already heard this story and was just humoring him. Knowing what he knows now, everything Lisa did was just to humor him. But in that moment, he didn't feel indulged and every time she leaned forward and looked into his eyes, he couldn't help but avert her gaze.

"By the time I got my mom to the door, the police had already arrived, and they scoop me up and run with me, while the others help my mom. While the police rush back into the house, my dad and my neighbor run over asking, *Did they get him? Did they get him?* And my mom asks, *Who?* So, long story short, Allie was choking on a human finger. The police finally came out of the house, dragging this dirty guy—I think he was a drug addict—whose right hand was just spurting blood from where his index finger used to be. So Allie saved our lives that night."

"Jesus fucking Christ," Lisa said.

Scott saw her withdraw a little. He wondered if the *Jesus fucking Christ* was because she'd heard "The Tale of the Choking Doberman" before—maybe at a sleepover, maybe some other man had used it on her—and was just realizing she'd been had—not by Scott, but by some other man, some other man Scott didn't want to think about.

"Is everything okay?"

"Yeah," she said. Sorry. "I just realized I cussed in front of a teacher."

"Well," Scott laughed. "I'm sure you've never had a teacher bore you with some stupid story from his childhood, either."

"Are you kidding? That story was amazing. I've been boring you this entire date with my crappy life."

"Did you say a date?"

Lisa smiled, and Scott stared at her Rush T-shirt. He had trouble looking in her eyes, but the truth was he couldn't stop staring at her breasts. And at this point, he'd already established he liked Rush, already established plausible deniability.

"You called me for coffee," she said. "You paid, so if you want this to be a date. . . ."

"Let's call it a date. Let's define it right now."

"Great. Fantastic first date so far, Scott. Can we talk a bit about my son?"

"Of course. Besides being a first date, that's why we're here, isn't it?"

Controlled Opposition

Scott's mother nudged him as his old photo from the DuClod-Mann website appeared on the TV screen. He'd always hated that photo, the way they'd coerced a smile from him, that they'd made him wear the school tie because he'd left his in the car. A graphic read "High School English Teacher Thwarts Mass Shooting." The host, a very pugnacious man Scott's mother despised named Patrick Donnelly, summarized Scott's story.

"You've probably heard about this story a lot on our network," Donnelly said. "Maybe you've seen the story from our friends at those other networks. Well, we're here to give you the truth. Last night, a disgruntled man named David Brightman walked into a Pizza Galley restaurant in Torrance, California with a gun. Some say he was there to kill his wife, while others say he was there because Pizza Galley C.E.O. Daniel Patrick McDougal, a friend of the show, donates money to the Republican Party. We're still not sure what went through Brightman's sick mind. Fortunately for the hard working folks inside that Pizza Galley, there was a hero on the streets. Meet Scott Bonneville, a man who taught Honors English at DuClod-Mann high school in Portland, Oregon before moving back to California in order to take care of his ailing mother."

"What?" Scott's mother said. "Bullshit"

"Fortunately, Mr. Bonneville had a gun on his person, and rushed in to save everyone in that restaurant from what was sure to be a bloodbath. Now look, we all recognize the right to bear arms is a very complicated subject and there are some valid points on both sides, there really are. Even I know that. But the fact remains: if Mr. Bonneville hadn't had his gun on him, not only would David Brightman have blood on his hands, but so would all of us. We've always said the best way to stop a bad guy with a gun is a good guy with a gun. We've always said this because it's the truth. Well, guess what? The good guy with a gun stopped the bad guy. Period. And thank God for that. Joining us to talk about the case is our friend Mills Burghardt, former lobbyist and board member of Liberty and Justice LLC, who is representing Mr. Bonneville in his quest for, well, liberty and justice."

Wilma sighed as Burghardt and Donnelly chuckled at their joke.

"Great to be here, Pat," Burghardt said.

"God, I hate that man," Wilma said. "Donnelly, that is. Although Mr. Burghardt isn't doing himself any favors right now."

Scott didn't like Donnelly much, either. The man was a full-throated supporter of the illegal wars in the Middle East and a known member of the Bilderburg group. Like everyone else in the mainstream media, Donnelly was part of the controlled opposition, a government agent in populist's clothing. His main objective was to distract everyone from the truth.

"Scotty," Wilma said. "We've never actually talked about what happened."

"What's to talk about?"

"Good Lord, Scotty. You were only there because you wanted to kill yourself."

She sat, elbows on her thighs, hands pressed together—she'd always pressed her palms together when she was upset. Scott had always hated it— partly because it meant she was upset, but mostly because it reminded him of prayer. He turned to his mother's face, the frown that had settled on her thin lips.

"Mom, I'm fine. Going through what I did cured me."

"Well, that may be. But the police keep calling asking if you'd like to talk to their crisis counselor and I think it might—"

"Mom, Mills says they're trying to trap me."

"Well then have Mills get a therapist for you. For God's sake, you shot a man to death. Don't carry that around with you."

He turned his head toward the hall, stared at the row of framed childhood photos, his eyes settling on a Christmas photo from when he was eleven, dressed in a Santa hat, holding a small black kitten they'd named Ziggy that night but would later be renamed Ursus three years later, much to his mother's chagrin.

"I'm not," he said. "Don't worry."

"You shot a man. How can you not carry that around? And if you're not carrying that around, how can I not worry?"

"Well Christ. I just can't win here. What's the right answer, Mom? Tell me what it is and I'll say it."

Wilma's forearms shook from the pressure being exerted upon her palms. He fought the urge to pull them apart. He rose from the couch and walked over to the photo of himself and Ursus. They'd fought when Scott decided the cat was no longer named Ziggy. Even then, she'd thought he was irrational.

"Scotty, you've been through a lot these past few months. I just don't want you to have a repeat of what happened in college."

"I got counseling for that and now I'm fine."

"So if counseling worked, why not try it again?"

"Because it worked so beautifully I don't have to go back anymore. I have no goddamn issues."

"You lost your job. You lost your girl. You sit holed up in your room playing video games all day. You tried to kill yourself but killed another man instead. You have actual issues, sweetheart, and it's okay to have issues."

Scott looked over at Wilma, sitting on the couch, her merged palms moving up and down, up and down. He looked into her eyes, hazel eyes that shook, practically rippled, until tears fell. He walked into the kitchen and poured himself a glass of water. He remembered purchasing the glass at Dodgers Stadium when he was twelve. He and Mitchell had gone to watch the Dodgers play the Padres. His room was full of things he'd purchased when Mitchell was around—a Lakers pennant, a canteen from a disastrous camping trip to Tahoe, the Revell fighter jet models suspended from the ceiling with fishing wire. He'd liked Mitchell, who passed away the summer Scott had graduated high school, and as he looked around the house, it seemed as though time had stopped after Mitchell died. His mother still had the same couch she and Mitchell bought when he was in middle school.

"I got this glass at Dodger Stadium," he said.

"I remember. You and Mitch brought home a matching set for all of us."

"Where are the other ones?"

"They broke during that earthquake, remember?"

The truth was, he didn't remember at all. Scott had awoken to find his mother in bed with him, holding him, telling him everything was going to be okay. At that point, he'd been desensitized to the idea of earthquakes. They were just a fact of life growing up, so he'd been angry she'd woken him. The glasses had fallen into the sink and shattered, along with a serving plate that had belonged to his grandmother. While he slept, his mother cried in the kitchen over that serving plate, as Mitchell did his best to comfort her. Scott hadn't even noticed the other glasses from that Dodgers game were gone until now. He didn't even remember they'd come in a set.

"That's right," he said. "I'd like to redecorate my room, if that's okay. Maybe a clean slate will do me some good."

"Of course."

My Dog Has No Nose

On January 11, 1968, a Hungarian composer named Rezso Seress strangled himself to death with an EKG wire that had been connected to his chest. He'd been admitted to the hospital after jumping from the window of his tiny Budapest apartment. Seress was a haunted man, having survived a Nazi labor camp in the Ukraine, having lost his mother to the murderous horrors of the Holocaust, having suffered the heartbreak of the love of his life deciding he was not the love of hers. But Rezso Seress' suffering went beyond the loss of these two women.

Two days before his own suicide, a young woman named Janine Holsapple parked her car in her Seattle garage and made love to a man named Morgan Jackson, a man ten years her junior, with the engine running. The two were discovered by her husband the next morning. A year earlier in Stockholm, a doctor by the name of Eriksson, heartbroken over the sudden death of his fiancee, walked into the waiting room of Karolinska University Hospital, put a pistol in his mouth, and blew out the back of his skull. In July of 1957, a young teacher named Adelbert Farkas murdered his wife and children before ingesting rat poison. Rezso Seress was haunted by the Farkas family murder-suicide, as it happened a mere five miles from Budapest, but he was haunted by all of these deaths because in his mind—and in the minds of others—he was responsible for all of them.

In 1932, Seress composed "Gloomy Sunday," one day after his fiancee broke off their engagement. A song about a heartbroken man mourning the death of his love, the song became widely known as "The Hungarian Suicide Song." Upon completing the composition, he sent it off to a music publisher, who promptly killed himself. The song eventually found a publisher, and a few months after the sheet music was printed, reports of strange deaths—deaths related to "Gloomy Sunday"—began to emerge. In Berlin, a young man requested a band play the song and then went home and shot himself. A young woman in New York stuck her head in an oven, leaving behind a note requesting "Gloomy Sunday" be played at her funeral. A young girl's body washed up on the shores of the Danube, clutching the sheet music.

Janine Holsapple, Dr. Eriksson, Adelbert Farkas—they'd all left suicide notes containing lyrics from "Gloomy Sunday."

During Scott's first date with Lisa Mesman, she'd asked him if he knew the story of the Hungarian Suicide Song. Of course Scott knew about it. And they talked about all the unfortunate souls who'd taken their lives after listening to the song. He told her how, in college, some girls in Scott's dorm listened to the Billie Holiday version over and over again "as a joke."

"There's this Monty Python sketch," he said, "where a man wrote a joke so funny, he died of laughter after reading the joke to himself. He just started laughing uncontrollably until he dropped dead. Then his wife picked up the sheet of paper next to his corpse, read the joke, and then died laughing, too. The sketch ended with the British military weaponizing that joke and using it on the Nazis. Now whenever someone mentions Billie Holiday, it reminds me of Monty Python."

"I never understood Monty Python. I just don't get why it's funny."

"My mom's boyfriend, loved them. He and I used to watch it all the time. I think I'm only a fan because he used to explain the jokes to me."

"That's sweet that he shared that with you. Are you two still close?"

"Oh, no. Mitchell died a few years back. Cancer."

"I'm so sorry. Your poor mother."

"It's fine. Anyway, where were we?"

"The Hungarian Suicide Song."

"Oh, that's right. Billie Holiday brought us here."

"Yeah, Billie Holiday. Totally. So anyway, one of my relatives, a distant-distant-distant cousin, listened to her version of the song before killing herself. She smoked a joint in the living room with her boyfriend while her husband was at work. Then after the record ended they went into the garage and had sex with the engine running. Her husband came home from work and found their naked bodies in the car."

"Wait. Was her name Janine Holsapple?"

"You know about her?"

"Well, it's a famous story. Everyone knows about Janine Holsapple."

"That is so crazy. Yeah, Janine Holsapple is a cousin of mine, a distant-distant-distant one."

Scott and Lisa's first date ended with Scott inviting her to his condo. He wanted to show her his Fender Jazz Bass—one piece maple neck with a thin "C" profile, high-mass bridge, black block inlays—the exact same kind Geddy Lee uses. He'd even signed it. She asked if she could have a drink, so he went in the kitchen. By the time he came back out, he found her bent over the back of the couch, her tights around her ankles. She asked if he had protection, and he told her he didn't, so she asked him to make sure and pull out. The truth was, he did have protection, but he didn't want his first time to be with a condom.

And he thought this was how loving relationships started—with a woman offering herself to him in such a desperate and brazen manner, with him lying when she asked for something as reasonable as a goddamn condom.

He told himself this lie wouldn't matter because he was going to be good to her, better than her piece of shit ex-husband, who'd abandoned her with a socially awkward son who needed the guidance of a man. As he wiped the small of her back with a dish towel, he knew he would be the good man she deserved.

Janine Holsapple had never listened to "Gloomy Sunday" with Morgan Jackson on the night they'd died. She'd simply planned on driving him home but they couldn't keep their hands off of one another after turning the ignition. It was all a stupid accident.

Totally Like a Virgin

Scott walked Lisa to her car. He'd wanted her to stay the night, maybe they could make love again—maybe they could do it seven, eight more times—but she told him Blake would worry. She'd already been gone too long. He asked her if Blake knew she was with him, and she said he didn't. Scott puts his hands on her hips, asked her if there was any way he could convince her to stay the night.

"I can stay for a cigarette," she said, "but I really do need to go."

"Can I see you again?"

"Of course. We'll see each other a lot. I mean, you're Blake's teacher."

She lit a cigarette, using a pink plastic lighter with flowers on it, and he declined when she offered him one. He watched the smoke shoot from her puckered lips and all he wanted to do was take her, right there, on top of her car. She licked her lips and then pressed them together, grinding them back and forth.

"You know," Scott said, "I think I'll take you up on that cigarette if you don't mind."

She popped another cigarette into her mouth and lit it. Before handing it to him, she licked the tip. Days later, she'd tell him she didn't recall doing that, but he saw it—she licked the tip of his cigarette. That she'd take his cigarette and light it in her own mouth felt so intimate. Who would think to do such a thing? Scott told himself he was going to love this woman passionately until— he stopped himself, and hoped he'd be the first to die. He pulled the smoke into his lungs, letting the tobacco burn and cut the insides of his chest. They locked eyes, and he told himself he wasn't going to gag—that cigarette had been in her mouth, that cigarette was a part of her, he was taking her into his mouth as far as he was concerned and gagging would have been a rejection of who she was. He tried to exhale in the most seductive way possible, smiling as it leaked from the corner of his mouth like dry ice.

A little black cat leaped off the brick wall and slinked around the parking lot. Lisa crouched and called for it, cooing and making kissing sounds until it strode towards them. It stopped and brushed itself against Scott's leg. Lisa held out her hand, letting it rub its cheek against her knuckles. Her eyes rolled up to meet his, and she smiled.

"It likes you," she said.

He took another drag, the blistering tingles digging into the back of his throat like carbonated nitroglycerin, and exhaled. The cat pushed against his shin and purred, while Lisa giggled at its little pink tongue.

"I used to have a cat just like this when I was a kid," he said.

The cat ran off, and Lisa rose. Scott stroked her cheek. She took a drag from her cigarette and playfully blew smoke into his face, laughed.

"What was its name?" she asked.

"Ursus."

"That's a weird name."

"It was the gorilla from *Beneath the Planet of the Apes*."

"I only saw the first one. They used to show it on channel 12 all the time when I was a kid. It used to give me nightmares, all those apes on horseback, chasing humans with nets."

"Me too. I couldn't sleep for days after seeing *The Planet of the Apes*. That's why I loved *Beneath the Planet of the Apes*. That was the one that ended with the entire planet dying in a nuclear blast. No more apes."

"No more humans, either though."

"True, but no more apes on horses chasing you through a field, right?"

"So there is a bright side to everyone dying."

Lisa laughed, and Scott laughed. She then asked him how they were able to have so many other movies if the planet had been nuked, and he told her three apes escaped the nuclear explosion in a spaceship, which took them through a time portal and back into present-day America. She laughed and said it was silly.

"It is, and it isn't," he said. "The whole idea is that by going back in time, they reset the clock—accelerated it, actually, setting the stage for a new planet of apes."

"So we're damned if we do, and damned if we don't."

"In a manner of speaking. You can argue these movies take a fatalistic view of the world, sure, but there are plenty of moments where people—and apes—take control—"

"If we make out right now, will you stop trying to blow my mind?"

That the inside of her mouth tasted like tobacco was of no concern to Scott, as he was more focused on the texture of her tongue, the way she sighed as he lost himself inside her mouth. He wanted to live there, inside her mouth, to become a part of who she was, to take over her entire person. He put his hand in between her legs, and she finally pulled away, told him Blake was waiting for her.

Scott couldn't sleep all night and had to fight the urge to call Lisa, text her, tell her he couldn't stop thinking about her. At around two in the morning, he went out onto the balcony and leaned over the railing, tried to lose himself in the pale turquoise shimmer of the swimming pool below. The black cat he and Lisa had seen in the parking lot slid under the iron gate surrounding the pool and curled up on a deck chair. He walked back inside and got his coat, drove to the 7-Eleven, where he bought a pack of Morley Lights, the same kind Lisa smoked, and then went home. He sat at the tempered glass deck table with his cigarettes and a Super Big Gulp, the cat purring against his fingertips. By the time the sun finally rose, he was officially a smoker.

Hashtag Good Guy With a Gun

"So you see," Burghardt said, we're starting a new movement. We're calling it the Good Guy with a Gun Initiative. We want the world to know that good men, such as Scott Bonneville, who is a fine Asian-American, outnumber the bad men. We're not pessimists like our friends on the radical left. We know there are more of us than there are of them. We know there are good Americans out there who do the right thing every day. So any time anyone stops a bad person, whether it be a mass shooting like Scott did, or if you prevent any kind of crime, be sure to spread the news on social media with the hashtag, 'good guy with a gun.'"

The text along the bottom of the screen read *#GoodGuyWithAGun*. The screen cut to a picture of Scott, with his coerced smile, with his stupid school tie, with the caption *#GoodGuyWithAGun*. Wilma took a deep breath. Scott waited for her exhale. The screen cut back to Donnelly.

"So from what I understand," Donnelly said, "this hashtag isn't exclusively for gun owners. Is that right?"

"That's right, Pat. Any time you want to celebrate any hero in your life, whether it be a teacher who went the extra mile for your son, or a policeman who took down a drug gang, a veteran—dear God we love our veterans—an elected official who went the extra mile to protect our civil liberties—anyone, really—be sure to celebrate their good work with *#GoodGuyWithAGun*. The mainstream media always celebrates death and destruction because it's good for ratings."

"Not me, of course," Donnelly said.

"Of course not. We're the good guys here, and that's the point we're trying to make. We need more news about good guys, and less news about bad guys. If the media wants to play the ratings game and scare us into believing the world is a scary place, that's fine. The rest of us don't have to. Let's show them how many good guys there are out there in the world."

They cut to a commercial, another campaign ad, a voiceover from the our eventual president promising to defend the 2nd Amendment. The commercial showed our proud tradition of gun ownership, both as sportsmen and defenders of liberty. Scott finally heard Wilma exhale. She may have exhaled many times before this moment, but this was the first moment he'd noticed. She told him these men were awful, and Scott told her he knew.

"But you think she's just as bad."

She kissed him on the forehead and stood up. She told him she going to take a walk, asked if he'd like to come. He told her he wanted to watch the rest of the show.

By the end of the night, *#GoodGuyWithAGun* was trending nationwide. Men posted about reporting teenagers who had no business in their neighborhoods. *#GoodGuyWithAGun.* Men posted about foiling shoplifters at the gas station. *#GoodGuyWithAGun.* Posted about veterans-turned-coeds who foiled college professors lecturing secular humanism. Posted about boycotting restaurants for refusing to serve cops. Posted about walking out on dates because the women were radical feminists, leaving them to pick up the tab, as per the tenets of feminism:

#GoodGuyWithAGun.
#GoodGuyWithAGun.
#GoodGuyWithAGun.

Ziggy's Ghost

When Scott was eleven, he got a black cat on the Christmas he'd asked for a dog. Even though it wasn't a dog, even though his mother had chosen the name, Ziggy, Scott tried his best to connect with the kitten, a timid little thing that spent most of his days under Wilma's bed with his legs tucked under his stomach. Having Ziggy as a pet had felt pointless, as he seemed to enjoy keeping to himself, and stiffened the hairs on his tail and back whenever Scott reached for him. She told him this was just how cats were, that Ziggy would come to him when the time was right, which only made him question the entire notion of cat ownership.

Other than the food dish and the litter box, the only time Ziggy wasn't sequestered under a bed or behind the couch or his mother's closet was at night. He'd sit on his hind legs, his body a straight line from his front paws up to the top of his head as if at attention, staring out the sliding door leading into the back yard. He'd meow over and over, and every time Scott suggested he might like to go outside, his mother would tell him it was out of the question—Ziggy was an indoors cat.

After a year of calling out through the sliding door, another black cat began appearing in the backyard. It always happened after midnight, and Scott used to watch it hop over the fence and crouch in the corner of the yard, used to watch Ziggy stare and paw at the window, call out to his companion on the other side of the glass. After a few weeks, the other cat finally made its way onto the patio, then the steps, and the two cats would stand on their hind legs, staring at one another. Scott's mother would tap on the glass in an attempt to scare the stray. Neither cat would move. They would sit there, face to face, for hours on end. Mitchell found it all very amusing, much to his mother's dismay.

"This is horrifying," Wilma said.

"I know," Mitchell said. "It's as if Ziggy's staring at his own ghost."

"Stop it, Mitch. It's not funny.

It became an inside joke within the household: Ziggy and his ghost. They'd eventually get used to the other cat showing up. They'd even taken to feeding it, even though Wilma refused to give it a name. Two years later, someone left the front door open, and Ziggy got out. They searched the neighborhood for weeks before giving up. The thing was, the other cat had also disappeared—it was as if they'd run off together. Scott's mother cried every time she thought of what might have happened to Ziggy—that he'd been mauled by a wild dog, or been hit by a car, or somehow got stuck in a drain pipe where he starved to death. Scott wondered if maybe Ziggy and his ghost were taking care of one another, and Wilma told him that was silly. Mitchell tried to tell her he was fine, that cats always find their way home at the right time. He'd watch Mitchell comfort her by placing her palms together, and then enfolding his hands around hers, and although it wasn't the first time he'd seen Mitchell do that, it was the first time he'd realized how frequently they'd done it. Honestly, even Scott himself found it comforting, knowing his mother had someone who gave a damn about her. From that moment, every time he and his mother fought, he'd made sure to concentrate on Mitchell placing her hands together in order to calm her down. That he took solace in the way Mitchell soothed her was, in Scott's mind, proof that he—Scott, not Mitchell—loved her.

They'd never been very affectionate, Scott and his mother. Even when they'd tried, it felt forced and unnatural. Scott often wondered if it had anything to do with his father. Whenever he thought about the children he knew in Lanai, he couldn't remember any of them every saying they loved their mothers and fathers, couldn't remember any hugs, or kisses, or hand-in-hand walks to the nightly service. No one in the Church of the New Millennium seemed to love anyone other than God, or maybe his father. In all honesty, he didn't mind all too much. Scott never really liked being touched, thanks to Neil McNeil, so knowing his mother enjoyed Mitchell's hands—that she was capable to accepting affection—gave him hope that maybe someday, he too would be able to touch another person in a loving way.

It was a little over a month before the cat finally returned—but something was different. The first night home, Ziggy hopped into bed and curled up next to Scott, and Scott realized it was the first time he'd ever heard Ziggy purr. Ziggy spent the entire night purring, and kneading Scott's chest with his paws. For the next two nights, Scott barely slept, spending most of the night staring at his cat in the moonlight. It was as if he were an entirely different cat.

"Mom, I was thinking about the cat coming home," Scott said one Sunday morning. "Maybe this is supposed to be a fresh start."

"Fresh starts are always wonderful," she said. "What did you have in mind?"

"You notice how much the cat's changed since he came home?"

"Well he certainly seems to have taken to you a bit more, that's for sure."

He didn't like the way she'd said that, the haughty bitterness in her tone, that she'd tacked on *a bit more*, followed by *that's for sure*. The way she'd begun the sentence with *Well*, without the implied comma, which would have indicated a thoughtful pause rather than the battering ram it became without it. As much as Scott tried to overlook the way she'd responded, he couldn't stop thinking about the way she'd tried to mask her own hurt feelings by dismissing them, by making them about him. When he brought it up later that night, she told him he was being crazy, that she didn't care, that it was supposed to be his cat anyway. *It*—that was the word she used, as if he were an inanimate object instead of the tiny creature she'd nuzzled all Christmas day, called *Baby* over and over again, cried over when he got out—she'd even taken to making sure the front door was closed behind him every time he came home, implying it was his fault Ziggy had gotten out in the first place. But for the moment, Scott tried his best to ignore her disdain.

"Well," Scott said with the implied comma, "I was thinking we could change his name."

"Why would you want to do that?"

"Because it's like we're starting over. I feel like after what we've been through, we deserve another—"

"You don't even care about this cat."

"Jesus, Mom. I'm just trying—

"I'm not listening to this."

Wilma walked out of the room. Later that night, Mitchell held her hands together as Scott tried to convince them Ziggy was a different cat now, that the name just didn't fit anymore, while she told him what a horrible idea it was, that his name was Ziggy, and for the rest of that cat's life, he would hear the dueling calls of *Come on, Ursus* and *Here Ziggy, Ziggy*.

Two weeks after Scott and Wilma fought over naming rights, Mitchell found the other black cat's stiff corpse in the back corner of the yard. Scott and Mitchell buried the cat where he fell, and every time Scott looked back into the house, he could see Ursus staring out, rubbing his face against the glass.

No. Stop. Wait. Let's Hear Them Out...

On November 6th, two days after the Pizza Galley Shooting, a young mother named Helene Nelson posted a selfie on social media. She was breastfeeding on a park bench, brandishing a Desert Eagle 50 caliber with a grin she herself would later describe as "shit-eating."

> *NO ONE TELLS ME WHAT TO DO WITH MY KID OR MY GUN!!!*
>
> *#GOODGUYWITHAGUN #1STAMENDEMENT* (sic)
>
> *#THANKUSCOTTBONNAVILL* (sic)
>
> *#FREEDOMBITCHEZ*

Nelson would spend the rest of her day assuring people she'd never place her baby in any harm, that the gun wasn't even loaded, imploring commenters to not call CPS. The rest of the thread was essentially women (presumably the "BITCHEZ" to whom Nelson was referring) telling men women could breastfeed anywhere they goddamn needed to.

That same day, "MurricanFreedom8741" claimed he'd been refused service over his red baseball cap but instead of getting angry, he'd asked the waitress why she'd supported liberalism and after she was done "screaming her dumb head off," he was finally able to explain the truth to her. To make a long story short, he said, the waitress realized the error of her ways, that feminism and the welfare state were the reason she was a waitress and not at a better paying job.

> *Shes now GREAT conservatvie!* (sic) *Finally true patriot who love America!* (sic)
>
> *#GoodGuyWithaGun*

Unfortunately, "MurricanFreedom8741" failed to disable the geotag on their post—which read Tartu, Estonia—which explained all the misspellings and the lack of definite and indefinite articles.

A soon-to-be-former Mercedes-BMW salesman named Bill Herrington deleted a post which recounted his argument with an Ethiopian woman in a Target parking lot. He'd told her this was America and people like her were on their way out, told her little son he wasn't welcome here, that he was stealing resources from American children (#*GoodGuyWithaGun*). That he'd deleted the post after the uproar didn't matter, as plenty of people had filmed the exchange. His deletion, and eventual apology, truly was of little consequence.

The hashtag was snapping its way through social media at such a dizzying rate, it was hard to keep up. Outliers like these were to be expected. There were plenty of successes as well, most of them were. Even the President's eldest son used the hashtag on a photo of him hunting big game in Zimbabwe.

The hashtag was fresh on Scott's mind as he sat with Burghardt in a small diner in Glendale. Television cameras captured everyone in the diner giving Scott a standing ovation as he walked in. The camera man was a stringer, a freelance journalist hired by Burghardt to capture the event. Elderly veterans, with baseball caps proudly displaying the names of naval vessels, patted him on the back, told him they were proud of him. Mothers told him that, as mothers, they were very grateful men like him were keeping their children safe. The proprietor, a small business owner through and through, told him he could come keep his restaurant safe any time. The stringer told Burghardt he'd gotten his footage and left. Scott and Burghardt ordered their lunches.

"You hired that cameraman?" Scott asked.

"He's an old friend. Does a lot of work for Channel 5, mostly car crashes and house fires. Very resourceful guy. He'll get the word out. You're a beloved member of the community, a local hero. It'll be great. So, I assume you watched Pat Donnelly last night."

"I did. It was very nice, the things you said. But I'm not home taking care of my sick mother."

"Actually, you are, Scott. She's very sick and you knew she needed you."

Over Burghardt's shoulder, Scott noticed a man in wraparound shades staring at him. The man turned away, looked out the window. He wasn't seeing things—the man was clearly staring at him. Scott could tell the man was staring, even through those blue, reflective lenses.

"The hashtag's really taking off isn't it? An intern at the office came up with it. Brilliant stuff."

"Yeah, it's everywhere. Do you think maybe we should keep a low profile?"

"God, no. The President's son talked about you last night."

"He's not the President yet."

"Not yet. He will be, though, God willing."

Scott looked up and the man looked away. He looked so nervous, this man, the way he chewed on his lower lip, the way he cracked and kneaded his fingers. It made Scott nervous. The waitress, the owner's wife, came to refill Scott's coffee. Scott thanked her.

"Did you see that man yell at the Ethiopian woman?" Scott asked.

"I did. It's unfortunate when a few bad apples can't get with the program."

"I hope you're talking about the man who yelled and not the Ethio—"

"Of course I am. Why the hell wouldn't I be? Look, Scott, I don't know where you lie politically but I'll tell you I'm a solid conservative. And I know people in your line of work think people like me are racists. Well, I'm not and I take exception to you implying—"

"I wasn't implying anything. It's just, how much longer before someone kills an Ethiopian and uses that hashtag? I get what you're doing, and I appreciate it, but aren't we playing a dangerous game?"

"Scott, you walked into a family restaurant with a loaded gun and shot another man in the chest and gut. My job is to make sure people realize you aren't a menace to society. Whatever risk I take right now is worth taking. If you want someone who's going to bury their head in the sand, then maybe we call some ponytailed homosexual from the Public Defender's office."

"That's not what I meant."

Scott looked up to see the man was gone. His stomach leapt into his throat as soon as he felt the man's presence at their table, standing right in front of him, looking down. The wraparounds were now perched on top of the man's head.

"Can I help you, sir?" Burghardt asked.

"I know why you went in there," the man said. "You know about the children, don't you?"

Scott stared into the man's bloodshot eyes. Of course Scott knew about the children. Aiden Iwakuma. Tasha Bennett. Hunter Moxley. Discovered by local government, clergy, and law enforcement. The locations of their bodies connected to form a triangle around Pizza Galley, Torrance, California, Store #631. Six, three, and one—all numbers in the Triangular Number Sequence. Scott knew all about the children, and the man knew Scott knew. How did the man know? He knew because his eyes were open, that's why. This man, men like this man, had most likely prayed someone like Scott would come along, do what they lacked the guts to do. And he'd failed.

Scott's hand shook as he reached for the creamer. He'd had a plan: infiltrate the Pizza Galley, hold the employees hostage until the truth was revealed. But he'd failed. The man pointed at Burghardt, told Scott to tell him about the children.

"Hey, buddy," Burghardt said, "I think you should leave. Now."

"Three children," the man said. "One black, one white, one Oriental. Tell him about the children. Tell him how the Rothschilds bankrolled their deaths."

Two men in orange construction vests dragged the man out of the diner. The man screamed for Scott to tell Burghardt about the children, that everyone had to know about the children. Scott took a deep breath. The waitress came and patted him on the back, told him everything was okay now.

"The Rothschilds had nothing to do with this one," Scott muttered.

"What was that?" Burghardt asked.

"Nothing. I'm just kind of disoriented, you know? What the hell just happened?"

The waitress brought their food. Scott picked at it while Burghardt discussed their case. The good news was everyone in the restaurant felt Brightman was the true threat, were grateful Scott happened to show up. The bad news was—Burghardt asked Scott if he was paying attention. Scott told him he was sorry, just a bit rattled by the man.

"Try not to think about it too much, Scott. The man was clearly sick in the head. Guys like that are only dangerous when you give them attention."

Burghardt stabbed his sausage, brought the fork to his lips. The Pizza Galleon, the ship drawn in every restroom wall in every Pizza Galley location, on every officially merchandized coloring book and T-shirt, was based on the San Nicolás, a Spanish vessel that had transported children, orphans who'd lost their parents in the Inquisition, from Spain to the Rome. Scott looked out the window. The man was gone.

II.

This American Carnage Starts Here and Starts Right Now

The Howls of Seven Virgins

One Spring Break, when Nina was seventeen, Jae found a bag of Brownies on the kitchen table and ate two. Miri was visiting a coworker who'd just given birth to a little boy, while Nina was—who knows what Nina was off to? When Nina came home and saw he'd eaten her Brownies, she became visibly upset. Jae apologized and told her he'd buy her more Brownies if she calmed down.

"Dad, you weren't supposed to eat those," she'd said.

"Why not? They were just sitting here. I didn't think it would be a problem."

"How are you feeling right now?"

"I'm fine."

Nina sat down with him and turned on the TV, the A's at the White Sox. She kept asking him how he was feeling, and he'd become so annoyed he demanded she quit asking him.

"Dad, I'm going to order a pizza," she said. "Will you split a pizza with me?"

"Are you buying?"

"Yes. Of course."

"I'm kidding. Just don't tell Mom."

"No, Dad. Please let me pay. It's the least I can do."

Jae looked at her and laughed—laughed harder than he had in years—the least she could do? What did that even mean? Wait. It's the bottom of the seventh already? Where did those six innings go? When did the White Sox tie the game?

"I don't know, Dad. I'm not really paying attention. Hey, can you tell me the story of Old Hwang?"

"What? Why?"

"I don't know. Because I like that story. Just tell it to me, okay? Just tell the story and really concentrate."

"The Sad Story of Old Hwang," a Korean folktale his grandmother used to tell him all the time—Nina had loved that story as a child, mostly because of the way he mimicked the moaning winds of his grandmother's village. The story had scared her back then, and Jae would have to lie next to her until she'd fallen asleep. Look at her now—all grown up. She looked like his mother. Nina had never really known his mother—the distance, the language barrier, how could he not teach his own child Korean? They'd call his mother, and he'd have to be on the other line while she spoke to Nina in order to translate. Why not teach Nina Korean? Why make it so hard for grandmother and grandchild to communicate. His mouth was dry, really dry, drier than it had ever been.

"Dad? Are you still there?"

"I'm really thirsty."

Nina told him to sit still. She bolted from the couch and ran into the kitchen, came back with a glass of water. She'd have to go back three more times. She asked once again for the story, kept telling him to relax and concentrate.

"There once was an old general named Hwang Hyun-soo," said Jae. "He had seven sons. Old Hwang was known throughout the village, the village my grandmother came from, as a coward because during the war, he hid from the Tang Chinese while his men were slaughtered. I mean, no one could prove he'd hidden while his men were killed, but how else could a general return home unscathed while his men were captured or murdered by the enemy? Did I tell you your great-grandmother was born in that village?"

"Yeah, Dad. You're doing great. Just keep going, okay?"

"Well, anyway, because of his cowardice, none of his seven sons could find families willing to give their daughters away as brides, even though they were all handsome and clever men. Until the winter of his sixty-sixth year, many thought this was his curse."

It was the bottom of the eighth, score still 4-4. The Sox hit into a 4-6-3 double play, ending the inning. When Nina was nine, he'd tried to explain the scorekeeping to her. The second baseman (fielding position #4) fields the grounder, and throws it to the shortstop (fielding position #6) to get the baserunner out. Then the shortstop (fielding position #6) throws the ball to the first baseman (fielding position #3) to get the batter out. He'd told her about the history of scorekeeping, how it had been very important as newspapers were the only way to track statistics. Jae wondered if maybe that was the reason she didn't like baseball. He loved baseball, wished Nina could appreciate it more. He loved baseball. Loved it.

"I love baseball."

"I know, Dad. It's great."

"Nina, what's a 4-6-3?"

"What? You mean a double play?"

"You remember. That's great, wonderful. Just wonderful."

"Dad, come on. Can we get back to the story?"

"I don't remember where we left off."

"Sixty-sixth year, remember?"

Every time Jae shut his eyes, he felt as though a string was pulling him into the center of his head. It was as if there was a tiny version of himself living behind his eyelids, and every time he closed his eyes, tiny Jae would float as if suspended in water, and the rope around his waist would go taut as an invisible force pulled it, hand-over-hand, deeper and deeper into his mind. And every time he opened his eyes, all the water would drain out, kind of like an airlock—no, exactly like an airlock, and tiny Jae was back on his feet. In his mind—not the brain, the mind. They were completely different things. The brain was an organ, while the mind was—

"Dad, the sixty-sixth year."

"On that fateful winter, while his virgin sons slept in their rooms, old Hwang stepped onto his porch and saw Jeoseung Saja, envoy of the afterlife, waiting for him at the gates of his home, and Hwang, coward that he was, fell to his knees and wailed."

Jae closed his eyes, filling his mind with water. He took a breath—it had been some time since he'd done the Old Hwang voice, the gruff Jeoseung Saja voice. What if he couldn't do them anymore? Nina had waited years to hear this story again. What if he disappointed her? What if she realized she didn't need him anymore? He exhaled, wanted to cry.

" 'Ohhhhh frightful emissary,' " Jae said, " 'Is it truly my time?' Jeoseung Saja stood silently in his black robe and wide-brimmed black hat. Hwang begged and clawed at the earth, praying someone would hear his cries and rescue him from his fate."

Nina smiled, told him he was doing great. Jae smiled and once again let the water rush into his mind. Inside the human body are organs. There are spaces between those organs. What lives in between those spaces? It can't be just cells. What about the places in between those cells? No one ever thinks about that.

" 'My entire life as a soldier, I have avoided death,' " Jae said. " 'But I only did so for my sons, to watch them grow into men, and husbands, and then fathers! Yet I have been cursed with the burden of seven virgin sons! I have failed in life! Surely the afterlife deserves better than the likes of me! I beg you—I am not worthy to walk alongside you!' Jeoseung Saja stroked his beard, and the leaves rattled in the wind. Many say the emissary took pity on the craven old man—how could anyone not pity the father of seven virgins?—and the breeze weakened, and the air was still, and the emissary finally spoke—You know, I'm not sure if I can do the Jeoseung Saja voice anymore."

"Sure you can. You have to try, Dad. I really want to hear the story."

" '*Youuu* speak the *truthhh*,' " Jae growled. " '*Yooou* are not *worrrrthy* to walk among us. When you *arrrre* worthy—if you shall *everrrr* be worthy—our paths shall *crosssss* again.' And with that, the wind roared, and Hwang shut his eyes and hid his face."

Jae took a sip of water, just a sip, and then the cup was empty. Where did all the water go? He asked Nina to refill it. Why was he so thirsty? The White Sox scored on a walk-off double, ending the game. Jae groaned and Nina asked him what was wrong. He told her the A's lost, and she told him to knock it off—he scared her. Why was she scared? He felt faint, told Nina he was going to take a nap. She told him not to, that he had to finish the story.

"When Hwang opened his eyes," he said, "he saw he was in his bed. It had all been a dream. He was convinced the dream was a good omen, that Jeoseung Saja had spared him because he hadn't achieved his one true purpose: to see his sons married off to good women. He put on his robe and sent a servant to gather his sons, so he could tell them good news. Once his sons were married to suitable girls, he knew the emissary would come for him, and old Hwang told himself he would gratefully go with him to the underworld. He heard the servant scream, and then the cook, and then the maids. He bolted from his room to see them all gathered in the courtyard, weeping in one another's arms. His sons, all seven of them, had died in their sleep."

The doorbell rang and Nina got up, paid for the pizza. Jae recognized the delivery boy, a kid from Nina's school. The two of them chatted for a bit before the young man greeted Jae, asked him if he was enjoying his Sunday.

"Boy," said Jae. "I don't think I've ever had a pizza come so quickly. Nina make sure to tip him well."

"Yeah, Nina," the boy said. "Make sure to tip me well."

"Shut up, haha."

After the boy left, Jae marveled at how quickly the pizza had been delivered. It seemed as though they'd just ordered it. How long does it take to tell the Sad Story of Old Hwang—three minutes? Five?

"Dad, it took him over an hour."

"What do you mean over an hour?"

Jae stared at the television. The A's were playing the White Sox, top of the fourth, 2-0 White Sox. Hadn't the game ended? Jae could've sworn Pierzynski drove in the winning run. How was it 2-0?

"Dad, it's a double-header. Just calm down, okay? Here, have some pizza."

"What was that boy's name. The pizza guy?"

"Jeoseung Saja."

"Jeoseung Saja?"

"No, Dad. Jeoseung Saja."

Jae stared at the pizza on the coffee table, the pepperoni curled into tiny bowls of grease. They were like little meat flowers. Better not say meat flowers out loud—Nina's immature enough to find that funny. Was that boy's name Jeoseung Saja? Of course it wasn't. But what was Nina saying. Nina sighed, put her hand on his shoulder.

"Dad," she said. "Look at me. His name is Jograj Sunishtha. Jo-Graj Sun-ish-tha. Jograj Sunishtha. You met his dad, remember? They own the pizza place next to Safeway. Jograj. But we call him Joe, remember?"

"Oh," Jae said. "I know him. Jesus—why didn't you just say his name was Joe?"

Nina laughed, gave him a hug, told him he was all right. Jae closed his eyes. He wanted to know where the rope was pulling him, what happened when he finally reached the center of his mind.

"Hey Dad, let's finish the story, okay?"

"Sure, sure. Here we go. Old Hwang was so heartbroken, he ran to the mountains, where he spent the rest of his days as a hermit. Some say, when the night is especially silent, you can still hear Hwang wailing from the mountain-top, tormented by seven virgin ghosts. In the village your great grandmother is from, every time the wind howls, like this, *Oooohhhh-Ohhhhh* . . . they know those virgin ghosts are once again tormenting their father. And they told us boys, that if we didn't want to end up virgin ghosts, we could never live like cowards, that we had to be brave. Every day of our lives, we had to be brave."

"That's new."

"What's new?"

"That last part about what they told you boys. Is that true?"

"Oh. Well, it's supposed to be a story about courage."

"That doesn't make any sense. They weren't the cowards, Hwang was. If anything, that story should be about fathers not being cowards, not the sons. Shouldn't it?"

Jae had never really considered it, but Nina was right. Why would they put the burden on the boys? Maybe "the Sad Tale of Old Hwang" was actually a story about fatherly cowardice. Cowardly men raised weak children—was that the real moral? Jae closed his eyes, tried to ignore Nina. He could feel the center of his mind getting closer and closer, but it seemed he'd never reach it. Why hadn't he taught Nina to speak Korean, so he wouldn't have had to translate for his mother? Was he afraid she wouldn't be seen as American as the other kids? A voice told him to stop asking questions he knew the answers to. He'd seen the way people looked at other families when they conversed in Korean. Everyone always looked so uncomfortable, the way they narrowed their eyes, cocked their heads. They'd done it to Jae whenever a Korean tourist or a student asked him for directions. No one was ever going to look at Nina like that.

Oooohhhh-Ohhhhh . . . .

He heard Miri's car pull into the garage, opened his eyes. Nina's face was bright and clear and always beautiful. She touched his face, asked him if he was okay.

"I don't know," Jae said. "That's how my grandmother told it and I was so afraid to become a virgin ghost, I never questioned it."

He couldn't remember the last time they'd laughed like this. By the time Miri walked into the house, the two of them were doubled over, their sides aching from the short, sharp convulsions. The next day, Jae called out sick. He slept all day. Nina told Miri it must've been the pizza. Miri told them they'd never order from Joe Sunishtha's family ever again, said it was bad enough they took forever, which saddened Jae and Nina. They really did have the best pepperoni.

Jeff the Killer

It was November 6, two days after Jae sent Scott into the Pizza Galley. He hadn't slept since, but he'd not been sleeping well these past four years anyway. Everywhere Jae went, he saw Nina. Officer Mercado, the nice Filipino fellow who checked in on him whenever he had the chance, asked him if he was doing okay. Nina was sitting in the back of Mercado's squad car. When Jae asked him why she was back there, Mercado told him the car was empty. Mercado handed Jae a bottled water and left. She was behind the counter at the coffee house—she was actually the one who'd sent the young man out to tell him he couldn't sit at the tables. A young man, with Nina's face, told him to stop staring at his goddamn kids. Three children, all with Nina's face—how was he not supposed to stare?

Jae sat at a concrete chess table in the park. No one ever played chess on these tables. He used to play all the time with Nina when she was a little girl, before she'd finally quit because he'd never let her win. He remembered the first time Nina had lost at Candyland—she was four. He'd decided just this once, he was going to win. She ran into her room, cried in her bed until dinner. What did they have for dinner that night? Was it Filet-o-Fish? It couldn't have been Filet-o-Fish—he'd had Filet-o-Fish last night, remember? Some woman, with Nina's face, and her husband had handed it to him in the parking lot of the Best Buy, said their daughter, who also had Nina's face, didn't want it. No, neither of them had Nina's face. They were both black. Were they black? He'd only remembered the husband's face, and he was definitely black. There was nothing wrong with that, but wasn't the fact he had to tell himself there was nothing wrong with that proof he thought there was something wrong with it? Nina had once told him that—focusing on someone's race was just another way to "other" them, a vestigial instinct toward those different from us, psychological baggage we'd inherited from our less civilized ancestors, something we did out of fear. How could he be so racist towards people who'd done nothing but show him kindness? Jae felt deep shame for his racism. All he wanted was a good night's sleep.

The lack of sleep had turned Jae's train of thought into a rollercoaster—loops, sharp turns, corkscrews, barrel rolls—all he'd wanted to a chance to get off, but it kept going, and going, and going and—

A group of young men—three or four of them, Jae was too delirious to tell how many there were—sat down at the chess table next to his. One of the boys called him Drunken Master, like the Jackie Chan film—Nina loved Jackie Chan when she was in middle school—and the others laughed. Jae had been living on the streets enough to know they were trouble, yet he was too tired to move. They were discussing Scott Bonneville. Jae closed his eyes, and every time he drifted to sleep, he was snapped back into the daylight.

"It's crazy, man. I used to go there when I was a kid. Now it's a crime scene."

"Yeah man. I used to have birthday parties there back in the day. It doesn't make sense."

"I mean, it kind of does. The dude that went in first went in because his wife was fucking around."

"Yeah but the Asian dude. Why'd he go in?"

No one could figure out why Scott had burst into the restaurant. Should Jae say something? Would they understand Scott's purpose the way Jae had? And why did they call him the "Asian dude"? Was it the same vestigial instinct that made the boy call him Drunken Master? A cool breeze smothered the sunlight on Jae's face. It was warm for November. One of the boys lit a joint. Musky smoke filled Jae's nostrils and settled in his eye sockets. He offered Jae the joint.

"Hey, Drunken Master, you want a hit of this?"

"Man, don't give that bum our shit."

"What, bums don't smoke weed? Hey Drunken Master, you smoke weed?"

Jae shook his head. They asked him what his problem was. He told them he was just tired. They told him to get some fucking sleep, then. A young man emerged from the cluster of trees on the West side of the park, walked to the middle of the field. He lit a cigarette and stared at the sky. Jae had seen him before, but only at night, the harsh orange tip of his cigarette warning everyone to keep their distance.

"Check it out. It's Jeff the Killer."

"Think he might want to hit this with us?"

"I don't fuck with that psycho."

"I heard he beat the crap out of some two-oh-four and the ese's didn't do shit about it."

"That's not what happened. He got into a fight with one of them at Del Amo, but it got broken up. One of dudes in the gang, his brother served with Jeff in the Marine Corps, so they let it slide on the count of that dude's brother telling him Jeff had PTSD and shit. It was an act of compassion."

"Bullshit, man. Those dudes have no compassion. I heard they just took it because he was psycho."

"Who told you that?"

"Dude, Chago's in two-oh-four. He told me—"

"Chago's not in shit, man. He's just some punk-ass weed dealer. If he was Varrio 204th, they would've skinned him alive. Besides, no one calls it two-oh-four. That should've been your first clue."

"Yeah they do. It's a tagger thing."

Jae had never seen Jeff in the daylight. He'd only seen him up close once. It was three weeks ago, Jae had relieved himself behind the restroom and turned the corner to find Jeff standing ramrod straight, holding a Pabst tallboy. If it weren't for the trail of smoke from the cigarette, Jae would have thought time had stood still. He noticed the scar on Jeff's face. It ran down the left side, grazing the corner of his eye. It rippled like a tiny pink snake. Time definitely hadn't stopped.

"Seriously feel sad for that guy, man."

"Yeah man. War messes up lots of dudes."

"I heard the first dude that went into the Galley, Doug Brighton or whatever, was a vet."

"I read that too. I don't know, man. I'm not about killing people. It's gotta mess you up. Hey, Drunken Master, you ever kill anyone? Like fight some Wu Tang swordsman or some shit?"

The others laughed. There was a time when Jae would close his eyes, and see himself floating inside his head. He'd first discovered he could do this seven years ago, after accidentally eating two of Nina's pot Brownies. Nina thought he'd never figured it out, but he had. How could he not have figured it out? After that day, every time he closed his eyes, he'd imagine himself suspended in dark goo, a place where the weight of his head and shoulders didn't hold his feet to the ground. Until it all ended, the day his Occupant left his body, hid itself away in the IBM 2314—after that day, he could no longer retreat inside his head. God knows he'd tried so many times.

"Hey, man, you finally sleeping or something?"

"You do realize," Jae said, "how racist you sound when you call me Drunken Master, don't you?"

"What's racist? I'm comparing you to a badass kung fu master, instead of being a bum. Which is what you are."

"Shouldn't you boys be in school?"

"I'm twenty-one years old, bro. Open your eyes, man. You're weirding me out."

"Let it go, John. Look, let's move to another table, man. Enjoy your time, sir. We're leaving now."

"Don't call him sir. And I'm not leaving because of some bum. He's the one that should go."

Jae tilted his head to the sky, the back of his eyelids reddening from the sunlight. No sleep, no floating—what was the point of shutting your eyes? One of the boys coughed a hacking bark that echoed through the park—just wouldn't stop coughing. The redness receded as Jae lowered his head. He imagined Nina lying in the grass, the grass where Jeff was sitting, reading a book. Jeff left her alone, of course, doing whatever it was he was doing in peace. Jae had no idea what he was doing right now—his eyes were closed.

"Twenty-one years old," Jae said, "and wasting your day smoking marijuana in a park where children play."

"I don't have to explain shit to you, man. Open your eyes, motherfucker."

"Come on, man. He's just trying to get your goat."

Jae felt a finger tap-tap-tap against his forehead as the boy demanded he open his eyes. The other boys tried to reason with the young man, who refused to listen. Jae told them he wanted to sleep, and the boy told him he'd put him to sleep as soon as he opened his eyes.

"Open your eyes, man. Open your eyes. I will Good-Guy-with-a-Gun you. I swear to God."

Jae found that threat stupidly funny. He began to laugh. As soon as he began laughing, he heard another laugh, a laugh that didn't belong to those boys. Jae squinted, the sunlight squeezing down on his eyes. The young man, the one who'd threatened him, had taken a seat next to his friends. They were all looking up at Jeff.

"Good-Guy-with-a-Gun is a verb now?" Jeff said. "That can't be right."

"What're you doing here, man?"

"It's a public park," Jeff said.

"I know that. I was just wondering what we could do for you."

"Yeah man. I mean, you're welcome to chill with us, but you know. No disrespect, but you usually keep to yourself."

Jeff pointed at the playground area on the other side of the field. Mothers and fathers and and aunts and grandfathers stood with their children, staring at the chess tables. The scar on his face moved up and down as if on struts.

"You're right," Jeff said. "I do keep to myself. And I know that as long as I keep to myself, those parents aren't going to tell the cops I'm scaring their kids. Right now, you're making a scene. When you make a scene, there's a chance people will turn their attention to me. I don't want that. I just want—"

"You're right, man. We're sorry. It's just this old man—"

"You interrupted me."

"Okay. Okay. I'm sorry. I didn't mean to be rude."

"You interrupted me again."

"I'm sorry, man. I'm not trying to—"

"Jesus Christ, Sherman, shut up dude."

"Yeah, Sherman. Stop interrupting me. It's rude."

"Dude, I'm sorry."

Jeff told Sherman to stand up, and Sherman asked why, and Jeff told him because he said so. Jae stared out at the grass. Nina was wearing a blue sweater, a blue sweater in this weather. Jae closed his eyes, tilted his head toward the sun, as if trying to pour water into the back of his skull.

When he opened his eyes, the boys were gone. Jeff was sitting on top of the chessboard, lighting a cigarette. Jae stared at the billowing scar as Jeff blew smoke from his nostrils.

"Man, that kid did not know when to shut up," Jeff said.

The scar said hello. Jae said nothing. He didn't want to speak. The scar told him he didn't have to open his mouth. They could speak in silence if he liked. Jae's chest began heaving as his lungs throbbed with pressure. Jeff stubbed his cigarette, asked him if he was okay. He put his hand on Jae's shoulder, told him to breathe in and out, that it was going to be okay. Jae concentrated on Jeff's hand patting his shoulder, was able to finally gulp in some air, in spite of the incessant questions from the Occupant.

"I'm sorry, man," Jeff said. "I shouldn't have smoked around you."

"It's not the cigarette," Jae said. "It's your Occupant."

"My what?"

Jae watched Nina mark a page and then move back to an earlier section, then another one, until she found what she was looking for. *Ha!* she mouthed, before continuing from the page she'd marked. This made Jae smile.

"My daughter," Jae said. "She's out there reading a book."

Jae pointed to where Nina sat. The scar told him Jeff couldn't see her. *I know that,* Jae told it. *I know you know that, so why point it out? Because I see her, that's why. You must really miss her—you think about her all the time. That's really none of your business. Whatever you say—I'm just glad you're finally acknowledging we exist. It isn't like you gave me much choice. Of course we did—you always have a choice. Is that supposed to be funny? No, but I can see why you'd think so—Ha, it is kind of funny, isn't it? No.*

"I don't see her. Are you sure she's there?"

"She's there."

"Well, I hope she's enjoying herself."

Jeff hopped off the table and walked toward Nina. He sat down, directly to her left, stared at the sky. Jeff motioned for Jae to come over. Jae shook his head, and Jeff shrugged before lighting another cigarette. A breeze blew his smoke into Nina's face. She didn't seem to mind at all.

Griefers

Scott was in his room playing *Code of Conduct* when Wilma returned from her walk. It had been a little over an hour after Burghardt's segment on Patrick Donnelly's show. She knocked on his door to see if he needed anything, watched Scott's M1 carbine mow down Japanese Soldiers in the South Pacific, watched as their chests exploded in a red mist, watched as they fell to their knees and collapsed in the jungle, watched as grenades severed limbs and spattered the screen with blood and dirt and God knows what else.

She kissed him good night and told him she was taking a bath, told him to get some sleep. Scott told her he'd be heading to bed soon, that he had a meeting with Burghardt the next day.

Scott wandered through the jungle, wondering if he'd ever run into Blake in the game. For months, he'd been searching for him—*GrieferBoi666* Blake called himself online—wondering what he'd do if they'd ever crossed paths. What could he do? It was just a video game. Besides, they weren't playing PvP mode—even if they had run into one another, it wasn't as if Scott could hurt him in any way. Scott's gamer tag was *JeoseungSaja1111*—he told himself maybe it was time to change the name. He, or rather his avatar, *JeoseungSaja1111*, snuck up behind a Japanese soldier, stabbed him with his melee weapon four times. He then pulled out his M1911 and emptied his clip in the dead soldier's back.

It was fitting, Blake calling himself *GrieferBoi666*. Griefers were trolls, idiots who joined online gaming communities for the sole purpose of harassing other players. That he'd affixed three sixes to his gamertag just further cemented Blake's intentions—you only invoke the number of the beast when you want to be a nuisance. Blake's entire life was an act of bad faith. He was the kind of kid who would loudly declare, *Boy I sure hope they don't find the drugs in my locker!* when policemen came to talk at school assemblies, the kind who wouldn't understand why a police officer might not find that sort of thing funny. Blake thrived on provocation, thrived in the aftermath—playing the victim, wondering how no one could see he was joking, agonizing over the ostracism that always followed, plotting ways to regain the attentions of those who'd shunned him through more provocation.

A few months before they'd started *Catcher in the Rye*, a young man named Tobias Kuykendahl fired shots in a Salt Lake City high school before taking his own life. Blake spent the next day sneaking up behind classmates, whispering, *Shooter,* into their ears. That he was only suspended for two weeks drew outrage from parents, but the principal felt the broken jaw he'd received was punishment enough, that he'd learned his lesson, that he wouldn't do it again. Both faculty and students got a good laugh from that.

A little note about the Kuykendahl shooting, one Scott saw so clearly, he was shocked no one else had made the connections. None of this was mentioned in the press, but Kuykendahl's Kill List was leaked onto a message board called *RE/Serch* by one of Kukendahl's classmates. Apparently, there were five main targets:

1. Brandon Corso, captain of the baseball team. Brandon had bullied Kuykendahl all through middle school. When he'd finally stopped in the tenth grade, he'd tried apologizing to Kuykendahl, but by then it was too late.

2. Angie Azarian, star volleyball player and Corso's girlfriend since the tenth grade. She'd lived across the street from Kuykendahl their entire lives and used to play together when they were children. In Kuykendahl's suicide note, he'd professed his undying love for her, even though he'd never forgiven her for dating Corso.

3. Dean Mulroy, president of the Drama Club. The most popular kid in school, known for his outgoing personality and beautiful falsettos in choir.

4. Nicholas Hwang, Student Body Vice President and Dean's boyfriend. Hwang's father was an award-winning realtor who ran most of Salt Lake County's commercial real estate. People loved Nic's self-deprecating sense of humor, particularly when it came to his family's wealth, as he'd loved referring to himself as Bourghwang.

5. Anika Sharma, the principal's daughter. No one could fully understand why she was on this list. She'd always been kind to Kuykendahl, kind to everyone, allowing him to walk her home. They'd had such lovely conversations. She'd even toyed with asking him to the Sadie Hawkins dance, just to be nice. None of it made any sense.

But Anika's inclusion on this list made perfect sense. During a fairly perfunctory news report on Kuykendahl—how quiet he was, his quick temper, his love of violent videogames and Japanese body horror comics—they'd showed a photo of Kuykendahl sitting in his bedroom. On the nightstand, on the bottom of a stack of graphic novels, was a copy of *Catcher in the Rye*. Selma Thurmer, the daughter of Pencey Prep's headmaster, sat next to Holden on the bus. He'd described her as very nice. Of course that's who the principal's daughter was supposed to represent. From there, it was easy to reverse engineer the truth. Nic "Bourghwang" Hwang: Holden mentions many times his hatred of Bourgeois values, how much he resents his own middle class upbringing. Dean Mulroy, president of the Drama Club: Holden hates movies and actors because of they're all phony. His inclusion on that short list made perfect sense. Angie Azarain: Jane Gallagher, the girl who used to play checkers with Holden when they were kids. At the novel's start, Jane Gallagher went on a date with the handsome and athletic Ward Stradlater, which of course led Scott back to Brandon Corso. The list was short, but it was also deliberate. Scott couldn't help but be impressed by its precision. But the truth was, Scott was more pleased with himself for once again cracking the code. Of course, he was impressed with the code itself, but failure to acknowledge that his devotion to logic had led to the truth would have been false modesty. He'd always told himself good things would happen as long as he stayed true to himself.

Three months after Scott solved the Kuykendahl shooting, Blake had written that response detailing his appreciation for *Catcher in the Rye*, which led to that fateful meeting after class, which led to Lisa coming in to retrieve Blake, which led to coffee, which led to sex. Good things always happen to people who stay true to themselves.

Then why did Lisa leave him? Hadn't he stayed true to himself the entire time? Maybe she'd changed him somehow—but hadn't she changed him for the better? Wasn't devoted lover the truest form one can take? Maybe he was meant to be alone, always alone. Perhaps that was his true self. After all, that love had been a lie—at least on Lisa's part. She'd never loved him. She even said so, herself. But he loved her, even now. Maybe that was the cause of his run of bad luck: loving her. He would've gladly stopped loving her if. . .No, no. He'd never stop loving her. Whether he liked it or not—which he did—whether she liked it or not—which didn't matter—he would always love her, in spite of the pain. If being with Lisa meant bad things would constantly happen, he'd gladly take it over being without her.

Dave Brightman's love for his wife had tossed all of Scott's plans into a burning dumpster. Had he known Scott planned on exposing the truth, on protecting children from sexual predators, would Brightman have changed his plans? If Scott had stopped him, offered him his last cigarette, told Brightman about the secret kill room in the Pizza Galley basement, would Brightman have agreed to just go home? Of course not. As much as Scott struggled to admit it, love will always be more powerful than hate. Scott entered Pizza Galley with hatred in his heart, hatred for those who'd sexually exploit children. Poor Dave Brightman went in because he loved his wife, even though she didn't love him in the same way. Scott knew Brightman wasn't willing to simply die for love, but willing to kill for it as well. He could never kill Lisa—God knows he'd considered it. Did he not love her the way Brightman loved his wife?

Blood spattered the TV screen and Scott's controller vibrated with every bullet he took. The map on the right hand corner of the screen showed no red Axis dots, only one blue Ally dot. Scott turned his character around to see another player, gamertag *Killary2016*, dancing in his field of vision. *Killary2016* fired a few more rounds into Scott's player, dotting the TV with flecks of blood. Because this wasn't PvP, Scott wasn't taking any damage but then why show the blood? *Killary2016* danced again, then gave a thumbs-down. Scott turned the game off.

They were all griefers. Every single one of them. Just by breathing the same air as he did. Scott looked at his hands. He could still feel the buzzing in his palms.

Wherever You Go, There You Go

During one of their final meetings together, Scott couldn't help but think about how he'd seen Dr. Ong at the park with her daughter two days before. It was clearly her daughter, looked just like her, but with red hair. He'd never seen an Asian child with red hair—granted the child wasn't full Asian, even Dr. Ong wasn't full Asian, but it still struck him as a bit strange, a little redheaded girl of Chinese ancestry.

Because of his upbringing, Scott had never fulfilled any of the expectations people had of Asians. He'd once joked he was terrible at math, but a fantastic driver, and Dr. Ong smiled while scribbling in her notepad. Where did the bad driver stereotype even come from? At the time, he used to see young Asian men driving around town in souped-up streetcars. If these boys were so bad at driving, why would they choose a pursuit that would only magnify how bad they were? Scott himself was a very good driver. He'd been taught by Mitchell, and he'd often wondered if learning how to drive from a white person saved him from that stereotype. He knew he should feel badly every time he'd wondered that—that it was a betrayal to think such things—but what, if any, allegiance did he have toward Asians? Mitchell himself had even joked about it—*Scotty, after we're done, I promise no one will ever accuse you of being an Asian driver*—and they laughed, laughed, together. Should he have been offended? Other than the jokes and slurs he'd endured, he had no context for what it meant to be an Asian. If he'd had the capacity to be honest with himself, he might have admitted he saw being Asian as a bad thing. Three months before leaving DuClod-Mann, Greg Kinoshita, the Chemistry teacher who'd told him about Boy's Day, asked him point-blank, "Scott, do you like being an Asian-American?" to which Scott replied, "I don't hate being Asian. I just hate being me from time to time," and that was the last time they'd had any substantive conversation about anything.

Every once in a while, Scott used to sit in the dining hall next to his dorm, and some handsome Laotian boy, or pretty Korean girl, would ask to sit with him, and then tell him all about all the clubs and organizations on campus for Asian-Americans like him.

"Thanks," he'd say, "but I'm not very Asian, you know?"

"You look pretty Asian to me."

"I know, haha, but I was raised by white parents, so I don't know what I'd really have to offer."

"Oh, hey! I was adopted too. That doesn't make us any less Asian, does it?"

"I wasn't adopted. It's a long story. I'd rather not go into it."

Eventually he'd made it so awkward, they all stopped asking. And this was what he'd chosen to talk about, rather than seeing Dr. Ong and her redheaded daughter.

"The Asian-American club on campus," Scott said, "do you think they're good?"

"Well, I think it's important for people with shared experiences to commiserate. I also feel it's vital for us to understand our history, so yes, I think they're very helpful."

"How do we move forward?"

"In what regard?"

"It's like we obsess over the past all the time. Even in here, all we do is talk about the past. What about the future? Do we ever think about where we want to go?"

"So where do you want to go?"

"I don't know, to be honest. But I know where I don't want to go, and that's the past. I mean, the only reason I'm here is because I set fire to that dumpster. Don't you think I've taken responsibility for that already?"

"I'm not sure if—"

"I know what you're going to say. You're going to say you're not sure if your feelings have anything to do with how I'm feeling."

"Actually, I wasn't going to say that. But how does one move forward without recognizing what's happened in the past?"

"What about clean slates? I mean, is there such a thing as a clean slate? You're making it sound like there isn't, and if there isn't, then what's the point of ever moving forward?"

A car alarm sounded in the parking lot, a short choppy siren radiating through the silence. Mitchell always had a joke every time an alarm sounded: *Looks like I set off the Cool Guy Detector.* Scott's mother would laugh every time, as if the joke hadn't stopped being funny years ago. Dr. Ong had once asked Scott if he'd loved Mitchell, and Scott told her Mitchell had nothing to do with his life—he was just some guy who kept his mother from complaining about Cary Bonneville.

The last time Scott saw Mitchell was at a hospice in Palos Verdes, two weeks before Scott went off to college. At that point, the cancer had weakened Mitchell to the point he couldn't smoke his own cigarettes. Scott's mother had to smoke it for him, occasionally blowing smoke into Mitchell's mouth like a bird feeding her baby. He'd asked Scott if he was excited about college.

"Sure," Scott had said. "I guess."

"Well, I'm excited," Mitchell said. "It's a good school, and I hope you can make some good memories there. One thing I've learned these past few weeks is it's important to have good memories."

Scott watched Mitchell suck the smoke from his mother's lips. The marine layer had created a torrent of wind—it was always windy in Palos Verdes—so his mother had to lean in extra close to make sure the smoke stayed intact. She leaned back, and the smoke dribbled out of Mitchell's chapped lips, tore apart in the breeze.

"It's like that old saying," Scott said, "Wherever you go, there you go."

"It's wherever you go, there you are," Wilma said.

"Sure, if you say so. But I like mine better."

Normally, they would have argued about whether his really was better. They would have argued over Scott's inability to admit he was wrong, her inability to just let him have his way for once. But she was too trapped in her sadness, and he was lost in the way the cancer had hollowed out Mitchell's cheeks, the fact he could practically see Mitchell's skull through the skin. She leaned in once more, the smoke seeping from her lips into Mitchell's lungs. The smoke leaked out of Mitchell's nostrils. He winked.

"Wherever you go," Mitchell said, "there you go. It's true. It's true."

Wilma smiled at him. She flicked the ashes, which confettied in the wind. She put her palms together and stared at Mitchell's limp hands. Scott put his hand on her back as she began to cry.

"C'mon, Willie," Mitchell said, "we're on a smoke break. You can't cry now."

She closed her eyes and took a deep drag, but didn't share the smoke this time. Mitchell stared up at the sky, marveled at the moon suspended in the daylight like a pale face breaching the cool blue waters.

"The moon in the daytime always feels like a mistake, doesn't it?" Mitchell said.

She took another drag and leaned over, fed him the smoke. She kissed his lips. Scott stared at the moon. It seemed to Scott that he saw the moon quite frequently in the daytime. Maybe not seeing the moon in daylight was the mistake, and not the other way around. Their heads jerked toward the sound of a fire alarm. A staffer came out and told them not to worry, that it was a false alarm.

"Looks like I set off the Cool Guy Detector."

"Oh, Mitch," Scott's mother said.

Mitchell hacked a watery cough. The phlegm percolated in his lungs. He'd be dead in three weeks.

"Scotty, could you take the cigarette for a second?"

"Sure, Mitchell."

Wilma handed him the cigarette, which he held pinched between his fingers like a dirty sock. Mitchell took her hands in his, her palms pressed together, sandwiched between his palms. He kissed her fingers, leaned back. Scott handed the cigarette back and stared at the moon. Mitchell and his mother spoke in a hushed tone, her voice raspy from the tears, his hoarse from the disease consuming his lungs.

On their way home, they stopped at a Ralph's to buy some groceries. Wilma cried in the Produce aisle, and then at the Dairy section, but they made it through without anyone really noticing until she cried again during checkout. Scott apologized to the cashier, told her about Mitchell's cancer. The woman said she was very sorry, and then avoided eye contact as she scanned and bagged their items.

As Scott pushed the cart of groceries through the parking lot, she began to shout, "No, no, no, no," as she stormed to their car, her arms gesticulating, shaking from the tension. A stray grocery cart had rolled into their car, scraping the passenger side door.

"Goddammit," she shouted. "How hard is it to put your goddamn carts away?"

As he pushed their cart, and the one that hit them, back to the front of the store—he took them all the way back to the store because he'd wanted his mother to have a chance to calm down—Scott glanced at the countless stations designated for carts. Each row had a designated area for carts. They were all over the goddamn parking lot. There was even a station four parking spots away from his mother's car—it wouldn't have taken any effort to put it away. As he made his way back to his mother, he couldn't help but see all the stray carts left in empty parking spots—one was even left capsized in front of a minivan, a seagull nestled within as if caged. The parking lot was filthy with seagulls, disgusting creatures who blanched the asphalt with excrement. Scott had always hated their presence in the city—their squawks should've evoked closeness to the ocean rather than the distance from it. He got in the car and held Wilma as she cried softly into his chest. A swarm of seagulls clustered in front of the car, picking at a pigeon carcass splayed behind the concrete wheel stop. Her hair smelled like cigarettes.

The car alarm shut off with a double chirp, and Scott was once again left in silence. Dr. Ong cracked a joke about how the alarm probably signaled the progress they were making. Scott placed his palms together, placed them under his chin. He immediately separated them and pressed them against his thighs.

"You know what superpower I'd like to have?" he said "The power to make people see the things they've done. To make them really understand how they've affected things."

"Okay," she nodded, "Yet you'd like to give yourself a clean slate. Don't you think there might be a disconnect there?"

"Sure, but what're you gonna do? "

"I, for one, would love to hear your thoughts on what can be done."

"I honestly don't know what to say."

"Take your time."

Scott took his time, eventually settled on a story about the time his cat went missing. The point of talking about Ursus was lost on him, and if Dr. Ong had any idea of what the point might've been, she didn't say.

It Honestly Wasn't Even That Great

Scott merged onto the 5 North. He hated driving into the Valley, but Burghardt had wanted to meet with him, discuss how they'd proceed in the wake of *#GoodGuyWithaGun*. Burghardt told Scott they couldn't meet anywhere in the South Bay, as everyone knew who Scott was, that the Valley might provide a little more anonymity—but wouldn't they know him in the Valley as well? It wasn't as though each city got its own newscast. It wouldn't be until Scott was ambushed by that cameraman and the well-wishers that Scott knew why Burghardt had wanted to meet in Glendale. He turned on the radio, tried to quell the rage of Killary2016's treachery. It had infuriated him to the point he could hardly sleep. Tom Petty sang about a small-town American girl who'd promised she'd find a better world for herself, even if it killed her—at least that had always been his interpretation. Lisa, of course, had another theory:

"Did you know 'American Girl' is about a girl that killed herself?" she asked.

Scott was splayed on the bed, naked, when the song began playing. Lisa was peeing in the bathroom. He closed his eyes, absorbed in the song when Lisa hopped into bed and told him her theory on "American Girl." Scott opened his eyes, Lisa seated next to him He looked up at her, put his hand on her naked thigh. He'd heard the story before. A girl at the University of Florida leapt to her death off a dorm room balcony. She'd been high on LSD and wanted to fly. Tom Petty had denied he'd written the song about this girl's supposed death.

"I don't know if that's true," he said.

"Why do you do that?" she asked.

"Do what?"

"Always contradict me."

"I do?"

"All the time. I say one thing, and then you always say, 'uH, WeLL, aCtUallY tHaT's NoT tHe CaSe. . . .' "

"Is that how I sound to you?"

"How do I sound to you? Like some kind of retard who isn't smart enough to know all the shit you do?"

"What? Why would you think that?"

"You're always talking down to me. All the time."

"No I'm not. I swear. You know what? I'm sorry. Please tell me more about the song."

Lisa slid off the bed and slid into her underwear. She bent over to grab her bra. Scott rolled out of bed, stood in front of her.

"Where are you going?"

"Home. I need to get Blake ready for school."

"School's not until the morning."

"I need to make his lunch."

"I'll buy his lunch—for the rest of the year. Please, just stay."

"We don't need your fucking charity."

"It isn't charity. I want to. I just don't want you to go."

He put on his robe and made her a drink—if she had a drink or two, she won't be able to drive—convinced her to stay, to talk it out. She had a rum and Coke, two of them, and then came back to bed one more time. By the time Scott's alarm went off, she was already gone. In class, Scott asked Blake if his mother was okay.

"Why wouldn't she be?" Blake asked.

"Could you have her call me?"

"What'd I do?"

"Nothing, man. Just tell her to call me, okay?"

Scott thought he was going to lose her that night. They seemed to argue about the dumbest things. As Scott inched toward the Glendale Freeway exit, he realized something about their stupid arguments—he was never wrong. His problem wasn't always being right, but the way she'd reacted to him. This had always been his problem, the way people reacted when he was right. Lisa, his mother, his coworkers—they'd always hated arguing with him because he was never wrong. Surely there were moments he was wrong, weren't there? There had to be. Scott searched his mind, tried to remember moments he'd admitted he was wrong—if he'd ever been wrong, of course he'd have admitted right away how wrong he'd been.

Nothing came to mind.

Did she leave him because she couldn't handle always being wrong? It had to be exhausting for her. Poor Lisa. How exhausting it must've been. Why couldn't he have been more understanding? Maybe they could've stayed together had he, for once in his life, let her have one. Maybe they wouldn't have ruined the great thing they'd had.

As he inched along toward the exit, he stared up at the pedestrian bridge. Someone had affixed a giant sheet across the chainlink retaining wall: *If both sides are wrong, then who's right?*

He changed the station, leaving Tom Petty and his American Girl behind.

The Literary Present

Okay, Scott tells himself, *I walk into the Pizza Galley, tell everyone I'm not there to hurt them, remind them they're innocent victims in all of this, just like everyone else. Of course they're not innocent—they're all complicit in their own ways—but I have to get them on my side. Then I tell them I know the truth, that I know about the kill room in the basement. There is no basement, they say. Bullshit, I tell them. Show me the goddamn basement. They realize I mean business, that I'm not just some random lunatic, but someone who's done all of the research—I show them everything I'm doing is deliberate and planned out. I go into the basement and take pictures, make sure to livestream the entire thing in case one of them tries something. I may not leave that place alive, most likely I won't. But everyone will know.*

There's something eternal about present tense, as if what's being described is always happening and will never stop happening. Moments become perpetual when described in the present:

> *In the* Sacrifice of Isaac *by Rembrandt, Abraham is horrified by the realization he's about to sacrifice his son, Isaac, who is resigned to his fate. In Caravaggio's painting of the same name, Isaac is the one horrified by his father's passive fatalism.*
>
> *Ophelia isn't merely the object of Hamlet's rage toward his mother, but toward all women, whom he views as dishonest corruptors of men. After Hamlet's rejection, her father's death, and her brother's absence drive her mad, Ophelia takes her own life. We can't even bring ourselves to view the pain of women as independent from the pain of men.*
>
> *So this guy says to me, What am I an asshole? So I says, Yeah. You're an asshole. And then this guy, you wouldn't believe what this guy does.*

Ophelia will always bear the brunt of men's cruelty. Abraham will always choose to sacrifice his own son. Assholes will always be assholes who do unbelievable things. Scott thinks about the literary present. When writing in MLA style, he'd told students, always write in the present tense. The author is speaking to you. It is a living conversation in the continuing present time. Huck Finn doesn't happen once—it happens again and again with every new reader. Gatsby wasn't doomed to failure—he is always doomed to failure. Holden Caulfield is, not was, an assassination trigger for sad, mostly young, men cultivated by the CIA. The past tense lends an air of finality to those things that have happened. The present tense underscores the fact stories are living, breathing things meant to be experienced over and over and over.

Scott sits in his car and watches the last family, a family of four—a pony-tailed man, his wife, two little girls—pile into their F-150 and pull out of the Pizza Galley parking lot. It's almost eight past ten on a school night. What kind of irresponsible people take their children out so late—to a place like this? Scott stares at the gold Pizza Galley token—a Dough-Bloon, they called it—in his hand, tells himself he's doing the right thing—he isn't here to hurt anyone. This is completely normal—no not normal at all. If this were completely normal, someone else would have done it already. Why hadn't anyone done this yet? Because they're scared, that's why. Everyone talks a good game about change—actual change—but none of them have the actual balls to carry through, to be the good guys, actual good guys, to make the bad guys pay. Man up, Scott. Man up. Stop being a fucking pussy.

"Subdivisions" by Rush plays quietly on the car stereo, and he remembers how Lisa used to sway to the synthesizer when the song came on. If only he'd sent the letter. If only he hadn't chickened out. His eyes clamp shut, and he wants to cry, but nothing comes out because what does he really have to cry about? Some bitch leaving him? Her asshole son screwing him over? Why cry for them when there are actual children out there in genuine pain? Why cry for anyone when most of us don't even care to know what's really happening?

The song ends, and Scott gets out of the car. One cigarette to pass the time, make sure the ponytailed dad in the F-150 doesn't come back. What if he forgot his cell phone? That's a reasonable thing that can happen. He sees a man walking up and down the sidewalk next to the restaurant. The man sits on the curb in front of the nail salon. Scott lights the cigarette, tries to look casual, smoking in an empty parking lot where every store on the strip is closed. What the hell's that guy doing here? Why's he just sitting on the curb? Scott walks to the other end of the strip mall, decides to walk his way down the sidewalk, casually. He starts at the children's clothing consignment store, then the computer repair shop—he's not here to hurt anyone—he stops in front of the pet shop, stares at the sleeping gerbils behind the window—just get to the basement—an old woman sweeps the floor inside the Vietnamese noodle shop, passes Subway—livestream the entire thing, make sure people see it—all the lights are out in Subway—will Lisa see the livestream? Of course she won't see it, at least not right away, unless she'd unblocked him an hour or so ago. Scott stops at the nail salon, takes a drag. He's giant, this man—shaved head, black leather jacket, dark goatee—not the kind of man Scott usually approached. If this asshole doesn't leave, he'll ruin everything. He drops his cigarette on the sidewalk, crushes it under his toe.

"Lovely night," Scott says.

The man says nothing, looking down between his knees at the blacktop. His hands are shaking. Scott doesn't know what to do. He's never been much for conversation—a man like this, what could they possibly talk about? Maybe Scott could annoy him into leaving. What else was there? How about them Lakers? What did Scott know about the goddamn Lakers?

"I used to come here all the time as a kid," Scott says.

"You need to get out of my face," the man says.

"Come on. I'm just trying to have a nice, friendly conversation—"

"If you don't get the hell out of here, I'm gonna conversate my fists all over your face."

Scott reaches into his pocket, runs his finger along the handle of his gun. What kind of cretin used the word conversate? It's not even a word. Were he a braver man, Scott would've laughed.

"Conversate isn't actually a word" Scott says.

"Maybe you should look it up."

"Where? In the dictionary? Because you won't find it there."

"Pretty sure it's there."

"It's not. Trust me. I'm an English teacher. Or at least I was, until—"

"My bitch wife is a know-it-all just like you. We looked it up. It's there, asshole."

Scott backs away as the man rises. The man lights a cigarette. He wonders if he could claim self-defense if he was forced to shoot this man. Just perfect. There's no way he'd get into Pizza Galley with this moron snooping around. Scott pulls the cigarette carton from his pocket. There's only one left. Seems like a good time to walk to the 7-Eleven down the street, let the closing crew get settled before he makes his entrance.

"I'm going to take a walk," Scott says. "By the time I get back, you'd better not be here."

"What if I am? You gonna shoot me?"

"If I have to."

The man laughs, stares right into Scott's eyes and laughs, his mouth stretched stupid, his shoulders hopping up and down. Scott reaches into his pocket for the gun.

"Let's hope you do, bud," the man says. "God knows my wife would appreciate that."

A breeze kicks up, the wind rumbling inside Scott's ears. An ambulance wails as it speeds by. The man watches the old Vietnamese woman and her husband lock up the noodle shop and walk to their car. He turns back to Scott and holds up his hands.

"Look," the man says, "I got no beef with you, man. So you go on your little walk. By the time you get back, I won't be here. You have my word. How's that sound?"

"Sounds good. Thank you."

"You're welcome."

"Enjoy the rest of your night."

"You too. Have a great night, man."

Scott turns and makes his way through the parking lot—turns out he's not such a bad guy, after all. It's about a quarter after ten. They'll cross paths one last time a half hour from now, the moment Scott will become famous for killing him inside the Pizza Galley, a moment Scott will relive over and over for the rest of his short life.

The Lady With the Dog

He lights the last cigarette and walks toward the 7-Eleven. The strong breeze rumbles in his ears—the rustling sound gets louder and louder. The cigarette smoke scatters in the breeze, immediately pulled apart as soon as it leaves his lips, as if vaporized by a ray gun. The waxing crescent moon hangs directly above his head. Lisa had once told Scott he was probably born under a waxing crescent moon because of his strong moral base, unshakable sense of pride, and an overpowering stubbornness that can lead to trouble when unchecked. She'd told him that after a fight, so Scott went online for a second opinion. What he'd discovered was those born under a waxing crescent were assertive, driven by achievement, and willing to risk everything to actualize their goals—so, she wasn't completely wrong. As far as he was concerned, her characterization was probably more accurate. At least it was honest.

Scott stares at the thin white sliver in the night sky—ponders his strong moral base, his unshakable sense of pride, the overpowering stubbornness—and takes a deep drag from his cigarette. Why is it that horoscopes and personality tests only give positive attributes? No one ever says, *Hey you're a Gemini—that means you're an asshole*, or *Hey, you were born in the year of the horse—you probably hurt animals for fun*. Chelsea Raban, the AP Psychology teacher at DuClod-Mann once told him it was called the Barnum Effect, how people come to believe vague, general personality traits that basically apply to everyone are tailor-made for them. She'd never told him that, not exactly. He'd overheard her telling others about it in the faculty lounge.

Scott remembers an online test he once took, posted on *RE/Serch*, the message board he stopped going to because they weren't serious people—*Which Star Wars Villain Are You?*—he got Grand Moff Tarkin because he was supposedly intelligent, and highly respected, and made decisions that favored strong tactics over emotion. Nowhere did it mention Tarkin being a cold-hearted, genocidal monster who'd forced a young girl to watch her planet die. This is the problem with the world—people only believe the things they want to believe. No one wants to believe that children are bought and sold on the dark web, that men in power have been pushing the benefits of child molestation since the ancient Greeks—it actually wasn't the ancient Greeks who were doing it, but a group of medieval scribes, conscripted by aristocrats and the Papacy, who'd invented the exploits of the ancient Greeks and Egyptians from whole cloth. These Papists were using "the Greeks" to justify their enslavement of children. These were cold, hard facts any idiot could research if only they'd wanted to know the truth. Scott tightens his lips and walks, exhales, the smoke pouring from his nostrils.

A group of kids hoot from the open windows of a speeding Honda Accord. What possessed people to do that—to hoot at random strangers from a moving car? How was that even fun? Scott reaches for his gun—he wouldn't shoot them, just flash it so they'd know he had it—but stops when he notices a motorcycle cop speed by.

He stops at the intersection and stares across the street. A man on the other side frantically pushes the button for the crosswalk. Scott wants to tell him it's useless, that everything's on a timer, that the light will change whether he does or doesn't push the button. As they cross paths, the man glares, keeps his eyes fixed on Scott, making sure to keep his head on a swivel. Scott turns and walks backwards, and the man finally turns away.

"You don't have to push the button," Scott says. "It's all on a timer."

He reaches the entrance to the 7-Eleven parking lot, in between a dry cleaners and a check cashing place. A swirling cluster of gnats dance around the lights hanging above the walkway. Scott drops the cigarette on the asphalt, crushes it beneath his boot, looks behind the glass. It's so bright inside the store, as if he's staring into a world that exists outside the one he's currently standing in. A group of pretty young girls laugh in their shorts and tight shirts as they pay for their Slurpees. The wind brushes past the back of his head. He walks to the DVD rental kiosk next to the sliding doors, waits for the girls to leave. They don't even seem to notice him as they pile into their little white car. The doors slam shut, and they laugh, their faces uplit green from the dashboard, gesturing with their hands, as they back out of the parking space— none of them buckles their seatbelts. Scott heads inside as one of them shrieks from behind the windshield.

He walks through the sliding doors and says hello to the man behind the counter. The man groans and points, tells Scott to turn around. Scott sees the tiny traces of dog shit left by his bootprints.

"Oh goddammit," Scott says. "I'm so sorry. I thought I'd wiped it all off."

"Every fucking night, the man says."

The man steps out from behind the counter and walks to the back, tells Scott not to move. Scott feels terrible, thinks about how he might have ruined this man's night—dealing with dog shit has a way of doing that. Lisa had once told him bad energy was contagious, that they'd done studies on it. Because she'd read it on a website called *The Natural Spirit*, he'd dismissed it as bullshit.

But here he is, transferring dog crap from one place into another, sharing a piece of his own bad mood with this poor man.

"What do you think the source of your bad energy is?" she'd asked.

"Is that even something we can know?"

"Of course it is. Anything can be understood."

"That's not what I asked, though, is it? I asked if it could be known?"

"Look, if you want to be in a bad mood just tell me, so I can find something productive to do."

"No, I'm fine. Let's just drop it."

Lisa had always believed stupid things to be true. It was one of her more annoying traits. But he loved her, still loves her, which was why he tolerated all of her bullshit. What if he was supposed to question her more? What if by not questioning her enough, he hadn't improved her life in any sort of way? Maybe he was supposed to tell her that ibuprofen and aspirin were better for pain than the natural supplements she bought at whatever headshop she bought her medicine. Maybe he was supposed to tell there was no scientific proof that essential oils eased the pain of muscle cramps. Maybe he was supposed to tell her sex on your period didn't cause UTI's. Maybe the reason she sent him away was because he wasn't acting the way a man should, but the way a loving boyfriend might. Maybe she didn't need a loving boyfriend, just a real man.

The man rolls out a yellow bucket, steering with the mop handle. The man swipes his mop back and forth, muttering in Spanish. Scott tells him he's sorry and the man waves his hand, tells him its fine. The man walks toward the entrance. The door slides open and he scans the parking lot.

"Can you tell me where you stepped in it?" the man asks. "I want to make sure no one else does."

"It was actually at Albertsons," Scott says. "She had this little pug and claimed it was a service dog."

Before driving to Pizza Galley, Scott stopped inside of Albertsons to get a cup of coffee. He tells himself he wasn't stalling—that he needed to be alert in order to function properly—but he knows he was. The woman in front of him was ordering a venti green tea while simultaneously having a very loud Russian conversation on her phone. At her feet was a pug wearing a red service vest. It was pissing on the floor. Scott tapped the woman on the shoulder. She was in mid-eyeroll when she turned to face him.

"Your dog," he said, "it's pissing on the floor."

The woman got off the phone and told the barista she was going to need a mop. The barista sighed and got on the intercom, called for clean-up.

"I'm very sorry," the woman laughed. "I didn't realize he had to go."

"Service dogs don't do that," he said.

"Excuse me?"

"Your dog's wearing a service vest. Service dogs don't piss wherever they like. They're highly trained. You're committing fraud."

"*Po'shyol 'na hui.*"

"I understand enough Russian to know what you said, and you should be ashamed of yourself. Your dog isn't a service dog. What you're doing is wrong."

"I have emotional distress, so thank you for understanding."

The woman blew him a kiss and stormed out. Scott had always hated Russians. He'd seen them move into Portland and do everything the clown running for president had attributed to other immigrants. Every interaction he'd had with them ended with some variation of *Po'shyol 'na hui.* He honestly had no idea what it meant, but he'd understood the context. Lisa's ex-boyfriend was a Russian. Scott was sure she was dating a Russian now. You couldn't throw a rock in Portland without hitting a Russian.

"Sorry that happened," he said.

"Oh it's fine, said the barista. No worries."

"These Russians, you know? No manners. They're a bunch of savages to be honest."

The barista turned and handed him his coffee. She glared as he paid. Her nametag read Irina. You couldn't throw a rock.

He left a five dollar tip, even though she said they didn't accept tips at this Starbucks. As he made it to the door, he turned around to watch Irina flick the five dollar bill off the counter. He felt a soft squish beneath his feet. The Russian woman was placing the pug into her car.

"Hey!" Scott called.

She turned around and leaned against her car. Then she slid into the open door and turned the ignition. Scott chain-smoked two cigarettes, while wiping the sole of his shoe in the dirt and woodchips, cursing this woman, wishing he had his gun on him—he wasn't going to shoot her, of course, but what if he did? What would it matter? He was going to be a marked man at the end of the night anyway.

The man turns and walks back inside. The door slides shut. Scott wants him to hurry the hell up—for Christ's sake, all he wants is a pack of smokes— but what can he say to a man he'd forced to mop up shit? Scott stares at the row of cigarettes behind the counter, behind the rack of bagged nudie magazines. Did people still buy nudie mags? Couldn't you just get anything you wanted on the internet? Wasn't that the problem—that everything was available to everyone at any time? How available had Scott himself been to Neil McNeil? His own father trusted Neil with his life—the entire church trusted Neil. Who wouldn't trust a former Chicago PD sergeant?

How available is any child in the eyes of predators? All they had to do was go to any playground, or theme park, or pirate-themed restaurant—the kind of places parents took kids as a distraction. Aiden Iwakuma was taken after getting lost in the woods. His parents were napping in the tent. They'd admitted they'd shared a bottle of wine. Tasha Bennet was last seen in GameStop playing video games, while her mother and grandmother were trying on shoes at the other end of the mall. Hunter Moxley's parents lost him in the crowd on the way out of a heavy metal concert at Staples Center. It seemed to Scott we were living in a golden age for pedophiles, an age where the parents wanted to be just as distracted as their children.

The man makes his way behind the counter, locks his fingers behind his head. Scott turns away from the girlie mags, which he wasn't really looking at anyway. They were sheathed in black, opaque bags—you couldn't see anything even if you'd wanted to.

"This woman at Albertsons," the man says, "she was a Russian?"

"How did you know?"

"She comes around here all the time, lets her dog shit all over the parking lot."

"Someone really needs to do something about her."

The man clenches his jaw, over and over again. Scott listens to the man's deep breaths, concentrates on the angry fissures forming on in between the man's brows. Lisa was right—bad energy is contagious. If it's contagious, then what is the source of Scott's bad energy? Surely it isn't the little pug—these things are always cumulative, aren't they? There's never just one thing. It wasn't the last straw that broke the camel's back—the last straw only completed the process of breaking its back. So what did it matter what the source was? What if he could trace his bad energy back to patient zero? Who cares? Who cares if Cary Bonneville's affair with Soo-mi was the source? Or if being left on the doorstep of a doomsday cult was? Maybe being taken to Hawaii and being left at the mercy of a pedophile was the source, or Millie Dufresne's bombing spree leading to a new understanding of CIA neurolinguistic conditioning. What does any of that matter? Once bad energy is out in the world, it's out in the world. One little smile won't change a goddamn thing, Lisa. It won't goddammit.

The man takes a breath and shakes his head, exhaling with the chuckle of a man who's already given up. Scott already knows this man won't do anything about the woman and her pug.

"The hell with it," the man says. "What can I help you with?"

"Oh," Scott says. "Can I get a pack of Morley Lights?"

Dream Sequence

Yu-jin had a dream two nights before Dave Brightman burst into the restaurant, two nights before she gave birth to Naomi. Adam had come home from Afghanistan and they'd gone out to celebrate. He was dressed in his Class A's, showing her the medals he'd earned while deployed. It was a strange conversation, as Adam spoke in a very formal manner, like a shy child showing his baseball cards to his parents' adult guest—in no way did it sound like a husband speaking to a wife. The medals were all very strange—awarded for things like *Most Drawings of American Flags Sent by Children from Across the Country*, and *Best Obama Impersonation*, and *Cleanest Fingernails*—not the sort of things the U.S. Army awarded medals for. They were in a loud pizza place with stained glass lamps, and Yu-jin was upset because Adam knew she didn't enjoy going out for pizza. Why would he bring her to such a place? Adding to her distress was the fact that the walls were tiled with framed paintings of Jeoseung Saja, and every time she turned from Adam's medals and looked around the restaurant, the paintings seemed to be staring directly at her. She told Adam we needed to leave.

"Relax, Jinny," Adam said, "they're not staring at you. You're just having a nightmare because you're pregnant. It's a good sign when pregnant women have nightmares. At least that's what Mom used to say. Besides, how many Jeoseung Saja dreams have you had in your lifetime?"

"I think 248," she said.

"Actually, it was 249. You're forgetting about the time you were eight and fell asleep in the care ride back from *Halabeoji's* funeral."

Of course, she thought. Her grandfather's funeral. How could she have forgotten about that dream? Wasn't there a tiger involved somehow?

The thing is, after she woke from that dream, she couldn't seem to remember ever having any dream about Jeoseung Saja, much less one with a tiger. She hadn't really given any thought to him since she was a little girl, when her grandfather used to tell stories of how he'd come the night before you died and watch you sleep.

She asked Brenda, her mother-in-law, if she'd ever told Adam it was good luck to have nightmares while pregnant.

"I don't think so," Brenda said. "No, of course not. I'd never say that. I mean, I'm sure it isn't bad luck but I'm pretty sure it isn't good luck, either.

Is it good luck to have nightmares? I have no idea. Why would he say such a thing? He was probably pulling your leg."

Six hours after the Pizza Galley Shooting, Yu-jin will finally bring Naomi Yu-na Walker into the world—November 5th, at 4:54PM. Four hours after her birth, Adam will die in a friendly fire incident—a counter-insurgency operation in Helmand Province, Afghanistan. A battalion of Afghan forces mistakenly opened fire on Adam's unit, killing three and wounding four. As Brenda wept at her side, the Casualty Notification Officer—that such a thing would even exist—assured them an investigation was underway, but what good would that do? Would she now be able to provide her twins sons, her newborn daughter, a nuanced account of how their father was killed by those he was providing support for? The CNO told her this in an attempt to reassure her, to let her know they were taking measures to make sure American lives weren't lost in careless accidents like this ever again. And she asked him if accidents truly were careless. And he told her he didn't understand.

After the CNO left, she locked herself in the bathroom because she couldn't breathe—not because her husband's death would never make sense, but because she finally remembered what Adam was talking about in the dream.

On the drive home from her grandfather's funeral, she'd cried herself to sleep in the backseat, dreamt a white tiger had entered her bedroom and curled itself at the foot of her bed. At first, she was afraid, but then she realized it was her grandfather. She pulled herself out of bed and sat next to him, stroking his coarse fur. The tiger's head snapped toward the door, and she saw the silhouette of a man in a wide-brimmed hat. A pale, white hand reached out and the tiger slowly rose, walked over to him. The silhouette kneeled, pushed its face into the tiger's, and she saw his long black beard, his glowing white skin. As the purring tiger nuzzled against his cheek, the man grinned through yellow teeth.

"Never forget who I am," the man said.

Yu-jin asked the man if her grandfather would be safe, and he became angry, said tigers never worried about safety. He told her she was a very stupid girl, and didn't deserve to see tigers, and said he was going to make her miserable for the rest of her life.

And as she sat with Jae behind the Pizza Galley, twenty-two minutes before Scott Bonneville kills David Brightman, she fought the urge to tell Jae about the dream. Instead, she listened as Jae talked about the rabbit in the moon, which was an odd thing to talk about as the moon wasn't even close to being full, and told him everything was fine every time he wondered why she was so quiet.

"Do you think we remember dreams the way they actually happened?" Yu Jin finally asked.

"I don't think so," Jae said. "Dreams don't work that way."

When she awoke from the dream, the one she'd had where her grandfather became a tiger, her father had to pull the car over. Her mother snatched her out of the back seat, held her until the screaming stopped. She will think about this moment over and over at Adam's funeral, praying her boys never had nightmares about their father, knowing they would because that was just how dreams worked.

A Night to Remember

Forty-three minutes after closing time, Yu-jin Walker came in through the back door to see David Brightman standing with a gun, yelling at someone on the phone, her staff seated at the tables closest to the prize booth. David motioned for her to sit down, told her not to worry, that it would all be over once Christian Gibbard showed up.

"I'm sorry you got mixed up in all of this, Jinny. I'm sorry for all of you. But this'll all be over as soon as I get my hands on Gibbard and his piece of shit mistress over here."

Dave's wife Darcy began crying, begging him not to do this.

"If he loves you," Dave said, "he'll bring his sorry ass here to save you. Otherwise, remember I'm the one who cared enough to be here."

Up to and including Dave's appearance, the entire night had been a disaster. They'd worked most of the night short-handed. Mark was supposed to work the kitchen that night, but had decided to call in sick because it was his birthday and no one would swap shifts with him. Abhay, who was set to work the kitchen with him and wear the Captain Pete Pizza costume for two birthday parties, called out sick with strep throat. As the night went on, two drunken mothers got into a fistfight, one hurling a beer mug at the other. She missed, and the mug hit a server named Amber in the face, and after the police reports were filed, Amber was sent to the Emergency Room with a broken nose. After closing, Yu-jin sent Ryan home early because he'd agreed to clean the shit streak in the tunnel slide for Rachel, who couldn't bring herself to do it. The agreement was Rachel would assume all of Ryan's clean-up duties as long as she didn't have to climb into the slide. After Ryan left, only Yu-jin, Darcy, Rachel, and an owl-faced woman named Morgan remained. During her maternity leave, Yu-jin would have to answer for closing the store with an all-female staff, which was against company guidelines.

On top of everything, she'd had to stop an angry man with a ponytail from fighting Ryan after Ryan had made the man's daughter cry. It wasn't all Ryan's fault—because Abhay had called out sick, Ryan had to wear to Captain Pete Pizza costume to entertain children. He hadn't wanted to wear the costume, as Captain Pete's giant head was cumbersome and poorly ventilated, and everything smelled like a thin layer of Lysol over mildew. But Ryan didn't complain, said he didn't mind at all, until the little girl kept hitting Ryan in the groin, laughing every time the giant pirate doubled over. The fourth time she took a swing, Ryan caught her little hand and wagged his finger in silent admonishment. The startled girl began to cry, as no one wants stern treatment from a man in a giant pirate costume, so her father shoved Ryan, who'd shown amazing restraint, all things considered. The ponytailed man told Yu-jin if she weren't pregnant he would have broken Ryan's jaw, and Yu-jin could tell he wanted her to be grateful, as if, somehow, her current state had anything to do with his restraint. He kept saying he didn't want to yell at a pregnant woman, but his voice seemed to get louder every time she'd asked him to calm down.

She'd sent the man away with a $15 Gift card and a roll of gold Dough-Bloons—a little under ten minutes after closing time—and the man told her he was going to use the gift certificate and Dough-Bloons at another location. He guaran-fuckin-teed it. Yu-jin had told herself the night couldn't get any worse. But that was before the streak of shit in the tunnel slide, before watching Dave Brightman berate his wife, before Scott Bonneville snuck in through the back door and killed Dave, before her water broke.

All in all, Yu-jin would joke to Adam the next morning, it was a night to remember, and for the rest of her life, she'd remember how his laughter had sounded over the satellite phone, she'd think about Adam, laughing in the desert, how he'd kept clearing his throat to hide he was crying, four hours before he was killed by Afghan trainees.

If You Ever Need Anything, Ask Someone Else

Yu-jin received a called from the President himself. He offered his condolences and apologized for her loss. He quietly listened as she told him he should've kept his promises, told her he understood as she yelled and screamed into the phone, as she told him he didn't understand and never would. Seven hours later, a man named Tom Baldwin, who was apparently an old classmate of Adam's, pulled a young boy named Sukraj Virk out of his car and strangled him in an IKEA parking lot. Baldwin shouted, *This is for Adam Walker*, over and over again as the crowd pulled Baldwin away, as he clawed at Virk's turban.

#GoodGuyWithAGun.

Yu-jin watched the President address what had happened to the young Sikh man, marveled at the deliberate and subdued manner in which he condemned the attack. He said he'd spoken with Sukraj's mother, and Yu-jin wondered if she'd yelled at him as well, if he'd told her he'd understood, if Sukraj's mother asked him how he could understand something that didn't make any sense.

CNN then cut to a response from the Candidate—you have to hear both sides, of course—who condemned the President's actions and spoke of how he'd always opposed the disastrous war in the Middle East. He said he had a secret plan to get us out and then offered his condolences for her beautiful husband—he called Adam beautiful—this beautiful man, this beautiful hero. He promised he'd only hire the best generals and promised to clean house in Adam's name. Not a word about Sukraj Virk, other than a terse, *I didn't like that.*

Yu-jin rang the doorbell a third time. It was a beautiful Colonial three blocks away from her own home. She told Brenda she'd like to take a walk. Brenda had told her to take as much time as she needed, that she'd watch the children. She'd immediately regretted the walk, all of the neighbors stopping her, hugging her, telling her how sorry they were, how grateful they were for Adam's service, *And what are you doing walking around in your condition?* Of course, they'd meant giving birth to Naomi, and not her fresh status as a widow, but Yu-jin would soon realize it's hard to separate the two. What bothered her the most was when people would say, *If there's anything you need, let me know*—why put the pressure on her to ask for something? Why not just offer something? Why say anything at all? It wasn't as though Yu-jin didn't know how everyone felt.

Jeff Logan finally opened the door, stood in the doorway as if blocking her path. She tried not to stare at his scar, the one that ran down the left side of his face, but what did it matter if she stared or didn't? Jeff smiled, and Yu-jin knew it was because she was staring.

"I'm sorry, Mrs. Walker," said Jeff. "Adam was a good guy. What happened to him was bullshit."

"Please call me Yu-jin, or Jinny."

"What can I do for you, Yu-jin? I'd invite you in, but my mom's not here."

"What does that matter?"

"I want you to feel safe."

"Are you a dangerous man?"

She'd heard the stories about Jeff Logan, that he'd come back from Afghanistan damaged, that he spent his days drinking in the park, that he'd nearly beaten a gang member to death at the mall, that he'd slaughtered women and children during the war, that he had a collection of ears he'd cut from insurgent heads (or fingernails removed from their hands). Adam had once heard the twins call him Jeff the Killer. Yu-jin had never seen him lose his temper with the boys until that day. They'd been told at school that Jeff the Killer had lost his mind in the war, that he now spent his nights dumping his victims in Machado Lake. Everyone had their own Jeff Logan story. Adam made sure the boys knew they were all bullshit. He'd even made them repeat the words, they're all bullshit.

"To be honest," she said, "I just gave birth and my energy level's a bit low. If I could come inside and have a seat, I'd really appreciate it."

"You did just give birth. Shouldn't you be resting?"

Yu-jin could feel people staring as they walked past, could see the discomfort on Jeff's face. She laid her hand on the white porch column, felt its coolness on her palm. She stared at the living room window and for a moment she was lost in the elegant pleats on the red curtains. Jeff's eyes nervously followed something behind her. She turned around to see a Del Taco Burrito wrapper scrape its way down the sidewalk. The white flowers on the jasmine tree swayed. She looked into Jeff's eye's as they sucked in the cool scent. It seemed once you smelled jasmine, all you wanted to do was keep smelling it. Jeff smiled a tight, nervous smile.

"It's a really nice breezy day," he said. "Come on in. You really shouldn't be on your feet anyway."

Before heading in, she looked back one last time to see three seagulls fighting over the Del Taco wrapper. After she headed in, Jeff stood in the doorway, staring at the birds. A red minivan sped by, sending the birds scattering.

"Disgusting birds," Yu-jin said.

"They're worse than pigeons," Jeff said. "So aggressive and obnoxious. It's funny but every time I see them, I'm reminded of how far away we live from the ocean and I start to resent them."

"That's true," Yu-jin laughed. "Someone should tell them they're not welcome here, that we call them *sea*-gulls for a reason."

"As usual, nature doesn't give a damn what we think. Story of my life."

Jeff smiled and closed the door. Brenda had always talked about the Logans and their money, but nothing prepared Yu-jin for the beauty of their home. It was as if the entire house had been built of sunlight. Dark, hardwood floors so glossy they looked wet. The way shadows nestled inside the crisp, white plaster molding that ran across the walls. How the light refracted in the chandeliers, every prism containing a tiny rainbow. It was no wonder Jeff didn't have to work for a living.

"You have a beautiful home," Yu-jin said.

"I don't know about that. It's just big."

Jeff led her into the dining room, pulled out a chair. Yu-jin took a seat. She recognized the table—solid oak base, elm and hardwood veneer top—from a catalog she and Brenda had looked through. It cost more than the mortgage on their home. Jeff brought her a glass of water in a rock-cut crystal glass, placed it on a hand-stitched leather coaster. He took a seat all the way at the other side of the table. Brenda had always mused on how lucky Jeff was, that he'd come back from the war to this home, to this family, as a poor man in his condition would definitely have ended up living on the street.

"I have to go to work soon," Jeff said, "but what can I do for you?"

"You work?"

"Of course I work. Why wouldn't I work?"

"I don't know why I said that. I'm sorry."

Yu-jin took a sip of water. She couldn't believe how crisp and cold it was.

"Really cold, right?" Jeff said. "The filter on the fridge. It's like it's being filtered through a glacier. The other guys used to ask me what I missed about California. Was it the beach? Was it the sun? Was it the girls? They never seemed to believe this ice water filter is the one thing I missed when I was away."

Yu-jin stared at her tumbler, ran her thumb along the condensation. Her husband had just died. She was away from her newborn daughter. And here she was, admiring swag valances, hardwood floors, and ice water filtration systems. Jeff put his elbows on the table and leaned forward. She noticed he wasn't smiling.

"Tommy Baldwin," he said, "the one that assaulted the Sikh kid, he's an asshole. Adam and I hated his guts back in the day. I'm sorry he thought he could use Adam as an excuse."

"My husband used to come here," she said, "after his first deployment."

"How did you know?"

"He thought I was asleep, but I followed him once. To your house. What did you talk about?"

Jeff stood and walked over to the refrigerator, poured himself a glass of water. He gulped it down and poured another, then leaned against the counter.

"Just stuff. We'd have a beer or two, which was weird because he and I didn't see eye to eye in high school. But it actually helped me out a lot, and I hope I was able to help him in any way I could. Mostly, we talked about things he didn't want to bring home to you and your kids."

"Was he in pain? Was he scared?"

Jeff looked out the window. His cheeks puffed up. Air leaked from his lips. Yu-jin stared at the scar. They say the scar was from an RPG—that a rocket hit a small home, buried him in the rubble, that they'd pulled him from the wreckage, that they'd had to remove a three-inch shard of glass from his face.

"No. I don't think so" he said. "He was kind of a true believer in this shit, really thought we were the good guys."

"You don't?"

Jeff took a sip of water. He drummed his fingers along the counter, then pounded his fist. He came back to the table, sat down.

"Your husband used to love Superman when we were kids," he said. "I mean, really loved him."

"He still has all the comics in the garage. I mean, we still have. . .we have all the comics."

"Yeah. I guess it's—well anyway, when we were in fourth grade, he found out I was a pretty good artist—for a fourth-grader—and he asked me if I could draw Superman fighting a giant robot. I told him no, but he wouldn't shut up about it. So I drew it for him. You should've seen his face when he saw it. You'd have thought I'd painted the Sistine Chapel. It was just a dumb picture, but he wouldn't stop telling me how good it was. It was really nice, him telling me I had talent, because my dad hated that I sat in my room drawing pictures all the time. That always meant a lot. For whatever that's worth."

Jeff stood and made his way over to her, handed her a box of tissues. She didn't realize she'd been crying. He put his hand on her shoulder, squeezed it, before apologizing and pulling away.

"Superman shoots lasers from his eyes and decapitates the robot," she said.

"Yeah. That's the one."

"He still has it. It's in a box with his comics."

"I know. He told me the last time he was here. Said he still looked at it from time to time. Kept going on about all the detail I put in the cape, the way it billowed in the wind. We got a pretty good laugh out of that."

Jeff laughed. Yu-jin blew her nose. His hand reached for her shoulder. He stopped himself, tried to pull away. She grabbed his hand, placed it on her shoulder. Jeff took a deep breath, held it for a moment that seemed like a lifetime.

"Listen," he said, "I can tell you it happened for a reason or I can tell you it was all meaningless, and neither one's going to make you feel any better about it. I can tell you how sad and angry I am, and I am, but what good's that going to do? Nothing I say is really going to matter much. Trust me, I've heard it all and I've said a good chunk of it myself."

Jeff fought to pull his hand away. Yu-jin finally let go. She'd never forget the way his hand shook like a frightened animal. It was a gentle struggle—there was nothing malicious in the holding on or the pulling away, merely two people doing what came naturally, two people acting in accordance with their personalities. Yu-jin thought about the drawing, the way seemed to move in the wind, the way it rippled and curled.

"Thank you for your time," she said. "If you ever need to talk, please know I'm here."

Jeff forced a weak smile as he massaged his hand. If he had anything else to say, she knew he'd never offer. It was as good as it was ever going to be.

Other People and Their Problems

During their honeymoon, Jae and Miri stood on the balcony of their hotel and marveled at the full moon, which seemed so much bigger and brighter than either had ever seen it. She told him about the man on the moon, how if you looked close enough, you could see two eyes, a nose and an open mouth.

"When I was a kid," she'd said, "I loved the full moon because I could see his face. I used to get really sad when the full moon would start to wane, and the face would disappear."

"In Korea," Jae had said, "it's a rabbit on the moon."

Jae pointed at the dark craters which made the ears, the body, the little hands and feet. He showed her how it was bent over a mortar, pounding rice to make rice cakes. He told her the story of the Moon Rabbit, how the Emperor of the Heavens had asked the rabbit, a fox, and a monkey to bring him food in order to test their devotion. The fox brought the Emperor a fish, and the monkey brought him fruits.

"The Rabbit," he said, "couldn't find anything to offer but grass, so he asked the Emperor to take him as food and jumped into a fire. The Emperor was so moved, he made the Rabbit guardian of the moon."

When Nina was little, Miri would take her out every full moon to show her the rabbit, and as the nights progressed, and the darkness encroached upon the moon's face, Nina stare into the sky and say, "Bye Rabbit. I'll see you next time."

When Nina was ten, they'd gone camping at Yosemite. One night, she and Jae stared at the moon, and she turned to him and said, "Hey Dad, you notice how there's smoke around the rabbit? It's like he's still on fire."

"It's funny you should say that. I keep trying to show Mama the smoke and she never sees it."

Jae wipes his tears as he stares at the Waxing Crescent moon, remembering his daughter, and the rabbit, and the smoke that aren't there. He misses her so much, misses Miri, and wonders why he doesn't miss them more, why he doesn't feel terrible for leaving them, and for the first time in four years, he wants to go home, and then wonders why he's never wanted to go home until now.

The night before, Jae had a dream. He was sitting in his home office, at the desk he'd left his goodbye letter to Nina and Miri—the note that told them he was sorry, that he was at peace—when he heard himself, it was definitely him, screaming downstairs. He bounded down the stairs and found himself in the basement of the IBM Almaden Research facility, Jeoseung Saja berating the IBM 2314 containing his Occupant.

"Stop being selfish," Jeoseung Saja said. "I want to go home too, you know."

And the Occupant begged the Emissary to leave it alone, told Jae not to listen, said this wasn't how dreams worked.

"If this isn't a dream, then what is it?" Jae asked. "Am I really home right now?"

"It's always other people and their problems, isn't it?" Jeoseung Saja asked.

He awoke from the dream, wondering what the Emissary's parting words even meant. It's always other people and their problems—what about his problems? Was he the other people? Jae looks up at the crescent moon. It looks like a dirty fingernail. Nina told him that once, too.

Jae smells cigarette smoke, sees someone turning the corner. He faces the Emissary—clear as day, it's the Emissary, himself—disguised as a young Korean man, cigarette rigid between his teeth. Jae marvels at the pleasantness of this boy's appearance—sad, nervous, with a hint of earnest desperation—nice looking kid. The Emissary stops dead, pulls a gun from his coat pocket and points it at Jae's head. Jae closes his eyes, but not out of fear. His eyelids become heavier and heavier as if he's drifting off to sleep—not because he's tired, but because sleeping would've meant waking up to another day. He opens his eyes with the sad realization it just isn't time.

"This isn't how dreams work," Jae says.

"Just leave and I won't hurt you."

"So then I take it you're not here for me."

"Why would I be here for you?"

Jae looks at the boy, shakes his head. The boy scowls as the gun quivers in his shaky hand. Jae lifts his eyes toward the moon, just hoping for a tiny glimpse of the rabbit, trying his best to shut out the Emissary's *Hey, hey*'s, and *Are you listening to me*'s. What a strange ruse—The Emissary disguising himself as this jittery boy. Jae bends over and picks up the paper plate holding his slice of pizza. He takes a bite and stares at the boy. He reaches over to the soda cup on top of the dumpster, takes a sip. The boy blows smoke from his nostrils.

"It's a beautiful night," Jae says. "I wish the moon were full, though. I hate when the moon is like that, the way it looks now."

"It's a Waxing Crescent."

"It might as well not even be in the sky. What's the point of looking like that?"

"Sir, you need to leave right now."

"During my honeymoon," Jae says, "I tried to show my wife the moon rabbit. I pointed up at the moon—just like this—and traced the outline of the rabbit for her. But I don't need to point it out to you, do I? You already know there's a rabbit up there. You see him, don't you—pounding rice for his rice cakes? Tell me you see him, Jeoseung Saja."

The boy lowers the shaking gun from Jae's head. He puts his hands behind his head and exhales, looks up at the moon, and then back at Jae.

"You know about *JeoSeungSaja*?" the boy says. "Who else knows? Are you on RE/Serch?"

"There's no research needed," Jae says. "I know what I know."

Jae points to Pizza Galley, just a guess, and the boy lowers his gun. Yu-jin hadn't closed it fully. She really needs to be more careful.

"Can you do me a favor?" Jae says." There's a girl in there, Korean like me and you. Her name's Yu-jin. Don't hurt her, okay?"

"I don't want to hurt anyone."

"Of course not. You're just doing your job."

Jeoseung Saja walks through the back door. Jae squints up at the moon, trying to will the rabbit to appear. He realizes it never does and never will, so he walks to the back door and clicks it shut.

"It's always other people and their problems," he says, as if he understands what that even means. He closes his eyes, imagines a full moon, imagines the rabbit, smoke leaking from its fur as it pounds rice into rice cakes. When he opens his eyes, he half expects to see the rabbit—he'd done such a good job picturing it—but this isn't how dreams work.

Psalm 23

Morgan takes Yu-jin's hand, asks her to pray. They lower their heads.

"The Lord is my Shepherd," Morgan says, "I shall not want—"

"Jesus Christ, Morgan," Dave says. "I told you you're not in any danger."

"How can you say that?" Rachel says. "You're pointing a gun at us."

"Please, Dave," Darcy says. "I'm sorry. Please."

"Sorry doesn't cut it," Dave cries. "I loved you. I loved you, you fucking bitch. And you cheat on me with that cocksucker?"

Darcy tells Dave it isn't what he thinks, even though it is, and Yu-jin begs Dave to calm down, to think about what he's doing, and Dave tells her not to tell him he needs to calm down, that he's calm as shit, that he knows exactly what he needs to do.

"At least let Morgan pray," Yu-jin says. "Where's the harm in that?"

"Do whatever you want. What do I care? I already told you I'm not here for you. If anything, your stupid prayers have already been answered. You'll be fine."

Dave motions his gun toward Darcy, who shrieks and buries her face in Yu-jin's shoulder, which makes Dave recoil. He kicks over a table and shouts. Dave paces the carpet, which has a wood paneling pattern in order to resemble the deck of a pirate ship, muttering about what he'll do to Christian Gibbard as soon as he shows his face. He clears his throat, the way Adam would clear his throat the next morning on the phone, four hours before he's killed by Afghan trainees.

"Did you know?" Dave asks. "Did you know about Darcy and Gibbard?"

"No," Yu-jin says.

"Well you should pray for her. She's the one who needs it."

"He maketh me lie down in green pastures," Morgan says. "He leadeth me beside the still waters. . . ."

But Yu-jin did know about Darcy and Christian. She'd caught them two months ago. She'd forgotten her phone charger in the countdown room and had to drive all the way back. She'd walked in to see them kissing, Christian's hand up Darcy's skirt. She tries to shake that image as she closes her eyes and bows her head, wondering what Morgan's prayer has to do with their current situation.

Yu-jin opens her eyes. She looks up to see Rachel's big blue eyes, a tear slides down Rachel's cheek and onto her fingers. She wants to reach out to her, to let her know everything was going to be okay. She hears gunshots. Rachel screams. Oh God. He's shot Darcy. She turns to Darcy, who wails *Dave, oh Dave,* over and over again. She doesn't have a scratch on her. Dave stares at the blood seeping into his shirt. He falls to his knees and drops dead.

Darcy runs to her husband, collapses on top of him. Morgan lowers her forehead to the table, praises Jesus. Yu-jin stands, turns around, sees a Korean man—he's clearly Korean—standing in front of the animatronic Calico Jacqueline. Yu-jin and Rachel hold hands as the man walks toward them. His chest convulses—he says he can't breathe.

She feels a tightness below her belly, doubles over. Rachel walks her back to the table, tells her to take a seat. The man begins to cry, asks Rachel if Yu-jin is okay. Police sirens get closer and closer. Yu-jin pulls Rachel in close.

"My water broke," she tells Rachel.

"Oh my God," Rachel screams. "The baby's coming. The baby's coming."

The man drops to his knees, and the room pulses with red and blue lights. The police burst in, guns raised, tell everyone to get on the floor. Rachel screams for help. A policeman rushes over and grabs Yu-jin's hand. He tells her everything's going to be fine now.

Little Donny and Big Don

They'd wanted to name Blake Donald, after his grandfather. They, of course, were the Mesman family proper and not Lisa, who'd found the name a bit silly. Jan had urged Lisa to reconsider, how it would mean so much to his mother.

"Do you want this kid to get picked on? What if other kids started calling him Donald Duck, or something worse?"

"Are you serious with this?" said Jan. "What's it matter? Do you know what life is like being a boy named Jan?"

"And do you want that for your son? *DoNaLd-duh-duh-duuuhhh-DoNaLd. hEy DoNaLd DuCk-duh-duh-duuuhhh*."

"You're being ridiculous. And do you know what I did when other kids made fun of my name? I popped them in the mouth, just like my father taught me to do, just like I'll teach my son to do."

"I don't want my son growing up violent. Besides, if Donald's such a great name, then how come you're not a Donald."

"I'm named after my mother's father—you know that."

"So what? Your mother gets her way again? No. I get to name my own fucking son."

"Is that language necessary? I mean, really? There are other words out there."

Lisa had always hated the way Jan patronized her. He'd always treated her like some kind of project. In her mind, Jan felt he was resigned to the fact of being stuck with her, so he might as well mold her into something he could live with, something his family could live with. Lisa wasn't like them. Donald had graduated from West Point and commanded an army. Cora was a school teacher, a classically trained cellist. Jan had gone to all the best schools and was a competitive sailor—he'd promised to take her sailing up to Victoria Island, but that was before he'd stopped calling her.

Lisa had always thought Jan felt cheated, marrying some server he'd met at a restaurant while on a date with some boring little Japanese girl. It was supposed to be fun and games for him. How quickly he'd asked if she was on birth control before tossing the unwrapped condom aside—it was all just another adventure to him. For her, Jan was a hope for something better—not in a financial sense, although his wealth was hard to ignore—but an honest-to-goodness nice guy who liked nice things, who read books and ironed his shirts and talked about how the moon affected the tides, a gentleman who would never utter the phrase *Drink Up* while on a date. She had no idea he was such a snob, a weakling, no idea he couldn't stand up to his own mother, a mother Lisa had overheard call her, "unsophisticated, to be charitable," during a phone call. Every man Lisa had dated up to Jan had despised their mothers to the point Lisa made them all stop talking about them. She'd often wondered if those men were attracted to her because she reminded them of their mothers, would eventually turn cruel because of them.

They'd fight over the name Donald all the way up to the delivery date. Eventually Cora would step in, tell Jan not to fight it anymore—and Lisa knew Cora had never forgiven her for it. Every time Blake made some little mistake—breaking a plate, spilling grape juice on the carpet, setting the garbage can on fire—Lisa would watch Cora's face pinch up, and they'd stare in one another's eyes, and she could read Cora's thoughts:

This never would've happened if his name was Donald.

Cora would have loved little Donald, forgiven every little thing that made Blake who he was. *Blake did this*, and *Blake did that*, would have magically become, *My Donald would never do such a thing*, of, *Oh no. Not my little Donald. Not my little angel. . . .*

So when Jan remarried—some pediatrician or podiatrist, some kind of doctor at any rate, and two months after the divorce, no less—of course he named his new son Donald. And of course Cora immediately took to Donny in a way she never had with Blake. Before Donny was born, Blake had spent every Sunday with Cora and Don—God forbid Blake spend time with his own father, God forbid the child interrupt whatever was going on with Jan and his new wife. Once little Donny was born, that all stopped—mostly due to Blake musing how funny it would've been had the baby died. Lisa remembered the phone call, how Blake had cried in the background:

"Cora," Lisa had said, "I'm sure he didn't mean it. He's just a child. They say things like that. No, of course I don't want Blake to hurt the baby. He loves the baby. Okay. I understand. But what about Blake? Okay, fine. What days is Donny not with you? Well, Jesus Christ, does this woman ever take care of her own kid? No, I'm not being fucking catty. Fine, fine, okay, okay. I'm on my way."

Donny and Blake had very little interaction, as Jan's new wife felt he was a bad influence on her son. But the fact was, little Donny Mesman was a nasty, spoiled little shit who was the center of the Mesman universe because he was everything a parent, or grandparent, would want in a little boy. He'd learned how to read at the age of four, while Blake still read at a preschool level in the second grade. He was a starting pitcher on his Little League team while Blake had quit Tee-ball in first grade, due to the team making fun of him, making him cry for picking flowers in right field and twirling around in circles during games. Piano lessons, Cub Scouts, language immersion—Donny excelled at every one of these things, all of the things for which Blake lacked the patience or competence. They'd even made T-shirts: Little Donny and Big Don. Jan's bitch of a wife really took every little opportunity to rub Lisa's face in it.

"He's just like his grandfather," Lisa had heard Cora say many times. Big Don had already taught Little Donny fly-fishing by the time Blake had mistaken Ike for a duck. Lisa knew what they'd meant when they called Blake a bad influence—they thought her son was a failure, and were afraid it might rub off on Little Donny. They saw Blake as a curse and Donny as a blessing—this Lisa knew. During Big Don's funeral, Little Donny would read a beautiful speech he'd written about how much he loved his grandfather, and how he was going to be a great man just like Grandpa Don. Lisa heard all about it when she checked in on Cora.

"Everyone was so moved," Cora had said. "He's already so eloquent. And he's only eleven, can you believe it? Don would've been so proud to see him up there. He was so poised and handsome."

And Lisa imagined all of Cora's friends, the ones who'd sighed when they saw Blake, the ones who'd rolled their eyes at him, the ones who'd tell him he had to settle down and be a good boy—he was a good boy, you stupid hags—the ones who'd made him shake hands with their grandsons, made him apologize every time one of their little bullies provoked him.

Oh Cora, they'd say, *Little Donny's speech truly made me appreciate Big Don's life. He's so insightful for his age,* they'd say. *You're so lucky to have been blessed with a grandson like that. I'm so sorry for your loss,* they'd say, *but remember that Big Don lives inside of Little Donny. And only Little Donny,* they'd say. *He'll go on to do great things in the Mesman name. Let's just hope the other one doesn't bring shame to your family first. Thank God he's not here. He'd probably make a scene, the way he always does. Oh goodness, he wouldn't know what to do with himself. That boy never knows how to behave. He'd probably talk all through the service in that loud voice of his. That boy doesn't ever know when to keep his mouth shut, which should be always. Everything he says is stupid. He's a stupid boy. A stupid, stupid, stupid boy. Did you know we popped champagne when Jan finally got rid of that wife of his? Oh, she was a piece of work, wasn't she? And thank God she stayed home, too. So ill-mannered. She probably would have worn a red dress to the funeral.*

"You know what he said?" Cora asked. "He said, When I grow up, I'm going to name my son Donald, so that he can also be great like my Pop-Pop."

Lisa should have been upset in the moment—of course, as the days went on, she would increasingly become upset Blake was excluded from the memorial—but was too amused by the thought of wearing a red dress—the slinky, low-cut one that drove Jan wild—to Big Don's funeral. That skinny little pipsqueak he was with now wouldn't have known what to do with herself.

An Objectively Horrible Boyfriend

Until Blake drove them apart, Scott and Lisa had only fought once. Of course, this wasn't true by any means, but in Scott's mind there was only one fight really worth remembering. They were seated at the table on his balcony for a post-coital cigarette. She looked down at the white lighter next to the ashtray.

"Did you know white lighters are bad luck?" Lisa asked.

"What?"

"They are. Jimi Hendrix, Janis Joplin, Jim Morrison—all had white lighters found in their pockets after they died."

"Well, that may be, but I'm sure at the time they only made white and black lighters or something."

"Yeah, okay, because they didn't have green or blue plastic back then. Kurt Cobain had a white lighter too. So how do you explain your *ThEy ONLy HaD bLaCK or WhItE LigHTeRs baCk ThEn?*"

He'd hated when she did that, the low, dull, *wHiCh WaY DiD hE gO gEoRgE?* tone she'd used when mocking him. He didn't even sound like that.

"Fine," he said. "Then you explain it to me."

"Oh I will," she said. "It was the DEA leaving those lighters to mock them."

"What? How?"

"If you'd stop cutting me off and maybe I'll tell you."

"Fine. I'm sorry."

"The DEA paid off Bic to make white lighters in order to make it easier to catch drug offenders. When you pack down a bowl with a white lighter, it's easier to see weed residue on them when cops checked their pockets. That's why you're supposed to avoid white lighters."

"But I don't smoke weed, so what's the difference?"

"You're an asshole. I'm leaving."

"What did I do?"

"You always make me feel dumb. Every time I say something, you point out how it's not scientifically possible, or that my views aren't logical. You do this all the time and then you do it to my friends."

"Is this about the vaccination crack?" Scott asked, and Lisa stormed back into the condo.

Before heading back to his place, they'd had dinner at an Indian restaurant with her friend Sasha and her boyfriend Rahni. His birth name was

Ronald McCutcheon, but he'd had it legally changed to Rahni Sage. The three of them—Lisa, Sasha, and Ronald McCutcheon—were discussing how Ivan, Sasha and Ronald's son, had been disinvited to a birthday party when the birthday boy's parents discovered Ivan wasn't vaccinated. They talked about how small-minded and brain-washed those parents were, how cruel it was to punish Ivan in the name of Big Pharma.

"Wait," Scott had said, "your kid's not vaccinated?"

He sat and ate in silence for the rest of the night. It just seemed better that way.

Scott followed Lisa into his living room, begged her to stop as she threw his robe on the couch and picked her clothes up off the floor. He held her by the shoulders until she calmed down. She sat on the couch with her clothes on her lap while Scott got her a beer from the fridge.

"You're really narrow-minded," she said. "You're not the only person who knows things."

"I know that. It's just, you know, I was shocked he wasn't vaccinated."

"Why?"

"Because I assume most kids are. So when you hear about a kid who isn't, it's a little odd."

"What's so odd about it?"

"Come on," Scott told her. "I'm sorry. I'll tell them I'm sorry too. Just don't go."

She sipped the beer. Scott took the bottle from her hands, placed it on the coffee table. He pulled her knees open, removed his shorts.

After fucking on the couch, they went back out for those cigarettes they'd never lit. Once again, they took their seats at the table. Scott felt self-conscious about the color of the lighter.

"It all started the night after Blake's DTap," Lisa said. "He was running a fever and fussier than he'd ever been, so I called the nurse, who told me it was normal. I swear I could practically hear that bitch's eyes rolling over the phone. The nurse suggested I give him a bath, that it might soothe him.

So I filled the tiny plastic tub with water and then put him in and I swear to God, Scott, his face just twisted with pain. It was like he was experiencing real actual pain for the first time. I just froze and looked at him. He was shrieking, his legs stiff, his tiny hands curled into fists. I mean, he barely cried when the doctor gave him the shot. The doctor even talked about what a little tough guy he was. And here he was, my little baby, just screeching like he was on fire. By the time my ex-husband burst into the room, I was sitting on the toilet holding Blake to my chest, the both of us crying uncontrollably."

"And you feel like it was the vaccine that did that?"

"What else could it be?"

"I don't know."

"That's right you don't know. You don't know because there's no other answer. I had to give him sponge baths after that, because every time I tried to bathe him, he'd just freak out. He couldn't bathe himself until he was ten years old. So yeah, I don't care what science says because I know what happened. And there's plenty of science to back me up too, by the way."

Lisa took a short drag, blew smoke in his face. He'd never seen her angry before, told himself he'd never make this mistake again. What else could they talk about? What would take her mind off of how angry she was? What would make her shut up and calm down? Scott settled on the story of Neil McNeil, someone he hadn't thought about since college, someone he wouldn't think about again until he sat alone in the police station, waiting to be interrogated. The only other person who'd ever heard this story was Dr. Ong, whom he'd told after hearing McNeil had been arrested for trying to strangle his father.

"When I was a kid, I used to take long hikes with this guy named Neil McNeil, who worked for my dad. We'd take these long walks, and he'd tell me stories about being a cop. All these stories about taking hookers into the back of his squad car. It didn't seem weird that he told so many stories about getting laid. I think he was trying to impress me. Actually, I know he was trying to impress me."

Lisa asked what his point was, and he continued, hoping she'd understand. After their hikes, they'd go around back to the private pool, he'd told her. No one had ever used it—his father being too busy, his mother not knowing how to swim—so it was always just the two of them. Neil had always gotten in naked, encouraged Scott to do so, even though Scott had always refused.

"One day," Scott said, "I think he'd had enough. While we were in the water, Neil kept dunking me under, over and over, and I begged him to stop. He'd pull me up, whisper no one would ever know, and then dunk me under again. He told me the only way I'd be safe was to wrap my arms and legs around him. So I did. For two days. Then on the third day, he started dunking me again, told me I needed to take off my trunks. So I did. Then I wrapped my legs around him. And it was like that until my mom took me away. I've never told anyone this story. You're the only person—"

"Why are you changing the subject?"

"I'm just telling you a story about my life that your story reminded me of."

"How do these stories even relate?"

"I don't know. You talked about Blake being in water, and that made me think about why I hate being in water."

Lisa set her cigarette on the lip of the ashtray. She got up and walked around the table, knelt between his knees, laid her head on his lap.

"I'm sorry that happened to you. I was molested too. I know how you feel."

And that was the end of the argument, the end of the conversation. The night she told him he couldn't see her anymore, Scott realized he'd never asked her about being molested. Maybe he wasn't a very good listener. Maybe if he'd only asked her about her experience, he could have comforted her, showed her was a compassionate and kind boyfriend he was.

If This is True Then Why Haven't I Heard About This?

The squad car stops in front of the 7-Eleven. That Russian bitch, of all people, is in the parking lot with her pug. The light turns green, and the woman sees Scott in the back of the car. He tries to turn away, but she sees him, smiles as the pug shits right in front of them. Once bad energy is out in the world, it's out in the world.

"That dog just took a crap in the parking lot," Scott says. "Service dogs don't go willy nilly like that."

"I thought I told you to stop talking," Officer McGill says.

"You guys really should crack down on that."

"Yeah, that's exactly the sort of thing we should be worried about tonight."

McGill runs a red light, begins whistling "What a Fool Believes" for some reason. McGill finally turns on the siren. Scott leans forward, is told to sit back and shut his goddamn trap. The ride back to the station, in the back of Officer McGill's squad car, Scott finally shuts out the infernal whistling by thinking of the day Lisa left him. Every time he thinks about her, he cries, but not tonight. Tonight he's too angry to cry. Whenever he thinks about how easily he pulled the trigger, the way the man dropped to his knees and fell over, the whistling gets louder. Every time he pictures that man's face, the way that man thwarted his plans, the whistling becomes more shrill, sharper. All he can do to make the whistling stop is think about Lisa and what Blake did to him.

Scott was grading papers the day Blake found out about what he'd been up to with Lisa. It was during his free period, and he'd skipped lunch, because he was three days behind schedule. He wondered if Lisa might want to go have to the Brazilian steakhouse later. There was a tap on the door, and he looked up to see Lisa tapping on the glass, waving. She opened the door and let herself him. Scott leaned back and sighed, knowing he'd now be four days behind. He'd spend days thinking about that moment, his annoyance at seeing her—was that a sign it was all coming to an end?

"I left work early," Lisa said. "Couldn't deal with today."

"What's wrong?"

"I don't want to talk about it."

"Well, you're here and I'm here, so we should talk about it. Clearly this is important."

She rolled his chair out from under the desk, sat on his lap. How Scott wished someone would walk by and see this, a beautiful woman, his girlfriend, sitting on his lap, at work. She leaned in. He could taste the tobacco on her tongue. He leaned back, looked through the door to see if anyone happened to walked past.

"So there's this girl I work with named Bich," Lisa told him. "She's new, and until we finally met her we all thought it was Bitch which is so hilarious."

Scott didn't think it was hilarious at all. Her name clearly wasn't pronounced in that way. If anything, Lisa and her coworkers should have been ashamed of their ignorance. He'd noticed her snide comments about Asians — "not Asian-Americans, but Asian-Asians" — and had wondered if she'd hated Asians.

"I like you," she'd replied. "Isn't that enough?"

And it was enough. He'd never mentioned it again. But every time something like Bich/Bitch came up, every time she'd mentioned how the dry cleaners didn't speak English, every time she mentioned seeing Kayla Chee's brother — the one who'd picked on Blake in fourth grade — every time conversation would shift to confronting Kayla Chee's mother — it always shifted to the mother — and she'd break into a combination of broken English and nasal bitch-tone, Scott would wonder when it would stop being enough. Hell, from time to time, she'd mused out loud how she'd never seen herself ever sleeping with an Asian — had she ever mused she'd never seen herself with a Dutchman or a Russian? What would happen after they'd had a child, Scott wanted children with her, would she still mock Asians in this way?

"Anyway," she said, "during lunch, I was telling everyone about why Mr. Rogers wore sweaters — do you know why he did? I just learned it today."

"I just figured it was in order to look friendly," he said.

"Haha, you're so cute. Anyway, it turns out that during Vietnam, Mr. Rogers was a sniper for the Navy SEALs. Every time he got a kill, he'd get a tattoo to signify he'd killed someone. So when he finally got a job on TV, he had to find a way to cover up those tats. Isn't that crazy? Sweet old Mr. Rogers was a trained killer."

"What?"

"Don't do that."

"Do what?"

"You're going to question me again."

"No, I'm just confused. I mean, this is all new information to process."

"My aunt posted it today and she's all about veterans. Anyway, I told Bich because she's Vietnamese, so I thought she'd find it interesting. And she's like, 'If this is true, then why haven't I heard about this?' and I was like, 'Um, you're hearing about it now?' And then she tried to pull up this website on her phone, during work hours, in order to prove it wasn't true, and I'm like, 'Do you always get off on this? Proving people wrong, really?' Besides, that website she was on is owned by a guy who helped gas Jews during World War II. Like I'd take anything they say seriously."

Scott wasn't sure what to do. Like most people, like himself, Lisa hated being challenged on her views. But wasn't Mr. Rogers on the air during the Vietnam War? She was always telling stories like this—she'd actually believed Justin Timberlake had a gallon of semen pumped from his stomach, even after he'd told her he'd heard it was Bon Jovi when he was a kid, she still believed it—and every time, he'd do his best to hold his tongue. And every time, she'd know he didn't believe her, and the only thing he could think to do was begin undressing her, which she'd never objected to—unless it was the time of the month, what with sex during your period causing UTI's and all.

"Anyway," she said, "let's blow off work together. Let's go back to your place and fuck like rabbits."

"I can't. I have to work."

"Come on, I don't wanna be by myself right now. Would you rather I went back to work and punched Bich in the face?"

"No, of course not. But I can't just leave."

Lisa began grinding on his crotch, the chair moved back and forth on casters. Scott looked up, hoping no one would see what was happening. She pressed all of her weight on his erection and tilted her head.

"Look what you've done," she said. "You don't want to take care of that?"

"I can't," Scott told her.

"I'm feeling the opposite of *I can't* against my leg."

Scott pulled her off of him, stood up, led her into the supply closet to the right of the white board, and bent her over. Before he entered her, she made him promise to leave work with him, and he told her he was already feeling too sick to stay.

When he unclamped his eyes, he saw Blake's horrified face standing in front of the closet door. Lisa pulled up her pants and dragged Blake home. Scott said he'd tell the office Blake had an emergency. Officer McGill's whistling breaks through, and Scott leans over again.

"Could you please stop whistling?" he asks.

"What the hell is wrong with you? I thought I told you not to talk."

That night, Scott went to Lisa's home—it was the first time he'd ever been in Lisa's home. She still had her wedding picture on the walls, family photos of Blake with her ex-husband. He sat in the dining room with Blake while Lisa smoked in the backyard.

"Blake," he said, "your mother and I are dating. Actually, we're in love."

"If that's true, then how come I'm only hearing about it now?"

Had Lisa never told Blake about the two of them? What did Blake think Scott meant when he asked, *How's your mom?* What did he think was happening when Scott had said, "I'm seeing your mom tonight?" What in the hell did this dense moron think when he'd said, "We should all go check out a movie sometime?"

"I thought you meant me and you should go to a movie."

"I said we should all go. We. All!"

"I didn't hear the all part."

"Jesus, Blake. What the hell, man?"

"What do you mean, what the hell? You're banging my mom in the closet. That's sick."

"How is it sick? I love her. She loves me. We're in love."

Lisa came into the house, smiled, asked how things were going. Scott said things were okay, that they'd have it figured out soon. Blake asked Lisa if he could have a cigarette.

"Mr. Bonneville can have one with you," she said.

"Wait, I can't smoke with a student."

"It's okay, Scott," Lisa told him. "I let him every once in a while."

Lisa handed Blake her pack of smokes. Scott and Blake sat on the steps leading out to the porch. Blake lit a cigarette, tossed the pack at Scott's feet, then the lighter, which bounced off the stairs and onto the patio. Scott bent over to reach for the lighter. Blake blew smoke in his face.

"You're never gonna see her again," Blake said.

"You have no say in that."

"Yes I do. She's my mom. You're just some guy who thinks he has power over us."

"I don't have power over anyone. If anything, your mother has all the power here. I love her. I've never loved anyone in my life the way I love her."

Blake took a long drag. The dog next door barked loudly. Scott lit his cigarette and stopped short of blowing smoke in the little prick's face. Control yourself. Control yourself. Let him know you're on his side.

"You're lying," Blake said. "You're using her, just like you used me to get to her."

"Why would I use her, Blake? Besides, your mother and I are adults. We can do whatever we want."

"Just watch, dude. Keep it up and see what happens."

Blake snuffed his cigarette and went inside. Scott looked at the butt—does half empty/half full apply to cigarettes? Could he be so optimistic right now? Lisa came out and sat with Scott. They stared at the starless sky. A dog barked, setting off a chain reaction of barking dogs. She asked if they could go to his place. They made love one last time and she told him she couldn't see him anymore. But he didn't believe her.

They pull into the precinct, and McGill gets out, and pulls him out of the car. They enter the building, and the desk sergeant shoots the most menacing smirk he's ever seen. He looks like a middle-aged Lee Marvin.

"Okay," the sergeant says. "Who do we have here?"

He and McGill chat, and Scott remembers the story of Lee Marvin at Iwo Jima, how he'd been shot in the buttocks, severing his sciatic nerve. His sergeant had apparently been Bob Keeshan, who went on to entertain children as Captain Kangaroo. Marvin would go on to say Keeshan was the bravest Marine he'd ever served with.

Lee Marvin, Captain Kangaroo, Mister Rogers—if Lisa were to come back to him, he'd tell her he believed her. Lee Marvin and Captain Kangaroo did move up the beach and defeat the Japanese. They charged the hill, their boots sinking in the volcanic ash beneath them, bravely staring down Japanese machine guns and heavy artillery. And Mister Rogers really was a sniper, and every time he went into his dressing room and removed those red, or blue, or sometimes beige cardigans, he stared at those tattoos in the mirror, framed by showbiz lights, haunted by the men he'd killed.

Move to California

The day after Blake caught him in the supply closet with Lisa, Scott was called into Jed Birkenstein's office. Birkenstein had told him Blake Mesman had come to see him. When he saw Rosa Valdivia, the union rep already seated in the office, he knew it had to do with Blake. Scott took a seat.

"You don't have to say a word, Scott," Rosa told him.

"Of course you don't," Birkenstein said. "It's not like this isn't serious or anything. Scott, there's no easy way to say this, so I'm just gonna rip the Band-Aid right off. Blake says you and his mother were engaged in sexual intercourse, on school grounds, during school hours."

Scott listened to the second hand tick, and tick, and tick. He stared at Birkenstein's old Marine Corps service photo on the shelf. That wasn't what happened at all. That little bastard. He'd actually followed through on his threat to take Lisa away.

"Scott?" Birkenstein asked. "Are you okay?"

Of course he wasn't okay. He'd been exposed by the most unremarkable boy in the school. That stupid little motherfucker. When he and Lisa finally married, how awkward was it going to be, having that lying sack of shit in the house? Maybe they could convince Blake's father to take him. Lisa had already done her time. It was someone else's turn to shoulder the burden.

"What did Lisa say?" Scott asked.

"Who?" said Birkenstein.

"Lisa, his mom. What'd she say?"

"She won't return our calls."

"Blake's just angry," Scott said. "I am, in fact, seeing his mother. He's trying to get back at me."

"So you didn't have sex with her?" Birkenstein asked.

"Oh Jesus," Rosa said. "Scott, please—"

"We've been seeing each other for months now. It's a consensual relationship between adults. That little—Blake is clearly angry he saw us, and I'm sorry about that. I really am, Jed. But, you know, things happen when you're in love."

Rosa and Birkenstein sighed. The second hand ticked, and ticked, and ticked. The young Marine in Birkenstein's service photo seemed to glare at him. Scott was immediately suspended pending an investigation. Rosa told him not to worry. She told him Birkenstein seemed amused by it all, that they'd find a way to play that into something good. He was to spend his days at a place teachers had jokingly dubbed the Vault, the warehouse-like facility where they sent suspended teachers until the district could find a way to fire them. The suspended teachers sat in the Vault and watched TV, graded papers, caught up on reading—Scott would never know what they did at the Vault, as he'd never go.

He got in his car and drove to the Optometry office where Lisa worked. She told him she was busy, and he asked her to take a break. He followed her around the office. She went into the restroom and locked herself in, told him to never bother her again. Scott banged the door, jiggled the handle until security removed him and walked him to his car. He drove to his condo and left fifteen voicemails, until she finally called back.

"We can't see each other anymore," she said.

"Why?"

"It's going to take Blake a while to get over what he saw."

"Come on, Lisa. He was bound to figure it out."

"Yeah well I've never seen my mom getting taken from behind, have you?"

"Lisa, please, come over. I love you."

"Scott, listen—"

"I love you. My mother keeps bugging me about taking her house. She wants to go live with her sister in Sedona. We can move to California, get a fresh start."

"Please listen—"

"Blake can come too. Look, I'm not as mad at him as you might think. I mean, sure I'm pissed, but you're right. That was a lot to take in. We'll get over it. We'll get along. Just give—"

"I don't love you, Scott. Listen, just listen, okay? I think you're a very sweet guy. But the truth is, you're the only teacher who showed any interest in Blake. Do you know what that's like? You know how he is. The fact that you seemed to care about him and thought he had potential—well, I got caught up in all of that."

He told himself his heart wasn't breaking, that it was all physiological. She'd simply triggered the part of the brain that regulated breathing and heart rate. If he'd concentrated hard enough, he could override that part of the frontal cortex—was it in the frontal cortex?—and restore normal body function. Besides, she couldn't have meant any of this—she was exaggerating, being overly emotional. All they had to do was think it through, use logic. But first he had to breathe. Breathe.

Breathe. Breathe!

"Let's be honest," she said, "you were using me, I was using you, and it was fun while it lasted. I talked to Mr. Birkenstein and told him it was all a mistake. That I'd never do it again. And they're moving Blake into independent study for the rest of the year."

Scott realized begging wasn't going to get him anywhere—of course he was pressuring her, but couldn't she see the logic?—but he kept it up anyway until she finally hung up. He tried calling her again, and again, and again, until Lisa blocked his number. Then he called Blake's phone, left a long voicemail begging for a chance to prove his intentions. He grabbed his keys and ran to his car. She wasn't going to do this to him, not over the phone, and Blake was going to have to answer for this as well.

He slowly drove past their house, saw a Multnomah County Sheriff car parked in the driveway. By the time he'd gotten to the end of the street, he'd already composed the letter of resignation in his head.

When the Roll is Called up Yonder

Four days after the Pizza Galley Shooting, the 45th President of the United States loses the popular vote by nearly 2.9 million votes. None of that matters, and that's exactly the point Scott tries to impress upon his mother. Wilma goes to her room and slams the door, partly because Scott can't stop laughing, but mostly because he tells her everything that's happened to him is her fault. Not once does she take into account how Scott avoided rolling his eyes, however tempting it truly was.

"She should be the president," she had said.

"What's it matter? We're all screwed anyway."

"You sound like your father."

"Don't ever compare me to that psycho."

"Oh you don't think you got that from him? He thinks the world is screwed. But what's it matter to him? He's got a seat at God's table. People like him are going to be just fine when men like our goddamn President finally blow up the world."

"What does that have to do with this election? Your anger at Cary Bonneville is separate from one incompetent liar losing to another incompetent liar."

"Some of us want a better world, Scotty. Not the afterlife, but the world we're on right now. Men like you, men like your father, are too full of hate to ever see that."

"Jesus Christ. This has nothing to do with—"

"You don't ever wonder why your father never shows you any sort of affection? Because it doesn't matter. You'll get all the affection you need when whatever goofy doomsday scenario he's hallucinating now happens. Cheat on me constantly? That's fine because he's creating more soldiers in God's army. Sure, I'll hate him, but in the end, he'll be rewarded for being fruitful."

"Mom, this has nothing—"

"Some of us have to live in the world you create, Scotty. Think about what you've done, going out there, shooting that man."

"I was contemplating suicide, but thanks for your sympathy, Mom."

She placed her palms together and placed her nose in the space her index fingers met, rested her thumbs under her chin. Her fingers shook against the weight being exerted against them. She lowered her hands without pulling them apart.

"What about sympathy for me? Where's my goddamn sympathy? My son tried to kill himself and then shot another man. He won't even talk to me about it. He won't even seek help because he's so caught up in being a prophet for gun nuts. That's just like your father. A man who cheated on his wife God knows how many times—"

"Calm down, Mom. Jesus. Settle down."

Her hands finally flew apart, and she held up her open palms. Scott wondered if this was how she might look if he'd pointed a gun at her, at least in a gestural sense. But her expression was not one of rage, not fear. He'd never seen her like this before, and he could feel his eyes widening. She jabbed her finger toward him. He flinched.

"Let me finish my goddamn thought. You don't tell me to settle down. A man who stole money from his parishioners so he could live a lavish island lifestyle. A man who paid me off to keep quiet about the child molester he'd hired as a bodyguard."

During the election cycle, Wilma used to joke that something was finally going to wipe that smirk off his face, and Scott would tell her he wasn't smirking, that she was seeing things. But in this moment, he could feel the corners of his mouth straighten out. His lips parted. It felt as though all the blood was escaping his organs and rushing up to the skin. Wilma's hands merged once more. She put them between her knees and pushed her thighs together, rocking back and forth.

"What did you say?"

"Your father's bodyguard, Neil McNeil. Two days before I took you away, before we moved back here, I caught him with two boys in the private pool. I'm sure you don't want to hear this—I know how fond of Neil you were— which is fine because I really don't want to talk about it."

Scott glared at the television—people in Georgia, Alabama, Texas, all cheering as if they'd done something special, the goddamn morons. They interviewed an auto worker in Ohio, who was wearing a T-shirt, *Good Guy With a Gun* emblazoned across the President-Elect's forehead in red Cooper Black font. Scott felt sick to his stomach. Of course there were other boys. Who were they? He scanned his memory, trying to remember the other boys on the compound. Was it Zachary Puller? Was it Todd Bolden? Those two seemed to hate Scott more than any of the other kids. It had to be them. Did they blame him for what Neil had done? He wonders if maybe they wouldn't have hated him so much had they known Neil had touched him too. Scott looked at his mother, the coward. All the children who could've been saved had she stayed and actually done something.

"And you didn't say anything?"

"Of course I said something," she said. "Your father promised to fire Neil, said it wasn't going to stand."

"What about the police?"

"This was our chance, Scotty. It was our chance to get away from him. I took it."

The auto worker from Ohio, Ben Bonneville was his name—Were they related? Of course they weren't related—smiles and flashes an A-Okay sign, forming a ring with his thumb and forefinger. In yoga, it's known as the seal of consciousness, the cycle of universal consciousness. To white supremacists like Ben Bonneville, clearly that's what this man was, the three upward fingers represented the letter "W," while the circle and the forearm represented the letter "P": White Power. Scott chuckled, even in this moment, knowing the man got one over on the media, knowing he understood this man's profane joke.

"You left all those children there with that man," Scott says.

"Your father said he was going to fire him."

"You left Brian."

Scott stared at his mother's hands, still pressed between her knees. He watched her legs press in and out, in and out, and he thought about Mitchell, how she would sit with her hands pressed between her knees after sharing those final cigarettes.

"Brian's fine. Your father promised to keep Brian away—"

"Pull your hands apart. I hate when you do that. Stop doing it."

"It was our chance, sweetheart. Don't you remember the flight here? The worst is always behind us, remember?"

Wherever you go, there you are, Wilma had said three weeks before Mitchell passed away. Scott stared at her clenched fists, the way they pulsed as she tightened them over and over.

"Do you have any idea how selfish you are?" Scott said.

"Who do you think paid for your house, Scott? Who do you think paid for your life? You think I could afford to live on a cashier's salary in this house? I made a choice."

"You're a fucking monster. Everything that's gone wrong in my life is your fault. You're the reason I tried to kill myself."

For the record, Scott had never seriously considered killing himself the night of the Pizza Galley Shooting. He hadn't thought that far ahead, hadn't once considered he might have failed, that he might have to bite down on that suicide pill. Failure wasn't an option. He knew he was bound to succeed. Had David Brightman not been a goddamn cuckold, he would have exposed the truth. There was no need to even consider suicide. But Wilma had no way of knowing this was a lie, or the lie that would follow. She reached out for his hand and then lowered it as she grasped air.

"Did Neil touch you?"

A group of young boys were standing behind the reporter, holding a sign that read *Greetings from Kekistan*. The reporter asked what the sign meant. One of the boys told him it was a land of magic and chaos. When he asked the boys if they were happy with the election results, the boys chanted, *Kek, Kek, Kek!, Kek, Kek, Kek! Kek, Kek, Kek!* until the host in the studio cut the feed.

"No," Scott said.

Scott watched the host roll his eyes, shake his head, knowing he'd just been had. This was all a joke, to be sure, but was it any more a joke than any other election? Wilma asked Scott to stop smirking, told him she was serious.

"Scotty, you have to tell me. If he touched you, then—"

"Relax. Your hands are clean."

Scott listened to Wilma breathe in and breathe out, in and out, in and out. *Kek, Kek, Kek! Kek, Kek, Kek! Kek, Kek, Kek!* The in-studio panel of journalists and political operatives sat stunned, even the ones who'd said he could win. Any other time, Scott would've laughed at the sight, all these phonies whose lies had caught up with them—and when they'd been forced to confront their bullshit, they could hardly recognize what they saw.

"Then you're just being cruel," she said. "I'm going to bed. I'll see you in the morning. I love you."

Wilma went into the room and slammed the door. For the past few days, Scott had thought about how strong he'd been in the face of all this adversity, thought about how, even under all of this stress, he didn't cry once. He'd always been a bit of a crybaby—Neil McNeil had said so many times—but he didn't cry after killing David Brightman, didn't cry in the squad car, didn't cry in the interrogation room. All three of those moments were emotionally intense moments, but he didn't cry—he didn't.

But here was, crying softly on the couch, watching throngs of his fellow Americans, some of them weeping for their futures, some of them rejoicing in the present, each of them too stupid to realize it was the past that truly killed us all.

The Pizza Galley Shooting (Closing Thoughts)

Yu-jin was breastfeeding Naomi when Brenda peeked behind the privacy screen to let her know she had a visitor. It was two hours before Adam would be killed by Afghan trainees.

"Hi Jinny," Rachel said. "Obviously didn't have to go to school today, so, you know. Anyway, are you okay?"

Yu-jin asked Rachel if she'd slept, and Rachel began to cry. She rested her head on the plastic railing along the bed and Yu-jin stroked her hair until she composed herself.

"How is everyone?" Yu-jin asked.

"Darcy's on suicide watch, I hear. Ryan and Abhay feel horrible. They both wish they'd been there, as if that would've done any good."

"They shouldn't feel bad. I'm glad they weren't. I'm sorry you didn't get any sleep."

"There was no way. My parents fell asleep next to me on the couch. I just sat there and watched news footage until the sun came up. That Asian guy who came in and saved us—did you know he was trying to kill himself before he burst in and stopped Dave?"

"No, I didn't know that. That's really sad."

Yu-jin gazed at Rachel's face. It was amazing how lovely she looked, after what they'd been through. You wouldn't know she hadn't slept a wink. She looked down at her daughter. Breastfeeding the boys had been a pain, so much so they were eventually bottle fed, but Naomi came out ready to latch, her lips puckered out as if ready for a kiss. They always say babies are a blessing, and of course they are, but Yu-jin had never really considered what a blessing they were until she was in the ambulance, speeding toward the hospital. The EMT, a wide eyed woman named Roshanda, held her hand the entire ride, told her how grateful she was to be there with her. When Yu-jin asked her why, Roshanda said she was just grateful everyone was safe. That she was taking a mother to deliver her baby was an absolute blessing. She told her they were bringing an angel into the world, and that made it the only good night she'd had all month. Yu-jin looked down at her little blessing, latched onto her breast—they'd had quite a night, the two of them. She couldn't wait for Adam to meet their little angel.

"Can I tell you something?" Rachel said. "It's about last night. If you don't want to talk about it—"

"You can tell me anything you want. You're the only person I'll talk about this with."

"It's just weird, you know? Four women all alone while two sad men burst in with their pathetic problems. I'm not a feminist or anything, but you know. There's something to it, if you think about it. I don't know."

"Sounds like you do know."

"Well, it's like, one guy's story is he wanted to avenge himself for being jilted or whatever. And the other guy's story is he couldn't take the pain of everything so he wanted to off himself. The news footage about Dave is all about how sad and put upon he was. I get that Darcy shouldn't have cheated on him, but it's like they forgot he came in with a gun. They made it so that he came off kind of sympathetic, you know? The other guy, I don't know, they talked to all his former students who called from their dorm rooms, and they all said he was a really smart teacher. And then it hit me. They didn't talk about us at all, just Dave and the Asian guy. Isn't this our story, too? Is anyone even going to remember us in this?"

"I'll remember," Yu-jin said.

"Then I was thinking about the election, how it's all, *Her husband* this, and, *Her husband* that. Why is it about him? Who gives a shit about him? When she becomes president, he better make himself scarce. Seriously, it's like we can't talk about women without talking about the men in their lives. I mean, we were there too. Doesn't that matter? And in all of this, you gave birth to a little girl. When people ask her about the day she was born, are we going to focus on those two assholes and their guns?"

"One of those assholes saved our lives, Rachel."

"But Dave said he wasn't going to hurt us, Jinny. I actually believe him."

"The other man saved Darcy's life. That has to mean something too, doesn't it?"

Yu-jin stared at the top of Rachel's head as Rachel ran her finger along the railing on the bed. Rachel grabbed the edge of Yu-jin's blanket, began rubbing it between her thumb and forefinger.

"I pissed myself, did you know that?" Rachel said. "That's why I just sat there staring at that napkin holder. The whole time, I was trying not to freak out about pissing myself. When you told me everything was going to be okay, all I could think was, *How? I pissed myself.* That's why I hid behind that cop. He said it was okay, that it happens all the time. But, you know, no one else pissed themselves."

Rachel reached out, stroked Naomi's hair, then realized Naomi was still attached to Yu-jin's breast and pulled back. She told Yu-jin she was sorry for doing that.

"It's fine," Yu-jin said. "Do you want to hold her?"

Rachel cried, said she was sorry, told Yu-jin she'd been crying all morning for no reason, which was proof she was never getting over this. Yu-jin wiped Rachel's tears, handed Naomi to her, and Rachel took the baby in her arms, pressed her nose against Naomi's forehead.

"Everybody cries for a reason," Yu-jin said. "I think crying is reasonable right now."

Rachel ran her finger along Naomi's eyelashes and smiled. Yu-jin will remember this moment two days later, when she'll realize Naomi's birth will always be connected to her husband's death. She'll think about how she'll have to explain who her father was, and the circumstances in which he died, and how that will always connect back to the day she was born. And then she'll wonder if Rachel was right: how does one talk about their own lives without the pain caused by men?

"I like her lips," Rachel said. "She has your mouth. You cooked up a good one, Jinny."

Five years later, Rachel will finally find a way to talk about the Pizza Galley shooting while minimizing Dave Brightman and Scott Bonneville. She'll talk about Yu-jin telling her everything would be okay, how calm and self-less she was. She'll talk about Morgan praying in the restaurant, how Morgan underlined passages in the Bible during her breaks. She'll talk about the last time she'd see Darcy alive—the way Darcy smiled and held her, the way she told Rachel she was sorry for what she'd done, how they'd wept when Rachel told her it wasn't her fault. She'll talk about how absolutely reasonable it was to piss her pants.

The rest of us will continue to fail.

Pizza Galley Shooting (Coda)

Two years after the Pizza Galley shooting, a journalist named Susan Fuentes will co-write a book about Scott Bonneville with a former detective named Holly Ramirez, entitled *"Good Guy with a Gun": The Truth Behind the Pizza Galley Shooting*, based off Ramirez's time investigating the shooting and Fuentes's Pulitzer Prize-winning reporting on the incident.

The book will be the first to draw a connection between Scott and Walton Pabst, the young boy who would shoot up a campaign rally on January 21, 2017—the day after Inauguration Day. Through the use of phone records, they'll prove Pabst had called *The Gordy French Show*, a right wing radio program, the night before, calling for the elimination of "Leftists" and "Social Justice Warriors," invoking both *#GOODGUYWITHAGUN* and his fallen friend, Blake Mesman. In spite of spending nine weeks on the best-seller list, the book will be panned for its lack of research, derided for its leftist, anti-gun agenda; for its supposed hatred of men.

The book will reveal Scott Bonneville posted in the RE/Serch message-boards under the name *JeoseungSaja1111*, prove he was at the Pizza Galley four days before the 2016 Presidential Election in order to prove a conspiracy theory involving a secret network of pedophiles who'd worked in concert with the Vatican and the political donor class. It will reveal Bonneville's obsession with Lisa Mesman, the mother of a former student. It will assert Bonneville was the product of the digital age, a man so damaged by his cult-leader father, so thoroughly blitzed by mass media, so wrapped up in the toxic masculinity of his era, he could no longer tell the difference between right and wrong. In short, Scott Bonneville will have been exposed as a fraud, vindicating Holly Ramirez, who'd received death threats throughout the Pizza Galley investigation until she was finally reassigned, supposedly for her own safety.

One of the main criticisms of Fuentes and Ramirez's book will be the ways in which its analysis depends so heavily on two other books. The first book will be *The Catcher in the Rye*, which will show up extensively on *JeoseungSaja1111*'s RE/Serch posts. Critics will say the authors spend far too much time tying Bonneville's motivations to the book without debunking Bonneville's claim of the novel being a CIA assassination trigger. Of course, the authors will see this as an unfair criticism, as their purpose was to point out the irony of a man decrying the book as a method of awakening sleeper agents, while being "awakened" himself (they'll even quote Nietzsche's Aphorism 146) but it will be a sticking point for many critics, who will feel the authors "bought into Bonneville's delusions." The authors will reference Bonneville's obvious mental illness as a counterpoint to his theories, how he'd wept the entire ride back to the precinct, begging the arresting officer to stop whistling (dashcam footage will reveal the officer never whistled during their drive back to the precinct), how he'd cried and wet himself in the interrogation room, begged for a lawyer, his mother, for Lisa—how he'd threatened to kill himself if Lisa didn't answer her phone—and how his differing accounts weren't lies, but the ironclad certitude of a sociopath. He'd actually believed he was calm and collected, actually believed the police were playing mind games, games he'd clearly won.

The book will also tell the story of Blake Mesman, the former student who'd despised Bonneville for loving his mother. Fuentes and Ramirez will explore the notebook discovered in Mesman's room by the Portland Police Department—speculate on his Oedipal impulses, the hatred for women, the crude drawings of muscular men with cartoonishly large genitals. It will mention the green hunting cap (yes, green) found in the front seat of the stolen car, tie it back to the copy of *Confederacy of Dunces*, a novel written by a shut-in who himself had lived with his mother, found in the car's trunk. The authors will mention the uncanny resemblance between Mesman and the book's author (underscored by Mesman's sophomore yearbook photo placed side-by-side with the author's jacket photo), make the connections between the book's protagonist, Ignatius J. Reilly, and the legion of sexually thwarted young men who lashed out on social media and internet messageboards. On a book tour, Fuentes will call Ignatius J. Reilly a "Proto-Troll, the Mitochondrial Adam of Incels," mention his love for Batman serials and penny arcades, his hatred for Doris Day's beauty. She will never know that Mesman hadn't actually read the book.

Oh, had Scott only been alive to read this. He would've had such a laugh. And if he weren't so wrapped up in his own sad and hateful fugue, might have even appreciated the insights.

III.

All That Work for Nothing

Things Begin to Fall Into Place

Blake never wants to think about Mr. Bonneville fucking his mother, or any man fucking her for that matter, but these things are not easily forgotten. How could anyone forget their mother bouncing up and down, their mother bent over against a wall, their mother's legs separated by the hairy body of some disgusting excuse for a man? Bonneville stood out more than the other times he'd walked in on her with men—that Russian drummer, her disgusting friend Rahni, his father two years after the divorce—because it was the one that had happened after he'd realized she was the only real-life woman he'd ever seen naked. The only breasts he'd ever seen were his mother's. The only ass he'd ever seen was his mother's. The only face he'd ever seen locked in pleasure was his mother's, and he despised her for it. What kind of woman had sex while her son was around?

He was a preschooler the first time he'd seen her. His grandmother had picked him up and dropped him home. She never stayed—as soon as Blake slammed the door, she'd begin backing out of the driveway. The door was locked, and no one answered. Lisa had always told him to go sit in the backyard if no one answered the door, so he unlatched the side gate and made his way to the patio, where he saw her and her boyfriend, a lanky chainsmoker named Ruslan, naked on a lawn chair. She quickly pulled her pants on while Ruslan laughed and asked Blake if he learned anything.

"My mom apologized," Blake said. "She told me she lost track of time. It really fucked me up. Think about being five years old and watching your mom put her shorts back on, like everything in full view."

Walt laughed until he began to choke, hacking coughs echoing through the hillside. They were sitting on the trunk of Walt's car, getting high before heading off to school. Walt leaned his back into the rear window, took a deep breath. He dried his eyes and passed Blake the pipe. Blake took a hit—he'd never forgotten the thick hair between her legs, the way Ruslan's giant dick—he'd never forget how big it was compared to the others—flopped against his belly as he cackled. Blake blew smoke into the air as his friend choked from the hilarity of it all. He handed the pipe back to Walt and hopped off the car, shoved his hands in his pockets.

"The entire time I've known her, she's only been with four dudes. And I've walked in on her fucking all of them. What are the odds?"

"Pretty fucking high, dude," Walt said. "I mean, Lisa's a good looking broad."

"Shut the fuck up."

"Come on, man. Seriously. You don't think that a nice looking woman might meet guys who want to sleep with her?"

Walt extended the pipe, and Blake slapped it away, knocking the glowing bud out of the bowl. The two boys rushed one another, Walt lifting Blake off his feet and slamming him into the gravel. Blake's palm bounced off the side of Walt's head—had Walt not rolled away, it might've actually done some damage. A little less than a year ago, Blake would never have considered fighting someone like Walt. A little less than a year ago, Blake would have taken it when boys talked about Lisa—he did take it a little less than a year ago, all the time. The guys in school never let him forget how attractive she was.

What the hell happened to you? they'd say. *Was your dad a scarecrow or something?*

Walt pushed down on Blake's face, shoving his cheek into the gravel. Blake flipped onto his stomach and tried to push off, which left him wide open for a rear choke.

"Okay," Blake said. "I'll get you later."

Walt rolled off and the two lay in the dirt, panting. Blake never understood how Walt always seemed to lock him in chokeholds—without fail, this was how Walt would best him.

"Lateral raises and shoulder shrugs today," said Blake said.

"It's bench day, dude."

"Not for me, man. I need to work harder."

"Whatever you say, dude. But seriously, your mom is hot. I'd fuck her twice if I wasn't her favorite son."

"Fuck off."

"Dude, it's normal. We all walk in on our parents. It's not like you're attracted to her or anything."

"That's sick."

"So that Asian dude she was banging. You see his dick?"

"No. It was kind of obscured."

Walt laughed. Blake stared at the evergreens that covered the sky. The wind shuffled through the branches like radio static. He could feel his skin expand like rising bread, and he suddenly felt awful for knocking the bud from the bowl.

"Obscured," Walt said. "Hilarious."

They sat up as they heard the gravel smash and crinkle, a jogger in reflective aviators and a University of Washington sweatshirt slowed in front of them. She removed her right earbud.

"You get a lot of shit about that sweatshirt?" Walt asked.

"Not as much as you'd think," she said. "Just so you know, some old man called the cops on you. Maybe it's time for you boys to go to school."

"Thanks, sweetheart."

"Yeah, my name's not sweetheart, Junior."

"So what is your name then?"

Blake saw Walt's smirk reflected in her aviators. She turned and jogged away without a word, replacing the earbud after the fourth stride. Blake stared at the back of her tights—purple with white daisies. Lisa had those exact tights. He told himself he'd never dream of staring at her ass the way he was staring at this jogger's. Walt asked if Blake was staring at her ass, and he told him he wasn't. He'd already masturbated two days ago, which was all he'd allowed himself for the week—discipline was one the hallmarks of a real man. Besides, even if he had allowed himself to cheat, Ruslan's cock would've probably made an appearance and ruined everything. It was surprising how often it did ruin the moment.

And Lisa wondered why he'd hated her so goddamn much.

It's Almost Over Now

Scott answered his phone. It was his lawyer, Burghardt. They talked a bit about the previous night's election, how it was going to help Scott—not only because the President-Elect was a friend to gun owners, but because it was going to take him out of the news cycle.

"This is great for us, Scott," he said. "We get to lay low for a bit, plan our next move."

"Why lay low? But things are going well."

"Look, I'm going to be honest. You left your last job under a cloud of suspicion. The press is already started to ask about that and your mental state during your rescue. I really wish you hadn't told the police you were going to kill yourself. It just raises a lot of questions we don't need right now. Anyway, the good news is, now they'll be so angry their precious lady got trounced, that's where they'll focus their attention. In the meantime, can we meet? We need to plan our attack."

The landline began chirping in the kitchen. Scott called for Wilma to get the phone. It was embarrassing, calling out to his mother to get the phone. He wondered what Burghardt thought of a grown man still living with his mother. Wilma came out and answered it, asked the person on the line if they'd called to gloat. Scott rolls his eyes.

"Don't worry, Scott. It's almost over now. My assistant will send you an email to set up a time to meet. It's a wonderful time to be alive. A great man won and he'll give us the great country we deserve."

"Sure, Mills. Whatever you say."

Scott ended his call, tried to ignore his mother arguing with her caller. Burghardt was right. This idiot they'd elected was going to take the heat off of him. It was probably a good thing he wasn't going to be in the news for much longer. He thought of another world, an alternate universe, where he'd succeeded in exposing Pizza Galley, realized how useless it would've been. *She* would have used it to campaign on. Hell, she'd already tried to capitalize on #*GoodGuyWithAGun*, countering with #*StrongWomanWithAPlan*. For the past few nights, she'd proclaim herself to be a hashtag Strong Woman With A Plan, and the left wing media would mock her for saying hashtag every time she used the catchphrase—why not just say "Strong Woman With A Plan"?—how her voice spiked in pitch whenever she said the word, *HASH-tag*. When the right wing media wasn't calling her "Wrong Woman with a Scam," they honed in the on the words Strong Woman, combining them to form the word *Strongwoman* to underscore the authoritarian policies she shared with her husband. She was like a cartoon character stepping on a rake, and then slipping on a banana peel, before falling face first into a cream pie.

If Scott had succeeded in his mission, there would've been no *#GoodGuy-WithAGun* to hide behind, no *#StrongWomanWithAPlan* for her to bungle. If he'd discovered the kill rooms, Daniel Patrick McDougal, the CEO of Pizza Galley, LLC, would have probably funneled more money into her campaign in order to destroy him. If she'd won, if everything had gone according to plan, it wouldn't have been newsworthy. The media would have given a few passing references to a woman being elected president and then focused their attention back to him, would have set about destroying his life. They were already trying to tie him to the so-called Culture of Guns—this sad, sad man who might have killed himself because he had access to a firearm. None of them focused on the fact he'd stopped a potential mass shooting. Think about what they might have said had he succeeded in exposing Pizza Galley, if he'd exposed law enforcement, the clergy, the wealthy elites who pulled the strings of our government. There were many alternate universes out there—ones where he'd won, ones where she'd won, ones where he exposed Pizza Galley, ones where someone else had. Her loss was the best outcome. And he knew people could come to see that life goes on, no matter which fraud occupied the White House.

The election had given Scott a new lease on life. For days, he'd despaired in his failure. But now, he saw the purpose of his failure. He was supposed to fail. He was supposed to stop Dave Brightman from murdering his wife, Christian Gibbard, possibly others. He realized everything happens for a reason—he laughed at that thought, imagine him thinking something so incredibly trite. But what if this was truly an opportunity to reinvent himself?

Scott had stayed up all election night thinking about what Wilma had told him, that she'd known what Neil McNeil had done to young boys on the compound. Had he been so wrapped up in saving other children he hadn't given much thought to saving himself? Maybe he should go back into therapy, just for what Neil had done, of course. Besides, could that garner more sympathy for him in the court of public opinion? They'd all been so upset over pussy-grabbing, what about the grabbing of children? Sure, they didn't seem to care now, but what if he could advocate for all those children? What if he could use what had happened to him to tell the truth about Pizza Galley—wouldn't that show Lisa he was a good and serious man? He could be an actual hero, instead of the one Burghardt and Patrick Donnelly had invented. Even Blake couldn't stand in the way of a real hero asking for his mother's hand.

Burghardt had already received tons of calls from friends, asking if Scott was interested in going on a speaking tour. Everything happens for a reason—there was that stupid notion again haha! But it was true. Thank God for this president.

Wilma hung up the phone, pulled her cigarettes from her purse. Scott asked if everything was okay.

"That was your father. Your brother's coming to visit."

"Brian's coming? From where? Why?"

"Palm Springs. He's going to borrow some money."

"Is he going to pay us back?"

"Your father's going to wire it to me. It's not our problem."

"But why here? You can wire money anywhere."

"He wants to see you."

"Why?"

"That's not my problem, either."

Wilma opened the sliding door to the backyard, stepped outside, pulled out a cigarette. A cigarette sounded nice, but it was clear she was in no mood for company—especially his. Brian was coming. Had McNeil touched him as well? Maybe this was the universe telling him to reunite with his brother. Maybe they were supposed to help each other heal. Scott turned on the TV, a local reporter stood in front of the abandoned toy store on the corner of Hawthorne and Lomita, the one Democrats had rented as a local call center. Someone had spray-painted #*GOODGUYWITHAGUN* across the glass storefront. Scott laughed so hard, Wilma poked her head in to see what was so funny.

"For Christ's sake," Wilma said. "Does everything have to be a joke right now?"

No Reasons, Only Excuses

Brian glanced, only glanced, at the naked girl moaning on the twin bed closest to the door. It was pure reflex—he had no desire to look at her, no desire to remember she was even in the room with them, but she'd coughed. What if she was choking on her vomit? What his friends had done to her was one thing, but letting her die would've been completely beyond the pale. It wasn't as if Neil McNeil ever left him to die, even though Brian had many times wished he would. His short stays in Manoa and ASU had both ended with him trying to finish what McNeil had started—a handful of sleeping pills in Manoa, severed cephalic veins in Tempe—he stared at his wrists, wondered if the girl might be better off with a pillow to the face. At least in death, she wouldn't have to remember what Nick and Vince had done. It would've been far better than what he'd been left with.

But maybe she wouldn't remember anything. Maybe she'd wake up and only remember the party, the "fun times" as Vince liked to put it. The girl moaned again, as if caught in a fever dream, and Brian told himself he wasn't a bad person, that he wasn't like his friends, tried to convince himself he hadn't done anything wrong.

Nick cradled her head in his left hand—it was almost tender, the way he did it—as his right hand brought the joint closer and closer to her lips. Brian wanted to stop watching, wanted to stop thinking about the tenderness he saw in Nick's left hand. He remembered that same tenderness in Neil's hands when he wiped away Brian's tears, when he gave Brian a burning hot swig from the flask, which he'd eventually learned to choke down.

"Here," Nick told her, "take a hit."

She looked up at him, dazed, took a sip from the joint and coughed. Nick put the joint between his teeth and gave her a sip of water, which she coughed up. He toweled off her chest. Brian hadn't touched her—he never touched any of them. That had to matter for something, didn't it? It never seemed to, but it had to. Brian turned back to the TV. Don't look at the girl, he told himself. Don't look at the girl and she won't exist. But he liked this girl. She wasn't like the other ones. She was funny and smart and flirted with him—she'd even called him the Rock when he told her he was from Hawaii. Until she passed out, everyone was having a great time. She'd even gone down on Vince, right in front of them, laughed about it. Maybe it was different this time. Maybe his friends were in the clear. Maybe she wouldn't remember anything.

Journalists and ex-politicians sat at a table, stunned as another man—tie loosened, sleeves rolled up—frantically explained the swaths of red and blue on a map of the United States. So much red—none of them could explain it—they all looked so broken. The disheveled man stood in front of the map as the anchor peppered him with questions. It was as if they'd wanted this poor man to justify what was happening on the map, as if it were a map of his own making instead of a map everyone had collectively painted red. If Brian had cared about politics, this might have mattered in some way. Instead, he thought about Vince sitting at the foot of the bed, the girl kneeling between his knees. He'd done that plenty of times himself, to Neil. Were things different then? Was anyone in the clear then? Brian reached over, took the joint from Neil's teeth.

Vince came of the bathroom, a towel around his narrow waist. The steam from the shower clung to his broad shoulders. He looked like a ghost, a glistening wet ghost, emerging from the fog, ready to drag them all to hell.

"What are we going to do with her?" Brian asked.

"I don't know," Vince said. "We'll drop her off somewhere."

"Like a hospital?"

"What the fuck is wrong with you, man?" Nick said.

"So then you admit you did something wrong."

"sO YoU AdMiT yOu DiD SoMeTHiNG WRONG," Vince said.

"Brian," Nick said, "she was down for all of this."

"Then why drug her?"

"Why say something now, man?" Vince said. "Why the fuck now?"

Vince dropped his towel and put on his underwear. Brian's lingered a bit too long on Vince's flopping dick, which Vince noticed. He jabbed his finger at Brian, took a sip of Wild Turkey, wiped his lips with the back of his hand.

"Brian," Nick said. "We're running low on money. If we wanted to, we could rob this girl. She has like sixty bucks in her purse. But we're not. Hell, I'll probably kick a few bucks her way just on the count of 'cause. Just chill, all right?"

"Next girl's all you," Vince said. "Me and Neil ain't touching her. You're in this, whether you like it or not."

"Not gonna happen," Brian said.

"So that's why you were staring at my cock. I get it now, man. Do we need to go cruising for dick?"

"Screw you."

"Yeah, you'd like that."

Nick rushed in between Brian and Vince, pushed against Brian's chest, told him to relax. The last time Brian and Vince had gotten into it, they took Vince to the E.R. to have his jaw wired shut. It took them three weeks to recover financially, mostly money squeezed out of Brian's father. The time before that, they'd had to remove bits of glass from Vince's forehead. He still had the scars. But Vince never really retaliated in any serious way—he knew he'd deserved it every time—other than the occasional questioning of Brian's sexuality. Vince pulled down his underwear, wiggled his hips, called Brian Little Fishie, told him to come get the worm. Nick had to tackle Brian, wrap his arms and legs around him to restrain him.

They'd known one another since childhood—Brian being the son of Reverend Cary Bonneville, while Nick and Vince were raised in the Church of the New Millennium compound in Lanai. They never talked about what Neil McNeil had done to them. They didn't even know he'd done it to all three of them. Only Brian knew, having snuck into Neil's room once to poison him. While squeezing an entire bottle of Visine into a carton of orange juice, he came across naked images of Nick and Vince in separate Poloroids. Their frightened faces upset Brian so much, he'd dropped the carton on the floor, spilling orange juice everywhere. Brian went and hid in his garage as Neil flew into a rage, storming around the compound demanding to know who'd broken into his room, vowing to kill whoever it was. Reverend Bonneville had to take Neil into his secret office, the one with all the liquor, for the rest of the night. Brian, his friends in the Poloroids, were all eight at the time. There were times Brian wanted to tell Nick and Vince he knew about the Poloroids, that Neil had done things to him too, but how do you even bring something like that up? Vince pulled up his underwear, the elastic snapping against his waist.

"I'm just fucking with you, Brian," he said. "Take it easy. Besides, we have other shit to worry about right now."

Brian could feel the girl tossing and turning in the bed, probably some kind of drug induced nightmare—he prayed it would exorcise whatever hell they'd put her through—he knew he'd put her through it as well, even though he'd never touched her—that she'd wake up relaxed and ready to move on with life. What were they going to do with her? He'd never seen anyone this catatonic in all the times Vince and Neil had done this. She wouldn't stop moaning. Definitely other shit to worry about right now.

"Like we're running low on cash," Vince said. "We're kinda fucked right now, thanks to Bobby."

Bobby was their contact at the CVS in Needles. They'd hit him whenever they were in town, buying Sudafed, Actifed, Benadryl—anything with pseudoephedrine—which they removed from the blister packs and sold in bulk to their wholesaler. Law enforcement officials called what they did Smurfing—the little Smurfs went into the forest to pick fruits and berries, which they took back to village and cooked up in Papa Smurf's giant pot—at least this was Brian's understanding of where the term originated from. Like the Smurfs, Brian and his friends foraged for cold medicines and decongestants they could sell to anyone who wanted to make crank in their giant pots. They mostly worked with the Legion of Blood, a biker gang that operated in, of all places, Palm Springs.

It wasn't much of a life, but neither was living on that compound, singing songs about the Second Coming, sitting through his father's sermons on the coming trials, convincing himself that not much of a life here didn't matter because something beautiful was coming once the seven angels blew their seven trumpets. That's what they all believed on that compound, that everything would work itself out in the end, that all was going according to God's plan, that something better was always on the horizon. The trouble with the horizon was it was always the horizon no matter how long you walked, how quickly you ran toward it, and no one really knew what lay beyond it. All any of them ever did was chase the horizon while Cary Bonneville moved the goalposts further and further away with every step they took.

If it weren't for Bobby, they'd have avoided Arizona altogether, but Bobby was very good at making supposed mistakes, and turning a blind eye, and playing dumb. It was only a matter of time before he'd gotten caught, which he had the night they'd pulled into this shit hole town. Now thanks to Bobby and a group of idiotic local Smurfers, Brian and his friends were running on empty.

"Okay," Brian said. "I'll call the old man. He'll get us more money."

Nick stared at the TV while Brian called the good Reverend Bonneville. "Yeah, it's Brian. I need more money. Five thousand dollars. You know why you owe me. No, this isn't extortion. You know why you owe me. I don't care. You don't think so? Try me. No it isn't. Try me. Why would I go see him? No, he's not my brother. Why should—You realize he's a murderer, right? I'm sure you think that but that's not true. Sure whatever you want to tell yourself to make yourself feel better. Yeah, I'm sure you're very proud of some dude who wants nothing to do with you. He's not better than me. You can think that but he's not. Okay, whatever you say. You know why you owe me. Stop talking about him. Any way you cut it, he straight up murdered that—No it won't. Fine, I'll go. But he better have the money. I'm not kidding, Father. Don't try me. You know why you owe me."

He ended the call, watched the TV. A group of women at a rally in Seattle tightly grasped one another's hands, tears streaming. They knew they'd lost.

"This is fucked up," Nick said. "I mean, I don't give a shit but really? That guy's the president now?"

Brian looked at the girl on the bed, told himself he felt sadness for her, when the truth was everything he felt for her was his own pain and distress. She was just like every other girl—the one in Boise, and in Reno, the sisters in Yuma. He wanted these girls to know that he had nothing to do with their pain—he was the good one—that his life would've been better had they never showed their faces.

"Seriously man," Nick said, "I can't believe this guy fucking won. My man's a straight-up assclown."

"I hear you," Vince said. "But that other bitch is almost worse. I mean, think about all the people she and her husband murdered."

"It's true," Brian said. "I remember Neil had a bunch of books about it. Her husband murdered their friend and made it look like a suicide. They covered it all up. He'd been doing shit like that ever since he was governor of Oklahoma, or Kansas, or wherever he was from."

"Well, holy shit," Nick said. "Fuck her too, then. And fuck Neil. Fuck Neil hard."

"Yeah man," Vince said, "and that's just the tip of the iceberg. It's really fucked up. We might have dodged a bullet with her. And yeah, Neil was a piece of shit. I'd love to get my fucking hands on him."

"Why's that?" Brian asked.

He regretted asking. Not only did it feel like an intrusion, but he didn't want his friends to know that he knew their shame, that he shared it. How awkward would it have been—three boys all damaged by the same man, in that way? Could the other two even look at him if he'd told them what Neil had done? Could he look at them if he knew what had specifically happened to them? What about the Polaroids? How could he tell them he'd seen those photos, those horrible photos with their sad, frightened little faces? It was better that only he knew.

"He's an asshole," Vince said. "What more do you need?"

"Yeah man," Brian said. "I hear you."

A Swift Continuation

Blake stops at a Shari's in Salem for breakfast. A reasonably pretty brunette asks for his drink order—a cup of coffee, black. She tells him they don't add cream and points to salad bowl stacked with creamer cups, jokes she can take those away if he'd like.

"Wait," she says, "Blake? Blake Mesman? Dude, it's me, Marla Crane."

Blake looks into her smiling face. Marla Crane, who'd been a year ahead of him at DuClod-Mann. She'd lost a bit of weight, just as he had. He flinches as she slaps his shoulder.

"Hi Marla. Good to see you."

"Holy crap, dude. You look amazing. Been hitting the gym, huh? Good for you, man."

Blake looks at his biceps, the cuff of his short sleeve wrapped below his deltoid like a tourniquet. Men were supposed to take great pride in how they looked, and knowing that had made all the difference in his life.

"So, what're you up to?" she asks.

"Not much. You?"

"Well, I work the morning shift here, then back to Willamette for classes."

"Cool. It's a good school."

"It's okay. I couldn't get into UO, you know—affirmative action and all. But seriously, man. You look amazing. What have you been up to?"

"Well, as you probably know, I got expelled from DuClod."

"No, I had idea. Oh God. Mr. Bonneville and your mom—I'm sorry, shouldn't have said that. None of my business."

Marla winces, but Blake doesn't mind what she'd said at all. She'd always been nice to him. More to the point, she'd always ignored him, which was as good as it was going to get for Blake at that point in his life. He pats her wrist, the softness of her skin, and tells her it's okay—really, he was fine.

"It's wild, right?" she says. "Him shooting that guy. I guess he saved a lot of lives."

"Sure, I guess. It's weird, seeing him on the news, knowing who he is and all that."

"I know. When I saw his face, I freaked out. I was like, Holy crap, that's my old English teacher, to my roommate. Anyway, Let me get your coffee. Seriously, though, I'm really happy for you. You really look great, man."

After his expulsion from DuClod-Mann, Blake was enrolled in Ronald R Swift Continuation High School, an alternative high school for troubled boys. Of course, that wasn't what the brochure said, but most of the boys at Swift Continuation were, like Blake, young men whose only remarkable feature was their penchant for making a mess of their lives. Lisa had to beg his father and bitch grandmother to help pay for tuition. Blake was told not to screw this up.

"Blow this," his father had said, "and we're done."

"We're already done, so blow this," Blake would have said were he a much more quick-witted boy.

The first day of school is always hard, of course, but when you're Blake Mesman, a boy whose own grandmother thought asked for it, it was unbearable. For boys like Blake, the notion of reinvention is a laughable one, and hoping against hope is always a fool's game. That he refused to take off his red hunting cap—his people shooting hat, as he called it—immediately made him a target of both teachers and students. In first period, the boys began calling him Elmer Fudd, and the teacher seemed more impressed kids their age actually remembered *Looney Tunes* than distressed by the obvious bullying— after all, Blake was the kind of boy who asked for it—so he offered a very weak, *Knock it off*, ignored all of the *Be vewy quiet*'s and *Dat wabbit in da dwess is hawt heh-heh-heh*'s.

"Maybe you should take off that hat, man," the teacher had said after class. "Maybe make life easier for both us."

Marla returns with his coffee, once again tells him it's so cool to see him again. He smiles and tells her he feels the same way, even though he doesn't. The Blake Mesman she knew is not the Blake Mesman he wants to think about. He'd killed that soft, doughy weakling through countless hours in a makeshift weightroom in Nelson Pabst's garage—the Blake Mesman she knew would never have dreamed of joining the Company of Men, of understanding the importance of reading history and philosophy, of personal grooming and hygiene. Blake remembers being afraid of taking baths as a kid, how Lisa had to give him sponge baths until he was ten, how even after getting past that fear, he'd never actually conquered it, how he'd avoided baths through most of high school, until Nelson Pabst finally pulled him aside and told him how horrible he smelled, how he wasn't welcome in his home until he learned to take better care of himself, how he'd finally learned to M.A.N. U.P. (Make A Note: Unlock your Potential)—part of the pledge every boy took before joining the Company of Men—because he needed Nelson Pabst's guidance, cherished Walt's friendship. Marla takes his order and leaves—there's something about her excitement towards him he can't quite place, something he's never felt in his eighteen years. He brings the coffee mug to his lips and blows, the shimmering film of oil swirling across the black surface.

It was after second period when he finally met his first and only best friend, his blood brother, a tall kid from California named Walt Pabst. They shook hands. Blake couldn't remember anyone ever offering their hand to him before, and here was this blond surfer-looking guy not just shaking hands, but then following it up with a hand-slap. He was actually slapping hands with another dude.

"Nice hunting cap," said Walt said. "Weird, but I like it."

"Thanks. It's my people shooting hat."

"Oh, that fucking book," Walt laughed.

"You know it?"

"Yeah, man. It's required reading—in school, anyway. See you around Blake."

Blake couldn't believe Walt knew his name. Of course he knew his name—they'd just introduced themselves—but he'd never had anyone acknowledge him like this. Even the new kids at DuClod-Mann, when they finally bothered to address him, had known to call him Sneetch. Of course, Mr. Bonneville had acknowledged him, but had turned out to be a bunch of bullshit. This seemed real, like real-real.

The boys who'd called him Elmer Fudd, the ringleader being Oscar Ramirez, all laughed at the idea of these two boys speaking. Was Walt a dork too? How could this be? He was tall, had blue eyes—if there had been any girls at this school, he probably would've been really popular with them.

"Holy shit," Oscar said, "Assblood fucks with Elmer now?"

"Just ignore them," Walt told Blake.

During lunch, Blake walked around the cafeteria looking for Walt, who was nowhere to be found. He sat in the stairwell and ate his veggie wrap, his gluten free brownies, by himself. He wouldn't see Walt again until after school, when Oscar and company snatched the people shooting hat off his head.

"Give it back," Blake said.

"GiVE iT BaCk," Oscar said. "Come take it."

"Give me back my hat."

Oscar put the hat on, cracked a smile. And that was when Blake saw Walt standing behind the boys. Walt winked, put his arms around the waists of

Oscar and the weird looking ginger they called Easy. Oscar and Easy recoiled, and Oscar shoved Walt, who kept his eyes locked on Blake's.

"What's going on, Blake?" Walt said.

"Get out of here, bitch," Easy said.

"Maybe they should give Blake his hat."

"Maybe I fuck you up right now," said Oscar. "Maybe I make you suck this motherfucker's dick."

"Is that what you want?" Walt said. "Seriously? Hey, Easy, you really want to watch me suck this dude off?"

Easy looked at Walt, then at Oscar. Were he a thoughtful boy, perhaps he would've given the obvious response a young boy might give to such a specific question. Oscar slapped Walt across the head. Walt shut his eyes, pursed his lips.

"Move it, Assblood," Oscar said.

Walt opened his eyes, took a deep breath. He reached into the back of his pants, underneath his peacoat, and pulled out a tiny revolver. The boys recoiled, backed away. Blake was completely still. Later on, Walt would talk about how unfazed he was, how very cool Blake looked.

"What are you gonna do, shoot us?" Oscar asked. "You shoot us, and this is all over man. Really think about what you're gonna do."

"Hey man," Walt shrugged. "We're a bunch of shitty kids in a shitty school. Maybe this is the only future there is. Me shooting you, going to jail, and everyone crying about how guns are bad, or that we're just a bunch of bad kids, and then no one cries because both the guns and the kids were bad—I don't know, man. Am I making sense? Maybe. Either way, maybe just give this guy his hat, and I make sure none of the guys at the school call you Pistol-Whip or whatever other totally not-retarded nickname they'll come up with."

"You better have that gun on you for the rest of your life," Oscar said.

Walt put the gun back in his pants. He nodded at Blake, and then pulled out the gun again. A flinching Oscar told him to knock it off.

"Give him back his hat."

Oscar removed the hat from his head, looked at Blake. He then cleared his throat, drew up some phlegm, deposited it inside the hat. Blake clutched his hat by the earflaps. He looked inside at the foamy blob surrounding the gleaming yolk of snot. Oscar's crew walked away. No one had ever defended Blake, ever. When things like this happened at DuClod-Mann, some teacher would tell the boys to cut it out—not leave him alone, but cut it out, and Assistant Principal Birkenstein would demand to know why he never stood up for himself, or Mr. Bonneville would tell him to use it as fuel (whatever the fuck that meant).

"You bring a gun to school?"

"Not in school. I leave it in my car. You want a ride home?"

"I can't. My mom's coming to get me."

"Call her. Tell her you got a ride."

"Why do they call you Assblood, anyway?"

"Call her, and I'll tell you all about it."

Marla comes back with his plate—two eggs, sunny-side up; two strips of bacon; hashbrowns; unbuttered wheat toast. She tells him if he's sticking around, there's a party off campus—a couple DuClod-Mann people will be there. They'd be tickled to see him. He tells her he can't, that he has to stick to his schedule, but thanks. She smiles and leaves.

So Blake called Lisa, left a voicemail telling her he was going to hang out with a guy he met, that he was getting a ride home. When he got home, Lisa would insist Walt stay for dinner, so thrilled Blake had finally made a friend—making sure to avoid asking how a nice-looking boy like him would end up at the kind of school her son would go, tried to ignore the fact her son's clothes smelled like pot, that his eyes were bloodshot slits. But until then, Blake and Walt sat in Walt's car, smoked from a chamber pipe, watched porn on his phone.

"Check out this dude's obliques," Walt pointed at the screen. "Goddamn this motherfucker's shredded, right?"

It was hard enough to enjoy watching porn with another guy, but having Walt constantly critique the men's bodies and technique made it downright uncomfortable. *Look at how strong his thighs have to be to hold her up like that. Maaaaan. . . the thrusting here. That's fucking power, baby. I like how his hand is practically palming her forehead like a basketball—look at the veins on his forearm. I mean, even all sleeved-up, you can see the definition. Shout out to him, man. See this guy's chinstrap beard? It's to hide his weak chin. You might want to think about growing one of those, man. Look at this motherfucker's lats, man. How many pull-downs and cable rows do you think he has to do to—*

"Hey Walt. Are you gay? I mean, it's cool if you are."

Walt took a suck off his pipe, held his breath, gave a sidelong glance.

"Why the fuck would you ask that, dude?" he croaked.

"Because you keep focusing on the guys. And, to be honest, it's a little weird."

Walt blew a giant cloud of smoke from his lungs, passed the pipe to Blake. Blake had smoked pot before, one of Lisa's friends, a manbunned cricket named Rahni, always made sure to sneak him a few puffs whenever they had parties. Although it had never really been sneaking, necessarily—Lisa had known about it, and it had become a bit of a joke.

Hey Rahni, don't you give my son any pot haha!

Oh, I wouldn't dream of it haha!

Blake sucked the smoke deep into his lungs. Through Nelson Pabst, through the Company of Men, Blake would come to know that Lisa's permissiveness was part of the problem. In every man's life, sneaking beer, cigarettes, drugs, porn, was a rite of passage. That Lisa had let him smoke cigarettes with her, that she'd sat down and shared cans of Coors Light with him, that she'd let that cucktard Rahni give him weed, showed his life had lacked structure. A man needs structure. He'd once heard Mr. Bonneville tell another kid, "You have to know the rules in order to break them," and he was right, that fucking prick. A man needed structure, because without structure, there was nothing to rebel against. And when a man can't rebel, he becomes complacent, weak. How could he break down walls if none were provided for him? That fucking bitch. It was Lisa's fault he'd turned out the way he had. Blake tilted his head and blew, watched the smoke ripple against the ceiling.

"Look man," Walt said. "You look like the kind of guy that doesn't understand the art of being a man, so I'm just trying to point shit out to you. I mean, look at these guys and be honest. Wouldn't you give your right nut to be doing what they're doing?"

"Sure, I guess."

"Well girls like this only go for dudes like that. So, logically, if you want to bang chicks like this, what do you think you have to do?"

"Become these guys, I guess?"

"Are you asking or saying."

"Saying."

"Good. So, after watching porn, I go home and lift."

Walt put the pipe to his lips and sucked in. Blake squinted, his lips moving like an idiot reading the side of a cereal box. Walt laughed so hard, he began to cough, and then Blake laughed, even though he had no idea what the joke was.

"My uncle converted his garage into a weight room. A bunch of guys go there and lift. You'd like it."

"I have to go home soon, but maybe later. If you can show me what to do, I'm in."

Blake finishes his breakfast, sips his coffee, stares out the window. "What a Fool Believes" plays through the speakers. In happier times, Lisa used to sing this song while washing dishes, while he and his father played Candyland. He looks behind the counter. Marla is laughing with another girl, a tiny Filipina, maybe Mexican—he's not quite sure. He thinks about the way Marla looked at him, wonders if Marla could look at him like that, could other girls as well? What if those girls he and Walt had talked about when they'd watched porn, their pre-workout ritual, were finally attainable? No, he's fooling himself. He still had no chance with girls like that. Only reasonably pretty girls like Marla were a remote possibility, but even the Marlas of the world had been so warped by RadFem—Willamette University, ha—they'd only give guys like him lip service before going off to sleep with androgynous college boys—none of whom had lived through the kind of pain that toughened you up, the kind of pain that landed you in Swift Continuation—the kind of soy boys who wore tights under their cutoffs in order to upset the natural order. Would Marla pull down her boyfriend's stockings before sucking his dick? Blake chuckles as Marla hands him his check, writes down her number in case he changes his mind.

"Hey, Walt. Why do they call you Assblood?"

"You really want to know right now, man?"

"Kind of."

Assblood's Story

"Okay, well, back in Redondo, I used to be a part of this group called The Half-Minute Brigade. We were just a bunch of dudes who saw how the world was going to shit and wanted to do something about it. Fifteen minutes from my house they were building something called a Women's Resource Center, and the brochure said it was going to be this place where women can have a safe place that provided things like counseling, shelter, and education for women who suffered from domestic violence. And we thought it was kinda bullshit because isn't that why we have cops? I mean, I get that women are sometimes abused, but you know, that's why we have families, to teach these women how to find morally upright men who won't hit them. That's what schools should be doing. They don't, but still. So, you know, we totally called bullshit on that.

"Anyway, what I'm telling you is this place was a front. What they were doing was taking a bunch of vulnerable women and then indoctrinating them into RadFem. And me and my friends saw right through that shit. We looked at the board of directors, and the head of the whole thing was a woman with a doctorate in Women's Studies. Why her? Why not one of the supposed psychologists who were in charge? Weren't they there to provide counseling? Why put someone who had no background in psychology in charge of a counseling center? You know why. It's because they wanted to teach women to hate men, that's why.

"So me and my friends Bobby and Aaron started talking shit online about how we lived close to it and we were gonna burn it to the ground. We weren't gonna do it for real. We were just a bunch of kids talking shit on the internet. But all these guys just kept egging us on. And these weren't bad guys. They were normal dudes like anyone else, just a bunch of guys who saw through that shit. Like for instance why isn't there a Men's Resource Center? No one ever asks that. Anyway, I'm getting on my soapbox here. Sorry, back to the point.

"But that is the point, isn't it? I mean, you make people feel special and unique and then they feel entitled to all kinds of shit. Women are no more special than anyone else. Why give them preferential treatment? Why give anyone preferential treatment? I mean, we're always taught that dudes don't deserve shit, but everyone else does. Mostly white dudes they say that about, but all dudes get shafted in one way or another, all dudes. Bobby was half-

Mexican, so it wasn't like a race thing. No one's more special than anyone else, and nobody makes men feel special.

"So one night, me, and Bobby, and Aaron did shrooms and just started tripping really hard. All I remember is we were playing *Code of Conduct* in my room, and then my house turned into a Safe House, and the only way for me to save the game was to go into the garage. So I led my friends into the garage to save the game. Then we grabbed my dad's toolbox and got in the car to continue the game. That's how we ended up at the Resource Center, like it was a side mission. I don't remember a lot of it, just that in my mind it was a side mission in *Code of Conduct*. We trashed the shit out of that place—slamming shit with wrenches and hammers, carving pentagrams and swastikas into the beams with screwdrivers. Then Bobby took a dump on the floor and started smearing it all over the walls. We thought that was hilarious, so we did it too. Could you imagine if you could do that in *C.o.C.*, just take dumps in the enemy camp? That would own so hard.

"Honestly, the next thing I remember is being on a stretcher in the E.R. with my ass burning like I was shitting razor blades soaked in jalapeno juice. There was blood everywhere because we'd wiped our asses with pink toilet paper that actually turned out to be fiberglass insulation. That's how the cops found us. All that blood and shit on the insulation led them to that E.R. We were ruined after that. No one wanted anything to do with us, other than to send death threats to our house and shit like that.

"Bobby killed himself in his garage. Aaron got sent off to military school in Alaska. All over bullshit. I mean, I guess what we did was a crime, but what about why we did it? What about the fact that there were thousands of dudes who felt like we did? No one ever considers that. They only think about the shitting and how funny that was, or that we're bad people for doing what we felt was the right thing to do. This is what they do, man. They focus on what we did instead of considering why we did it. I'm not some kind of gangbanger fuckup. I'm a straight A student—we all were. We were good kids, and they punished us because they hated our ideas. My friend fucking died because of them, man. It's all fucked up. It's fucked up, man. Fuck those people. Fuck all of them.

"So anyway, once they found out who I was at Swift, the name Assblood just kinda stuck."

Blake stared at the ceiling of the car, the sound from Walt's porn seeping into his ears and settling into the back of his head. What struck him was Walt's assertion that no one considered why people sometimes did horrible things. Walt and his friends had committed vandalism—Blake could easily concede that point—but at the same time, they had good reasons for doing what they had done. Grandpa Don had once told him that back in the old days, you could tell a woman how beautiful she looked and she understood it was a compliment. These days, you could get sued just for saying something so harmlessly friendly. What if this resource center really was going to brainwash women into hating men? Blake wondered if women from Grandpa Don's day would've found him friendly and complimentary. Maybe knowing they would might have helped him open up with girls. Part of the reason he'd never talked to girls was because they all seemed to think they were better than him. It was bad enough guys thought they were better than him, but when girls looked down on him, it just seemed to hurt more. When the boys called him Sneetch, it didn't feel like they were making fun of his body, that they found him disgusting, the way it had when girls called him that. If only one girl could've been nice to him in some small way—

"Hey Blake. You okay dude? Anybody home?"

"Yeah, just zoned out a little."

"Dude, were you even listening to me?"

"Yeah, man. I was totally listening. I'm sorry they call you Assblood. It sucks when a nickname sticks."

"Doesn't matter. I have bigger fish to fry, you know?"

"My mom always says that. But it's like, I can't even fry these small fish, know what I mean?"

"Maybe you need some direction in your life."

"Probably. I don't know."

My Neck, My Traps

Blake knows he can make it into California without stopping, but pulls over in Medford to pump gas anyway. Something tells him it's time to stop, mostly the Adult Store next to the gas station. A stork-faced boy in a blue polo sits on the curb smoking a cigarette. He runs over to Blake's car and says hello. Blake hands him fifteen dollars and walks into the gas station to buy a Gatorade. He opens the door and sees the bull-necked bruiser behind the counter. They lock eyes. He has a half-cut just like Blake, a U.S. Marine Corps insignia tattooed across the top of his right forearm. Blake admires the man's neck, his traps—those were Blake's trouble spots. They nod at one another. Blake walks to the cooler and pulls out a Glacier Freeze. The man at the counter, his name tag reads Steven, taps his fist on the counter twice, he pauses and rotates his neck, then taps four more times. Blake smiles, reaches for a Glacier Cherry to go with his Glacier Ice, and makes his way to the counter.

"Double Glacier, huh?" Steven says.

"Would you like one?" Blake asks.

"No Green Apple, huh?"

"Isn't Green Apple for bitches?"

"Then I'll take the Cherry."

"In a better world, brother, we all take the cherry."

Blake pays for the Glacier Ice and Glacier Cherry, hands the Cherry to Steven. Then they perform the Company Handshake. Other than black coffee, the only flavored drink the Company of Men are allowed to drink is Gatorade—no sodas, no juices—and only Glacier Ice and Glacier Cherry. The Double Glacier Test is a gesture of brotherhood between two men. Every other flavor is, as Blake put it, for bitches. Giving your brother the Glacier Cherry symbolizes sacrifice, as giving another man the cherry is the equivalent of giving him your woman, proving that you are willing to truly give your brother the things he desires most, even if it means you'll be depriving yourself. By giving a stranger the cherry, you are demonstrating your hospitality. Once two men become friends, after one has proven his sense of hospitality, the Double Glacier involves two Glacier Cherries, as sharing the cherry is an act of brotherhood. The rules were now public knowledge, thanks to some assholes on the internet who tried to turn it into a joke. It was only a joke to the slimy little cucktards who'd never have the conviction to live life by a code.

The Glacier Ice represents the man—powerful, resolute, with a strong moral base that lies beneath the surface. The Glacier Cherry represents the woman—a watered-down sweetness that could always use a little sugar. No two men can drink Glacier Ices at the same time. In a group of men, only the recognized leader may drink a Glacier Ice. Everyone else must drink the Glacier Cherry. There was absolutely nothing funny about any of this. All men had to live in a world of rules. The only rules meant for breaking were rules not worth following, rules not created by real men. For boys like Blake, this all made perfect sense.

"What brings you to Medford, brother?" Steven asks.

"I'm on my way to LA," Blake says. "On my way to fuck some shit up."

"That's what I'm talking about. Need any help?"

"No, I'm good. This guy I'm going to see is a complete cucktard. No need to waste your time."

"If you need anything, I know some dudes in Long Beach. One phone call and they got you."

Blake looks out the window at the Adult Store across from the pumps. Oregon is littered with Adult Stores, places for lonely travelers to stop in and catch a show in the arcade.

"How's that place?" Blake asks.

"It's clean. The guy who works it deals Oxy out the back, but otherwise it's not bad if you mind your own business. Looking to test your might?"

"I could be."

The stork-faced kid pumping Blake's gas gives a thumbs up to let Blake know he's good to go. Blake gestures at the kid, who replaces the nozzle and closes Blake's lid.

"That kid need a Glacier?" Blake asks.

"Hell no," Steven says. "Look at him."

The boy ambles back to the curb, his noodle legs practically dangling from his baggy denim shorts, the fair hairs on his pale calves sparkling in the sunlight. The boy wipes his nose with the back of his hand and takes a seat, slides earbuds into his giant Dumbo flaps. There was a time when Blake was that kid, a gangly dork with no sense of pride in his appearance, of his intellectual development, no understanding of his rightful place in this world built by men. He pities the kid, remembers what it was like to live without kindness or charity.

"Ring me up for a Green Apple?" Blake says.

"Godspeed brother," Steven laughs.

They give the Company Handshake and Blake leaves. He hands Stork Boy the Green Apple, the kid gushes over his generosity. Blake gets in his car, looks in the rearview mirror, the adult store. Stork Boy gives a thumbs up as Blake pulls away.

Sanctuary

Four years before the Pizza Galley shooting, St. Catherine United Methodist Church in Torrance, California had been left a sizeable amount of money from a widow who'd passed away in a nursing home in Boulder, Colorado. The widow, Margaret Wellington, had grown up poor in Torrance and on many days, the only food she and her brothers had to eat was due to the generosity of St. Catherine's parishioners. She'd never forgotten the kindness of the pastor, an elderly man named Bill Rogers, how he'd let her and her brothers study in his office when they couldn't bear the thought of going home to their alcoholic mother. Pastor Rogers had even let them sleep in the sanctuary when he couldn't convince them to come stay with him and his wife. Margaret went on to earn her Bachelor's from South Bay State College and then married a heart surgeon before earning her JD from the University of Colorado, going on to become one of the first female judges in the state of Colorado.

On the night Grace Halbermann became the pastor of St. Catherine's she'd received a phone call from Margaret Wellington. They spoke candidly about Margaret's failing heart, celebrated the fact Halbermann was to be the first female pastor St. Catherine's had ever had, expressed gratitude for the path God had set both of them upon.

"Listen," Margaret said, "my husband and I had no children. Lord knows we tried. I've been very fortunate in my life and now I have no one to share these blessings with. Could you do something for me?"

At the time, Margaret's brother Raymond happened to be the mayor of Torrance. She'd already spoken to him, and he was going to pull every string, twist every arm. Margaret was going to leave her entire fortune to the church, on the condition they built a fully-staffed homeless shelter in honor of Bill Rogers. And with that, they broke ground on the Bill Rogers Homeless Sanctuary three months after Margaret's death.

Of course, Raymond lost his seat in the next election. No one wants a homeless shelter near their homes. But within a year, the Bill Rogers Sanctuary was up and running, gaining national attention for its outreach and education efforts, particularly with homeless veterans. The president had even visited the premises, praising the legacies of both Bill Rogers and the Honorable Margaret Wellington—it was a great honor.

It was three days after the Pizza Galley Shooting. Jae had spent the night sleeping in the woods behind the park, the park he'd seen Nina lying in the grass. She lay there all night, reading her book, guarded by a trio of seagulls who slept next to her on the grass. Jae sat next to the trees, watching her, making sure she wasn't cold, that she was safe. When he woke up, she was gone.

Two hours after Jae awoke, Jeff came back to the park with a brown bag and two coffee cups in a cardboard holder. He sat at the chess tables and called Jae over.

"I saw you sleeping here last night on my way home from work," said Jeff.

Jae said nothing, just stared at the empty patch of grass that contained no trace of Nina. He didn't remember falling asleep. It was the first time he'd slept in days.

"Got you some coffee. There's donuts in the bag if you want."

The coffee burned the roof of Jae's mouth, so badly he could hardly enjoy the donuts, which he devoured. He hadn't been back to Pizza Galley since the shooting. He wondered if Yu-jin was okay—if Jeoseung Saja had kept his word and spared her.

"Listen," Jeff said, "I work at this place. We give shelter to guys like you. I would've told you yesterday but you refused to come see me. Plus, I lost my shit in front of you and was kind of embarrassed to be honest. Sorry about that."

"You were sitting next to my daughter," Jae said.

"Is she still here?"

"I fell asleep. She's gone now."

Jae dropped his chin to his chest, sobbed. Jeff put his hand on Jae's shoulder, told him it was going to be okay. And then Jae realized it wasn't Jeff telling him it was okay, but Jeff's scar. *I told him about you.* What did you tell him about me? *That you knew.* Knew what? *Knew about me.* Does he know about you? *Kind of. He thinks he's going crazy.* Maybe I'm crazy. *No, you actually understand us.* I don't understand anything anymore. *Sure you do.* No, I don't.

"This scar on my face," Jeff said. "It wriggles. Did you know that? I see it in the mirror. It moves the way a worm moves its segments."

Jeff took a long drag from his cigarette. The scar pulsed as he exhaled. Jae took a bite of the last donut. The scar asked Jae to talk to Jeff, tell him what was happening, and Jae shook his head.

"I don't know why I told you that," Jeff said. "Honestly, it just came out. Forget I said anything. Sorry to freak you out."

You should tell him. I'm not going to tell him. *Why not?* Because I'm not supposed to. *How do you know that?* I just know. *But he knows about us.* No, he thinks he's losing his mind. *So do you!* Look, if he's supposed to know he'll know soon enough; it's not my job to—*But he's in pain.*

"I'm not going crazy," Jeff said.

"What?"

"You just said I think I'm losing my mind."

"I didn't say that."

"You've been muttering to yourself this whole time. I don't know the other stuff you've been saying, but I definitely heard you say, 'He thinks he's losing his mind.' "

"I should go."

"Just sit for a second, okay? Look, I work at a place called the Bill Rogers Sanctuary. It's run by the Methodist church two blocks from here. You know it?"

Jae nodded. He watched the seagulls pick at a bag of Cool Ranch Doritos. One of them finally lifted the bag by the corner and tipped it over, and its two companions began fighting over the tiny chip fragments that fell onto the grass.

"I told Pastor Grace, my boss, about you last night. She'd like for you to stop by. I told her I didn't think you would, but—I don't know man. It's up to you. Please go. She's a good person and she can help you. And you need help. I have to go now. I'm not feeling well."

Jeff got up and turned around. Jae watched the back of his shoulders jolt up, watched Jeff seize and drop to his knees. Jeff curled into a ball and began groaning, hands clamped over his face. The seagulls began screeching, beating their wings. Two of them flew away, staggering mid-flight as if caught in a tornado of some kind, as the other lay on its side, twitching with its head buried in the Doritos bag. Jae backed away as Jeff's Occupant began leaking out between his fingers.

By the time Jae stopped running, he was dizzy and completely out of breath. He fell to his knees and vomited doughy chunks of black coffee all over the sidewalk, right in front of the St. Catherine United Methodist Church.

Sports!

They'd watched the election results at Nelson's house, as they did most of everything at Nelson's house, and everyone seemed to find the returns hilarious. The men in the room especially liked watching the males cry, those bearded gender traitors who'd sacrificed their manhood in order to project a facade of virtue. They hated that facade, the men in the room. Thanks to RadFem, modern women had been taught to favor false virtue over strength. In turn, a generation of boys grew up to become weak-minded peacocks who displayed the feathers on their backsides rather than face forward like real men. To watch false virtue finally fall victim to strength, true strength, was, in the minds of all in the room, truly a sight to behold.

Blake smiled, as it was enormously satisfying to watch the smug weaklings finally put in their place, but he wasn't quite sure why his brothers applauded every time the President-Elect was onscreen. Walt backhanded Blake's chest, smiled.

"Can you believe this shit?" Walt said. "This fucking guy."

"Yeah it's pretty funny I guess. But honestly, why do we care that he won?"

Nelson put his hand on Blake's shoulder, took a sip of Glacier Ice. He rubbed Blake's head and took a seat.

"The question here is," Nelson said, "why don't you care?"

"I mean, I get it's funny to watch the cucktards cry their bitchtears, but, I mean, look at him. Look at his sons. He's not one of us, you know? If anything, he's just like them."

When Blake said "his sons," he wasn't just talking about the two weak-chinned stuffed shirts the President-Elect had sired, but also his son-in-law. In Blake's eyes, the son-in-law was the worst of the three. He looked like a sickly prince, the kind of pale, anemic weakling they'd forced beautiful princesses to wed in fairy tales, right before the rugged conqueror came to rescue her from a life of misery. This President-Elect was a slovenly narcissist who hid behind baggy suits and hair plugs. He tanned himself like a woman. Blake sipped his Glacier Cherry and watched the son-in-law on TV, his hollow bird chest, his scarecrow neck. Nelson shook his head and smiled in that way Nelson shook his head and smiled to let Blake know he just didn't get it.

"I hear you, Blake," Nelson said. "And I appreciate your thoughts. But here's the thing: you like basketball?"

"What?"

Nelson told him about his past as a high school basketball player, how much he'd loved the game when he was younger, back when it was more pure. Blake listened as Nelson told him what a great player he was before he stopped giving a shit. Nelson took another sip of his Glacier Ice.

"Anyway," Nelson said, "this president is that pasty-faced, 6'9" Power Forward—probably has a crew-cut, maybe a bit of adult acne."

Blake watched the son-in-law put his bony arms around his gorgeous wife. This was what the world had become—a place where cosmopolitan wimps like the son-in-law ended up with women like the President-Elect's beautiful daughter. Rugged conquerors were no longer heroes, but savages. Women had come to view weakness as desirable because RadFem had showed them the way to true power. A real man would never let a woman lead them around the nose the way these cucktards did. Blake watched the son-in-law smile the stupid smile of a smug fucker who'd never suffered, and all he wanted to do was pulverize that goddamn phony's face with a hammer.

"Everybody fucking hates him because he's an uncoordinated, unathletic goon," Nelson said, "but he grabs boards and throws elbows, pulls on the backs of jerseys—an absolute foul machine. And we love him because he's an agent of chaos, just like this president. Every time the other team cries about fouls under their basket, the Speaker of the House is gonna kick it to the Majority Leader for an easy, uncontested lay-up. Now, you're right. We shouldn't care about any of these cucktards, but these guys are going to salt the earth. And then men like us will be able to move in, reclaim what's owed us."

"I just don't know about this guy."

"Sometimes, half the fun of sports is watching a guy draw blood. And he's going to draw a shit-ton of blood, and the other team isn't going to know what to do about it. They're going to whine about sportsmanship, and the entire time they're whining, they're going to be losing. For me, I don't necessarily give a shit if either team wins, but I do sure as shit care who loses, and I'm gonna enjoy watching those libtards lose over and over and over again."

This reminded Blake of another conversation they'd had the day after the Pizza Galley shooting. They couldn't figure out which man was the one—it was either Bonneville or that other guy—but the brothers were convinced one of them was there to expose the Satanic pedophilia ring run by Daniel Patrick McDougal, the Papist that ran Pizza Galley.

Blake had asked if these men really worshipped Satan, and everyone had laughed.

"Yep," Nelson had said, "but they do it knowing Satan doesn't exist. They know that worshipping the devil is only going to upset decent people. They get off on it, the idea that devil worship upsets people. And I get why they think it's funny, because it is in a sick way. If what they were doing wasn't so fucking evil, I'd probably think it was funny too."

"So they do it sarcastically?" Blake had asked.

"Remember how those Nazi cocksuckers drank milk to prove racial superiority?"

"No."

"Oh, that's right—a little before your time. The white supremacist cucktards got it in their stupid heads that non-Western cultures had higher rates of lactose intolerance. It's true, by the way, white physiology does handle milk better than non-white. But anyway, they all started drinking milk in order to trigger people of color, to show them the strength of white genetics by chugging gallons of milk. It was fucking stupid, but it did its job. People lost their shit and it was admittedly kind of funny—I mean, for a bunch of Nazis. And that's what the elites are doing with all their Satan worship. It's their way of provoking us. Every time they swear allegiance to the devil, they're probably laughing under their breath."

And as he watched a man stand in front of a map of the United States, watched the man sputter as he stared at the large swaths of red, Blake wondered if Bonneville had been triggered by the Satan worship. The other man, Brightman, was there to kill his wife for cucking him, so it had to be Bonneville who'd gone in to expose the pedophilia, to save the children.

"Hey Walt," Blake said, "you think my old teacher knew about the Satan worship inside Pizza Galley?"

"What are you thinking about that for?"

"I don't know. It just came to mind."

"I think he was a patsy. Hey guys, you think Ching-Chongeville was a Pizza Galley patsy?"

"Hey man, that racist," a kid named Russell said. "Put some respect on the guy who banged Mesman's mom."

"Shut the fuck up, Russell," Blake said.

"Seriously bro," Russell said. "For an Asian dude to land a prime piece like that, how can you not put respect— "

Blake leapt on top of Russell, who was a good twenty pounds heavier than him. Russell tossed him to the carpet and slapped Blake across the neck. The brothers all jumped in and pulled them apart, making sure to get their licks in because rules had to be enforced—no one fought in Nelson's house, you took that shit outside.

"You know the rules, fellas," Nelson said. "I'll see you tomorrow."

Nelson pointed at the door. Blake and Russell headed out. Once they reached the driveway, Russell threw his arms around Blake.

"Thanks for sticking up for yourself, brother," Russell said. "I respect you as a man."

Blake returned the bear hug, and the two swung back and forth, each caught in the other's affectionate grip. These fights were never personal. The reason any of them fought one another—only open hands, no closed fists— was out of respect. Russell was his brother and sometimes, the only way to defend your brother's honor was to engage him in battle. Just a few months ago, Blake would've cowered at the thought of facing someone like Russell.

"Thanks brother," said Blake said. "I respect you as a man."

Russell kissed Blake on the temple and they let go. He rubbed the top of Blake's head. The warm residue of Russell's touch slowly cooled, dissipated from Blake's scalp. As they walked to their cars, Russell decided he'd answer Blake's question. Bonneville wasn't a patsy. The other guy, Dave Whatever, was the patsy. It was all a false flag op. Patrick McDougal knew people were getting wise to his child trafficking ring, so he needed to garner some sympathy by sending Dave Whatever in to shoot up the place. Dave Whatever being ex-military made him psychologically pliable—they brainwash soldiers in Basic Training, using the techniques the CIA perfected during MKUltra—and they flipped the switch, making him believe his wife was cucking him. Bonneville showing up to stop it was just dumb luck.

"I don't buy what everyone else says about Bonneville," Russell said. "I think he really was there to kill himself. Maybe because of your mom or something—no offense, just being honest."

"Naw man, she's not worth that."

"A man loses his job, loses his woman, what's left? Even if she's not worth it, even if your job is a shit job, it is what it is. You lose that, you got jack shit. Honestly, bro, I feel bad for the guy. Can you imagine the world crushing you so fucking low like that?"

Blake remembered Bonneville asking him about how Lisa was doing, every day before class, taunting him. It was no different from any other punk fucker asking about Lisa. How could he have fallen for it the way he had? Blake and Russell bumped fists.

"Thanks man," Blake said. "I respect your opinion."

"Hey, you really stepped it up these past few months. Proud of you. We all are."

Blake left Nelson's house and went home. He did fifty push-ups and two hundred crunches, then took a shower. Lisa was asleep in bed, stinking of wine and cigarettes. Blake touched her face one last time and then went to his room, crawled into bed.

The clock read 3:33. Blake had been in bed for over an hour. He got up, pulled out his copy of *Catcher in the Rye*, the one he'd stolen from the DuClod-Mann library, began to read the pages he'd dog-eared, passages he'd underlined. He got to chapter 24—with Mr. Antolini, and Oral Expression class, and the simple joys of digression—when a tiny envelope fell out of the dust jacket, Christmas card sent to Lisa from Mr. Bonneville. Blake had come home to find it in the mail and hidden it from her—it was nothing she needed to see. The address was for a house in Redondo Beach. Blake read the card, Mr. Bonneville's neat handwriting, asking if Lisa could think of him this arduous Holiday season the way he was thinking of her.

Arduous Holiday season?

Who even talks like that?

Bonneville, that piece of shit, that sexual pervert—Blake knew what needed to be done. He tucked the envelope back into the dustjacket, tossed the card in the trash.

He left a note for Lisa, telling her he was staying over at Walt's. He packed a bag—deodorant, toothpaste, toothbrush, hair gel, phone charger, his copy of *Catcher in the Rye*—and got into his car, and headed toward I-5.

Grit Your Eyelids and Scream

Blake pushes the turnstyle, walks into the Adult Store. He walks to the counter. A male sits behind a glass wall, smoking a cigarette, reading the newspaper. The front page is a large photo of the President-Elect, and the headline announcing his victory reads less like a declaration and more like an incredulous mutter. The entire room smells like cigarettes. Blake asks how to pay for the arcade.

"Just swipe your card," the male says.

"All right. Thanks."

"Can you believe he fucking won?"

"No. I can't believe he fucking won."

"He's gonna really shake things up, man. Just watch."

A state trooper pushes through the turnstile, doesn't acknowledge Blake's nod. He walks up to counter and holds up a picture. The male groans and shakes his head. There's been news, the trooper says—she was last seen in Medford. The male behind the counter shakes his head. The trooper tells him that it might not be a good idea to smoke indoors. The male asks if there's any law against smoking indoors. The trooper tells him that there are, in fact, laws against it, and the male snuffs his cigarette. The trooper then turns to Blake, shows him the picture. A little blonde girl named Caitlyn—her last name was some Russian or Ukrainian shit Blake couldn't pronounce—smiling innocently in her green Oregon cheerleader outfit, pom-poms held aloft by twiggy little girl arms.

"I don't know," Blake says. "I'm not from here."

"Not what I asked, sir," the trooper says.

"I've never seen her."

The trooper gives the picture to the male behind the counter, tells him to post it on the glass.

"You mean next to the other picture of her?" the male asks.

"Yes," the officer says. "Next to the other picture of her, and the one next to that. Is that all right with you?"

"Sure thing, officer."

He then leaves, tells Blake to enjoy his stay in Medford. Blake begins walking toward the booths when the male calls out to him.

"Look," he says, "we're all here to have a good time. Don't make a fucking mess, and don't piss in the trash can."

Blake enters a booth, pays for fifteen minutes. During the seven-week probationary period, every boy pledging his loyalty to the Company of Men is in no way, shape, or form allowed to masturbate. During that time, the pledge must watch porn with a group of brothers for two hours a day and then drop and give 100 push-ups. After the probationary period, you are allowed to masturbate once a week—but never to pornography. The only other sexual release must come at the hands of a woman.

After his probationary period, Blake found it very easy to abstain from masturbation. The only time he'd masturbate, every Saturday or Sunday evening, felt perfunctory, like a medical procedure, or flossing.

"Jerking off to porn is a sign of weakness," Nelson had said. "You're watching another man fuck some woman, and the only pleasure you're getting out of it is watching that other man get off. What kind of sick shit is that? Do we celebrate that man, or do we want to be that man? Do you think that man jerks off to you? Of course he doesn't. He's too busy fucking."

Mostly, when anyone in the Company of Men watched porn, it was for instructional purposes, which was why they focused their attention upon the men in the scenes, rather than the women. Porn was, to these boys, both educational, and aspirational. Because they studied these scenes the way athletes studied game film, there was no sense of shame. Because they didn't bring themselves to orgasm while watching, there was no sense of self-loathing. Admire the stubble, admire the abs, admire the way they made the girls grit their eyelids and scream.

Blake watches the scene, three men, one woman. It was dizzying, trying to keep up with the way these men maneuvered around the woman. He focuses on their serrated obliques, glistening like fish scales. He lifts his left arm, runs his hand along the side of his shirt, admires the slight bumps beneath his fingertips. The first time he'd hung out with Walt, Walt had asked him if he'd wanted to be like these men. Blake wonders when he would finally be like them. He'd built his body, sharpened his mind, strengthened his moral core—when would his time come?

What the hell is he doing here? He has a long drive ahead of him. Why is he wasting time like this? He slaps himself in the face, again, then again. That goddamn phony, the one who'd pretended to care about him just to get into Lisa's pants, he had to confront him. Blake had to show him the man he'd become. He has no idea what he's going to do when they meet, but it has to happen. Think of all the children Bonneville has led astray. Did he pretend to care about them as well? Why did he do it? And the children from the

Pizza Galley, how did Bonneville know they were being held in the basement? Russell was wrong—Bonneville knew something and Blake knows this in his heart. He knows it. What if Bonneville had known the entire time he and Blake had known each other, but did nothing because he was too busy screwing Lisa? Guys like Bonneville always took advantage of Lisa. She usually dated morons, so when a smart one like Bonneville, like his father, came along, she lost her wits. Bonneville probably made her feel smart and special, the way Jan Mesman had—of course she was easy pickings. All women were easy pickings for guys like that. Guys with their money and their fancy knowledge—guys like Blake didn't stand a chance in the world as it was, a world that crushed him so fucking low like this.

Blake stands up and leaves the booth, shoves his way out the turnstile. He walks to his car and removes his copy of *Catcher in the Rye*, walks over to the garbage can. He pulls out the envelope that once contained the Christmas card sent by Mr. Bonneville, and then tosses the book in the trash.

Everything Ends the Way It's Supposed to End

Jae found himself at his old kitchen table. He looked at his fingernails, clipped and clean, looked down at his black SDSU sweatshirt. He brought the sleeve up to his nose, snorted the crispness of fabric softener. The kitchen looked exactly as he'd left it four years ago—white kitchen cabinets with glass doors, the old green countertops he'd always promised to replace, the white Samsung refrigerator he'd bought two weeks before running away—he touched his smooth face, ran his palm along his cheek over and over. He'd forgotten what being clean-shaven had felt like. The fridge was full of take-out boxes— Chinese food, spaghetti and garlic bread clam-shelled in Styrofoam, an uneaten McDonalds Filet-O-Fish next to a Happy Meal box—it all seemed so wasteful. Miri and Nina would never fully appreciate a home-cooked meal the way he did. He'd always told Nina he was willing to play dumb, as Miri hated McDonalds, as long as she didn't bring it home. Maybe Miri's attitude had changed in the time he was gone. What kind of grown woman still eats Happy Meals? Jae chuckled and closed the refrigerator.

The note on the refrigerator door read, *Dentist Appt 4 Jae, 230pm DO NOT FORGET TO BRUSH YOUR TEETH*. Miri's beautiful handwriting, so small and precise, the doublecase "*a*" seen in typeface, rather than the simple D'Nealian single story "*a*" used for handwriting. Jae had lost four teeth in the years he'd been away. He wasn't looking forward to this visit.

Nina came home from work, some textbook company in Santa Clara. He didn't know much about it, but how wonderful was it that she'd cleaned up her act and gone back to finish school? When he'd left, she was working at a sushi restaurant outside San Pedro Square. The entire time he'd been away, he'd hoped she'd find it in herself to go back to school. He asked her how her day was and she shrugged—some things stayed constant.

She opened the refrigerator and grabbed the Happy Meal. She tossed the plastic toy on the dining table and pulled out the cheeseburger. Jae sat at the table, listened to the crinkle of the wrapper. He asked if he could have the Filet-O-Fish and she asked what Mom would say.

"She'll probably assume you ate it," he said.

He bit into the Filet-O-Fish. He'd never had one cold. While living on the streets, he'd eaten a lot of McDonalds, mostly given to him by mothers who'd pitied him, and there was something wonderful about eating this fish sandwich out of his own refrigerator, the refrigerator he'd purchased two weeks before his Occupant left his body, a fish sandwich his daughter had purchased because her eyes, as Miri liked to say, had always been bigger than her stomach.

"Hey Dad, can I ask you something? You ever wonder what would've happened had Old Hwang married off his sons? Like is there an alternate universe where Hwang was right, that he was supposed to live until he married off his sons?"

Nina finally took a seat at the table. She'd always had a habit of eating standing up. Miri had always told her not to do it, something about it being bad for digestion. Of course, Nina and Jae had always laughed about that notion—people eat standing up all the time—but Miri had insisted she'd read it in a health magazine. Jae thought about the question, an alternate universe where Hwang Hyun-soo's seven virgin sons came to him and he told them about his dream, that Jeoseung Saja had spared him so that he may see them married off. It seemed so implausible, but only because he'd never considered any other outcome.

"I doubt it," he said. "The story ended the way it's supposed to end. There really could've been no other outcome."

"I don't know about that. I always felt bad for his sons, that they died because of him."

"You shouldn't feel bad. They didn't die because of him. They died because it was their time to go."

"But that's not how the story works, is it? It clearly sets up this idea that they died because he was a coward who needed to suffer."

"He was already suffering because no one wanted to marry them."

"Yeah, because he was a coward."

Jae gazed out the kitchen window, into the back yard. The tool shed was in bad shape, paint flaking away like birch bark, and the lawn was pocked with mangy brown spots.

"Exactly," he said. "That was his curse."

"No, the story says that's what he thought his curse was, meaning his real curse was being haunted by his dead sons. That means their death was his punishment."

"But death doesn't come as punishment. Death comes because it's time to die."

"Then what's the point of that story? If he wasn't being punished at the end because he sucked and there's no moral to it, then what's the point?"

"It's just a sad story about a man who misunderstood why death came to see him."

"So then do you think death came to see the sons?"

"Of course he did. They died, didn't they."

"No, I mean, did Jeoseung Saja visit them the way he visited Old Hwang?"

Nina's face warped, as if her nose were the eye of a storm, sucking her mouth, her eyes, into the vortex. Her entire face fell victim to Coriolis effect, sucked down the hole, replaced by a new version of her face.

"The story doesn't say," he said.

"But did Jeoseung Saja visit them individually, or did he visit them altogether as a group?"

The kitchen floor buckled and rolled like water. The dishes stacked in the cabinet, rattled and clinked. Nina asked him if he was okay. He told her he was fine—it was just another episode.

"That's not the story, Nina."

"Not for us, but what if there's a world where the story ends with all his sons marrying and then he redeems himself before he dies?"

"How could he redeem himself?"

"I don't know. He finds a way."

"This is the world. There is no other version of the story. Everything ends the way it's supposed to end."

Ready

help

Syntax error

"Dad?"

Ready

test

Syntax error

"Dad are you okay?"

Ready

dir

Syntax error

"Dad?"

```
*** STOP: 0x000007E
(0xc000005,0xF88FF190,0x0xF897BA0,0xF89758A0)
```

"Dad? Hey, Dad. Hey. Hey."

How come right when something amazing is about to happen, you always wake up?

Accidents Happen All the Time

Jae awoke on a cot inside the Bill Rogers Sanctuary, surrounded by other homeless men, some without their Occupants, others with distended bellies, and faces, and forearms which screamed for Jae to help them. He stood up and made his way to the door. His hand was inches away from the handle, which turned as if willed by force. He recoiled as the door opened. A tiny gray-haired woman, Jae assumed they were around the same age, stood in the doorway.

"Hello," she said. "My name's Grace. Are you okay?"

"I need to go," Jae told her. "I want to see my daughter."

"Oh, is she waiting for you?"

"She's in San Jose."

"We could call her if you'd like."

"No. Thank you for your generosity but I should get going."

Grace put her hand on his shoulder, looked into his eyes. The Occupant swam beneath the skin of her forehead. *Hey you should stay. She doesn't have much longer and the next bus to San Jose doesn't leave for another five hours. You have plenty of time. Get something to eat. You can shower here. Get a fresh change of clothes. Do you really want Miri and Nina to see you like this? Look at you. You're disgusting.*

"You're right," Jae said. "I could use a shower."

"I can make sure you get one. Can you stay and get something to eat? You got really sick outside and I'm sure you're stomach's pretty empty."

Jae's stomach sounded like a balloon rubbed against human skin. He winced as it compressed and churned. Jeff's donuts were the first food he'd had since the shooting—no, he'd had a chicken strips and tater tots the morning after. Nina—no, not Nina—some young woman had handed it to him, apologizing because it had sat in the car overnight. Even so, he was fully aware of starving. Grace smiled, put her hand on his shoulder. He looked into her eyes and she smiled.

"Okay. I can stay for breakfast. Then maybe a shower."

He sat in the dining hall with a group of mostly men, a few mothers with their children. He focused on the men, men he'd seen around singing in the parking lot of gas stations, sleeping behind shuttered strip malls, weeping as they asked him why their Occupants left them. Every door and window was opened wide, fans placed strategically throughout the room. He thought of

Lucinda, the homeless woman who used to stand in front of the Rite Aid near his home, how every time he'd seen her inside, she was parked in front of the Thrifty Ice Cream dip cabinet, the glass display case that held tubs of ice cream. Nina was around five at the time. Lucinda always made sure to buy a scoop of strawberry ice cream. Not for herself, but for the little boy who helped push her cart, carry her things. He'd always made sure Nina avoided that Rite Aid, making her wait in the car, doors locked, safely hidden behind tinted windows, any time he had to go inside.

"Too many kids here," Jae said.

"Yes," Grace said. "It's really sad. We do what we can."

Jae took a bite of scrambled egg. He could already feel the coming heartburn from the orange juice. He saw a little girl, no older than four, sitting on her mother's lap, chewing a piece of toast. The last time he saw Lucinda, her little boy had dropped his ice cream on the pavement. It wasn't his fault, the scoop just fell off. Jae told them not to move, ran inside to get another scoop for the boy. When he came out, they were gone, although he didn't look too hard for them.

The entire drive home, he stared at Nina in the rearview, licking the ice cream cone—the distinct joy of a child with an ice cream cone—and he never understood why he'd hated himself the way he had in that moment.

"Why do they let these people keep their kids?" Jae asked

"I don't understand, Jae. Why wouldn't they?"

"We just don't take care of people is all."

"You're right. But I don't see how that's the fault of the parents."

Jae watched the little girl chew on her toast. He used to tell Nina not to chew with her mouth open. His father-in-law would tell him to relax, that this was how little kids ate. Wasn't it enough she was enjoying the food? When they got home from the Rite-Aid, Miri had gotten upset at the strawberry stains on Nina's shirt. How could he buy her ice cream when they were about to eat dinner?

"Are you the gentleman Jeff was telling me about?" Grace said.

"I don't think he's doing so well right now."

"He's not, oddly enough. He called a bit ago to tell us he's feeling under the weather. I hope he's okay."

"It's different for everyone."

"What do you mean?"

Three days after Miri had gotten upset about the ice cream, Jae saw Lucinda's face on the news. She'd been killed in a hit and run right outside a trailer park. The suspect had left her on the side of the street, didn't even stop to check on the woman she'd hit on the way to the golf course. Jae knew this woman, the suspect, from the driving range. Her name was Jana, a doctor of some kind, on the younger side, drove a Turquoise Jeep Cherokee with a Stanford Medicine bumper sticker. She'd always been very friendly and engaging—Jae had often wondered how a sweet, pretty girl like her was still single. Nina had once asked Jana if she was a princess, and she'd smiled and given Nina her sunglasses. Jae couldn't believe the smug cruelty of Dr. Jana Sensenbacher's mugshot, couldn't believe Lucinda Thomas from Coalinga was only thirty-two years old, as Lucinda looked at least ten years older than Jana, who was only thirty-six. Miri would never know why Jae had cried and raged at the television, never know that Jae wasn't crying over Lucinda's death or how the young doctor had the tiniest smirk in her mugshot—he wasn't even crying over Lucinda's boy, whose whereabouts were unknown—but over the memory of Nina humming "Under the Sea" to herself, ice cream dripping down her chin, asking him if they could have Thrifty ice cream every day.

"Jae," Grace said, "can I tell you something?"

"Of course."

"I'm a firm believer God has a plan for all of us."

"What's his plan for me?"

"Apparently, it's getting you home to San Jose."

"That's not God."

"Maybe not. But you being here, the day after Jeff told me about you, finding you passed out right in front of our parking lot. That doesn't seem to be accidental, does it?"

"I'm not exactly understanding what you mean."

"You run into Jeff Logan, who tells me about you, then we find you passed out right outside our doors, just as I was wondering if Jeff had happened upon you on his way home from work. That's pretty amazing, if you ask me."

"I ate coffee and donuts after not having had a decent meal in days. I ran for some reason, and then threw up. That I did it at your doorstep was just an accident."

"I don't believe that. I don't believe in accidents."

The little girl finished her toast, smiled at Jae, opened and closed her fingers at him—Nina used to wave like that. He remembered when Nina was that age, how much she'd loved eating, how she used to call for French fries in her sleep. Did this little girl cry for French fries in her sleep? What sort of accident was this girl's life—being born to a mother who couldn't support her? What sort of accident brought Lucinda Thomas from Coalinga to San Jose, led her to step in front of Jana Sensenbacher's Jeep Cherokee? What sort of accident caused the scoop of strawberry to fall from that cone?

"My ex-husband was a psychiatrist, just retired three months ago. He said my so-called problem is called apophenia: finding patterns and meanings in otherwise unconnected and meaningless things. He used to always joke that it was a precursor to schizophrenia, that apophenia was what drove conspiracy nuts to find patterns in things that were totally unconnected. Whenever I'd get like this, he used to ask me if Elvis had hidden behind the grassy knoll. He was never as funny as he thought he was. Anyway, I think it's normal for people to make connections, to think that everything is part of some greater meaning. God's plan, so to speak."

"Maybe so, but I could've thrown up and passed out anywhere. That I stopped where I did was just dumb luck".

"Something led you to stop here and I don't think it's just dumb luck. And I don't believe in accidents, but I do believe in consequences. You already said you had coffee and donuts after not having a decent meal in days. Then you ran for some reason, which led to you throwing up. Right in front of our building. That chain of events led you here. May I ask why you were running? The fellas out front said you looked scared."

Jae tried to shake the memory of Jeff writhing in the grass, holding his face as if someone had thrown acid on him. He told Grace he'd rather not say. She nodded and told him she understood, asked him to think about what they'd discussed, told him if he wanted to call his daughter, to come see her or any of the staff. Jae showered and grabbed a change of clothes from the portable garment racks in the changing room. He couldn't stop smelling himself, wanting to make sure he didn't stink when he finally saw Miri and Nina. On his way out, Jae stopped and stared at the broken beer bottle glittering on the other side of the parking lot. He made his way to the sidewalk, glanced over at the shattered glass.

The white graffiti under the shards, read GOD IS A WHITE MAN.

Let It All Burn

Blake listens to the audiobook in his car, a book Walt had told him to read. It was his one sneaky indulgence, this audiobook. The Company of Men viewed audiobooks as intellectual surrender—*I lack the moral discipline to read things myself, so why don't you just tell me the story?*—but he didn't have time to read the book, and Walt had been bugging him for a full year now, asking if he'd read the book. As far as Blake was concerned, it was unabridged, and at least he wasn't masturbating or drinking alcohol, or smoking cigarettes. Besides, so many of them smoked weed—of course, not Nelson—and he gets that weed is natural, that the Founding Fathers used to grow it, but it all seemed so hypocritical. Blake was still only coming once a week. A lot of the others would pay for lap dances in order to ensure weekly masturbation wasn't their only outlet for joy. On the scale of transgressions, an audio reading of a Pulitzer Prize winning book seemed mild compared to the degeneracy of lap dances.

Blake stares at Mt. Shasta through his windshield, notices the smaller mountain off on the side called Black Butte, wonders if anyone else thinks it looks like a broken molar. He laughs as the protagonist, a portly New Orleans hot dog vendor who sees the world for all its ridiculousness, reads from his journal. It feels good to actually enjoy a novel—he had no idea literature could be so funny. Sure, his teachers loved cackling their way through Shakespeare and Chaucer, but were those really actually funny? And the few students who'd laughed, the ones people like Bonneville genuinely liked, only seemed to do so in order to feel smarter than the rest of the class. They'd explain the jokes, talk about the clever wordplay and Blake often wondered what it might feel like to punch those kids in the throat.

Blake remembers Tobias Kuykendahl, the kid from Salt Lake City who'd shot all the classmates on his kill list before shooting himself in the head. The shooting had happened during the Fall of Blake's junior year, back when he was still at DuClod-Mann. At the time, Blake had identified with Kuykendahl, both being of Dutch descent, both not only having been misunderstood, but suffering through the pain of other people refusing to understand. Blake would spend the day after the shooting sneaking up behind other kids and whispering *shooter* into their ears. It had all been a joke, but no one seemed to understand why it was funny. Even Blake didn't quite get why it was funny— he just knew it was. By the end of third period, word had gotten out that Blake was doing this, and a kid named Samuel McMasters broke his jaw, even though Blake hadn't whispered in his ear. The next day in the Principal's office, Mr. Birkenstein asked him to explain himself, and then repeat himself, to slow down, try to enunciate, as his jaw had been wired shut. Mr. Birkenstein had finally had enough.

"Blake," Mr. Birkenstein had said, "if you have to explain a joke, then it isn't very funny."

But Blake hadn't been trying to explain the joke. There was no explaining the joke, only that it had made him laugh, that it had brought him joy. Blake sits in the car, listening to the protagonist's journal entry, wondering if perhaps Shakespeare's jokes were like the joke he'd whispered after the Kuykendahl Shooting—a mystery you either get or you don't. Blake stares at the broken tooth that is Black Butte and thinks about the Kuykendahl Shooting, which was so clearly inspired by *Catcher in the Rye*, it wasn't even funny. It was so obvious. How could everyone miss that?

Blake had once read about how the pity we'd felt for others was just a projection of our own self-pity, and that had made sense during the time of the shooting, as he was just as weak and pathetic as Kuykendahl had been. But hadn't he changed? Wasn't he a stronger, better man? Nelson had once said there comes a time in every man's life when he must let the bad things burn in order to keep the good. Hadn't he done that? Why waste time thinking about Tobias Kuykendahl?

After watching the porn, after getting high, after dinner with Lisa, Walt and Blake drove out to the woods, came to a clearing where they set the People Shooting Hat on the dirt. Walt doused it in gasoline. The flames whooshed as the match hit the fuel.

"Sorry about your hat, man," Walt said.

"It's weird, but I kinda don't give a shit anymore."

"Yeah man. That book's a piece of shit anyway."

"Why do you think that?"

"It's for babies. Once you realize that, you start to see what a pile of crap it is."

They stomped out the fire and then drove to Walt's place, where he lived with his uncle Nelson. Nelson was a tall man, muscles and tattoos—he looked like a comic book villain, with his shaved head and black beard. He told Blake to remove his shirt, which he did after Walt insisted.

"Build out your chest and shoulders and go down a pant size," Nelson said. "Then we'll talk."

Nelson told Blake to put his shirt back on. They sat and drank black coffee while Walt told Nelson what had happened with the bullies. Nelson shook his head. Blake had seen enough disgust in his life to recognize it on Nelson's face, but there was also something else, something Blake had initially thought was pity, but would later come to see was compassion.

"So you can't fight for yourself, huh?" said Nelson.

"No, sir."

"It's okay. It isn't your fault. A lot of kids your age don't know how anymore. There used to a lot more bullies in the world before we got so feminized. Now they're so few and far between, kids like you have no proving grounds. It's sad."

Blake thought about how he'd seen bullies his entire life. He wondered where this place was, where bullies were few and far between, but said nothing. If Nelson was right, if Blake had been on the proving grounds, he'd failed, and he didn't want Walt to know he'd failed—even though he suspected Walt had already known.

"So what exactly did these kids do?" Nelson asked.

"They spit in my People Shooting Hat."

Walt leaned over and whispered in Nelson's ear. Nelson said, "Oh, that," and nodded. They took Blake into the garage, and taught him how to spot on the bench press. Then they laid him on the bench and made him press eighty pounds. During the second rep, Blake's arms gave out, and the steel bar pressed against his breastbone. He called for help. Nelson leaned over, cupped his hands under the bar.

"I'm forty-four goddamn years old, Blake," Nelson said. "You have no excuse. Pick that shit up. No excuses."

Blake looked up to see Walt and Nelson looking down at him. He could feel the blood rushing to his head.

"I'm not making excuses," Blake croaked. "I just can't pick this up. It's my first time."

"Come on, man," Walt said. "Just push through."

"You know what your problem is?" Nelson asked. "You're weak. And as much as I pity you right now, you need to toughen up. Do you want to be like all the other boys in your school? Do you really want to be like those little fuckers?"

At the time, Blake wanted to be like each and every one of those fuckers. He wanted to be confident, have lots of friends. He wanted teachers to get off his case, to say hi to him in the halls and pat him on the back. He wanted girls to notice him—not go out on dates or anything like that—just notice him. He wanted to know how to talk to them, to know what sorts of things they liked to talk about, to know why they didn't pay attention to kids like him. And then Blake watched flecks of spit, his spit land on Nelson's smiling face. His arms quivered as they pushed the bar off his chest.

"That's right," Nelson said. "Only bitches quit. Are you a bitch?"

"No. Fuck no."

The bar clanged as it dropped onto the rack. Blake tried to sit up, but stumbled off the bench and onto the floor. His eyes tingled. Nelson and Walt helped him to his feet. Walt slapped him on the back.

"I'm gonna throw up," Blake said.

"Puke in my gym and I'll beat your ass," Nelson told him.

They sat on the concrete floor. Nelson pulled out a Gatorade from the mini fridge, told Blake to drink. He'd eventually get used to the taste of Glacier Cherry, and although he'd never admit it, he'd actually come to prefer it to Glacier Ice. Then Nelson told Blake about the counterculture, and all it had done to damage American men. He tied it back to *Catcher in the Rye*, the book breaking down societal structures through its mistrust of adults and parents, how the book helped weaken family bonds—the way all 60's youth culture had.

"They've slowly eroded our values," Nelson said, "until we were left with this. The world used to belong to men like us. But the males gave it away, piece by piece. In the old days, they worshipped soldiers, and laborers—real men. Books like yours made it so people sitting in their rooms, staring their bellybuttons, took everything men like us built."

Nelson got up, told Blake to come back tomorrow, that they'd work on his arms and back. He told them good night, said he was going to take a shower, to lock up when they left.

Blake sat in the garage with Walt and talked about the things Nelson had said, what it had all meant—the difference between males, who were mewling subhuman trash, and men, true men; how RadFem had indoctrinated women into making the wrong choices in life, how that had led to the date rape epidemic; how Bonneville's stupid book had filled young boys with a sense of hopelessness, how adolescent males aspired to be the whiny simp from the book, instead of the handsome jocks the simp had derided as phony.

Blake pulls over to stare at Black Butte. He sits in the car and lights a cigarette—a menthol, which The Company of Men smoked for ironic reasons. Four crows pick at a deflated deer carcass, their beaks rhythmically pecking through the exposed rib cage like hammers hitting piano stings. He stares into the deer's eyes, and it's as if the deer is staring back, and wonders if this was how the deer looked when hit by whatever car ran it over. He wonders if these eyes are those of a creature stuck in the moment of instantaneous death or those trapped in the final moment of suffering. It all feels so intrusive, like the time he caught Lisa and Mr. Bonneville in the supply closet, the way his eyes locked with Lisa's, how after that moment, the eyes from that exact moment were the only ones he'd see whenever he saw her face.

The audio book describes a photo of a naked woman sitting on the edge of a desk, her face obscured by a book, a pornographic photo that distresses the portly hot dog vendor. He turns off the stereo and smokes his cigarette, the crows hammering into the carcass, oily bits of pink flesh scattering onto the gravel.

When he sat with his brothers, watching the election coverage in Nelson's house, Walt had turned to him, smiling, repeating the phrase, *Let it all burn down*. It was something they'd always said to one another, and something Blake had always thought about even before meeting Walt and the Company of Men. Let it all burn down. Destroy everything, and then rebuild. Maybe then, the world would be a fair place.

The hot dog vendor had a notion, degeneracy would lead to peace. He had a plan: infiltrate the government and military with flamboyant homosexuals. These men would be too busy preening and fucking to start wars. They'd settle differences through orgies. They'd put on ballets and Broadway musicals in order to boost morale. The hot dog vendor, being a wise and educated man, would advise them and help shape policy. Only then would the world truly be a peaceful place.

Blake found that passage hysterical, soldiers in tight-fitting uniforms with sequins and feathers, so impressed with one another's appearance, they'd have no time for actual battle. Degeneracy would lead to peace. It was a nice thought, and for the first time since the election, Blake feels pretty good about the outcome. Burn it all down. Destroy everything, and then rebuild. Maybe then, the world could be a fair place.

He turns the ignition, let's the engine run. The crows hardly seem to notice.

Take the Fucking Yo-yo and Get Out of My Face

Vince pulls the car into a trailer park outside of Palm Springs, two miles outside the Marine base. Once Vince cuts the engine, the desert heat chokes the climate control out of the car and every time Brian takes a breath, it's like he's breathing through a space heater. A shirtless boy sits in a white kiddie pool stained with dirt. He stares at the four Harleys parked next to the pool and begins hyperventilating. Vince tells him to call down.

"How am I supposed to calm down?" Brian says. "We're short. You don't think Chavo's gonna notice that?"

"We're not short man," Vince says. "We're just not bringing what we normally do. We don't owe these guys anything."

"Yeah man," Nick says. "It just means they're not gonna pay as much. That's all. Just relax, okay."

They get out of the car, and Brian clutches the black gym bag to his chest. He can already feel the zipper cooking in the sun. A man everyone called Beertruck comes out of the doublewide—shirtless, his smooth white belly like a boiled dumpling—chugging a Budweiser. He belches, then wipes his mouth with the back of his hand and smiles at Brian.

"Hey there, Smurfies," Beertruck says.

He crouches next to the little boy in the pool, kisses him on the top of the head, points at Brian and his friends.

"Look at those Smurfies, Colt. You ever see three cute little Smurfies in your life?"

The boys approach the trailer and Beertruck groans as he rises to his feet, tells the boys to never get old.

"Chavo around?" Vince says.

"Only if you got something," Beertruck says.

"We do," Bryan says.

He hands the bag to Beertruck, who unzips it and looks inside. He walks into the trailer with the bag. Brian watches the little boy, Colt, laze in the pool. He can see Colt's white scalp through the wet, matted hair. Vince glares at Colt, who doesn't seem to notice.

"Hey, Colt," Brian says. "How's life?"

"Uncle Beertruck took me to the Dinosaur Museum."

"That's awesome, man. You like dinosaurs?"

"You're twelve years old," Vince mutters. "Haven't you outgrown that shit yet?"

Brian glares at Vince. Beertruck opens the screen door, motions for them to come inside. Brian tells Colt it was nice talking to him. Vince tells him not to talk to the kid anymore. Brian tells him he's sorry.

The inside of the trailer is a mess, crushed beer cans and Legos scattered all over the tiled floor. It reeks of cigarettes. There's a stack of pizza boxes next to the garbage can, which is empty, save the used condom clinging inside the cylinder like one of those rubber octopus wall crawlers found in vending machines outside of drug stores. Corey Stephenson stands in the kitchen smoking a cigarette with Black Derrick. Brian walks over and gives her a hug. She kisses him on the cheek, tells him he's becoming a handsome young man. Black Derrick says they should jump him in. Everyone laughs.

"Hi, Vincent," Corey shouts.

"Hello, Corey," Vince says.

"You say hi to Colt?"

"Nope."

"Boy, you better straighten up," Black Derrick says. "Show your mom and your little brother some kindness."

Brian has known Corey and Vince Stephenson for most of his life. She'd come with Vince to the Church of the New Millennium when Brian was four, looking to start a new life with her six-year-old son. They'd come to Lanai in order to escape Dennis "the Menace" Stephenson, Vince's father, one of the most feared enforcers in the Legion of Blood, an outlaw biker gang that had all but cornered the drug trade in east Riverside County. On September 8, 2000, three days before Cary Bonneville had predicted the End Times, Corey and Vince were kidnapped on the streets of Lanai by a group specializing in deprogramming cult members. The Legion of Blood had paid for the group's services, each member setting money aside in order to help Dennis get his family back. Three weeks after reuniting with his family, Dennis was told by a specialist he had three months left to live. According to the Legion of Blood, Dennis was completely at peace.

"It was like he was ready to die, knowing you guys were safe," Black Derrick had told Vince one night.

According to Vince, however, Dennis became increasingly resentful toward his mother, berating Corey for stealing his son, for robbing him of the proper time needed to mold Vince into a man. Vince ran away three days before Dennis passed. By the time Vince came home, after a stint in San Diego

Juvenile Detention Facility for assault, Colt had already been born. No one was quite sure who the father was, but it didn't seem to matter in the long run. Everyone treated Colt as their own, just as they'd always tried with Vince.

Chavo sits on a blue sectional, watching women's tennis on a 32" plasma screen, stroking the purple hair of some young girl in cutoffs who was laying on his lap. His other hand rests on the black gym bag Brian had given to Beertruck. The bottoms of her bare feet are filthy. Brian notices the orange koi tattooed on her thigh, until a look from Chavo reminds him not to notice such things. Chavo taps the girl on the head, and she gets up and makes her way out of the trailer. Brian and his friends take a seat on the couch. Beertruck stands behind the couch, his belly resting between Brian and Nick's heads.

"What happened?" Chavo says.

"Our guy in Needles got pinched," Vince says. "Was a bit of a dead end. We still got about twelve-hundred in there."

"Twelve-hundred my ass," Chavo says. "This is nine, maybe ten, tops."

"No, we counted that shit. There's fucking twelve in there. It's not my fault the cocksucker got pinched."

"Hey," Black Derrick says from the kitchen. "Watch your language around your mother."

Vince glares at Black Derrick. Corey raises her hand, stopping Black Derrick in his tracks. She takes him by the hand and they go into the room all the way at the end of the hall. It always amazed Brian the way Vince talked to Chavo, the way Chavo tolerated Vince talking to him in that way. He knew if he'd ever spoken out of turn like that, Palm Springs PD would find his body washed up on the shore of Lake Hemet.

"You look like your pops when you get pissy," Chavo says. "I loved that man like a brother, but man when he got that bug up his ass about the tiniest things."

Chavo laughs. Beertruck slams his palms on Brian and Nick's shoulders, laughs with Chavo. Brian jumps, but only because Nick did. He tells himself it wouldn't have been so startling had he not seen Nick flinch first. Chavo stops laughing, looks up at the ceiling.

"Fucking Dennis the Menace," Chavo says. "Beautiful man, your pops. I'll give you fifteen."

"Seriously?" Vince says.

"It's a going-away present. Me and your mom were talking. This isn't the life your pops wanted for you, not the life he'd want for Colt."

"Colt's not his fucking kid. He wouldn't give a shit."

Brian smells the weed coming down the hall. The barefoot girl comes back inside, leans against the wall. The koi on her thigh curled in a backward C, its mouth practically kissing her inner thigh.

"Doesn't matter, Vinnie. I never felt right about you Smurfing. None of us did. We been carrying your sorry ass for too long."

"This is bullshit, man."

"It is what it is, little brother. You, your friends, you're out. We find out you've been Smurfing for some other cook. . . ."

Chavo looks to the girl on the wall, motions with his head. She walks down the hall, knocks on the door. The door opens and then closes.

". . . Man, I better not find out you hooked up with anyone else. Matter of fact, I'm gonna make a few calls. You even start sniffing around, you can watch your friends get killed on sight."

Nick's hands begin shaking. Brian taps Nick's thigh, tells him it'll be all right. Beertruck begins kneading Nick's shoulder with his hand, and Brian looks up. Beertruck winks.

"So because Mommy says she finally gives a shit, you're gonna just cut me out? Over her?"

"What are you," Chavo says, "thirty-one? Thirty-two? You've done nothing with your life. That's my fault. We promised your pops we'd take care of you, and I fucked that up. We felt bad for you, so we kicked a little money your way here and there, gave you odd jobs to do, but we did you wrong."

"Your pops loved you," Beertruck says.

"You hardly knew him," Vince says.

"Don't get fresh, little fella," Beertruck says. "I don't wanna make your mom cry over you, but I will."

Chavo glares at Beertruck, who crosses his arms, rests them on top of his belly. Vince clenches his jaw, narrows his eyes, pulls out a cigarette and lights it. His leg shakes so hard, Brian can feel it through the couch.

"It's time to grow up now," Chavo says. "We been kicking the can down the road, and we need to stop that shit cold. You wanna go to some kind of trade school, I'll pay for that shit with my own money. Go be a mechanic or something, man. Be a good role model for your brother."

"Can we get another 2K?" Vince says. "Give us that and I'll consider it."

"What are you doing, Vince?" Chavo says.

"Don't mean to speak out of turn," Beertruck says, "but this reminds me of a story."

Beertruck puts his hands on the back of the couch, leans forward. He and Chavo lock eyes. The couch shakes from Vince's leg. Chavo nods and leans back into the couch.

"I used to work at Pizza Galley when I was a kid, Beertruck says. You've all been to Pizza Galley—remember how they used to give you tickets for every game you played?"

Beertruck waits for everyone to nod. Vince takes a long drag from his cigarette, blows smoke into the air, flicks the ashes into a Harley Davidson ashtray already heaping with butts.

"Anyway, kids loved those tickets. It was like you were getting rewarded for playing games. They loved those tickets until they didn't, and they stopped loving those tickets when the time came to cash out. You get hundreds of goddamn tickets and you think to yourself, 'Holy shit. I'm gonna use these to get that PlayStation,' when in reality all you can probably get is a fucking Calico Jacqueline keychain or some stupid inflatable sword if you were lucky. Anyway, long story short, any time those little brats complained about what their tickets were worth, I'd say, 'Did you have a good time? Yeah? Then take the fucking yo-yo and get out of my face.'"

The room falls silent and Beertruck crosses his arms. What does this even mean? Is he saying everyone should be grateful for the money they're getting and leave? That was probably what he was saying, but Brian can't help but wonder how relevant Beertruck's story actually is. The tickets were a scam, just another way to incentivize children to play more games. What did that have to do with Vince needing to grow up and live the life of a responsible citizen? It didn't make sense at all.

"Hey Beertruck," Nick says, "can I ask you something?"

"Sure thing, little brother."

"All that stuff about Pizza Galley and the pedophiles—is that true?"

"Fuck no. Jesus Christ, man. When did we get so retarded that we believe everything we read on the internet? Were you even listening to my story? I was trying to make a goddamn point. Asshole."

Corey stumbles down the hall, takes a seat on the couch. She grabs Vince's hand, kisses it. The living room fills with the sound of Black Derrick and the barefoot girl having sex. Chavo sends Beertruck into the kitchen. He comes back with a stack of bills, tosses it into Vince's lap.

"I think it's time for you to go now," Chavo says. "Call me when you're ready to grow up."

I Guess This Is Goodbye

Jae sat on the bus stop bench at Hawthorne and Lomita, watched the sunset. He had no idea how he'd gotten there, or how he'd spent his day since leaving the Bill Rogers Sanctuary—all he knew was the sun was setting behind the empty Democratic call center that was once a toy store. He hadn't even given much thought to what Grace Halbermann had said about the nature of fate and destiny, and seeking connections people said weren't really there, even though they were. Or maybe he had. He couldn't really remember.

After the sun finally sank into the horizon, he watched as people pumped gas, their skin powdered blue by the LED lights hanging over the pumps. Some of the people pumping gas had Occupants that spoke out to him, others didn't bother speaking out at all. What did it matter at this point? He was going home. Back to Miri, and Nina, and their tempered glass cabinets, their sun-damaged tool shed, the ugly green tiles on the countertops. He promised to spend whatever time he had left with his family, if they'd even have him back.

Jeff stepped out of a black Honda Accord. Jae tried to turn away before he was noticed, but it was too late. Jeff made his way from the pump to the bus stop, took a seat at the bench. They stared at the empty call center.

"Are you okay?" Jae asked.

"That used to be a toy store," Jeff said. "My family owned it."

"I heard the owner of the building jacked up the rent," Jae said. "I'm sorry that happened."

The palm trees flapped as the wind picked up. Jae could only see the right side of Jeff's face. Without the scar, it was a kind and gentle face, a patient one. Jeff smiled. He had sad eyes when he smiled, as if the mere act of showing joy had made him wince at the same time.

"We actually made out fine," Jeff said. "The smartest thing my dad ever did was marry into money. Honestly, he was ready to retire anyway."

"It must've been nice, being a kid who owned a toy store."

"It was amazing. I was like a kid in a candy shop, except the candy shop was filled with toys."

Jeff turned to Jae and laughed like a man who hadn't laughed in quite some time. It was a tentative laugh, as if he was out of practice. Jae laughed as well, just to show him what laughter could sound like. Jeff began to cough from all the laughter, and Jae patted his back until he recovered his breath.

"Waiting for the bus, huh?"

"I want to go home."

"What if you don't make it?"

"I might not."

An elderly woman in a red tracksuit stopped at the bench with her tiny white dog. She asked Jeff if he remembered her, Susan Ontiveros, who'd gone to school with his mother. He told her that of course he remembered her, asked how her son was doing. Julio was doing fine, she told him, was working as a hospital administrator in San Antonio, had two little girls, pulled out her phone to show him pictures. Jeff smiled and told her he was glad to hear it. Before leaving, she thanked him for his service, told him how wonderful it was that brave young men like him had served this country. He nodded as she walked away.

"You don't like that, do you?" Jae said. "People thanking you for your service."

"It's not her fault. No one really knows what else to say."

"But you'd prefer it if they said nothing."

"That would actually be better for me."

A woman came out of the gas station with the employee. They stood in front of Jeff's car. She pointed at the car and then threw her hands up. The employee tried his best to calm her down. Jeff stood up, offered his hand.

"I guess this is good-bye."

They shook hands and Jeff walked back to pump his gas. The woman who'd complained, yelled at him as he put his card in the pump. He didn't say a word, just quietly filled his car until she stormed off and got into her car. Jae laughed as she peeled out of the station onto Hawthorne Blvd. Jeff honked before driving away.

Jae got on the bus and took a seat. The bus was silent—no squeaking brakes, no running roaring engine, no hydraulic hiss—it was as if no sound could exist inside. Jae couldn't even hear the outside world through the windows. Even the people were silent, but that made perfect sense—there wasn't anyone inside to speak for them. It was refreshing, a bus full of strangers with no Occupants crying for help. He turned to the woman next to him.

"Where you headed?" he asked.

"Just up the street," she said. "You?"

"San Jose."

"My sister lives in San Jose. I'll probably never see her again."

"Probably not."

"Oh well."

The bus turned into the hospital. The woman told Jae this was her stop, so he stood to let her by. She wished him good luck and got off, made her way toward the hospital, her hands tucked in the pockets of her robe. Jae closed his eyes and went to sleep.

A Cheap Metaphor

Three days after burying her husband, Yu-jin saw Jae on the news. It was a little after three AM. She was feeding Naomi when she saw the report—a retired software engineer who'd been missing for over four years, all of the sudden discovered in the basement of an IBM facility, banging his head against a data storage unit. A photo of Jae, clean-cut and healthy, on a fishing boat, smiling through wayfarers with a beer in his hand. Yu-jin saw his daughter, Nina, making a statement on behalf of the family, expressing gratitude to IBM security for finding her father and contacting the authorities. She had his nose and chin, his high forehead—she was clearly a Korean girl. The goodbye note Jae had left for his family—a hand tracing, like the kind the twins made to draw turkeys during Thanksgiving, a smiling comet emerging from the palm—flashed on the screen.

Don't be sad, the note read in hangul, *I have to go away for a bit. We'll see each other sooner than you think.*

Yu-jin stared at the note, and knew Jae wouldn't last the week. It was strange, seeing such beautiful, clean penmanship next to that crude, childish drawing. Why would they show such a thing on TV? Didn't he deserve some dignity? It seemed cruel, showing the world his mental state in such a horrible way.

For the past two nights, Yu-jin had dreamt of Jeoseung Saja, who'd told her she'd died the night of the shooting. He told her Naomi carried her essence, and no matter how many times she'd asked, the Emissary wouldn't tell her what that meant. After putting Naomi to bed, Yu-jin had another dream. This time, the Emissary came with a tiger, who asked her why men always excused bad behavior by invoking their own pain, their own suffering.

"Do they do that?" Yu-jin asked.

"Remember the time Adam cheated on you?" Rachel said.

And then she noticed the tiger was gone, replaced by Rachel, who asked to take a walk with her. No one mentioned the tiger had even been there, so Yu-jin assumed it had never been there. They left Jeoseung Saja behind and had the same conversation they'd had in the maternity ward the morning after the shooting, until Rachel disappeared and she was at Adam's funeral with Jae—just sitting, as if she'd been sitting the entire time, because she'd been sitting the entire time, even remembered sitting the entire time.

"How come right when something amazing is about to happen, you always wake up?" Jae asked.

And Yu-jin woke up, remembered none of it. But for the rest of the day, she couldn't stop thinking of the time Adam confessed to sleeping with a lieutenant from the Nurse Corps while deployed. It was before the twins were born, and she'd thought of leaving him, but he cried and swore it meant nothing. He told her about all the death both he and the other woman had seen, how they'd both needed to forget the pain they'd suffered. Yu-jin would wonder why she couldn't stop thinking about it, something she hadn't thought about in years—it had only been days since Adam's funeral, so why were her thoughts turning toward things that made her resent him?

Later in the afternoon, Brenda sat on the deck, staring at a dead hummingbird. Ants had already begun to swarm around the body, clustered upon the bird's breast like grapes.

"We should move this, before the boys see it," Brenda said. "I don't want them to see any sadness if I can help it."

"I'll get the broom," Yu-jin said.

"It's fine, honey. I'll do it."

Yu-jin sat, the two of them staring at the ants pooling around the bird. Neither wanted to admit it was fascinating and beautiful in its own way.

"I was thinking," Brenda said, "something my grandmother used to say. She said, 'Men see the world as a mirror while women can only see it through a window.' Do you know what that means?"

"It's true."

"Well it shouldn't be."

Yu-jin gasped, her hand shooting up to her mouth like in the movies. Tears fell down her cheeks. She couldn't breathe.

"Jinny, what's the matter?"

Yu-jin began to cry, as the skin on the side of Brenda's neck began to ripple. *It's okay,* the ripples said. *You're just seeing things.* She ran inside, into the nursery, and pulled Naomi from the crib. She clutched her baby to her chest, heaving sobs as if she were disgorging her soul. Brenda calmed the baby and put her back in the crib, gave Yu-jin a Unisom tablet and put her to bed. She didn't dream at all.

This Is Bad

Brian reluctantly returns his hug. They go inside and Scott asks Brian if he'd like a beer. The plan was for Brian to sit and chat until he got the money, to occupy Scott and Wilma in the living room while Nick and Vince rummaged through the backyard and took everything they could sell. Scott goes into the kitchen and comes back with two beers. Brian texts his friends, let's them know the coast is clear. Brian takes a seat on the couch, asks if he could turn the TV on.

"I just figured we'd talk," Scott says. "I haven't seen you since you were a baby. Actually, that's not true. I saw you on the beach with Father—you know, when the world was supposed to end."

Brian remembers that night, standing on the beach with the torches, crying as he sang "We Shall See His Lovely Face." He remembers the excitement of the Lord coming to take him away, to rescue him, to help him forget how Neil McNeil had tasted. He remembers the pit in his stomach during the end of the second verse, the realization no one was coming for him, the tears skating into his mouth like snakes.

"Oh yeah," Brian says. "What a complete crock of shit that was. I'd actually like the TV on if that's okay. We can still talk, but I, uh, you know, the election. I'm pretty pissed about it."

"Sure. Okay."

"Where's your mom?"

"She went to get the money. She'll be back."

Brian stares at Scott, and Scott stares at Brian. It amazes him how much he and Scott look alike. When Scott smiles, it's like seeing an alternate version of himself, a version who'd lived in a world where he was born to a Korean mother, a world where his father's white wife stole him away from Neil McNeil, a world where he could live a somewhat normal life, become a teacher, and then a hero after foiling a mass shooting. Scott nods in the awkward way Father used to nod, and then sighs the way Brian sighed, and it's like seeing a seeing a version of himself he wants to punch in the nose, over and over, until he can feel the bone fragments crush like the shell of a hard-boiled egg.

"So, you've been through some shit, huh?" Brian says.

"Yeah, I guess you could say that. I've been through some shit. Just don't believe everything they say on TV."

"All I hear is that you're a hero."

Scott takes a sip of beer, smiles. Brian stares at that smile, that smile that left with the mother he never knew, the mother he'd learn was never his mother—that smile that left him alone on the island with their fraud of a father, that left him alone with Neil McNeil. Scott grabs the remote and pushes the button, flips from a cooking show to a split-screen argument between a talking head in Houston and a talking head in New York.

"I'm just happy to be alive," Scott says. "That's why I'm glad you're here. I think it's a sign, you know? I know that sounds really dumb, but you coming to see me after all these years, maybe that's a sign I'm going to turn it around."

"After all we've been through with Father, you still believe in bullshit signs?"

Scott turns to the TV, tightens his lips. Brian takes a sip of beer as the woman in Houston fails to address the issue and the man in New York completely misses the point. Brian watches the muscles in Scott's jaw pulse.

"Sorry, man," Brian says. "That wasn't for you."

"We both have reasons to be angry. Look, while we wait for Mom to get back, I wanted to ask you about something. It's going to be really personal, so if you don't want to talk about it, I understand."

Brian's phone buzzes—a text from Nick telling him to come to the back door.

"Everything okay?" Scott asks.

"Yeah, can you hold on a second? Just sit tight."

Brian gets up and walks to the back. He reaches the sliding door leading to the back yard. Nick stands in front of the glass, the phone illuminating his face. Vince stands behind him, a gun at Wilma Bonneville's head, his left hand over her mouth. Brian shuts his eyes, taps the lip of the beer bottle to his forehead. Those fucking idiots. He opens his eyes and Nick mouths, *open the fucking door.* Wilma's eyes enlarge. A muffled scream.

"What the hell is going on?" Scott says. "Mom? Brian, what—"

Brian turns around smashes the bottle over Scott's head, takes Scott to the ground and punches twice. He gets up, wipes his bloodied hand on his pants, unlocks the door.

"What the hell happened?" Brian says.

"I don't know," Nick says. "She just showed up."

"Nick," Vince says," go to the car and get the zipties."

Brian looks at Wilma. He recognizes her from the newspaper clippings in the compound. Father had gotten rid of every photo of her years before he could understand she wasn't his mother. He touches her face with his finger.

A tear falls onto his fingernail, pools before sliding off. He wonders of a world that could have easily existed—one where Wilma Bonneville had taken both boys to Redondo Beach, one where he was never touched by Neil McNeil, one where maybe he actually finished his Engineering degree and worked at Chevron, or Northrup Grumman, or the Department of Water and Power. Why did she leave him behind? Was he so horrible as a baby?

He asks her if she got the money and she nods. He snaps the purse from her shoulder and reaches in, pulls out the envelope.

"This is bad," Brian says.

"No shit it's bad," Vince says. "It's fucking terrible."

In-N-Out

Traffic is horrible, breaklights as far as the eye can see. Blake pulls up his phone. There's been an accident two miles ahead of him. He pulls off the 405, heads to an In-N-Out Burger in El Segundo. Walt had always said In-N-Out burgers were the best he'd ever had, always said it was the only thing he missed about California.

Blake thought it was fine. You couldn't get bacon on the burger, but as a burger, it was fine. It was like any other burger you'd get anywhere—you could get a burger like this all over Portland. The fries were terrible, like mashed potatoes stuffed into limp french fry casings. But overall, it was fine. A little boy stands in his booth, leans against the back of his seat. Blake smiles and points at him.

"Tyler," the boy's mother says, "leave that young man alone."

"It's okay," Blake says. "How ya doin, man?"

"Do you like your Double-Double?" Tyler asks.

"It's my first one ever."

"Ever?"

"Yeah. Ever. It's pretty good. There's a place near my house called Burgerville. It's about the same."

"Oh you're from Portland," the mother says.

"Is Burgerville good?" Tyler asks.

"It's not bad," his mother says. "It's no In-N-Out."

"I beg to differ," Blake says.

"Well, maybe you're not ordering the right stuff," Tyler's mother smiles.

Tyler's father comes back with their tray of food. They begin eating, and Blake wonders what that means, not ordering the right stuff. It was a simple menu: burgers, fries, sodas, shakes. Why can't this woman just accept the food isn't very good? Of course, he knew about the secret menu, but the implication these people have a right way and a wrong way to order their food is ridiculous. If an item is available to eat, then put it on the menu. Why have this kind of exclusivity over goddamn burgers and fries? Goddamn California snobs. Look at them: these tan little girls in their short little shorts, these knock-kneed boys sockless in their boat shoes. Blake notices the Bible verse on his burger wrapper: Revelation 3:20. He looks it up on his phone:

Here I am! I stand at the door and knock. If anyone hears my voice and opens the door, I will come in and eat with him, and he with me.

Unless you order the wrong goddamn thing, of course. Blake dumps his food in the trash, heads for the door. Tyler waves.

"Bye," Tyler says. "See you never again."

Tyler laughs. Blake smiles and salutes.

Burgerville, U.S.A.

A week before the Pizza Galley Shooting, Blake was at Burgerville when he felt a tap on his shoulder. He turned around to see his half-brother Donny looking up at him—the goddamn Duck Boy himself. Blake used to call him Duck Boy, as was the custom for anyone named Donald—of course, in the current political landscape, a more obvious insult would make itself known, but Blake hadn't seen Donny in four years. He wanted so badly to pound the goofy little fucker, with his braces, his silver and black Marcus Mariota jersey.

"Blake?" Donny said. "It's me, Don. Your brother, remember?"

"Well holy shit," Blake smiled. "The Duck Boy. What's up, little man?"

"Come on man," Donny said. "Anyway, Dad saw you come in and said I should say hi."

Blake laughed. They slapped hands. He had no idea why he'd even offer Donny his hand to slap. Of course the old man would be here today of all goddamn days. Blake sees the old man sitting at a booth. He barely nods before turning back to his fries, fat phony that he is.

"Did he really? Did he really tell you to say hi, Donny?"

"I go by Don now and, well, you know. Who cares? He's a dick. Anyway, that's a great shirt, man."

Donny stared at the blue long sleeve compression shirt, red and gold Superman logo centered on the chest. Of course he'd be wearing a Superman shirt today of all goddamn days. Blake didn't like how the boy admired his body. It made him very uncomfortable when men admired him, even when his friends complimented him—all of whom had been hitting the weights harder and longer than he had—something didn't feel right. It wasn't as if they were gay, or that he was—hell, even he'd been known to admire the work men had put into their appearance—it had more to do with the silence of women. It seemed only men noticed the way he'd transformed himself from a Star-Bellied Sneetch to the bare minimum of what a man's body should look like. And that's what it was to Blake, the bare minimum. He still could've used some work on his neck and shoulders, his calves—what the hell was so great about how he looked?

"Man," said Donny. "You must work out every day."

"You have to."

"Yeah, I gotta really bulk up. I want to make varsity next year."

"Football?"

237

"Uh-huh."

"Kinda small aren't you?"

Donny stared at the floor, nodded. Blake rolled his eyes. Pick your head up, you little bitch. Be a goddamn man and stand up for yourself. He saw the old man glaring at him.

"I know," Donny said. "But I'm fourteen. And a half. Besides, you're tall. Pop-pop was tall. I'll grow. I hope. Hey do you use Creatine?"

"Hell no, man. You just have to work hard."

The last time they'd seen one another, Blake was fourteen and Donny ten. Grandpa Don had been sick, so the boys spent the weekend with him while Grandma Cora was off at an old coworker's funeral. Blake remembers the moments that led to them never seeing one another again. They were in the backyard, reading Donny's comic books—all of them Superman.

"Do you have any other comics?" Blake had asked.

"No. I only like Superman."

"Really? Only Superman? What about Batman?"

"Batman's stupid. Superman could beat him in a fight. He can beat anyone in a fight."

"What about Hulk?"

"The Hulk is just big and dumb. "

"I like Hulk. He's awesome."

"The Hulk is stupid. Superman's a good guy. The Hulk's just a big stupid monster."

And that was when Blake finally had the kind of thought he'd been waiting for his entire life—the kind of witty retort that made people pause and really consider the words coming from his mouth, the kind that made people scrunch their noses and look into the sky and think to themselves, *Maybe this guy isn't the retard everyone says he is.* When he was asked what his proudest moment was, this was the moment he'd think of—while trying to avoid the fallout of his retort—before shrugging and saying he didn't know.

"Maybe Hulk is so dumb, he doesn't know when he's hurt," Blake had said. "And maybe Superman's so good he'll feel sorry for him and stop hurting him. But Hulk will never stop hurting Superman because he's just too dumb to care about Superman's feelings."

"That's not true," said Donny. "Superman—"

"Hulk smash. Hulk smash Superman. Hulk smash stupid, puny Superman."

"But Superman—"

"Hulk smash. Hulk smash."

"Stop it."

"Hulk smash. Hulk smash Donny. Hulk smash Duck Boy."

"Don't call me Duck Boy."

"Hulk smash Duck Boy. Hulk smash Duck Boy. Hulk smash Duck Boy. Hulk smash—"

By the time Grandpa Don had pulled Donny off of him, Blake had already tasted enough of his own blood to know it was time to run behind the shed and cry. He could already feel his lip plump up, and it burned every time he sniffled. If he'd wanted, he could've killed Donny, he'd sworn to Lisa, but then everyone would hate him even more than they already had. He remembered lying in bed that night, Lisa and the old man arguing in the living room, how he'd wished the tears falling into his ears would've plugged them up so he couldn't hear what was being said.

"Relax, Lisa," the old man had said. "It was just a disagreement between brothers."

"A disagreement? He busted Blake's lip and broke his nose. What's your son's fucking problem? Who loses their shit over a disagreement?"

"A fourteen-year-old got his ass kicked by a ten-year-old. I don't think Donny's the one with the problem."

The girl behind the counter called to Blake, handed him his bag. He flirted with her, just so Donny could watch her laugh. The old man called Donny back to him, told him to finish up, Grandma was waiting for them.

"I better get going," Donny said. "Good seeing you, man."

"Seriously, Donny, stay away from Creatine. No shortcuts. I find out you've been touching that shit, I'll beat your ass."

"Okay, Blake. See you, man."

He watched Donny make his way back to the booth. The old man sighed deeply, waved Blake over. Blake smiled and shook his head, mouthed, *Nope*, made his way to the exit.

Blake stood next to his car, placed his food on the roof, pretended to make a phone call, stared as the old man lectured Donny. He should've felt bad for the kid, the way he'd mouthed, *Yes sir*, every time the old man shut his mouth. The old man looked up and glared out the window.

Donny turned to see Blake roll his eyes, ball his hand into a fist and simulate jerking off. Blake got in his car and backed out of the parking lot.

No Witnesses

Scott comes to, flinches when he sees Brian kneeling over him, tries to shout through the gag in his mouth. Brian tells him not to move, tells him he's trying to pick the glass out of Scott's head. Scott winces as Brian pulls the flecks of glass.

"I didn't want this, Scott," Brian says. "I swear. I'm really sorry."

One of the men, he'll later learn his name is Vince, kneels in front of him. Scott's hands are bound behind his back. The hard plastic cuts into his wrists.

"She just showed up in the backyard," Vince says. "I'm really sorry it's gotta go like this, man."

"Vince," a third man says, "she won't stop crying."

Scott sees the other man, sitting cross-legged on the floor, wiping Wilma's tears away. He will learn this man's name is Nick. Not that it'll matter in the end. It's almost tender, the way Nick caresses Wilma's head, tells her no one was going to get hurt. This, of course, is a lie. Scott knows he and Wilma are going to die, that Brian can't leave any witnesses.

"We have to leave the money," Brian says.

"What?" Vince says. "No way. We take the fucking money."

"Leave the money, that way I can say we never made it to the house."

Vince throws his hands up, then kicks the air like a child. Wilma whines as the third man shushes her and speaks to her in a soothing whisper. She looks up at him, tears skating down her cheeks.

"Look," Brian says. "We're going to need an alibi. If I take the money, then they're gonna ask more questions. Leave the money, and I can say we were never here."

"Then where were we?" Vince asks.

"We'll figure that out later. Let's just grab some shit to sell and leave."

"What about them?" Nick asks.

Brian looks into Scott's eyes. Scott marvels at how much Brian looks like their father. He looks at his mother, muffled sobs pulsing through her gag like a barking dog. He knows this is how it ends. Scott wonders if his last thoughts will be of Lisa. They should be of Lisa. He closes his eyes, tries to shut out everything that isn't Lisa. He wonders if Lisa will be heartbroken, if she'll be sorry for letting him go. Maybe if she hadn't let him go, they could be together here in this house. Maybe if she hadn't let him go, Brian would have had to go to Sedona to collect the money, leaving Wilma to die alone. Then maybe Lisa would comfort him, hold him on the couch while he stared at her picture.

"Scott," Brian says, "I know about what Neil did to you and I'm sorry. Father told me that's why you and your mother left. I just want you to know he did it to me too. That fucker hurt both of us."

Nick stops caressing Wilma's hair, locks eyes with Scott. He stands up, walks to Brian.

"What did Neil do to you?" he asks.

Neil McNeil, that piece of shit. Scott remembers sucking in water, how the chlorine congealed in his throat, remembers Neil shushing him, telling him everything was going to fine. Trust old Neil, and everything will be fine.

"What did Neil do to you, Brian?" Nick asks. "Seriously man, tell me right now."

"What's it matter?" Brian says.

"Did he do to you what he did to me and Vince? Did he?"

Brian looks at Nick, and he knows he doesn't have to tell him what Neil McNeil had done, if it was the same thing he'd done to Nick and Vince. They'll discuss it later, away from the chaos of the Bonneville home.

"Did you know she was blackmailing Father?" Brian says. "Your own mother was using you to extort money. She didn't go to the cops like she should have, like a real mother. She knew—she fucking knew—and just took the money and ran. She left me, a fucking baby, behind, knowing what Neil was capable of."

Brian walks over to Wilma, taps his toe against the top of her head. She does her best to shriek, coughs violently, choking on her own spit. Nick sits her up and slaps her back, then begins rubbing it. He puts his arm around her, tells her he forgives her, that it doesn't matter anymore. "Fuck it," he says, "you were just trying to protect your kid." She cries on his shoulder. The insides of Scott's throat constrict like a bent hose.

"The day my father told me you weren't really my mother was one of the best days of my life," Brian says. "Sure, I would've figured it out eventually, but you have no idea what it feels like, knowing your own mother didn't leave you behind. I used to cry for you every night, that you'd come back and take me away. You have no idea the things that fucking monster did to me and your son over there."

"We're wasting time," Nick says.

"Then stop wasting it," Brian says. "Go help Vince."

Nick once again mutters, "Fuck it," and walks into the hallway, tells Vince he's on his way. Brian lifts his foot, rests the sole of his shoe against her forehead, knocks her back to the ground. Scott stares at Wilma, who refuses to look at him. She rolls into the wall, buries her face into the white wooden molding, and wails. Scott remembers the argument from election night, the one about Neil. Had Lisa not left him, had she moved to California with him, Wilma would have been an occasional phone call from Arizona. They never would have had that election night argument. None of this would have happened had Lisa never left him. He could have mourned Wilma's death at Brian's hands like a good son. Why, Lisa? Why did you do this to us? Look at me, Mom. Look at me. Look at me, goddammit.

Scott hears glass break in his room, and a startled Vince shouts. Then the living room window shatters and the curtains go up in flames. Scott sees broken bottle, the burning rag, the puddle of fire. Another bottle flies through the window, shatters on the floor. Flames explode like a water balloon, and then another bottle hits—red, orange, and yellow, dance their way up the couch. Vince and his companion run into the living room, both holding overstuffed gym bags.

"We need to get the fuck out of here," Vince says.

Brian looks at Scott, then at Wilma. His friends grab him by the shirt and pull him away. They run through the kitchen, out the back door. Scott watches Wilma, curled up against the wall like a pill-bug, her arms ziptied behind her waist. He turns to the TV, watches the President-Elect shake hands with well-wishers in the lobby of some building, probably one he owned.

Wires spark as flames crawl up the entertainment center. The TV screen goes black.

The Horwitz Conundrum (Revisited)

Bonneville's car is parked in the driveway. It still has a sun-damaged DuClod-Man bumper sticker on the trunk. There's a black cat curled on top of the roof. Was it Bonneville's cat? It raises its head and they lock eyes. It lowers its head and goes back to sleep.

The home is a modest little cottage, an overgrown juniper bush in front of the living room window, which is to the left of the front door. Another juniper stands in front of the window to the right of the garage. A giant palm tree sits in the front yard, its trunk framed by rocks. It's not as nice as the other houses on the block. The lawn would've used some upkeep, weeds pushing their way through the cracks in the driveway, the rim of the rain gutter pushed outward like a lower lip—it's insulting that Bonneville wanted Lisa to come live in this dump.

Blake lights a menthol and opens the rear driver's side door. He grabs the People Shooting Hat in the back seat, the green one Walt gave him for his birthday, and puts it on before leaning inside. It came with a book, this green hat. Blake remembers staring at the cover: a fat man in a green hunting cap, the flaps hanging over his ears—it was the hot dog vendor whose exploits he'd eventually listen to on the drive to California. The buttons on his red overcoat bulge from the man's girth, ready to pop. A yellow parrot rests on top of his head. Blake had wondered if Walt was making fun of him, saying he was the fat man on the cover.

"Happy birthday, faggot"

"He looks like Super Mario," Blake says.

"Super Mario is based on this book."

"Seriously? Wow."

"No, man. What's wrong with you?"

Walt laughs and punches Blake's shoulder. Blake laughs, but he does look like Super Mario. How was he to know it wasn't really about Super Mario? A yellow parrot did seem like the kind of stupid power-up you'd see in a video game. He pictured the parrot carrying Mario by the head, while Mario tossed fireballs at killer mushrooms and zombie turtles. It was perfectly reasonable to believe it was a book about Super Mario.

"Seriously," Walt said. "Just read it. It's an awesome book. The guy who wrote it killed himself because no one would publish it. Then twenty years later, it won the Pulitzer. Think about that. This guy was rejected his entire life. Then he dies and everyone has to admit how wrong they were. Can you imagine making people eat shit from beyond the grave?"

"Yeah but he wasn't alive to enjoy it."

"Doesn't matter, man. Everyone else was alive to know what they'd done. Could you imagine being some cucktard bookworm who got off on how smart he was, only to find out he turned his nose up at a Pulitzer Prize-winning classic? Not so smart now, are you, bud?"

Blake wondered what exactly it was that everyone had done to this author. He doesn't doubt people had done him wrong—he just wonders exactly what it was. Had they ignored him his entire life? Had they shoved him against lockers, tripped him in the halls, offered high-fives with pushpins wedged between their fingers? Blake wished the man had been alive to know how successful the book had become, wished he could actually enjoy making people eat shit.

But maybe Walt was right. Maybe it was better this way—to make those who'd wronged him regret their choices, to make them live with their regret, to make them eat shit from beyond the grave like some avenging spirit haunting the wicked for the rest of their lives.

"Anyway," Walt said, "I thought I'd replace your stupid book with this one. Your book will rot your brain."

"What do you mean?"

"J.D. Salinger was MKUltra, dude. He used to interrogate Nazis during World War II and then went on to become a CIA neurolinguist after the war. *Catcher in the Rye* contains a secret code that awakens sleeper agents. Read that book too many times and it'll drive you insane."

Walt told Blake about Lee Harvey Oswald and the guy who shot John Lennon, how they'd both read *Catcher in the Rye*. He told Blake about others. The one that stood out was a college girl in Oregon—who'd gone to the same school Bonneville had gone to—how she'd set off a bunch of pipe bombs because of her obsession with the book. Blake remembered watching a documentary on her, how everyone had thought it was Muslims, how freaked out they were when they realized it was just a pretty girl from a good family.

Blake reaches behind the back seat, pulls the crate of Molotovs closer to him. He's read *Catcher in the Rye* five times, wonders how many times is too many times. Bonneville taught the book every year. How many times had he read it? Blake lifts the crate and crosses the street, the glass clinking with each step.

He stops at Mr. Bonneville's shitty car, places the crate on top of the trunk. The cat steps down the rear windshield and smells the crate. It purrs against Blake's fist, runs its tongue along the knuckles. Blake gently swats the cat in the face until it leaps off the car. It takes one last look back before sprinting behind the side of the house.

He takes a bottle and lights the wick, makes his way to the window to the right of the garage. The light is on, and he wonders if Bonneville's home. He thinks better of looking inside. He hurls the bottle through the window, and runs back to Boneville's shitty car.

"What the fuck!" someone screams from inside the house.

He grabs another bottle, lights it, throws it into the living room window. The curtains immediately catch fire. The frantic voices of men inside the living room—maybe Bonneville has friends over. He lights another, throws it through the window, and then tosses another at the front door, watching it shatter, the fire clinging to the door like flaming mold. There's one Molotov in the crate, next to a spray paint can. The spray paint can rattles as he shakes it. He kneels behind Bonneville's car and begins writing one last final *Fuck You*, the kind of *Fuck You* that can never be rubbed away.

Before sprinting to his car, he takes the last Molotov, lights it. He takes a look at the burning house, aims for the DuClod-Mann bumper sticker on Scott Bonneville's shitty car. As the flame trails from the bottleneck, he sees the black cat sitting on the roof, licking its front paw. The bottle crashes against trunk, and Blake turns the ignition.

As he peels out, the shitty car explodes and burns. Through his rearview mirror, Blake sees neighbors running out of their homes. The horror that must've been all over Bonneville's face, Blake wishes he was inside the house to see it. How helpless does Bonneville feel right now? Two nights earlier, Blake had lost his virginity to some girl everyone called Pepper, who'd agreed to come back to his place with him and Walt in exchange for weed. He was told it would be good for him, that it had been arranged by Nelson and the guys. Walt had told him in no uncertain terms, that he wouldn't be welcome back if he didn't go through with it.

"I just didn't picture my first time to be like this," Blake had said.

"Who cares what your first time, second time, one-hundredth time is like? You just do it because you're supposed to. Are you a fucking man or not?"

"I am, but you know."

"No, I don't. Just get in there, man. Stop being a bitch."

The entire time he was in his room with her, Blake couldn't stop thinking about how, other than Lisa, Pepper was the only real live naked woman he'd seen—but she wasn't even a woman, just some seventeen-year-old who'd been held back twice because she kept cutting class. What if Lisa came home while he was doing it? Would she be disappointed in him? Would she ask him about it? Why did that matter? The entire time he was on top of Pepper he couldn't stop thinking of Lisa in the closet with Bonneville, her left breast flopping out of the top of her shirt, the furious concentration on Bonneville's stupid face—the entire time he was with Pepper, he wondered if he had that same stupid face.

Blake removes the green People Shooting Hat, tosses it to the passenger seat. The next day, after the news of his arrest, people will talk about what Blake had spray-painted on the driveway, the sad irony of Scott Bonneville dying at the hands of a former student, #GOODGUYWITHAGUN scrawled at the foot of his car, on the cracked concrete, like some kind of curse.

People with way too much time on their hands will wonder why Blake had written that on the driveway. They'll say it was a message from the FBI—that they were wise to the movement, and Blake was their messenger, letting the world know anyone who'd used that hashtag was now a target. Some will say Blake had exposed Scott Bonneville as a fraud, Controlled Opposition, and Blake was reclaiming the hashtag from the elites who'd co-opted it. Others will say the Pizza Galley Shooting and Blake Mesman's murder of Scott Bonneville was all a false-flag operation, a ruse cooked up by the government to keep us distracted from the real child trafficking-ring run by the CIA, the same CIA that undermined the President, the President who'd come to office and shake things up, burn it all down.

And the rest of us? I'm sure we'll read some eloquent think piece on how fanning the flames of gun culture finally caught up with Scott Bonneville, how he's emblematic of the toxic world we live in, how this is all the fault of *CheetoBoyFuckBagTinyHandsHashtagResist*. And of course, we'll be right because we're the only ones who know anything. We, and only we, will ever know the truth because the world is a window and all those other poor saps think it's a mirror.

This is who we are now. RT if you agree.

Thumbs Up

Heart

Sad Face

Angry Face

Charles-Foster-Kane's-futile-attempt-at-starting-a-round-of-applause-for-Susan's-opera-performance, dot gif.

When the police ask Blake why he'd spray-painted *#GOODGUYWITHA-GUN*, he'll tell them this story, and it will be the only answer he'll ever give:

I remember this one time in class we were discussing the duck scene in Catcher in the Rye. *All these pretentious morons kept saying it was all about how the ducks represent innocence and lost childhood and all that crap. And I raised my hand, and when Mr. Bonneville called on me, I said it wasn't any of those things. It was just a kid asking a question he was curious about and the old cabbie got pissed because he didn't know how to answer it. That's all it was—just a kid asking a question and the old man not listening to him.*

Then Mr. Bonneville asked me if it was like the sound of one hand clapping, and I told him maybe. I didn't even know what he was talking about, to be honest. Then he nodded and said, Well put, Blake. And then moved onto another point. I never said another word about that book, even though he kept encouraging me to speak up.

And you know? That was the only time I ever actually liked the fucker.

Jeff Chon's stories and essays have appeared in *The Seneca Review*, *The Portland Review*, *Barrelhouse*, *Juked*, and *The North American Review*, among other fine places. He currently lives in the Bay Area with his wife and children. This is his debut novel.